THE
ECHOED
REALM

A. J. VRANA

THE PARLIAMENT HOUSE

ISBN: 978-1-7333868-3-8

The Parliament House

www.parliamenthousepress.com

Cover Art by: Shayne Leighton

Edited by Malorie Nilson, Emily Peters, Megan Hultberg

PRAISE FOR A. J. VRANA'S THE CHAOS CYCLE DUOLOGY

THE HOLLOW GODS

Vrana's dark, folklore-infused debut, the first of a duology, introduces readers to the residents of Black Hollow, who hold their daughters close and their twisted secrets closer...Vrana crafts a unique local mythology and draws from existing lore to create a sense of creeping dread. Vrana is off to a strong start with this solid, suspenseful tale.

   – *Publisher's Weekly*

This dazzling debut pulls you in with its compelling characters and horrifying mystery and keeps you in its thrall until the final page. The writing sizzles with menace, and the dark mythology A. J. Vrana weaves from dreams and nightmares is unlike any I've ever encountered, in and out of books. A perfect story for contemporary fantasy readers who love their narratives razor-sharp and their secrets dark and deadly.

– Katya de Becerra, author of *OASIS* and *WHAT THE WOODS KEEP*

A. J. Vrana's debut The Hollow Gods is an exciting contemporary horror-fantasy that shines when it declines to play frights, which are easy, and instead explores dread, collective and generational grief, trauma, and historical responsibility...The fragmented, surgically precise narrative builds from the utterly, painfully ordinary to the absurd and fantastic.

– *Three Crows Magazine*

Grounded in secrets, myth, fantasy, and alternate reality, Vrana's debut installment in The Chaos Cycle series is a fast-paced, deeply intriguing urban fantasy. Prepped with intriguing details, the narrative is both engrossing and vivid, the writing assured, and the pacing perfect. Exploring varied themes of grief, depression, trauma, and collective guilt, Vrana hooks the reader from the very start, leaving them anxious for the next installment.

– *The Prairies Book Review*

THE ECHOED REALM

"Good vs. evil is cleverly turned on its head as Vrana pulls readers down the rabbit hole into her strange, folkloric world."

– *Publisher's Weekly*

The Echoed Realm cleverly expands Vrana's wholly original Dreamwalker mythology beyond the town of Black Hollow, with blood-chilling consequences. Gods are more powerful, possibilities are endless, and threats are more sinister than ever. Miya and Kai are haunted by the past, literally, while the lines between dreams and reality, lore and fact, and obsession and possession are paper thin.

– Katya de Becerra, author of *OASIS* and *WHAT THE WOODS KEEP*

The Echoed Realm is the perfect sequel to Vrana's stunning and original debut, *The Hollow Gods*. Brimming with sharp edges, dark nightmares, and menacing villains, this book will haunt you in all the best ways. Compulsively readable, with complicated characters and expansive world-building, this is an epic, macabre folktale for a new generation. Vrana's lyrical writing is a mix of poetry, chaos, violence, and energy, blending to create a wild and wonderful potion, and I can't wait to read more from this rich new voice in contemporary fantasy.

– Kim Smejkal, author of *INK IN THE BLOOD* and *CURSE OF THE DIVINE*

"*The Echoed Realm* pulls no punches and offers a masterfully crafted supernatural horror that's not afraid to face the hard truths and imagine a different kind of world. *The Echoed Realm* leaves an aftertaste of a promise, of something bigger and better, deeper and even bolder than this. Look out for A. J. Vrana in NY Times bestselling lists in the next couple of years.

– *Three Crows Magazine*

"Everything about this book has a dark and spellbinding edge...an emerging threat in your peripheral vision, a creeping dread. Horror, supernatural, and fantasy push the threads of realism to its very edges."

– *The Coy Caterpillar Reads Book Reviews*

This book deals with themes of domestic violence, however, there are no depictions of domestic violence on these pages.

If you are or have been experiencing domestic violence and would like more information or assistance, here are some resources that can help:

National Domestic Violence Hotline (United States):
https://www.thehotline.org/
1-800 799-SAFE (7233)

Ending Violence Association of Canada:
https://endingviolencecanada.org/getting-help-2/

Crisis Text Line:
https://www.crisistextline.ca/

For those who embrace the shadows between absolutes.

The most painful truths are never grand. It's the little things that kill.

— *THE SERVANT*

❧ I ❧

ECHOED WHISPERS

❧ I ❧

MIYA

THE STREET WAS as empty as the eye of a storm. Save for the wind scattering autumn leaves over cracked asphalt, a lone young woman stood in the middle of the road. Her long, dark brown hair whipped around her face, and her muddy green eyes prickled from the sharp cold that howled at her to go home.

Home, however, was a long way from here.

She canted her head at the sound of a shrill cry echoing through the vacant night. A mass of black feathers and a sharp, curved beak entered her periphery. Talons dug into her shoulder, but the animal trilled contentedly.

"Hey, Kafka." Miya scratched the raven's breast, enjoying his silky plumage.

He squawked back, beating his wings as he clung to her.

Miya trained her gaze on the house up ahead. Lily-white paint chipped from the rickety paneling, and the bumpy driveway, with its patchy interlocking and overgrown weeds, reminded her of a world she longed to forget. But

3

Summersville, West Virginia was no Black Hollow. A faded, grey sign was splayed on the lawn, the text barely discernable: *As seen on—*

Ghostventures.

America loved its ghosts. Amateurs armed with EVPs and electromagnetic readers went barging into people's homes, yelling taunts and expecting answers. Did they think proof of the supernatural would keep the demons at bay?

Truth was never an antidote—only a drug too short in supply to meet the demand.

Taking a deep breath, Miya clutched the pendant that hung around her neck—a copper raven with its talons contoured over the top of an iridescent stone. The dream stone—a piece of it, anyway.

As she started up the porch steps, her companion flew away and perched on the blackened compass atop the roof. Kafka-the-boy—the one who'd gifted her the labradorite—had been absent from the dreamscape for three long years, but she suspected he was watching through Kafka-the-raven. He always stayed close.

"It'll be ok," she whispered to herself. "You've dealt with much worse."

Refusing to use the ghastly colonial doorknocker—a brass lion's head clutching an ornate hoop between its jaws—she rapped on the door three times before it swung open.

The woman who answered looked like she'd stumbled back from the afterlife or was on her way there. The only sign of animation was the bare look of surprise on her face as she took in her visitor.

"Are you the..."

"I'm the witch," Miya cut to the chase. She didn't have the patience for dishonest terms like *medium*, *psychic*, or *empath*. Strictly speaking, she wasn't a *witch* either, but it was the closest thing to her true nature that people understood. Outside of Black Hollow, no one knew who the Dreamwalker was.

"R-Right," the woman stammered. "I'm Dawn. We spoke earlier?"

Miya strained a smile, and the corners of her lips felt like they were chapping. "I remember. I take it the *Ghostventures* crew didn't help?"

"No, they didn't." The door whined as she opened it further. "Please, come inside."

Dawn's slouched shoulders obscured her otherwise robust figure. Miya wondered if she was having trouble eating; her clothes hung loose, and her cheeks sagged. Her light brown hair was parched, peppered with silver strands that almost looked gold against the dim orange light of the hall.

"I'm sorry it's so cold in here." She wrung her knobby hands as she led Miya towards the kitchen. "The heat's technically working, but it's just...always so cold."

"Asshole spirits will do that," Miya mumbled. She clutched her dark mauve leather jacket around her sides and lifted the hood over her head. It helped her stay focused when she knew she was surrounded by malevolence. Dawn took a seat at the table and rubbed her arms with a sigh.

"It started a year ago, when my husband got his new job. We were struggling, and this house was such a steal. We figured it was because the town was small, too far from any major cities, but strange things began to happen almost right away."

Miya helped herself to the chair across from her client. "Weird noises? Bad dreams?"

"The noises didn't bother me." Dawn fiddled with a wine bottle that'd been left on the table, then poured herself a glass. She'd obviously been finding ways to cope.

"But the dreams...My husband, Greg, didn't think they were a big deal. He thought I was being dramatic, or that I had a sleep disorder."

Miya snorted; the narrative was almost cliché. "It's always the husband who won't believe."

Dawn hesitated, then nodded slowly. "I suppose so." She offered a tepid smile. "So, are you really a witch?"

Miya curled her fingers under her palm. "Sort of. I don't worship the devil or eat kids if that's what you're asking."

Dawn's voice grew quieter. "Do you believe in the devil?"

Miya caught her client's gaze. "I believe in far worse."

Dawn bowed her head and clutched the cross around her neck. "Anyway, the dreams kept getting worse—more vivid. Most nights, it felt like I hadn't slept at all. A few times, I woke up elsewhere, in the basement or the back-yard. I did what Greg asked and went to see a doctor, but my test results came back normal. Nothing was wrong with me, so I figured it must be the house."

"Why not move?" Miya asked.

"Greg refuses." Dawn's voice fractured, frustration bubbling to the surface like boiling water licking the lid of a pot. "It's like he's waging war against this *thing*, only he doesn't even believe in the thing he's fighting!"

"And what do you think this *thing* is?"

"I-I don't know. Our church preaches that spirits aren't real. There's heaven and hell. Nothing in between." Dawn covered her face with her hands, her shoulders trembling. "But I know it's real, no matter what my faith says."

Miya's heart clenched. She could feel this woman's pain, and it sundered whatever distance she'd worked to keep. "I believe you," she whispered. "Even if you moved, there's no guarantee *it* wouldn't follow."

Dawn's breath drew in. "Is it a ghost?"

Miya shook her head, scanning the room. Claw marks

were etched into the wall, revealing the entity's path. "Ghosts are human spirits. This one's not, and it isn't friendly, either. To tell you the truth," she stood and reached into her back pocket, "I've been hunting this one for a while."

This was her life now—not out of choice but out of necessity. Miya never could have imagined just how many malicious spirits preyed on people in their dreams, and as the Dreamwalker, she was in a unique position to help them. She enjoyed it, but it wasn't altruistic. The monsters haunted her too.

A crack, jagged like lightning, splintered the drywall, oozing something black and tarry. A low, wet gargle reverberated through the kitchen.

"It's happening!" Dawn yelped, knocking over her chair as she jumped up.

Miya's hand steadied on her back pocket. She glared down the fissure in the wall—or rather, a fissure in the seam of reality.

"Dawn," Miya said evenly. "Get behind me and stay in cover."

The older woman scrambled to the other side of the kitchen and ducked behind a cabinet. Grateful Dawn didn't peek, Miya pulled a single playing card from her jeans.

It was the king of spades, copper stains marring him from a nightmare long ago.

She threw it down, face-up, and unsheathed a hunting knife strapped to her belt. "I didn't think we'd do this here," she called to the spirit, and it answered with a ferocious roar that ruptured the drywall around the blackened rift.

Miya winced as she dragged the blade across her palm. Clenching her fist, blood ribboned around her fingers and speckled the card on the floor.

She grinned into the oncoming void. "Long live the king."

Wisps of black mist slithered upward and coalesced into the shape of a man.

The house rumbled in dissent, and the border between Dawn's world and the dreamscape pulled taught. Something sinister was lurking.

Normally, Miya had to lie down and let her spirit descend into the dreamscape, but the demon spared her the effort and shunted her wholly across realms. The quaint kitchen, decorated in canary yellows and smelling of fresh casserole, stilled like a film on pause. The lemony hues melted to muddy browns. Tables and chairs fused into ghoulish shapes. A vase levitated from the crumbling windowsill, then hurtled towards her.

The man made of smoke extended an arm, clipping the vase just enough to slow it down. Miya stepped aside, watching, unfazed, as it drifted past her nose and dissipated.

The house was gone. Miya found herself in a sea of black fog, the laminate counter and spring-coloured backsplash sinking like sand through an hourglass. The plywood chimera, fused from fragments of domestic life, roiled in the dark. Its misshapen wooden joints screeched painfully as it tottered away. The stench of sulfur wafted with the haze, and Miya clamped her jaw to keep from retching. The spirit's true form glinted up ahead. With the dream stone glowing against her chest, the darkness parted around its lavender light. She could see a silhouette: an imposing figure with long, slender limbs and fingers that dangled like knives.

"Are you the dream demon that calls itself Drekalo?" Miya stopped several feet from the grotesque creature, spindle-like with a head too large for its elongated neck. Its dappled skin was a chalky grey, scaly and splintered like a stone gargoyle.

The phantom's jaw unhinged, and it released a bone-shattering shriek, its sharp teeth bound only by strings of thick, red saliva.

"How did you come here, witch?" its reptilian voice quivered.

"It doesn't matter how. I needed more time."

"You can't kill me," Drekalo slavered. "This is the dreamscape, where all is timeless. Death doesn't exist here."

Miya regarded the demon, then shrugged. She was waiting for the man made of smoke to become flesh and blood. Slipping off her leather jacket, she watched as it evaporated into the fog. When the last specs of mauve disappeared, she turned to the demon.

Throwing her arms back, she cut across the expanse. Her hand shot out to wrap around Drekalo's throat. His gangling body careened to the side, but he couldn't escape. Violet swirls enveloped Miya, then erupted into a billowing cloak of spectral feathers. A raven beak made of bone drew over her face, black and purple bleeding onto the ivory like oil mixing with water. The bottom edge of the mask cut over her lips in a sharp V, and she flashed the demon a wicked smile.

"Let's take you somewhere death exists."

Drekalo gasped—the start of a protest that never came. Miya hauled Dawn's tormenter into the in-between—a sliver away from either realm. She could see the faint outline of the kitchen—all blurry lines and morphing shapes floating behind an ethereal curtain. The in-between was neither here nor there; it was a cell, trapping the demon where he couldn't roam.

The bars to this cell were open to the blade, and the executioner always struck from the earthly plane.

The demon shrieked and flailed as Miya released him. "Y-You're no witch!" His voice sounded garbled. "You're—"

Drekalo's accusation died in his mouth when a knife was thrust through his throat, then twisted for good measure. The man, it seemed, had finally arrived, and he'd reclaimed his beloved weapon.

The fissure in the wall sutured shut, and Miya returned to Dawn's kitchen. She snatched up the half-full wine glass from the table and raised it in a toast.

Wiping his hunting knife, slick with black viscera, Kai turned to the Dreamwalker. He took the glass from her and spilled its contents onto the floor, then tossed the delicate crystal aside. Tilting Miya's chin up, he swooped down and stole a kiss before she could say the words. He pulled back, grinning rakishly, and said them in her stead.

"Long live the fucking king."

THE DREAMSCAPE'S iridescent sky greeted Miya as she tore through the veil, Kai stumbling in tow. Pallid at first, the pearly sheen melted into a blanket of azure that bled into warm hues haloing the hanging star. Rings of amber and marigold, then pink and wisteria, radiated from its core into the sea-coloured ether.

The journey back was gruelling every time, but it was worth the spectacle that awaited them. Their corner of the dreamscape was a kaleidoscope of colour. Vast knolls of emerald and dandelion sprawled across the landscape. Save for a few high hills, the lush earth was blanketed in a thick forest that blossomed around a low river valley, the water sparkling like ice on a winter's day. If Miya could peek into the dream stone and glimpse the world inside, she imagined this was how it looked.

The fragrance of lilac trees washed over her, and the wind whistled its welcome alongside the song of a nearby thrush. Miya knew Dawn was safe. She would try to make sense of the ordeal, to give an order to the chaos, but it was futile. Her mind would do the only thing it could: blur the details and treat it like a bad dream. Her memory would be fuzzy, and Kai, who'd manifested from shadow and blood, who'd ended her nightmare, was only a mote in the mural.

Kai's job wasn't as simple as stabbing a spirit with a pointy object from the physical plane. First, Miya had to address the entities on their terms. The boundary between the earthly realm and the dreamscape was murky, but the place where spirits could actually *die* was the microscopic middle of a Venn diagram—a limbo that was both worlds at once, and yet neither.

"That's the twelfth one." Kai inspected his hunting knife, now back in his possession.

"They're getting tougher," Miya sighed, plopping down on the slope. Each hill in their nook of the dreamscape was named after a precious stone: amethyst for the lavender fields stretching over the knoll to the west, ruby for the lumpy mound sprouting with red dahlias, and peridot for the clover-leaved grass peppered with milky aspens. She loved perusing the clovers, searching for the one that'd bring her luck. If anything, she needed some good fortune.

Miya was tired from travelling. Dreamwalking was easy; her physical body remained, but her consciousness departed for the dreamscape. It was effortless, like sinking into a warm bath. On the other hand, moving flesh and bone from the dreamscape to the earthly plane and vice versa was like plodding through a current of mud.

"So many nightmares out there..." she trailed off. "It's tough to tell if people are haunted or just stressed."

"The ones that go on a murder spree are probably haunted," said Kai, smiling wryly.

"It's not only that. I feel like there's a new Black Hollow every day."

Kai scoffed and wrinkled his brow. "There's only one place bat-shit enough to be Black Hollow."

Miya threw herself back and stretched her limbs. The summer grass was inviting, and a small cottage awaited in a glade nestled in the woods overlooking the peridot hill— past the flaming oak swaddled in a copse of birch trees, beyond the willow's canopy, and through a gateway only they could see.

The stone cottage boasted a thatched roof with a sturdy chimney. A hedge of white roses decorated the front wall near the door, the thorny vines sprawling across the stonework and snaking around the windows. The snug interior was furnished with a hearth for cooking meals and newly lacquered chairs around the table. There was a bed— an actual *bed*—with a walnut frame and a quilted blanket for the rare nights when Kai's body heat wasn't enough to keep the chill away.

Miya didn't know if they'd dreamt it into this reality or if it'd always been there, but she didn't care to question it. It was home, and that was enough.

The smell of smoke and the madness of the mob was still fresh, even after three years. Miya had been in the dreamscape during the worst of it, but her physical body had absorbed the mayhem. The memories had sunk into her bones. Of course, she also had Kai's colourful narrative to fill in the gaps.

Miya rolled over onto her stomach. "Come take a nap with me," she offered, and Kai joined her on the grass, slumping against an aspen's bole as he pulled her into his lap.

He stroked her hair back and clipped her ear with his teeth, earning a squeak of protest.

"I said a nap, not a nip," Miya slurred as she began to drift. Kai half-heartedly made his displeasure known with a grunt that rumbled against her back.

"Sorry." She patted him on the thigh. "Dimensional

travel takes it out of a girl."

His arms tightened around her briefly. "At least you get to travel."

Miya's heart sank. After Black Hollow, they'd found that she'd unwittingly tethered Kai to her like a familiar to a witch. He could only enter the physical realm when she willed it, and neither of them understood why. Worst of all, he couldn't be there alone; Miya's consciousness needed to remain with him. They'd learned *that* the hard way. The first time they'd returned to explore the material world, Miya tested the reins on her abilities. She was pleased to discover she could willfully dreamwalk while her body slept in the earthly plane. It was easier than breaking physics and moving bodies through dimensional doors. But barely twenty minutes into her descent to the dreamscape, Kai's panic, palpable like a splinter in her skin, tugged at her to return. When she made it back, he was writhing on the floor in agony. Eyes wide and bloodshot, he gasped for air like his lungs were filled with cotton. He later described the sensation as something like being eaten alive by starving fire ants.

It was a rude awakening to learn that Kai's body couldn't sustain itself in the physical world without Miya's consciousness there to anchor him. If left on his own for too long, his body began to disintegrate, tearing itself apart cell by cell.

Miya shook away the memory. She didn't understand why things worked the way they did; all she knew was that once Kai was in the physical plane, he needed her there—specifically, he needed her awareness of him. Eventually, they accepted this as their new norm. Or at least, Miya had.

"We can go whenever you'd like, not just for hunting," she said. "Like a date night!"

Kai snorted back a laugh.

Miya pushed her back against his chest and looked up at him, his face upside down. "Oh, come on! Everyone likes to be wooed occasionally. Movie and dinner?"

He clicked his tongue. "Cliché. Try harder."

"All you can eat steak and...?"

His lips grazed her ear, his breath a seductive whisper. "Start a bar brawl with me."

"Such a...hopeless romantic..." Her muscles were letting go, everything fading as she fought to keep touch with the conversation. Thoughts melted into obscurity. Her lips moved but formed only an incoherent mutter.

"Sweet dreams," she heard Kai say, the words muted like they'd been spoken underwater. She melted into familiar warmth, no longer aware of where her body ended and where his began.

Sticky heat pressed down on Miya's skin, the shapes of soaring cypress trees and winding boughs barely visible in the steam. She was in a swamp, the plant life saturated and drawing sustenance from water flooding the landscape. Leviathan tree roots protruded from the bog in slithering arches. Her feet submerged, she stumbled forward as tall grass caught her ankles. She knew this was a dream —a dream within the dreamscape.

The dreamscape was a world she could step into like one stepped into a room, but she always carried her dreams with her; they come from inside, swallowing her up while she slept. It didn't matter whether she was in the dreamscape or the physical plane.

"Don't be afraid."

It was her *again. Miya thought* she *would've gone by now, but even after three years, the ghost of her past clung to her like a shadow.*

Miya steadied herself against a cypress tree, taking stock of the flooded forest around her. There were no animals, no birds or even insects. It was too quiet. Coal-coloured clouds rimmed with amber darkened the sky, and the narrow path opened towards a black lake with algae strewn across the surface. It was perfectly still save for a single ripple that roiled from a circular cay. A crooked grey elm sprouted from the islet, and beneath its leafless branches, a figure peered out over the water.

Miya walked into the lake and waded through the green slime, her toes barely scraping the bottom. She shook the sinewy weeds from her hands and feet as she clambered onto the shore. As she approached the elm, the figure grew clearer: a tall man with dark, dishevelled hair and a warrior's build.

"Kai?" she called, pushing forward until she could reach out and touch him.

His expression was vacant as he turned and stared right through her like his soul had been carved out, leaving only a husk behind.

"Hey, what's wrong?" She waved her hand in front of his face, but his eyes didn't follow.

Instead, his hands shot out and wrapped around her throat. He plunged her into the water and squeezed. Miya grappled against his hold, her vision tinted mossy green by the plant life glazing the bayou. She opened her mouth to scream, but her voice dissolved into the liquid abyss. All the while, Kai held her down, his face smearing like a painting blotched by a spill.

He was too strong to fight off, but she'd be damned if she was snuffed out by a nightmare-puppet. Twisting underwater, she clawed at his arm and managed to resurface just long enough to see the elm looming overhead.

A silhouette hung beneath it.

The umbral mass glided closer, obscured by Kai's towering form. Miya's gaze trained on the space behind his shoulder. A woman's hands—grey, putrid flesh—slinked around Kai's neck. Gaping slits slashed diagonally across her boney arms like gills. Gradually, the rest of the creature emerged. She was something between woman and fish. Her unruly hair resembled the lake algae and clung to her rot-speckled face. Cheekbones protruded like marbles in a worn *leather sack, and inky shark-eyes with slit-green irises shone from the caverns under her brow.*

Blackness bloomed across Miya's vision as she was submerged again. She was drowning. Fear raked up her throat as Kai's fingers clamped tighter, ensuring the terror remained locked in place.

"Open your eyes."

A familiar voice.

"Open your eyes, Dreamwalker."

Miya gasped for air, her heart racing through her ribs as she scoured the empty, white void. The swamp, its macabre resident, and the distortion of Kai were gone.

"Psst, over here."

Miya squared her shoulders towards the beckon. It was the echo of the original Dreamwalker—Miya's first incarnation, and the entity who'd haunted her while she was still just a girl in a village. She'd stayed like an imprint from a past life, following Miya after her awakening. A shadowy, feathered cloak billowed around her, and a bone mask disguised her face, though Miya knew it was likely her own.

"What's happening?" asked Miya. "Who was that woman?"

"You must hunt them." Urgency laced the command.

"Hunt who?"

Her reflection from another life strode forward. "The demons. Hunt them." A sharp smile cut across her face, splitting the edge of the mask. "They're already hunting you."

A blustering wind ripped past them, blocking Miya's vision as her hair was swept up. "But why?" she called over the blaze. "Why am I being hunted?"

"You keep wandering, stumbling into nightmares where you don't belong." Her predecessor's lips stretched further over her teeth. "Demons love the smell of a lost lamb."

The Dreamwalker had a knack for getting lost, no matter the lifetime.

"I can't help it," said Miya. "I don't know how to find my way."

The spirit's smile retracted. "Use the stone," she advised. "Follow the raven."

She raised her arms, her cloak swelling. Throwing her arms against the wind, she thrust herself skyward. Black and violet bled from her garbs and swirled through the air like dye through water, devouring the white void.

The dark fabric encasing them unravelled, and Miya tumbled through the rift below.

3

MASON

MASON THOUGHT he'd eventually get used to this. Gripping the folder between his fingers, he allowed himself a moment —for composure, he told himself—to breathe away the pounding in his chest. His stream of success could never wash away the bitter suspicion that *one day* he'd fail again. He flicked the folder open to the first page and immediately found himself dizzy with relief.

Today would not be that day.

He burst into his office, barely able to contain his excitement. "Great news, Miss Nassar! Our tests show you're officially cancer-free." He looked happier than his patient—a biology student at UBC whose life was put on hold after her diagnosis. Her family had flown in from Egypt to spend the first month of treatment with her, but she'd done most of the heavy lifting alone.

Dania Nassar pulled back her ferocious curls, her sculpted eyebrows drawing together. "Seriously?" she asked, breathless. "The leukemia's gone?"

"It is," Mason nodded, feeling a twinge in his chest. This was his second leukemia case with a university student. He imagined Amanda smiling, reminding him of the journey she'd put him on three years ago.

Dania's mouth dropped open before a bright, dimpled smile spread across her cheeks. "I can go back to class? Take my exams?"

"You can!" Her excitement was infectious.

"I can go to med school!"

Dr. Mason Evans signed his patient's release forms. He could hear her chuckling quietly, trying to contain her mirth. "Dania, I have no doubt you'll go to medical school if that's where your heart is."

"Hey, Dr. Evans? Is it hard treating people who might die?"

Mason finished his notes. *A clean bill of health.* For now. "It can be," he admitted, then leaned back and clicked his pen. "I wish I could tell you there's a way to prepare for it, but it's different for everyone."

Their celebration tapered into a prolonged silence. "Do patients die a lot?" Dania asked.

Mason smiled, his thoughts wandering elsewhere. "Even one death feels like a lot, but when you help someone survive, it feels like you've saved the world."

Dania smiled back. "I think that makes it worthwhile."

Mason stood up to shake the young woman's hand. "I'll see you for your check-up in three months."

He flopped back into his chair after she left and rubbed his eyes. He had plenty of open cases to review, and at least a third of them didn't look great. Reaching for the pile, Mason skimmed through his remaining patient files, his heart sinking at one in particular.

Ronnie Kaplansky, male, eighteen, aggressive non-Hodgkin lymphoma. Mason took a deep breath. Ronnie was his most difficult case, and he was one of several doctors working to improve the boy's chances of survival. As a medical oncologist, Mason worked with radiation, targeted therapies, and immunotherapy, making him responsible for the chemo and antibody treatments. He was impassioned by Ronnie's situation, and that scared him. He didn't need another Amanda worming into his heart. Mason struggled to strike a balance between Lindman's pessimism and his own savior complex; it was a slippery slope in either direction. He wondered where Ronnie's fight would take him.

"Shall I tell your fortune?"

The woman's voice tugged Mason out of his thoughts. He hadn't heard her enter, her striking amber eyes and silvery-white hair seizing him.

She simpered and cocked her head. "You seem apprehensive."

"Ama," he finally managed.

"It's been a while. Three years, is it? You seem well."

Mason whipped his drawer open and sifted through until he found the fractured, iridescent rock, then held it up to the light. "Gavran broke it." He sounded accusatory. A *specific* raven had pilfered half the stone while Mason was unconscious in the hospital.

"It's not yours," Ama replied. "I don't think Gavran expected you to be so possessive of it."

Mason chuckled. "And here you are offering to tell my fortune?"

Ama shrugged. "If you'd like."

"Is that wise? Telling someone like me the future? You know I'd just drive myself crazy trying to change it."

The wolf's smile fell away as she regarded him. "You've changed."

Mason tutted. His eyes were hollowed out by dark

memories. "It would be absurd not to change. I was the only one who survived."

"You were the only one who remained," Ama corrected.

Mason waved her off. "Semantics. Why are you here, anyway? I haven't gone rambling about your secrets."

Ama blinked, feigning innocence. "Just saying hi to an old friend."

"I don't believe you."

Ama only replied, "You didn't believe in *her* either."

"You mean the Dreamwalker?" If he was to trust what he'd seen, then Miya and Kai were alive. Besides, their bodies were never recovered.

"She needs that stone in your hands more than you do," said Ama. "But Gavran understands you need it too. That's why he broke it."

Mason sighed. "You'll have to give me more than a riddle, Ama."

Sombre clouds drifted over the sun, and her honey eyes seemed to glow as a shadow drew over the room. "A storm approaches," she warned. "Guard the stone. Keep it close until the time comes."

"The time for what?"

Her lips quirked, a single pointed tooth gleaming on her lip. "To make her whole."

A knock sounded on the door, jostling Mason from the white wolf's spell. "Come in!" he stammered, swatting at the papers on his desk.

"Ama, you should probably—" *step out*, he was going to say, but she'd disappeared like an apparition. Had she really been there at all?

"Dr. Evans?" someone called from the now open door. "Apologies for the intrusion. Are you busy?"

"No, please, come in," Mason stood and gestured to the empty chairs in front of his desk.

A middle-aged couple poured in. He knew the man from somewhere—his tall, lanky frame and salt and pepper hair —but Mason couldn't place him. The man guided his wife to one of the chairs, then unbuttoned his suede jacket and sat in the other.

"We apologize for taking time from your work," the man started. His green eyes met Mason's. "My name is Raymond Delathorne, and this is my wife, Andrea." He extended a hand, which Mason hesitantly shook.

Andrea remained silent, offering a ghost of a smile. Tired circles rimmed her lashes, and she wrung her hands together as she pressed her elbows against the armrests. Wavy black tresses framed a stunning heart-shaped face, and Mason imagined her bronze skin glowed like the sun when she was well-rested.

He remembered thinking Miya looked nothing like her father, and now he understood why.

"Delathorne," Mason breathed out.

"Yes," said Raymond. "You may remember our daughter, Emiliya."

Sweat pooled at the back of Mason's neck. Why were they here? The events of *that* night were so long ago, yet still so fresh. "I—"

"We believe our daughter is still alive." Andrea finally spoke for herself. "Her body was never found."

"That's not uncommon in missing persons cases." A gut-level urge to squash their hopes overcame Mason. He knew Miya was alive, somewhere, but Andrea and Raymond Delathorne were probably better off believing otherwise.

"No," Andrea replied. "She's not dead. There've been sightings, reliable ones. Her best friend saw her in New York."

"New York?" Mason's eyes darted between the couple.

"Her friend, Hannah, moved there from Burnaby last

year for work," Raymond explained. "We hadn't heard from her in years, but several weeks ago, she called us out of the blue."

"We were skeptical," said Andrea, "but Hannah insisted. She said she was certain."

Certain enough to stir the grief back up. Perhaps Mason's attempt to cast doubt wasn't for Miya's parents' sake. There wasn't a single day that went by without Mason fighting the impulse to investigate. No, it wasn't her parents who would've been better off thinking their daughter was dead. It was Mason.

"That's wonderful news," he feigned with a tense smile. "But, may I ask, what's this got to do with me?"

Raymond's mouth twisted like he was perturbed that Mason hadn't gleaned their purpose. "You were the last person to see her alive."

Mason swallowed. "I was?"

"That's what the police report says, on the basis that you were the only surviving witness that day."

"Right," Mason exhaled.

"Are you all right, Dr. Evans?" Raymond's concern struck Mason as artificial.

"Hon, take it easy." Andrea unclasped her hands to touch her husband's arm. "I'm sure it's a traumatic memory for him as well."

Mason hung his head, and his façade peeled away. "I spent a year in therapy after that night, coming to grips with what happened."

"And what *did* happen?" pressed Raymond.

Mason strained a laugh. "Well, that's just it. Turns out, *coming to terms with what happened* is impossible, because I have no idea what the hell happened. What I really had to come to terms with was *not* knowing. I had to accept that I'd never know." Saying it out loud made his voice quake with resentment. He still hadn't accepted it; he'd simply learned to suppress it.

"Would you be willing to share your experience?" asked Andrea, leaning forward in anticipation. "I can't imagine how difficult it must be, but if there's anything—"

"Nothing that could help you find Miya," Mason interjected, then added after a pause, "It was the town's fault. They didn't see her when she was right in front of them. They were going to kill her." He skipped the part about Raymond being complicit.

Andrea pulled back like his words had struck her across the face. Raymond was still as stone, his knuckles paling as he clutched the armrests. The expectation of propriety wore thin.

"If Miya's out there and hasn't come back by now, it's because she doesn't want to be found," Mason said.

"I see." Raymond eased his grip and stood. "You have a point, Dr. Evans."

The concession caught Mason off guard. When Raymond roused the crowd at the church, declaring that Miya had been taken by something out in the woods, Mason reckoned he was dealing with an austere man who had little capacity for self-reflection.

"I wasn't there enough. Work preoccupied me, and I failed as a father when my daughter needed me." He nodded to Andrea, who rose to her feet and joined her husband. "But we cannot overcome this if we pretend to be dead to one another."

"Dr. Evans, if you'd be willing to help us in any way, you are always welcome." Andrea's invitation sounded more like a plea. "We're working alone—just two heartbroken parents trying to find their missing girl. The police can't be bothered with a cold case, and our PI has lost interest. You must understand, you're our *only* lead at this point."

Mason ran his hands over his face and tried to swallow down the guilt. How many nights had he spent thinking about what he could've done differently? How many hundreds of times had he replayed the memories until he wasn't sure which parts he'd embellished and which were accurate? "I understand, Mrs. Delathorne. And I'll consider your proposal," he lied.

This seemed to appease her; she smiled brightly, her face coming alive with hope. "Thank you."

Raymond opened the door for his wife, then stalled on his way out. "It's interesting." He glanced back. "According to the police report, you didn't know our daughter at all."

Mason looked up from his paperwork, perplexed by the comment. "I didn't."

Raymond Delathorne caught him with the edge of a cold smile. "Yet only her friends know to call her Miya."

Before Mason could respond, Raymond stepped out and shut the door behind him.

As sharp as his daughter, Mason thought with a rueful chuckle, though his insides were churning. It was a threat— a hostile gesture belied by a calm, calculating exterior.

Bubbling under the thin membrane of alarm was a bone-deep ache, a ravenous hunger he'd been ignoring for three years. His appetite for the truth had yet to be slaked. Again, he found himself bouncing between the stages of grief, fumbling towards acceptance but finding only a sopping illusion of it. It was a consolation prize—another kind of denial.

If I could just have something, he bargained with the empty room. *Anything*.

But at what price?

"I don't care," he said aloud, his voice cracking. "I survived last time, didn't I? What more harm could come from some truth—a taste of closure?"

A searing pain on Mason's left arm severed him from the tangled web of emotions tugging loose. He unbuttoned his cuff and yanked up his sleeve. At the inside of his elbow, pink, swollen flesh framed a black crescent moon. It looked like a fresh tattoo, yet it burned like hot coals.

"What the hell?" He pressed his finger to the sickle, jolting as fire shot down his arm. The mark was hot to the touch like it'd been branded into his skin. He heard a whisper from his periphery and knocked his chair back as he shot to his feet.

"Ama?"

No response. The room darkled, shadows lurked in every corner, and something lurked in the shadows.

Get a grip, Mason tried calming himself, then snatched up the dream stone and clutched it tightly in his hand.

A voice crept into him.

To what does one grip, young doctor, when there is nothing left to hold on to?

4

KAI

KAI WASN'T one for long stretches of sleep. The human custom of conking out for a third of the day seemed tedious, if not dangerous. Naps kept him alert; if Shit were to meet Fan, he'd have no trouble evading the spatter. A wolf always had to be ready.

Kai was wrenched from slumber when Miya ploughed upright, then toppled over like a freshman at a kegger.

"You all right, Lambchop?" He squinted through the dregs of sleep.

Tears framed her eyes. Pushing Kai's arm away, she sat up and pressed her hands over her face, her breath falling heavy against her palms. Clumps of mushed-up grass streaked her forearms.

"The dreams are getting worse," she told him. "I still can't control it."

Kai propped himself up on his elbow. "Got lost again?"

Miya nodded. "Never anywhere nice, either." She

scooted closer and rested her forehead against his shoulder, her voice dropping to a whisper. "She was there again."

"The DW?" Kai liked the shorthand. Black Hollow had branded her name a slur, but the acronym made it sound tender to his ears again. He hoped it did the same for Miya.

Her breath tickled his skin. "Yeah, but it makes no sense. I *am* the Dreamwalker."

"Maybe your past life just wants to gossip?" Kai offered. "Either way, nothing makes sense here. Who the hell dreams in a dream world?"

"Me, apparently," she scoffed. "Every time I fall asleep, I hear something—like a dripping faucet. I try to ignore it, but it pulls me in, and it always leads to a monster. I see the monster, and the monster sees me." She plucked a clover from the flattened grass. "I think she's trying to protect me because I have no clue what I'm doing yet."

It'd been like this since Black Hollow; every time Miya dreamt, she was pulled to the things that go bump in the night. Honing the Dreamwalker's abilities didn't come with a manual, and no matter how hard she tried perfecting her technique, the results proved erratic. It was as much of an art form as a five-year-old finger painting on a housecat.

Their clumsy shambling hadn't all been futile, though. Three years ago, Miya's blood spattering the king of spades had thrust Kai into the dreamscape while Abaddon tortured her in a nightmare. It'd been an accident then. Now, she'd harnessed that ritual, using the card and her blood as a catalyst to tear the seam of reality and push them both to the other side—literally. Still, the ride was bumpy, and Kai often wondered if he'd one day find himself rearranged like a mangled doll with its limbs stitched on wrong.

Kai's arms tightened around her. "You'll learn."

"Will I?" Miya questioned. "She tells me to hunt them

so they don't hunt me, but I'm sick of dragging myself back and forth just to play exterminator. I never meant for us to become some demon-hunting duo!"

"At least you *can* go back," Kai's voice dipped. "You have that option."

Shit. The words were out before he could stop them. He'd been stuck in this three-legged race for years, though it sometimes felt like Miya was the one racing, with Kai getting dragged on his ass behind her. Realizing he was tethered to his partner right after dislodging Abaddon was like getting cudgeled by a giant chain-link. He coped well enough at first; he liked his Lambchop, and after a decade of solitude, the companionship was welcome. When it became clear that they weren't finding any answers—not to the *why* or the *how the fuck do we make it stop*—Kai's prickly frustration grew into something more cutting, and he didn't like where it was pointed.

Miya's face twisted with...guilt? Regret? Kai couldn't always tell the difference. Feelings were layered, weaving into a larger tapestry until the threads were indiscernible, but tapestries had patterns, and with enough practice, he'd learned to recognize them. Kai saw her lips part to apologize and stopped them with his own. He crashed his mouth to hers and devoured the rift between them, along with the guilt and regret trapped there.

She didn't question it, wrapping her arms around his neck and pulling him over her.

"It's fine," he said, then flashed her a wolfish grin, "because you're taking me to start a bar brawl."

"Yes," a voice drawled from behind. "Take your puppy to the park. He could use some exercise."

Kai was up and snarling by the second syllable. Crouched over Miya, he glowered at their uninvited guest at the top of the hill: a skinny kid he recognized too quickly for his liking—a raven wearing a corpse. He was a ventrilo-quist tugging strings from inside his own doll. Miya called him Kafka-the-boy, but Kai knew that wasn't his real name.

The little shit gave Kai a toothy grin, and his inky irises glistened with glee. *Teeth and claws are no match for wings*, his face said.

"It's been a long time, Dreamwalker." The words were directed at Miya, though his gaze remained fixed on Kai, staring him down.

Kai thought back to that grisly night in his cabin. The black mist puppeteering the bloodthirsty mob had crashed against the Dreamwalker's apparition while she and her raven stood guard over Miya's comatose body. The spirit united with the girl, and with the raven's help, plucked Kai from his violent battle and hurled him into the dreamscape. He'd woken up alone in the ethereal plane, determined to wait under the willow until Miya found him again. To Black Hollow, they'd vanished into thin air. Miya had become the Dreamwalker, and the remnants of the spectre that'd saved them existed only as an ancestral voice, bossing his Lambchop around in her sleep.

Then, the nightmares started, and the monsters they featured were *very* real. Three years and a dozen dead demons later, they were no closer to finding a way off the hamster wheel.

Miya pulled herself to her feet. "I haven't seen you since I arrived. I know you've been watching over me, Kafka."

The skin-bag shuddered in delight, his hair bristling like feathers. "Gavran," he hissed. "I'm a raven, not a crow."

Kai heard Miya's heart squeeze behind her ribs. She knew the name. Kai did too, but not because he'd heard it before. It was carved into Kai's heart like a scar, and the mention of it made the lesions ache with familiarity.

"Gavran," Miya breathed out like she was testing how it sounded.

"Take me to the Emerald Shade," said the kid.

Miya tilted her head. "What's that?"

"The willow tree." At least, Kai thought so. The leaves on its whip-like branches reminded him of green shards, and the cool shade underneath was the perfect place to come to after a nasty bender.

Gavran smiled so widely Kai thought the corners of his mouth might tear. "Lead the way, pup."

Kai wanted to rip Gavran's head clean off that noodle-thin neck, but he resisted. The raven was their only anchor to this place, and he'd finally shown his face after Kai and Miya had been unceremoniously dropped into the dream-scape three years ago. Miya scrutinized Gavran like she was trying to dissect him, tease apart the fleshy exterior and find his core. If anyone could do it, she could.

Kai turned on his heels, glared over his shoulder, and disappeared through the barrier of closely-knit trees bordering the hillside. Miya's footfalls softly followed, but the forest demanded attention even in the dreamscape. One misstep, one momentary lapse in focus, and the damn labyrinth would rearrange itself. The trees' bony arms reached for one another, twining and tugging until the shadows shifted and the earth moved.

The hanging star curled beneath the horizon, and night blanketed the sky like a spotless curtain torn by a sickle moon. Kai's eyes trailed the grove of birch trees hugging the oak with fire-red leaves. They burned even in the dark, and he could have sworn he saw pieces of ashen bark flaking away like scorched paper.

In a world that looked like an endless acid trip, his nose led the way as it always had. The willow smelled different from the wet, earthy odour of the forest. Its scent was sweeter, subtler, like a pleasant memory from a different life, and it was strongest after moonrise when the darkness swallowed the shadows.

"I'm impressed," Gavran patronized.

"With what?" asked Miya.

The brat gave a throaty snicker. "With how difficult he is to trick."

"He's a wolf," Miya chuckled. "He's lived in forests a long time."

"These forests are not those of Black Hollow," Gavran whined.

Kai pulled back a wiry branch, then released it once Miya was in the clear. The little shit barely ducked in time, leaves catching in his hair as the limb swept over his head.

Miya whacked Kai's arm as he sniggered, then said, "No, they're not. Every forest has its own personality and its own memories. But there's something common to all forests, no matter what world you're in."

"And what's that?" asked Gavran.

Kai stopped where the trees opened into a glade—a yawning mouth in the black woods. As they approached, the mammoth willow's silhouette rose, and its wispy boughs whistled their greeting as they danced in the wind. Moonlight trickled trough them like silver threads and stippled the little green blades.

Kai smirked down at the raven wearing a corpse, his mahogany eyes glinting their triumphant red. "They don't like it when you see with your eyes."

Fleeting surprise flashed across the boy's face. "Funny," he choked. "I recall telling a foolish detective the same."

Kai stiffened like a dead raccoon at the mention of foolish detectives. He'd suspected Mason Evans couldn't untangle Black Hollow's secrets on his own, not with his hard-on for rationalism and those wasting chicken legs.

Whether the guilt-ridden doctor wanted to admit it or not, he was incapable of digging his way to the truth without an excavator—a malfunctioning one at that. From what Kai had gathered, Golden Boy hardly noticed the dipper scratching at the walls of his sanity in the form of a shit-for-brains bird.

"You egged him on." It wasn't a question. Miya's lips tugged in disapproval as she continued studying the raven-boy.

"He was making too much noise," hissed Gavran. His blue-black hair stood on end, his teeth cutting across his lips as the hiss devolved into a snarl. "Crunch, crunch, the twigs and leaves screamed, their bones ground to dust under his grief. Every step—crunch, crunch, snap, snap." His eyes widened and twitched. "He grieves too loudly."

"We're here." Kai gestured flippantly toward the willow. He secretly relished Gavran's disdain for Evans, but he wasn't naïve enough to express his solidarity, let alone anything that stank of vulnerability.

Gavran's shaking shoulders stilled. "Yes, we are."

"Emerald Shade, huh?" Miya approached the tree. "I didn't know it had a name."

"Every gate," whispered Gavran, scratching giddily at the trunk, "must have a name."

"Gate?" Miya echoed. "Between worlds, you mean?"

"Yes," the boy said. "Every tree has veins and roots. Follow them to find the right one."

"Why can't I just walk directly to the tree?" Miya asked.

"Things aren't always in the same place, not always aligned. This you have seen. But the roots never change. They are sturdier than the world."

Kai peered up at the willow. "Does this one always lead to Black Hollow?"

"Smart puppy," Gavran crooned. "As does mine. The Red Knot."

"Is that how you find your way?" asked Miya. "You know all the roots, so you know which ones to follow to get to the right tree?"

The raven-boy only grinned, his jagged little teeth filling the entire crevice of his gargantuan smile.

Miya crouched down and stared at the ground, her fingers tracing a line in the soil. "How do you see the roots?"

"Look with different eyes," Kai and Gavran advised in unison before the wolf smiled balefully at the raven.

"Maybe you're not needed," he goaded.

"Oh?" Gavran sneered. "Will you draw the map to the Grey Gnarl yourself, wolf?"

"The fuck is a..."

"Precisely."

"So, the willow is the Emerald Shade," Miya interrupted, circling the hefty bole. "What kind of a tree is the Red Knot?"

Gavran pouted as if disappointed that she didn't already know. "A redwood. Tall as the sun."

"The Grey Gnarl, then..." she trailed off.

Gavran's lips slithered out. He stepped forward and poked Miya between her eyebrows. "Look with different eyes," he repeated, his finger trailing down her nose and then sinking towards the ground.

Miya followed his motion and frowned at the leafy soil. Dropping to her knees, she brushed the dried willow leaves aside and burrowed her fingers into the earth like she was reaching for something.

Gavran cackled, the sound sputtering in the air like a firecracker. "Too soon," he hacked, "too soon!"

Miya withdrew her hand, then smiled sheepishly. "Guess

I don't know what I'm doing."

"Come," the boy beckoned. "I will take you there."

He pranced towards the willow, then jumped directly through the trunk and disappeared.

"Wait!" Miya called after him. To Kai's dismay, she followed without a moment's hesitation.

"Oh, sure!" Kai threw his arms up. "Just follow the creepy corpse child straight into a magical tree-portal."

Cursing under his breath, Kai went after his straying lamb. He half expected to break his nose against the bark, but as he braced for impact, the fossilized wrinkles gave way to a warm breeze and glaring white light. He lifted his arms to shield his eyes, then plunged forward, the world tipping until he was face-to-face with the ground. When Kai could stand again, he was on all four paws.

Sour swamp water rushed into his nostrils as he recovered from the whirlwind fall. He glimpsed Miya following the raven through ancient cypresses, her pace languid even as Shit-for-brains barrelled onward. The trees framing the murky stream were tall as skyscrapers, disappearing into stodgy clouds. Some twisted together, their mangled trunks looming oppressively as globs of moss drooped over low-hanging branches and caressed the stale water.

The bayou was shallow enough to pass through but deep enough to hinder Kai, and the overpowering smell of must dizzied him. Up ahead, Miya climbed over a giant, protruding root. It roiled at her touch, the drowning cypresses now crawling, closing in on her. Kai bolted forward, struggling to keep sight of the raven—now a tiny black blob hurtling through the miserable sky.

The tape grass tugged on his legs until he stumbled and found himself submerged in putrid green. His eyes stung, and he strained to hear the distant flap of wings.

He listened and listened, searching every frequency,

until finally, he managed to pick one up. Or rather, it picked him up. A woman's voice, soft as silk yet hard like stone, melted through his senses.

You poor, lost, little wolf.

The grass curled around his paws, pulling him deeper.

Can't even keep up with your straying lamb.

Kai clawed at the muddy floor, but he only sank further.

A lamb that's collared you so tightly...

The slender blades cut into him like wire until his elbows ached and his heart squeezed with fear.

...choking the life from you.

Lungs burning, Kai stopped his futile attempts to swim up and instead dove deeper, gnawing at the restraints and tearing himself free. But the voice came louder, angrier.

She'll strangle you with her chains!

Legs like needles scuttled against the sparse fur around his scalp, and something crawled into his ear. Pushing off his hindquarters, Kai launched himself towards the surface. The moment the water broke, the voice plummeted into the depths and disappeared.

With a soft whimper, Kai paddled down the river until he caught sight of land—a pea-sized island in the middle of a dark, algae-covered lake. He could see Miya there, waiting for him with Gavran at her side. Behind them lurked a lifeless elm tree, its crooked branches erupting from the blackened trunk like Medusa's snakes.

"Did the dream dampen your senses?" Gavran mocked as the wolf hopped onto the cay. He shook himself out from head to tail, water droplets spraying the boy.

Gavran shielded his eyes and scowled.

"The only thing that's damp is you and this swamp," Kai replied as he straightened into a man. It was all he could do to keep from squealing with apprehension. *It's over*, he reasoned, yet his prickling skin disagreed. Kai ran his palms over his arms, smoothing down the bumps. The dreamscape was full of unsavoury personalities—not unlike a dive bar on a Monday night. Whenever he and Miya waltzed off from their wholesome cubbyhole with its rainbow skies and hills like bejewelled ass-cracks, they could expect to meet a wayward devil or two lurking in the shrubs. Still, this felt...different.

It *knew* how he felt about the tether.

Miya huffed, grabbing Kai by the hand and tugging him towards her. "Aren't wolves and ravens supposed to get along?"

A sobering hum threaded through Kai's every nerve. The warmth of Miya's skin melted away the cold, waxy residue of whatever had touched him. For the first time since dropping through that hellish tree-hole, he felt the air fill his lungs with ease.

"In a relationship of convenience, perhaps," Gavran muttered as he combed his feathery hair back. "Shall we?"

Miya approached the elm, gazing up at its misshapen limbs. "It looks so twisted up."

"That's because it is," replied Gavran, his abysmal eyes trained on Miya. "You've been wandering. Dangerous places, they draw you. They hurt you."

Miya whirled around and squinted at the landscape. "I know this place! I came here recently."

"Yes," Gavran agreed.

"I saw something. A monster." She turned to Kai. "She wanted you to hurt me."

A chill coiled around Kai's spine. Was it the voice that'd spoken to him in the water?

"The original Dreamwalker's voice—my predecessor's, I guess—pulled me out. Told me to hunt them." Miya probed Gavran, "Is the monster from my dream next?"

"This tree—the Grey Gnarl—is the gate that will take

you to the monster. The Grey Gnarl is where she re-homed herself after fleeing her birthplace. Here, she finds new victims, untainted by her past." Gavran's slender fingers plucked at the bark. "It will take you where you must go— to the place where she haunts the living, feeds on their sorrows, their fears, their fragile egos." His head swivelled around like an owl's, and he peered at Kai. "She adores weak-willed men."

A growl simmered in Kai's throat. "I'm not a man," he seethed, yet uncertainty riddled every inch of him.

"Do we walk through the tree again?" Miya interrupted their duel. "To get to where we're going?"

The boy chortled. "No, sweet Dreamwalker. That would only send you to another part of the dreamscape, and you have yet to learn the winding roads of this realm."

"But we hopped right through the willow to get here," Miya observed.

"That may be how it seemed. When you find new eyes, you will see that it's less simple." He tilted his head to an impossible angle. "I followed the right root to get here."

"How do we get to the other side?" Miya asked. "Which root do we follow?"

"You do not follow the roots to find tears in the stitching." His hand ran over the elm's trunk, his long nails clipping every crevice. "You lose yourself in them."

"Lose myself?"

"Tangle yourself in the roots, Dreamwalker, and descend, as only you can."

A smile tugged at Miya's lips. "That, I can do."

So that was how the DW got around—by drowning in tree guts. Kai cracked his neck and pulled her to the ground. "Any idea where this will take us?"

"Not a goddamn clue," Miya replied, stealing his knife

and cutting her forearm with it. She dug the king of spades from her pocket and smeared him up.

Kai figured it was Dreamwalker witchy-woo-woo. He wondered if it had any purpose or if Miya had only imbued the ritual with meaning. Either way, it seemed to bolster her ability to blur the line between worlds—like the king of spades turned her blood into some chemical destabilizer for reality. She twined her fingers with Kai's, lay back, and clinched the card with her other hand.

Kai hated this part. He felt like a Lego toy being dismantled. His mind went blank, and his body felt weightless like he wasn't even real. Miya relished the challenge; every time they hopped realms, she strove to make the ride smoother, ecstatic whenever Kai managed not to puke.

He heard her inhale and exhale as she relaxed against the earth. Normally, this part didn't scare him, but something about the gnarled roots of the elm left him squirming. They looked like they could snuff him out if they vised around him tightly enough.

Kai closed his eyes. *Time to get wigged out*, he thought.

The air was stale and windless, the soil clammy as he felt himself sinking. Craggy bark scratched at the backs of his legs and writhed over his limbs. Kai held his breath, pushing down all the ugly things he didn't have space for. If he didn't try to breathe, he wouldn't find out that he couldn't.

All the while, he clutched Miya's hand—he'd shit himself if he let go—and hoped this leap of faith wouldn't get him killed. Everything quieted, and he gradually went numb as the boundary between worlds fizzled away.

KAI RASPED FOR BREATH. Blood raged in his veins like a river of fire as sweat slicked his skin. Returning to the world he'd spent most of his life in hurt worse than getting mauled by a bus. Every damn time, his body rebelled against the limitations of the physical plane. Only when he adjusted to the jarring switch did the pain let up. Maybe that was why *the change* always hurt like hell here, but in the dream-scape, he shifted seamlessly between forms.

"You okay?" Miya brushed his forearm, and his hairs stood on end. Some part of him was still spooked, and for a brief moment, he saw decaying fingers curl into his skin like a claw.

Kai shook away the vision, reminding himself that he was supposed to be over it. He shoved his anxiety away and corked it like a bottle of rancid wine. Why dwell on it when Miya was pressed against him? The swell of her breasts and the warmth between her legs nudged him awake, and heat twisted in the pit of his stomach. It was true that the physical world slapped him around a bit, but there were two sides to that coin. Everything felt more intense—the good and the bad.

Kai bit down on his primal impulses and sat up, his surroundings washing over him. It was humid as Satan's balls. Everything stank like pickle juice and wet clay, the air wobbled with smog, and a choir of cicadas and mosquitos nettled his ears. He looked down to evaluate the damage.

In the dreamscape, clothes were a projection of personal desire, and while they often transferred to the physical plane, sometimes Kai found himself lying naked in a muddy ditch with nothing but road rash on his ass. This time, he was pleased to find himself in light cargo pants and a black tank top, the lack of sleeves providing his armpits with much-needed ventilation.

"It's like a sauna here," Miya groaned, wiping the sweat from her brow. She groped around for the bloodied playing card, wedged between parched blades of grass, then tucked it in her jeans. Somehow, it never suffered any damage through all their dimensional travel.

They were on a riverbank at the edge of a massive swamp. Kai glanced westward where the orange sunset poked over the horizon and saw the outline of buildings around a sparsely populated road. It looked like a shithole, but shitholes usually had cheap bars. Dragging himself to his feet, he offered Miya a hand.

"I'm sure we'll find a lead in that town," she remarked, dusting off her jeans and peeling away her mauve jacket to reveal an old grey t-shirt. Her once coltish limbs had thickened with lean muscle; it wasn't easy running alongside a wolf. Miya pulled her hair back, several of the dark, wet strands catching her collarbone and neck. Her olive skin glistened with moisture, beads trickling down the side of her face.

"Mm," Kai mused, his eyes trailing the lines of her figure.

She peeked at him and snickered, a knowing quirk at the corner of her mouth. "Later."

Kai grinned. "Not into swamp sex?"

"Gross."

He gave her behind a playful smack, eliciting a surprised squeak. "Let's go, Lambchop."

As he started down the slope, she swatted him back, then hooked her arm with his and laughed. It was a short walk to the two-lane state highway that led into town. They passed a shoddy welcome sign Kai suspected had once been white, the washed-out print barely legible.

Orme's Rest.

Jewel of the Pearl River.

Beneath the town name and motto was a blue flag with a dirty pelican feeding its chicks.

"State of Louisiana," Miya muttered the words printed under the flag.

Kai was less concerned with their geographical location. "It had to be another small town," he murmured.

"Yeah," Miya sighed. "Not exactly my favourite destination."

Her arm tensed as she hugged his elbow tighter. He couldn't blame her; there was something about this place that smelled worse than the swamp water. It was the stench of Black Hollow...or at least something like it.

"Come on," he coaxed. "Let's get a drink."

The languid town was chockfull of chestnut oaks, their long, winding branches draped in Spanish moss. Stately white mansions and old brick townhouses bordered the main road, most of them serving as storefronts for boutique shops. Colourful flower baskets hung from the terraces and

A. J. VRANA

lampposts. Only an occasional car whizzed by, the quaint street otherwise empty.

"It's so wholesome," Kai gagged. Pulling Miya along, he turned the corner into a cobblestone alleyway. An antique sign hung from one of the few doors along the wall. It squeaked invitingly and swayed in the soupy breeze, the tavern's name scrawled across it in black paint.

The Mangy Spade.

"I think we found your watering hole," said Miya. "It's perfect."

Kai narrowed his eyes at the sign. "A little too perfect."

Lambchop tugged him inside. Red paint chipped off the door decorated with playing cards. They were trapped against the wood under clear resin, the king of spades greeting him with a dark-eyed stare as they passed.

The interior was dimly lit. Grungy leather armchairs and tattered sofas that looked like they'd been picked out of a garbage dump framed the dilapidated tables scattered around the space. Burgundy velvet stools lined the bar up front, the underlit wall behind it covered in shelves of booze. A burlesque chandelier hung from the ceiling, though it barely gave off light, most of the amber glow spilling from lanterns mounted on the walls and smudgy candle jars peppering the tables. Muffled rock music from the '90s and aughts droned from speakers strung up near the ceiling. Wincing at the gritty tones of an indistinguishable vocalist, Kai turned his attention to a mini grandfather clock tucked between two bottles of Jack. It was just shy of eight o'clock.

Besides one guy eating soggy nachos and drinking beer at the bar, the establishment was empty.

The Mangy Spade was a fucking dream come true.

"What's your poison?" the bartender asked as they strolled up to the counter. She was wearing a navy-blue tank top, her shoulder inked with a tattoo of Batman punching Hitler. Kai glimpsed a giant praying mantis on the inside of her forearm, the word *MANEATER* stamped underneath. The top of her undercut was dyed bright pink while the buzz remained bleached. There was something off about her—a tenor in her aura that quivered, slow and listless—like she was barely hanging on.

"Whisky," said Kai, eyeing the purple lipstick stain on her glass, the smell of gin and citrus wafting out of it.

"And for the lady?"

"I'm good with just Pepsi." Miya smiled sheepishly as she settled into the stool. "Isn't it usually Captain America punching Hitler?"

"Smart girl," the bartender guffawed. "Captain America's overrated. I like me some dark justice, you know?" She threw back the rest of her gin, then tossed Kai a wink. "Brains *and* beauty. Aren't you a lucky one?"

The man sitting a few stools away pushed his empty stein towards her. "You sure like the girls, don't you?"

"Gay as a fuckin' unicorn. Now go home, Clint. You're drunk."

The asshole belched and slapped his bloated belly. "You just need a good dickin'."

The bartender grimaced like she was biting back a vicious retort.

"Who'd want to touch your dirty dick?" Kai turned with a searing glare, a smirk crawling up the side of his face. He relished watching the blood flood Clint's blotchy face.

"Hey, screw you, man!" Clint shot to his feet, his eyes a cocktail of rage and humiliation.

"Nah." Kai grinned, canting his head towards Miya. "I'm spoken for." He rose slowly and loomed over his prey. "Don't think anyone here wants you."

Kai was ready for the swing. His fingertips tingled,

begging to curl into a fist as Clint's elbow pulled back—but the strike never came. Miya dashed between them and grabbed the drunkard's arm, pushing it down against the counter.

"Hey!" she snapped at Clint. "Cool it!"

Clint yanked himself free, wringing his wrist like she'd splashed boiling water on him. His teeth clamped shut as he all but frothed at the mouth. Silent with indignation, he slapped a twenty onto the bar top and tore his jacket from the hook underneath. "Cunt." He spat at Miya's shoe, then stormed out of *The Spade*.

"Goddamn," the bartender muttered, shaking her head. She shot Kai a pointed look. "Unnecessary, dude. But I think we could *all* use a drink after that—except Clint, that is." She reached for the bottles. "First one's on the house."

Kai hardly cared about what was *necessary*, especially when it came to fun. He would have enjoyed a good brawl with the blame easily pinned on the other guy. He already felt cooped up with too many unanswered questions bouncing around his brain. His fist breaking a few teeth might've settled his nerves. Shrugging in non-apology, he plunked down on the stool and pulled Miya onto his thigh. He nuzzled her hair and whispered against her ear, "Should've let me eat his heart out, Lambchop."

Miya scoffed and prodded him in the ribs. "And get the bartender into shit?" She asked more loudly, "Any reason you don't ban him?"

"Can't afford to. Business is tough nowadays, and Clint's a regular. He only gets this way sometimes, and by then, he can barely stand." Their host pushed the drinks forward. "Name's Crowbar."

Kai reluctantly accepted the gesture, swirling the tawny liquid around the ice cube. "Crowbar, huh? That your weapon of choice?"

She laughed, the sound light and airy—a strange juxtaposition to her cutting demeanour. She flicked her thumb over her shoulder at an iron lever mounted on the wall above the register. It looked like a trophy. "Few years back, some dumbass came in looking to hold me up for some easy cash. Thought a little girl behind the counter would be an easy target."

Miya sniffed the drink she'd been offered, though Kai caught a whiff of gin and lime from a foot away. Lambchop wasn't getting any Pepsi here; soda was for the weak. "What happened?"

Crowbar ran her tongue over her teeth, pouring herself more gin. "Sucker thought wrong."

"Guess you don't need me to kick a man's ass." Kai raised his glass in a toast. "Hope you broke a few bones with that thing."

"Oh, at *least* a few." Crowbar clinked glasses with him, then downed her shot. That one was followed by another, and then several more.

The last specs of sunset had disappeared, leaving the rat-sized windows of *The Mangy Spade* entirely dark. With time catching up to him, Kai's stomach cramped with hunger.

"What's good to eat around here?" he asked, flipping through a menu on the bar top. He peered over the laminate with a raised eyebrow. "Taco beef mac and cheese?"

Crowbar shrugged. "Whatever meat's leftover from the nachos, we throw into the mac and cheese." She winked at Miya. "Waste not."

Kai slapped the menu shut. "I'll take it."

Crowbar refilled on an umpteenth shot and shouted the order into the kitchen. By the looks of it, she was planning on getting sloshed at work.

Miya sipped her gin and smacked her lips in appraisal,

then had a little more. "So, what's got Clint drinking at the bar regularly?"

Crowbar passed her a glass of water. "Wife left him a few months ago."

"Well, he doesn't have to be a jerk about it." Miya glanced at Kai as he threw back his whisky.

Crowbar poured him another, continuing to help herself to the gin. "People can be far worse," she muttered, her voice suddenly soft, shaky even.

"You okay?" Miya asked.

Kai was always amazed at how readily Miya pried out people's crap. He didn't have her emotional intelligence, but he had his animal instincts. Crowbar's heart rate came hard and fast when she spoke, almost like the beating mass in her chest was trying to hurt her. She'd been so steady when Clint was hassling her, but now the smell of her sweat had changed—stress hormones running amok. She swallowed more often, probably because there was a lump in her throat.

Crowbar was about to cry.

"Ah, it's nothing." She smiled at Miya, her eyes a little glazed. Her voice was tight, the slight wobble giving her away. The booze had done its job to loosen her up, but instead of helping her forget whatever was eating her, it was stirring it up to the surface.

Miya took a large gulp of gin, her face scrunching and her cheeks turning ruddy. She grabbed the water to clear away the bite, then blew out a hefty breath. "Hey, I'm sure you listen to a lot of people vent. No shame in having them return the favour."

Crowbar laughed hoarsely and wiped a stray teardrop from her cheek. She picked up the gin, then set it back down, seeming unsure if it was worth drowning her sorrows any further. "It's just...I lost my sister recently.

Though I guess it's more accurate to say she was taken from me."

Kai held the rim of the glass against his bottom lip, the whisky burning through the dry cracks. He clacked it down on the counter. "By whom?"

Miya rapped him on the leg—a gentle admonition. "You don't have to tell us anything if you don't want to," she quickly swept over his blunder.

"Nah, it's all right." Crowbar picked at her nail polish until it flaked off. "It was her husband. Kind of grim for bar-talk, but it's not exactly news around here. Small town and all."

Kai felt his ears prickle with unease. He'd known there was something off-kilter when he'd first walked in. Something had latched onto this woman, something putrid like death ignored for too long. It was gnawing its way through her heart.

A hulking, broad-shouldered man with bleached dread-locks and dark skin burst through the kitchen doors, his entrance breaking their stony stares. "One taco mac and cheese!" he announced, the plate diving in front of Kai's nose. The chef wiped his hands on his greasy apron, speckled with dancing pink elephants, then gave Crowbar a hearty slap on the back.

The smell of sharp cheddar, chili powder, and cumin drew Kai's attention. He barely remembered to unwrap the fork from the napkin as he scooped the goopy pasta and shovelled it into his mouth. He nodded towards the big dude and said, "Good shit."

The chef offered a satisfied grin, leaned against the doors, and glided back into his kingdom.

Once the squeak of the hinges halted, Kai's gaze shifted back to Crowbar. She was drawing circles into the bar top with condensation from her glass.

"I'm sorry for your loss," Miya whispered, the air thick like vapour.

"It's ok," Crowbar shrugged. "I'm just glad the piece of shit's getting locked up for life."

Kai tilted the dish, watching the yellowed oil pool into one corner. "Why'd he do it?"

Miya's head snapped towards him, her lips pursed as she cut him with a glower.

Crowbar chuckled and shook her head. "It's all right, girl." She patted Miya on the arm, then topped up Kai's whisky with a sloppy tilt of the bottle. "To help with digestion," she told him before resting against one of the shelves.

Kai lifted the drink in thanks before helping himself to the social lubricant.

"Honestly, I'm not sure why he did it," Crowbar began. She was slurring a bit now, but the words kept coming. "They were happy. As far as anyone could tell, Vince adored Syd, but a few weeks ago, Syd said he started to change. He got cold, distant, snappy. Started avoiding her and everyone else—guy just wouldn't talk to anyone." She paused, her hand trembling before she locked down the grief with her nth drink. She'd been slamming back shots with Kai for over an hour now, the count long gone with the daylight. It seemed she hadn't spoken to anyone about her sister, or maybe it was just easier talking to strangers in a town where there were no secrets. With strangers, the stakes were low; it was a purge without commitments. That was how Kai kept afloat before Miya cracked him open like an expired egg.

Crowbar squeezed her eyes shut as she swallowed too fast, the liquor probably burning in her throat. "First, we thought he was having an affair—that maybe he'd killed her because he couldn't deal with the guilt."

Kai scraped the last of the cheese from his plate.

"Doesn't sound like something you'd do to someone you love."

Crowbar nodded, pointing a finger at him while she still clutched the glass. "Right! It just didn't add up. Police went through his stuff and didn't find anything—no phone numbers, emails, dating site accounts, bank withdrawals. Nothing!"

Miya grew fidgety, furrowing her brows as she stared at the table. "I don't know. Men kill women they love pretty frequently." Her voice was low, her posture stiff—tell-tale signs she wasn't speaking her mind.

A sour taste rose in Kai's mouth. Miya's father had nearly killed her. Could he really say it *wasn't* about a twisted kind of love? Just like in Black Hollow, there was probably something sinister exploiting that warped affection. Kai knew in his bones it was the *thing* Gavran had warned them about—the monster from Miya's nightmares. The one that'd pulled him underwater.

The Grey Gnarl was *her* gate.

A shiver wormed up his spine. The demon left pieces of herself wherever she went, and her stench clung to Crowbar. It'd found him too, and for one chilling moment, Kai swore he felt her decaying breath caress his neck. A soft, sickly-sweet giggle danced through the air, and his heart seized.

Crowbar pressed her forearms to the counter. "Police didn't give a shit. Just said it happens all the time. Tried to make it sound like he was ill, but I don't buy it. After it happened, Vince was heartbroken. He just kept saying he had no choice—not that it made it any better." She shook her head and cussed under breath. "Don't know what's worse—having someone you love get murdered for a deranged reason or having them murdered for no reason at all."

"The second one," said Kai, unable to shake the monstress' putrid scent. He raised his head and caught Crowbar's gaze, though his words were intended for a second audience. "If someone's going to end me, they better do it with some fucking purpose. Anything less and I'll haunt them 'til they find their grave."

Miya choked on her drink, beating a fist against her chest. "You sound like your dearly departed brother," she said between hacks.

Kai smirked and clinked his glass against hers. "Guess it's in the blood."

The unnerving presence was finally gone.

"So, what're you two doing here?" Crowbar interrupted their exchange. "Orme's Rest isn't exactly a tourist grab."

Miya and Kai traded glances.

"Looking for our employer," Miya answered.

Crowbar's mouth twisted into a frown. "Not sure I follow you, girly."

Miya smiled, her muddy green eyes softening. "I got called here for work. Nothing exciting, I promise."

If she'd said that horse shit smelled like roses and tasted like red velvet cupcakes, Kai would've believed her.

Crowbar's interest appeared to wane as she washed out her tumbler. "Yeah, man, the gig economy's tough. Takes people everywhere." When she hit the pump, dish soap erupted from the dispenser and splattered over her jeans. Swearing, she pulled some plastic cards from her pocket and slapped them down on the bar top.

Kai let his eyes drag past the glassware and settle on her driver's license. *Dahlia Rose Baron.* So that was her real name.

"We should go," he said, digging out his worn leather wallet. He leafed past his scrap of lilac birthday card—all he had left of Alice—and fished out a few bills. "Keep the change," he nodded as he folded the crumpled notes under his plate.

Miya washed down the rest of her drink with water and slid off her stool, smiling at Crowbar. "It was great to meet you."

Crowbar beamed in return. "Hope to see you again while you're in town. Really, I mean it."

"I'd like that too," Miya replied, tucking the stool in.

Kai didn't bother with the platitudes. Before Miya could stop him, he was already out the door. His fingertips brushed over the king of spades, a quiet nostalgia stinging like wooden splinters burrowed in his hand.

❦ 6 ❦

MASON

MASON STARED at the giant map of North America stretched over his corkboard. He'd wedged thumbtacks into various locations across the continent—all potential candidates for the Dreamwalker's interest.

How was she travelling? Her passport had been left in Black Hollow. She couldn't cross national borders without legal documents, and there was no record of her license being re-issued by British Columbia, at least according to the PI Raymond hired. As far as the file opened on Miya detailed, there had been no bank account or credit card activity, much less any indication of a government-issued ID matching Miya's age and description.

Mason considered that she didn't need earthly transportation, but that wasn't a theory he could indulge. Not because he didn't think it was possible, but because Raymond and Andrea Delathorne were unlikely to accept it.

It was ironic how readily they believed in the Dreamwalker's malevolent schemes while remaining intolerant to the possibility that their daughter was skipping across the world through alternate planes.

Mason scratched through his wiry, blond curls, his jaw clenching and releasing as he tried to puzzle out where to begin. This was an after-hours project, an extracurricular activity. He hadn't *really* agreed to anything, but he had to remind himself that he had a job and people to look after.

Yet the desire to drop everything and fly to New York simmered like a hot pot about to boil over. Miya had been spotted in NYC by a childhood friend, Hannah Cleary, who'd landed a highly coveted job there as a make-up artist. Despite her busy schedule, she'd agreed to a phone call after Miya's parents passed on her contact info in an unsolicited email.

Mason plunked down in his armchair and dialled the number. After several rings, a woman answered.

"Hello?"

"Ms. Cleary, this is Mason Evans. I hope I'm not calling too late?"

"Not at all! Thanks for getting in touch...Dr. Evans, is it?"

"Just Mason is fine." After leaving Black Hollow, he'd retired the title outside of his practice.

"You can call me Hannah, then," she said, the sound of crinkling grocery bags in the background.

"Of course. Hannah it is."

"So," she ventured, "I guess you want to know about Miya?"

"Yes..." Mason trailed off, unsure of where to begin. "Not to be facetious, but I just want to confirm—you're absolutely *sure* you saw Emiliya Delathorne?"

Hannah laughed, and Mason felt the tension melt from his shoulders. She had a sense of humour. "I understand why you'd doubt me," she said, "but I'd bet my own life on it. I've known Miya since we were kids. She's always been different."

Mason felt his brows knotting. "What do you mean?"

"I don't know," Hannah sighed. "She's got a sixth sense about things."

Mason sat up and reached for his notepad. "Are you suggesting she's psychic?"

"No, not quite." There was a pause, followed by the sound of pasta or rice being dumped into a pot. "It's more like she's got her finger on everyone's pulse. She knows what's going on beneath the surface, and it comes at the expense of her own mental health."

Mason traced over the question mark he'd drawn on the blank page. "I'm sorry if this is a bit intrusive, but do you believe in the Dreamwalker?"

Hannah's breath drew in. "Yes. I know it sounds stupid, but how could I not after everything that's happened in Black Hollow?"

"It doesn't sound stupid," Mason murmured. "I'm just curious if you think Miya was really possessed by her."

"Honestly," Hannah mused, "it's hard to say who would possess who."

Mason knew the truth—that Miya *was* the Dreamwalker. He'd seen it with his own eyes, but he was curious if Miya's friends knew her better than her family seemed to. As far as Mason could tell, Miya was lucky; her best friend knew her quite well.

"Is there anything else you can tell me, Hannah? Anything at all."

"Well, she looked pretty good when I saw her," Hannah

scoffed. "She could have called, but I'm sure she has her reasons for staying away."

"You're not concerned?"

"No." Another pause. "New York City is...a haunted place. St. Paul's Chapel, Mulberry Street, Poe's residence while he wrote *The Raven*—there's no shortage of weird stuff here. If Miya's somehow tangled up with the Dreamwalker, I guess it makes sense she'd be visiting places that have a history. Maybe it's her way of making sense of what's happening to her, without Black Hollow's baggage."

Mason glanced up at the map. Hannah wasn't wrong. Canada's neighbour to the south was quite superstitious. There was no shortage of local news reports, blogs, and ghost hunting documentaries that detailed hauntings and demonic possessions, but Mason had no way of figuring out if Miya was involved in any of them. His eyes trailed over New York State, stopping on one notorious name from Long Island: Amityville.

Perhaps he could narrow the search.

"Thank you so much for your insight," he said, hurriedly bringing the call to a close when an idea clobbered him over the head.

After exchanging goodbyes, Mason jumped to his feet, dove into his chair, and skidded to his desk. Haunted houses were a dime a dozen, but if he found the worst ones in recent memory, maybe he'd have a hope of catching Miya's trail.

Mason browsed dozens of websites, yet few cases seemed dire enough to warrant a visit from the Dreamwalker. He needed something big that flew under the radar of popular media—something like Black Hollow.

There was consistent mention of two states: West Virginia and Louisiana. Since West Virginia was closer to

New York, Mason began his dig there, and he didn't have to dig deep.

Dawn Macintosh accuses realtor of failing to disclose haunting in under-priced Summersville home.

Mason skimmed the article, his interest piqued.

After spending thousands to hire popular ghost hunting team, Ghostventures, Summersville resident claims that the malevolent forces terrorizing her home only grew stronger. Shunned by neighbours and turned away by her local pastor, a desperate Mrs. Macintosh reached out to a specialist in an undisclosed practice, which she described as "a kind of witchcraft." The unnamed witch allegedly worked free of charge to cleanse Mrs. Macintosh's home. Mrs. Macintosh reports that the intervention was successful, but she has not provided the name of the specialist she contracted, describing her as a young woman who claimed to be "something like a witch."

Mason opened a new tab and searched *witches for hire* in West Virginia, but he found nothing that matched Dawn Macintosh's description. The fact that Mrs. Macintosh herself appeared dodgy about the details in her interview with the journalist only aggravated Mason's suspicion that the woman in question—*something like a witch*—was the best lead he had. The chances were minuscule, but something in him burned to know if his hunch was right. Besides, why would anyone work for free unless they had no use for the money?

Mason scratched at his arm, nails digging into the prickling flesh. The itch was somewhere beneath the skin, somewhere close to the bone.

If only he had a way of *knowing.*

The itch sharpened into a sting, and Mason's fingertips turned slick with something moist. He'd drawn blood from the inside of his forearm, right next to the peculiar black crescent that'd appeared after Miya's parents visited.

He'd tried ignoring it, foolishly hoping it would disappear. But there it was, a mark that hadn't been there before.

The voice—wasn't there a voice?

If you seek truth, I shall give it.

Mason jolted upright, spinning his chair so fast one of the wheels came loose.

"Who's there!" His voice cracked as his eyes darted around the empty room.

A servant, the voice answered.

Mason didn't trust it, but he knew better than to disbelieve.

"Am I—"

You are not hallucinating. The voice was gentle, reassuring. *Remember, you resolved to discard such rationalizations.*

Mason squeezed his eyes shut. He hated to admit it, but the thing speaking to him was right. No one in his family had a history of psychosis, and aside from his stint in Black Hollow, Mason's perceptions had never been medically suspect. He'd concluded that his experiences in Black Hollow were real—every last one of them.

Was it farfetched that he'd again be plagued by mysterious voices and otherworldly truths the moment he resolved to search for Miya—the Dreamwalker and the missing girl all in one?

No, it wasn't.

"How can I trust you?" Mason asked shakily. He leaned back in his chair and surveyed his office.

I do not ask for your trust, the voice replied. *I promise only truth.*

"That's vague," Mason countered.

The voice was silent for a moment, as though considering Mason's unease.

I can tell no lies, it said at last. *Whatever question you have is mine to answer.*

How Mason wished he had Ama with him. She'd know what to do; she always did, but he had no way of beseeching her advice.

He would have to brave the storm alone.

"All right," Mason huffed, glancing down at the mark on his arm. The wound was starting to scab, the burning itch fading to a tingle. "Who helped Dawn Macintosh cleanse her home?"

She is the one you seek.

Mason's heart pummelled the inside of his chest. His instincts were right. "Is she still in Summersville?"

No.

"Then where is she?" he demanded.

I do not know.

"I thought you knew everything," Mason muttered, disgruntled.

I never claimed that. Only that your questions were mine to answer truthfully.

"Why don't you know the answer to *this* specific question?" he interrogated.

Because your target is not human. She is a living god. Gods go where they please, sometimes without a trace. This one is chaos; she is not bound by the laws of your reality. She transcends them.

Defeated, Mason leaned his head back and closed his eyes. "How do I find her then?"

There was a lull in the air before the voice spoke.

Your god was born of violence, and to violence she will return.

Mason's eyes shot open. Of course. God or no, all people were creatures of habit. They were driven towards the familiar, to the patterns they'd learned in life—or in Miya's case, throughout multiple lifetimes.

Gavran had told him repeatedly. Mason could still see those eerie, depthless eyes and that wide, cutting grin, sharper than a knife.

Everything beats in cycles.

7

KAI

KAI HAD a singular purpose when he pulled Miya from *The Mangy Spade*. His eyes flickered across the rust-coloured wall until he caught a narrow lane stretching behind one of the buildings. The hunger coiled inside him, urgency rising, and when he couldn't stave it off any longer, he snatched Miya's hand and led her into the dark.

The bone-coloured moon hung heavy in the sky; it was past nine, and there was no one for miles. Even if there was, Kai didn't really give a damn. Want burned in the pit of his stomach and crawled up his ribs where his heart released a jostling thud.

He pushed Miya to the wall and caught her lips between his teeth, his hands already at her hips. Her gasp was like music—sweet and sharp as she grabbed his wrist and guided his hand between her thighs. A heartbeat later, she kicked her pant leg free and yanked at his belt.

Fucking was better in the physical world. It felt more real—the smell of her skin, the taste of her sweat, her breath ringing clearer in his ear. Even the orgasms were better. His senses buzzed with life when he felt her coming, her thighs clenched around him as she muffled a cry against his shoulder and released a long, shuddering breath.

In the dreamscape, it was different—like some vital piece of him was missing.

When her feet met the ground, she groped for her jeans, splayed over the cobblestones, and tumbled forward against his chest. He wrapped both arms around her, enjoying the warmth of her body before she pulled away and smiled.

"Couldn't wait until we got a hotel room, huh?" Her face was still flushed as she wiped the moisture from her brow.

Kai thumbed the scratch marks on his abdomen where she'd clawed at him beneath his shirt. "More fun this way."

Miya pointed at his cargo pants as he zipped up the fly and re-fastened his belt. "But those could have come all the way off if we'd waited."

Kai shrugged, unconcerned, then walked over and slung an arm around her shoulders. They meandered from the narrow lane, bricks scraping his shoulder as they tottered clumsily with limbs like soft rubber. "I like watching you put men in their place."

Heat rose to her cheeks. "Is that what got you going?"

Kai hummed in contemplation. "I was already going. But that was probably the last shot of blood my nether-regions could handle."

Miya cackled as they strolled onto the main road. "Sorry, not sorry."

"You *monster*," he murmured in her ear, then nipped her lobe.

As they emerged into the lamplight, Kai nearly bumped into a bewildered passerby and twisted to avoid collision. Colour drained from the greying man's face. His saucer eyes wobbled over Kai's imposing figure as he reeled back, then scurried away.

Kai glared after him, the rhythmic cry of cicadas pulverizing his ears. He couldn't tell if the sticky feeling on his skin was from the mid-summer humidity or something else. Wherever he went, he stood out like a bloodstain on a white shirt. Sometimes, he wondered how much of his rage leaked through his pores. Could people smell a loaded shotgun with the safety off? Wrinkling his nose, he shoved down the impulse to yell after the sod who'd gawped at him like he'd murdered a basket of baby rabbits.

"This town smells like zombie shit," he seethed quietly. Miya ran a hand up his back, trying to distract him. "I can't smell it, but I can feel it. We need to learn more about Crowbar's sister. She's definitely the reason we're here."

A mosquito whirred, and Kai slapped a hand to his neck in a half-hearted attempt to squash it. Between the bloodsuckers and the serenades of dying, overgrown flies, he wasn't sure which would break his sanity first.

Kai glanced down the darkened street, lit only by the meager, piss-coloured glow of lantern-shaped sconces sporadically lining the storefronts. Insects hurled themselves at the muggy glass before dropping dead into the planters that hung from the light fixtures' ribbed necks.

So human of them, Kai thought, remembering his last night in Black Hollow. The way flesh tore and bodies fell limp with empty thuds and quiet gargles.

"Could break into the police station and steal Vince's records?" he suggested, vaguely wondering how many lives he'd ended that night. Ten? Fifteen? Maybe twenty?

Miya glanced sideways at him. "Overkill much? Besides, the police won't be able to give us anything we can use. Pretty sure they don't jail demons for murder."

He shot her a narrow-eyed look. "Out of my head,

Lambchop." She only blinked, befuddled by his meaning, so he pulled her along in the direction dread filled him fastest. It was unsettling how empty Orme's Rest was. The townspeople seemed to hide as soon as the sun dipped below the skyline, like they knew not to fuck with the funky stench caking the air. Black Hollow was a superstitious cesspool, but people still went out at night, getting trashed, dealing drugs, looking for a lay. In this lethargic stink-hole with its ye olde-timey roads, drooping trees, and plant beds full of daisies to mask the animal shit, doors were slammed shut and crucifixes clutched tightly alongside grandma's pearls. At least, that's how Kai imagined it.

There was no one to snatch up and squeeze secrets out of, and although there shouldn't have been any rush, Kai could hear Crowbar's clock, sandwiched between two liquor bottles, ticking against his temples like a warning. They didn't have much time.

"Other ideas?" Kai scrunched up his face as he imagined Miya raising Crowbar's sister from the dead. "I'm *not* going gravedigging."

Miya reached for a row of dappled pink lilies planted around latticed benches. The petals brushed her palms as she ambled onward. "Why would you need to dig up a dead body? I just need something that can give me a glimpse."

"A glimpse? Into what?"

She rolled her neck and pulled the scrunchy from her hair, shaking out her dark brown mane. "Spirits leave a residue on the things they touch. If we had access to Sydney Baron's murderer, I'd know right away if he was influenced by something. He's in custody, so we need to find the next best thing."

"Like something that belonged to the victim?" Kai asked.

"That would be good, but we can't ask Crowbar for her sister's stuff without one hell of an explanation."

Kai slowed and squinted at her. "Not. Going. Gravedigging."

Miya tied her hair back up into a messy bun. "Like I said, I don't need her *body*. Maybe there's something around her tombstone we can use."

"Fine," Kai huffed. He hated cemeteries. They were places where the dead were immortalized, commemorated for those left behind. Every death had left Kai with little to remember the loss by. His parents had never been buried. Their bodies disappeared into the earth—rotting corpses desiccated by scavengers and the unyielding attrition of time. Alice had no relatives, no savings to speak of. Her body was cremated by the coroner, her ashes clumsily thrust into the hands of an angry, confused teenage-boy-who-wasn't-actually-a-boy. Her crumbling bungalow was fore-closed, and Kai's application for emancipation was tossed on sight. He had a history of juvenile delinquency and anti-social behaviour. *Conduct disorder*, the shrink had called it. As far as Child Protection Services were concerned, he belonged in a foster home or an institution. He was a dumpster fire they weren't willing to let loose.

Kai never got the chance to visit old Alice's bones, and now every graveyard he saw made his insides writhe with longing for all the things he'd never know.

Fuck, how he'd changed. Three years ago, the sight of a tombstone would've made him feel like a Molotov cocktail begging to be thrown. He couldn't have known that deep under that hardened rage was something brittle, something that made him look back and regret that he hadn't done better than a goddamn birthday card to enshrine Alice's memory. That emotion, he'd learned, was guilt. And it stung worse than an acid-coated knife shanked between his ribs.

Anger had always been so much less painful.

"Hey." Miya tugged on his shirt. Her murky green eyes riffled him with concern. "You okay? If you feel that bad about it, we can go back and ask Crowbar."

"No." Kai shook his head. "We're hunting the thing that attacked you. We shouldn't get anyone else involved." Of course, he didn't mention the thing from the swamp had already made contact...twice.

Miya plumbed him with a dubious stare. She knew he was hiding something. "All right," she let it slide. "Which way to the cemetery?"

Kai tilted his head back and inhaled. In a healthy city, the scent of death wasn't present outside the usual places— butcher shops, graveyards, funeral homes, crime scenes, accidents. Death was contained, isolated. Here, the flower nectar, the earthy aroma of trees, and the waft of grilled seafood could barely mask the grizzly undertone of rot. It was strong—so strong that he'd already found himself following it.

"Same way we're headed." He pointed eastward, the sky like a sprawling, black plume.

"Okay." Miya hooked her arm around his, still scanning his face.

"I miss Alice," he answered her probing gaze. "Threw her ashes to the wind—and not in the romantic way. I threw her *out*. Now that I want to go back, I can't. I can't visit her because I destroyed what was left of her."

Miya's hand slid down his arm, and she entwined her fingers with his. "You were going through a rough time. I don't think she'd hold it against you for not knowing how to react."

Kai's breath hitched, his mouth curving into a ghost of a smile. "She'd probably laugh if she knew her ashes ended up as bird feed."

"Then maybe the ashes aren't what's important," Miya offered. "But if you'd like, we can always make her a little shrine in the dreamscape. Maybe we can get a sapling from somewhere?"

"Maybe," he murmured, then clutched her hand as he strode forward, away from his own brooding.

He silently counted the cracks in the sidewalk as he trailed the scent of death to its final resting place. The Orme's Rest Cemetery was perched on a mound behind the local church: a modest, white-paneled building that looked like a farmhouse with a red-brick spire poking through the front of the roof. Windows lined the side of the rectangular structure, though it was dark inside.

They followed a two-pronged dirt path that looked ploughed through the tall, unkempt grass. No one was around, and it didn't take long to spot several new graves with fresh dirt swelling before the tombstones.

"There," he said as they passed one. "Sydney Maria Baron."

Her name was carved in dark stone that glittered in the moonlight. In the center was a sepia portrait of a young woman with shoulder-length, curly hair. *Beloved sister and daughter*, the epitaph read. Kai was surprised by its simplicity, as though the brevity revealed how much couldn't be expressed.

A bunch of white roses in a blue-tinted vase sat next to the slab. They seemed freshly snipped off a bush, lacking the polish of a store-bought bouquet.

"White roses are my favourite," Miya said softly. "It's strange, feeling sad while admiring something you love." She crouched down. Her fingertips grazed over the petals before she pinched a thorny stem and plucked a flower from the bunch. "This'll work."

Kai raised an eyebrow. "A single rose?"

"I can feel so much on it." Miya examined the flower, still speckled with dew. "Crowbar got these recently. It's like they absorbed all her emotions the way they absorb water. But there's more—something under the grief. Something... sticky. Unwelcome."

Kai dropped his nose to the flower. It was true—he detected Crowbar's scent, but it mingled with something else: the same rancid odour he'd picked up in *The Mangy Spade*. The thing that'd breathed down his neck.

"Let's get a hotel room," Miya instructed. "I'll need someplace quiet to concentrate, and the trail won't last more than a few hours."

Without waiting for his input, she turned on her heels and headed down the slope. It was the three-legged race again, and Miya always led the way. Perhaps if he knew *why* they were tethered—why he had to shadow her every move —he would have felt more at peace with it. He wondered if she even noticed he was like a dog on a two-foot leash. She had the freedom to move between worlds; he couldn't even stay in this one without her.

Back on the main road, it didn't take long for them to spot an inn close to Kai's new watering hole—a three-story, yellow-brick townhome with a sign out front that read *Mildred's Guesthouse*. As they stepped through the whining door, Kai was assaulted by the smell of dust. A bespectacled woman with greying hair looked up from her mystery novel, apparently befuddled by the presence of customers in her establishment. She was accompanied by a bean-shaped, bushy-tailed tuxedo cat loafing on the desk and a cross the size of a welcome sign hanging on the wall behind her. The cat stretched and yawned, then slithered around the woman's hand before hopping to the floor.

"Can I help you?" she asked, her tone nasally and suspicious. She glanced at the clock—half-past ten.

"We're looking for a room," Miya said.

The woman—presumably Mildred—blinked like her brain was processing at the pace of a '90s PC. When she finished computing, her mouth popped open, and her eyes widened. She looked between the two of them, then asked cautiously, "Two beds?"

"One bed," Kai warned. Fuck her puritan virtues. That, and he was short on cash.

Mildred shrank back, her disapproval quickly buried under Kai's menacing glare. "Of course."

Miya thwacked his thigh and hissed, "Be nice."

Just then, the stubby feline brushed against Kai's leg, its plump tail snaking around his ankle. The hairs on the back of his neck stood on end as he beat down the urge to consider the cat a dinner option.

Lambchop shot him a warning look, and Kai glowered back, then picked up the fat cat. Nose to nose, he stared the furball square in the eye as its limbs dangled pathetically. "You're a meager shadow of your ancestors."

Miya's hand shot in front of his face as she clasped the aluminum nametag between her fingers. "Petunia," she read aloud, "is adorable."

Mildred looked perturbed, but Kai wasn't finished. "This is how I feel about golden retrievers," he said. "Your species has ruined a perfectly good apex predator."

Miya frowned. "What's wrong with golden retrievers?"

"They eat rocks and cat shit! They have floppy ears!"

Miya blinked at him, then smiled pleasantly at Mildred. "How much for that room?"

"Eighty dollars please," she stammered, closing her book. "We take credit."

Kai slung the cat under his arm like a football and dug through his pocket. Miya was uncomfortable charging for her services, but Kai understood the world ran on money, not kindness. Those plagued by a need to showboat their wealth made easy targets, and Kai's deft hands never missed their mark.

His lioness tolerated it so long as he stole from the right people, and Kai was always happy to ruin a rich man's day.

He moseyed over and slapped the dough onto the desk with one hand, then plopped the cat down with the other. Petunia trilled and scuttled into her owner's lap, pleased to have her feet on something solid again.

Mildred cleared her throat. "Thank you." From her drawer, she retrieved a key with the number *301* written on the attached tag, then reluctantly surrendered it.

Kai closed his fist around the faded digits and blithely smirked back. "You're welcome."

The room was one of two on the third floor—small and simple, with cream-coloured carpets, a brass-framed double bed, and a back lane window adorned with peachy drapery. The walls were pastel green, decorated with dried flowers locked behind picture frames.

"Yuck," Kai said as he inspected the bedside table only to find a bible.

"How's that libido?" Miya snorted.

"Like I stuck my dick in the freezer."

Miya wandered into the bathroom, turned on the faucet, then returned with her rose safely resting in a glass of water. She set it down by the lamp and tugged on Kai's belt.

"What happened to fading trails of demonic energy on delicate flower petals?" Kai asked, his eyebrow arched.

Miya shrugged. "I said it'd be good for a few hours. The rose can wait twenty minutes."

His mouth quirked as he was pulled towards the bed, his hands sliding up the inside of her shirt. "Sage words," he cracked as their clothes came off piece by piece.

She was right; being naked and alone was better than desperately fumbling in an alleyway. He pushed Miya onto the bed and pinned his knee between her thighs, then cast the rose a cursory glance. "We won't be long."

Miya burst into laughter and pulled him into a hungry kiss. Her body rose to meet his, her lips tracing his jaw as she whispered breathily against his ear, "Let's give Mildred something to blush about."

❦ 8 ❧

MIYA

MIYA CLOSED her eyes and let her fingers run over the petals, feeling every vein and groove for what she knew didn't belong—something she couldn't name. All she knew was that it felt *wrong*, like a viscous powder layered over the rose, slowly snuffing it out. Miya's brow creased as she concentrated. The residue stirred as if responding to her call, but the moment her concentration slipped, the dregs of its foul odour fled back into the flower.

Miya's eyes shot open. "This isn't working."

Kai was still lying in bed, watching her idly. Their clothes were back on, but he'd opted to remain horizontal while she worked. "I witnessed no failures," he quipped.

She turned to him, her tone apologetic. "I need to get closer."

His lips pursed into a tight line. "...In the dreamscape?"

Miya nodded, her stomach churning with guilt. She held out the rose. "I can't tap into it from here. I'm not good enough yet. But if I dreamwalk, I should be able to learn more."

Kai let out a shaky breath and sat up. He ruffled his coarse hair, and for a moment, Miya swore she saw a tremor in his hand.

"I won't be long—fifteen minutes at most. My body will be right here; it'll be like a power nap," she promised. "I just need to see if there's some memory I can access. I can do that more easily from the dreamscape."

"I know," he murmured, his eyes fixed on the duvet.

"Please, Kai?" She crawled over to him and wrapped her arms around his midsection. "Have a little faith."

His face twisted like she'd stuck a knife in his side, his gaze halfway between torn and angry. "You know I can't stay here alone, even if you're just dreamwalking. I want to, believe me. But I *can't*."

"I know," she whispered. "I know it's scary, but you have to trust that I can do this and get back in time." She reached up and cupped his face with both hands, searching him for a shred of confidence. "I *will* be back in time."

His breath halted, and the moment drew out for what seemed like an eternity until he finally nodded.

Miya pressed her mouth to his. "It'll be okay," she reassured, but he remained guarded. They could physically go back to the dreamscape together, but each trip through dimensions was a burden; one too many in succession and the tether would snap. Kai could get stuck between realms —a gamble with too high a price.

"If you don't want me to—"

"No," he said evenly. "I trust you." His shoulders finally let go as he exhaled. "Just feels like I'm on a leash sometimes."

Miya bit back the bitter taste in her mouth. She knew he felt trapped. She knew he hated being stuck in a world of endless illusions. He missed being here, where touch, smell, and sound reigned—where it was imminent. It was the one place he'd lost the freedom to go.

Miya opened her mouth to apologize, to swear to find a way to break his shackles, but she was arrested by an abrupt change in his expression. His eyes were frozen wide, staring at something in the distance—something that made his hands shake and his muscles harden with fear. She heard him swallow, his breath hiking behind his clenched jaw.

"Kai?" She grabbed his arm. "What's wrong?"

He jolted back, blinking away whatever had gripped him. His brows knitted together as his lips pulled back into a grimace. "Nothing."

"That's a fucking lie," she rebuked.

Kai closed his eyes and rubbed the bridge of his nose. "It is, but now's not the time for my shit." He nodded towards the rose. "You're on a time crunch, yeah? We can talk about me when you get back."

Miya was about to protest when her confidence faltered. Even if she had a few hours, she didn't want to cut it too close. The vestiges of otherworldly energy were dissipating with every passing moment. "All right," she reluctantly agreed. "We'll talk about it when I get back."

She settled back onto the bed and looked up at Kai. He tangled his fingers with hers, running his thumb over the back of her hand. Miya touched the rose to her mouth, letting the floral scent intoxicate her as the plush petals brushed against her nose. If there was anything she'd gotten good at, it was descending into the dreamscape without Ama's help. She felt it calling her back the same way the Dreamwalker had three years ago. Miya wondered if her connection to the dreamscape was like an elastic band. It stretched as far as she needed it to when she traversed the physical realm, but eventually, it snapped back into place, pulling her along with it.

She could feel it tugging on her now, straining to hold an impossible tension.

Miya's eyelids grew heavy as she imagined the deathless star in the sheer white sky, the shimmers of purple, azalea, gold, and emerald—like the dream stone hanging around her neck. If anything helped her find her way, it was the stone Gavran had gifted her.

Slowly, the sensation of Kai's skin against hers melted away, until their hands felt as one. Miya's body sank into the abyss, below the seams of the material plane, and far into the boundless world of dreams.

❦ 9 ❦

W*HEN* M*IYA* OPENED HER EYES, *she didn't expect to find herself staring at a row of metal bars. They fluttered like hummingbird wings as the air danced and undulated in a hazy, milk-coloured current. The quivering iron emanated a low hum that ricocheted off the walls of the enclosed space. The song grew louder—more urgent —until the quiet buzz ripped into a shriek.*

It was a nauseating orchestra of pain and vertigo, and an icy draft battered Miya's right shoulder. Distant, muffled cries filtered through her awareness as she swooned, then caught herself on the bars. The quaking stopped, and the room stilled as the voices grew louder, clearer. Miya's vision focused, and she homed in on a large mass on the floor. A man was crumpled in a fetal position, his eyes wide and blank, his mouth agape.

"What the hell happened!" someone demanded as they barged into the cell. "Suicide? How?"

"Maybe he OD-ed on something?" a second guard suggested.

"How, genius? We searched him! He had nothing!"

"Heart attack?"

Silence. A defeated sigh.

"Maybe, yeah."

Miya needed to get closer. The moment of death had just passed. She could still reach him and uncover what happened. If she could touch him—

"I'll spare you the trouble, Dreamwalker."

Miya's breath caught as the stench of decay assaulted her. She clamped a hand over her mouth and gagged, her body lurching forward. Her watering eyes darted across the room in search of the figure.

"Right here," *the voice, smooth as silk, directed Miya to a shadow lurking in the corner. The creature stepped forward, and although she was familiar, it took Miya a moment to place her. It was no wonder why; during their first encounter, her flesh was old, sagging leather. Her pallid skin was now firm and smooth, her shark-eyes vibrant where they were once hollow. No longer like tangled algae, her slick, dark green hair flowed over her breasts and clung to her curves like a perfectly draped garment.*

"You killed him," *said Miya as she backed away from the foul odour.*

The demoness lowered her gaze to the body. "Vincent here took his own life." *Her ashen-blue lips widened into a curved bow.* "We made a deal, he and I." *She stepped over the body, droplets of water stippling the tiles and burning through like acid. A black spider with a taut, bulbous body scuttled out of Vincent's ear and up the woman's leg. Its thin, disjointed limbs left needle-point impressions as it routed over her arm and settled on her fingertips.* "In exchange for his life and his soul, he'd be spared a dreadful fate." *She opened her mouth wide, her jaw unhinging as the spider crawled back home.*

"What could be worse than having your soul devoured by a rotting swamp monster?" *Miya retorted.*

The insult rolled off her as she laughed, the sound sickly-sweet. The bars were shuddering again, the thrum pounding through Miya's skull. "You of all people know what happens to spirits who die in great agony, who struggle to forgive their own mistakes." *The demoness canted her head, her eyes softening, her smile almost sympathetic.* "Do you really want another Abaddon?"

The evocation of his name was enough to thrust Miya against the cell wall, but her body didn't hit the concrete slab. She fell through like a stone in an empty pool and plummeted into a shallow stream of cloudy bog-water.

Where are you? *a familiar voice implored.* Just give me a lead, anything!

Miya swivelled on her knees to find herself staring at Mason Evans's back.

She's alive, I know she is, *her mother cried desperately from somewhere within the fog.*

We'll find her, Andrea, I promise.

Miya wheezed painfully as a figure walked straight through her—his anguish, frustration, and stubborn determination crashing over her in a thundering wave. It was her father.

I won't give up, *his voice shook,* I'll never give up.

Her parents joined Mason. He was staring at a map of the United States, a single thumbtack piercing the town of Summersville, West Virginia.

Mason and her family were searching for her.

Her insides clenched until her ribs began to ache. Her parents hadn't moved on. Mason hadn't moved on. They were still clinging to the threads she'd left dangling behind her, hoping those traces would lead somewhere.

"No," *Miya found herself muttering.* "No, no, no!" *She climbed to her feet, stumbling as the world teetered.* "I'm fine," *she called to them.* "Please, just let me go!"

"Leave them," *a voice hissed in her ear.*

Miya didn't bother turning; she knew it was her predecessor—the original Dreamwalker.

"They cannot know you live," *she warned.*

"Why not?" *demanded Miya.*

"They were not made for this world."

Miya sucked in a shaky breath and faced the raven-beaked mask. Violet-black feathers licked her skin as they flickered from the spirit's iridescent cloak. "I've tried not to think about it," she confided. "I can't, or I'll hate them."

For three years, she'd evaded the memory of that night. She knew her parents had been complicit—that they'd participated in the town's bloody hunt for the Dreamwalker's newest victim: their precious daughter who they hardly knew. Would her father have murdered her just as Elle's father had? She'd never know for certain, but historical precedent was enough to scare her out of finding out.

She wanted to hate her parents, but realizing they hadn't forsaken their search for her tore open the near-mortal wound they'd inflicted. Why were they looking for her? They practically built the pyre; all that'd remained was to pour the gasoline and light the match.

Because they love you, *a tiny voice chimed.* They're your parents.

They hadn't acted purely of their own volition; she knew they'd been manipulated by Abaddon, yet this was no salve. Yes, Abaddon might've twisted them up, but there must've been something for him to grasp onto first.

They love you, *the voice repeated.*

God, how much easier it'd been to cast them off when she believed they'd let her go. Now, she just wanted them to understand.

The Dreamwalker's fingertips—cool as a winter's breeze—grazed Miya's cheek. With her other hand, she lifted the mask from her face. Miya's own reflection stared back at her—murky green eyes, lush brows, and dark ash-brown hair cascading past her shoulders in waves. "She wants you to follow them," the spitting image warned. "She wants to break your resolve."

"I know," said Miya. "But what if I met them halfway? I could send them a sign—something to ease their minds until I'm ready to open my heart to them."

"*No!*" *her predecessor pleaded, but it was too late. Miya was already running after the three figures as they faded into the mist.*

"*Mason!*" *Miya called. Even though she was sprinting through shallow water and the doctor only meandered, she was unable to catch him. Every step pushed him further into the void.*

Vines shot up from below, trapping Miya's legs. She gasped as they yanked her into the water, forcing her to her knees. When she looked up, the architect of Vincent's death was in front of her.

"*So young and naïve,*" *the woman tutted. She crouched so they were level.* "*You followed the breadcrumbs quite well, Dreamwalker. But you're still too callow to roam the dreamscape unguarded.*" *With a Cheshire grin, she curled her bony fingers around Miya's throat.* "*I could crush you bare-handed, but that won't do me any good.*" *Her words were hoarse like the spider was jittering in her voice box.*

Miya scrabbled at her putrid captor—flesh soft and sticky like spoiled fruit. "*Rotting...swamp...monster...*" *she cursed as she struggled to wrest herself free.*

"*My name,*" *said the demon,* "*is Rusalka.*"

"*Rusalka,*" *Miya repeated, straining to speak through the pressure on her windpipe.* "*Who says I needed guarding?*"

Miya dug her fingernails into Rusalka's wrist. A torrent of shimmering smoke ripped through the river like a bullet, pummelling the landscape before crashing into the two women. Dark vapour woven from amethyst and obsidian enveloped Miya's form. It slithered over her hair, down her face, and hardened into a bone mask, the beak a knifepoint over her bottom lip. Feathery tendrils spiralled down her arm and coalesced into a raven, its wings spreading before talons clawed at Rusalka.

She gasped and pulled back, flailing to shake off the spectral bird. She turned to Miya, glowering with fury. "*Enough of your tricks!*"

The sea of violet eddied around Miya's body and erupted into a billowing cloak. "*I didn't realize it was a trick.*"

Rusalka's scowl warped into a humourless smirk. "And neither is this."

Kai's anguished scream gouged the stillness of the dreamscape.

Stomach sinking, Miya realized her mistake; she'd gotten carried away and lost track of time.

"No," she breathed, panic welding her to the ground. Forgetting Rusalka, Miya spun around to find herself staring through the swamp.

She had to get back to the Grey Gnarl.

But how?

All around her were towering cypress trees drowning in the mossy shallows. They were the same ones that led to the dead elm in her dream, yet she had no idea which way to go.

"You're too late," purred Rusalka.

Miya clasped the dream stone around her neck. Ignore her, she chanted.

Gavran said to follow the roots. Dropping to a squat, Miya pushed her empty hand into the water and dug beneath the slimy grass. She tuned out her surroundings and forgot her fear of the monster at her back, listening instead for the right pulse—slow, languid, and dying...like the residue on the rose, like the grief clinging to Crowbar.

Somewhere in those writhing depths, Miya saw the pearl-coloured flower petals and the Grey Gnarl's brittle roots.

The stone hummed to life against her fingertips.

It had picked up the scent.

Miya propelled herself forward just as Rusalka dove for her. The demon plucked several strands of Miya's hair, but they morphed into iridescent feathers and floated from her grasp. Rusalka's gaze shifted to the fleeing Dreamwalker, but Miya didn't dare look back twice. She squeezed the stone as she bolted across the cypress roots, her chest aching with furious desperation. She was dizzy with fear, the ghosts of her family still floating before her eyes as Kai's pained cry pressed down on her every cell.

She'd promised him she'd be back in time. He'd trusted her, and she'd failed him.

When the drowning forest cleared away and the black lake crept into sight, Miya stumbled into the water and waded across. Algae wrapped around her limbs and tugged her down, but she persisted.

The Grey Gnarl rose from the horizon like a stygian star. Although she half expected Rusalka to intercept her, the islet remained barren of movement. Miya clambered onto land and rushed to the tree, its crooked limbs towering over her.

As the barrier between the dreamscape and the physical world thinned, Miya felt the horror wracking Kai's body carve into her heart. Tears stung her eyes as she reached for the elm's bole, the craggy bark cutting into her palms like gravel.

The Grey Gnarl's deathlike aura sneered a grim farewell as Miya tore through the suture between realms and tumbled back to her wolf.

❦ 10 ❦

KAI

THE MOMENT MIYA LOST CONSCIOUSNESS, Kai felt the tickle beneath his skin. It started as a pinprick in his fingertips, crawling towards his heart. Every itch was an omen of what was to come. His blood was sand in an hourglass, his body an interloper. Miya's departure had tripped the wires; he was living on borrowed time until reality gathered its wits and corrected its existential algorithm.

Kai didn't belong in this world.

His body and soul were incompatible with the red earth that'd formed him. It was his cradle, and now it would kill him. Without Miya there to anchor him, he would be ripped to pieces, particle by particle. He hated not knowing why, hated that he had no control. He'd dedicated every scrap of affection and willpower to accepting it, reminding himself that it was better than being alone.

It didn't work. He *couldn't* stomach the chains anymore.

He'd hoped Miya would find a way to free him, but after three years, she'd given up, leaving him in a gilded cage. As she wandered off into the dreamscape, the gilt flaked away like a cheap coat of paint.

His heart pounded like his ribcage was trying to crush the muscle that kept the machine running. Kai shrivelled with fear as the seconds ticked by—literally—he could hear them clicking from the black-rimmed clock on the night-stand. Sixty seconds, then a hundred and twenty. A hundred and eighty. Two hundred and forty. Fuck, he'd lost count after three hundred.

Kai shuffled next to Miya and leaned back against the headboard. He held his breath as long as he could, then let go when the dull ache in his chest became too much. The prickles came quicker, harder—like someone was jabbing him with a sewing needle.

He thought back to what he'd said—that he felt like he was on a leash. Those words weren't his own. They'd been planted into his subconscious, burrowing until he couldn't dig them back out. Kai had no idea how far the roots had spread, but he was ill at ease with his own mind. Something had hatched inside him, and it was preying on his fears and frustrations.

The words he'd spoken belonged to the *thing* that'd accosted him in the swamp, dragged him underwater, and held him until he nearly drowned.

He'd managed to resurface, but his lungs still burned for air. Moments after regurgitating the monster's shit about leashes, he'd glimpsed her in the corner of the room, simpering as ice pumped through his veins. He had to tell Miya the truth when she got back. *Fuck*, how he wished she'd hurry up.

Kai opened his mouth to drag in another breath, but his throat closed with a raspy pull. His heart seized, gravity pressing him from all sides. Oxygen no longer worked for this body. He tried again, gulping down what he could.

Vision mottled with colours, his eyes shot to the clock, and he realized three hundred seconds had turned into twelve hundred. Twenty minutes had passed.

Kai turned his torrid gaze to Miya's sleeping form. The bitch was cutting it close.

Pain shot through his ribs and coiled around his heart like a snake, squeezing until he collapsed onto his side.

What the hell was that? *Bitch?*

No. This wasn't him. He would never—

Never say never, my sweet pup.

Kai craned his neck, his vertebrae threatening to snap. He could smell her—the sour stench of death and swamp.

She's forgotten you, little wolf. The voice was salty-sweet. *How could she, that—*

"Fucking bitch!" Kai finished her sentence. His eyes were trained on Miya, but he didn't know which woman he was referring to.

He didn't know which one deserved his wrath.

You're looking at her.

"No," Kai choked.

The voice laughed like chiming bells. *She promised she'd be back in time. She's not, that lying little—*

"No!" Kai roared, the outburst shredding his already weakened lungs. He retched and coughed up blood.

Stubborn pup, the demon cooed against his ear. *You'll be torn limb from limb while she sleeps peacefully, wandering her dreams like an innocent lamb.*

The taste of iron was bitter on his lips. Somewhere through the haze, Kai located Miya's face. She looked so relaxed, her hands folded over the rose stem. He swallowed down the bile, but he couldn't stem the onslaught. How could she just lie there? How could she abandon him? Didn't she know what would happen to him?

End her, came the devil's offer, *and the pain will stop.*

The solution seemed so simple. Everything faded until all he could think about was easing the pain...and punishing the one who'd foisted it on him.

With his remaining strength, Kai pushed himself to his knees, his muscles tearing like tissue paper as he trained his glare on the object of his ire.

The one who'd lured him from his home.

The one who'd robbed him of his greatest pleasures.

The one who'd stripped away his freedom.

The one who'd locked him in a cage to which she was the only key.

The demon slid her miry hands up Kai's back, her voice like honeyed poison as she spoke the name burning on the tip of his tongue.

The Dreamwalker.

MIYA

SHE TORE THROUGH THE DARKNESS, reaching for the ripple in a swirling sea of shadow and light. Somewhere beneath it, Kai screamed—a distinct *no*—the refusal muffled like he was underwater. He was close, just beyond the stitching of the dreamscape.

Puncturing through the veiny seam, Miya shot upright and gasped for air. She found herself staring wide-eyed at dried lavender that was encased in a chestnut picture frame mounted on a mint green wall. A shiver slunk up her spine as her skin crawled with goosebumps. Something was in the room.

"Kai!" He was collapsed on the floor, several feet from the bed, his head near the door. Was he trying to get away from something?

At the sound of her voice, his shoulder twitched. He pushed himself to his knees, then rolled back into a squat. Miya swung her legs over the side of the bed and stood.

"Stay back." It was an order, his voice a menacing growl.

"What? Why?" she demanded.

He remained turned away. "It's not safe," he said tightly. "*I'm* not safe."

Miya swallowed the lump in her throat, the air suddenly smoggy. Eyes darting around the room, she searched for the source. "What do you mean you're not safe?"

Still crouched, he pivoted to face her, his fingers clawing into the carpet as though he were preparing to lunge. That, or he was holding himself back from lunging. When he finally looked up, his eyes were a firestorm. His lips pulled back, canines gleaming.

"I almost died because of you," he seethed, his restraint slipping.

Miya's breath hitched, and she shambled back, her legs bumping the bedframe. "I-I'm sorry," she stammered, but her mind was reeling too fast to provide an explanation— that she'd seen her family, that they were searching for her with Mason.

She was preoccupied with trying to tune in—to figure out what was lurking in the room with them. It was like the walls had eyes, and they were leering with sinister anticipation. Surely, those eyes belonged to someone. She caught Kai slowly rising to his feet, his chest rumbling as he bit back a wolfish snarl.

He's going to attack, something inside her stirred. *You need to find the parasite.*

Yet what if Kai wasn't under any influence, and the anger was his own? What if *he* was the danger she sensed? Doubt pelted her focus as panic crept in.

No, that was *impossible*. In all the years she'd known him, she'd never once felt unsafe. Barring a single fight when they first met, he never so much as raised his voice.

What of the others he's harmed? Did they deserve it?

Usually, it was self-defence, but needless confrontations

weren't uncommon. He always sniffed out reasons to pick fights—good and bad ones.

"Miya," he warned through clenched teeth, and her gaze wrung back to him.

His face was a flood of rage and sadness that twisted into a single, anguished glance. She could see him fighting for control even as he reached behind his back and unsheathed his hunting knife.

The air around him crackled, and Miya glimpsed a shadow reflected in the glint of Kai's blade. Sour breath wafted past her, and as though the veil had lifted, Miya finally found what she was looking for.

Rusalka was standing behind Kai. She peered over his shoulder with a serpent-like smile tugging open her taut cheeks. She had a hand on his arm, her velvety fingers caressing him with sickening tenderness.

A flash of silver sliced through the air.

"Lambchop." Kai's voice was a ghost of a whisper, a plea that nearly sank beneath the silence before it reached Miya's ears. His knuckles whitened around the leathery hilt as his arm shook against Rusalka's touch. His dark mahogany eyes rose to ensnare Miya for one paralyzing moment as he spoke a single command.

"Run."

Kai thrust the knife downward. It disappeared into his leg, crimson blooming over his faded green cargo pants. Rusalka gasped as the wolf's defiance staggered her out of her own spell. Kai tore the blade up his thigh and released a scorching scream, the sound slashing through the air and maiming Miya's already battered heart. Kai's knee buckled, and he crumpled to the floor.

Miya's stomach churned as the blood pooled around him and dyed the carpet red. Acid clawed up her esophagus alongside the blistering fury, her every breath ragged as she pierced the demon with an icy, tear-brimmed stare. "I'll cut out your fucking spine and hang you from that rotten tree."

A wide, appreciative smile slithered across Rusalka's face. She seemed to welcome the threat—delight in it, even.

Come and get him if you dare, she sneered.

Miya knew better than to be goaded by a demonic siren. She wouldn't let Kai's sacrifice go to waste. He looked up, his eyes a sea of torment.

"I'll fix this," Miya promised.

She snatched her mauve jacket off the chair and rushed to the window. Pushing it open, she slipped through to the fire escape that led to the laneway. While Kai was the sword that cut down their enemies, Miya was the hand that wielded it. She needed to be smart, or they would both end up dead.

Miya didn't dare look back, terrified she might waver. Her hands trembled as she climbed down the narrow black stairs, each footstep reverberating against the hollow metal. Rusalka didn't come after her, opting instead to hang on to her new prize.

Miya snagged her lip with her tooth as she bit down too hard. She had to endure, no matter how unbearable it was to know that Kai was trapped with that *thing*. He would do no less for her.

When Miya's feet hit the ground, her body seized as she considered her surroundings.

Where would she go? To whom could she turn? Kai would be ripped apart if she returned to the dreamscape. God, how she hated herself right then—her utter lack of focus. She was like a magpie drawn to a shiny gem.

Miya clutched the dream stone around her neck and began walking, her strides quick as her ankles and toes froze in her sneakers—not from the cold, but from the foreboding. If only she'd spent more time practicing, maybe she would've been able to call the raven to her. If she were a more competent Dreamwalker, maybe she wouldn't have run after her family like a dog chasing a strip of bacon. She could've evaded Rusalka and made it back to Kai in time. She could have kept him safe.

Could've, should've, would've. None of that mattered now. Rusalka was right; she *was* wet behind the ears.

Miya rounded a corner into an empty alleyway and crashed into the bricks, grains of mortar scraping her jacket as she slid down and collapsed into a squat. She buried her face between her knees, her insides a volcano waiting to erupt. Everything she'd shoved down came spuming up. Salty tears flowed free. Sobs broke from her tightly pursed lips, but she snuffed them out with her sleeve.

She thought back to what she'd seen in the dreamscape —Mason, staring at a map of the United States. Her parents, searching desperately for their only daughter—the child they'd spent years raising only to lose in a single night. How she yearned for the protection of her mother's arms now. The desire to reach out to them was overpowering; it would only take a phone call. Yet her predecessor's warning still rang clear in her mind.

They cannot know you live, she'd said. *They were not made for this world.*

Those words were so much weightier now.

She had to reach Gavran and his fledgling in mischief: a lifelong friend with a stunning white coat and piercing amber eyes. Her black nose had once curiously poked through the bushes when Miya was a child searching for magic in a mundane world.

Miya wiped away her tears. Had she just lost her fortress? She didn't want to believe it, but she knew Kai wouldn't have wounded himself so viciously unless he really believed he'd been compromised.

He thought he was a danger to you.

Miya would have to win him back at any cost. He was her home, her one constant amid boundless dreams and finite reality alike.

She was the Dreamwalker. All she had in the world was her wolf under the willow.

❧ 12 ❧

MASON

"Your daughter was in West Virginia."

The couple sitting across from Mason didn't move.
Raymond Delathorne blinked once, then twice.

"How do you know this?" he asked with a suspicious
squint.

Mason's fingers curled into the itchy flesh of his left
arm. He could feel the mark burning under his sleeve. "She's
tracking events similar to those of Black Hollow."

Andrea tilted her head to the side. "I don't understand.
What events?"

Mason's expression turned dour. He'd noticed the
Delathornes' reluctance to acknowledge their town's
actions, but were they really so obtuse?

"Hauntings, possessions." He paused, then added,
"Violence."

"You mean the Dreamwalker," said Raymond.

Mason fidgeted with the cuff of his sleeve. "I think she's

travelling across the country, going places where people claim spirits are causing problems."

Raymond's mouth opened and closed.

"I spoke with her friend, Hannah," Mason continued. "She thinks Miya's looking for situations like her own. To make sense of things."

"But what's there to make sense of?" Andrea asked.

The words of the entity that called itself a servant echoed in Mason's mind.

Your god was born of violence, and to violence she will return.

Mason placed his elbows on the desk and clasped his hands together as he leaned forward. "Mrs. Delathorne, you must understand something. Your daughter experienced a massive trauma. The whole town came after her. They tried to kill her under the guise of saving her. I was there, I saw it. The whole thing was unreal." He tried to bite his tongue, but righteousness ensnared him like sweet nectar in a desert of depravity. "She had every right to leave the people who tried to end her life."

Andrea pulled back, disarmed. Her brows knotted together as she averted her gaze, her eyes glassy. He'd struck a chord. Raymond reached around his wife's shoulders and rubbed her arm.

"Dr. Evans, I appreciate your honesty," he began, "and I understand that you yourself must have been deeply impacted by the ordeal."

Mason swallowed. "Yes, I was."

"Perhaps, then, you would be well-suited to approach our daughter."

Mason's head snapped up. "What?"

Raymond sighed and exchanged a forlorn glance with Andrea. "We're concerned that if we approach Emiliya, she'll run from us."

Mason leaned back in his chair, staring idly out the

window. Miya's parents had supported the search party that attacked Kai's cabin. Mason wasn't innocent either; he was complicit in the townspeople's actions, even if he told himself he was trying to find Miya before they did.

"We'd like to pay you to approach her for us," Raymond reiterated. "She trusts you."

Trust? Could it really be called that? Mason, Kai, and Miya had been united by circumstance—or was it fate? Either way, their alliance was one of necessity, not trust.

"I'm sorry, I can't do that," answered Mason, the inside of his forearm blistering in pain. He ignored it. "I have a job here. Responsibilities. My patients need me."

"Surely, they could be transferred to another oncologist?"

"No!" Mason fought to keep himself restrained—partly from the ache, and partly from Raymond Delathorne's gall. "I have a good relationship with my patients. I can't abandon them for a side project."

Extending the shelf-life of an expiring mortal or chasing a living god? This is no quandary.

Mason bit the side of his tongue. The servant's voice came more frequently now.

"I-I can't," Mason stammered, despite that neither Raymond nor Andrea had responded.

Raymond cleared his throat and straightened out his blazer. "How many patients do you have, Dr. Evans?"

"Two," he responded meekly. "I'm on consult for a third."

"Do you have any appointments scheduled with them?"

Mason clamped his mouth shut. Raymond was a conniving, manipulative son of a bitch. Was he trying to twist Mason's arm? He wanted to lie, but the thought of Raymond calling his bluff was paralyzing. "I'm meeting one this week, the other two next month." Ronnie was his only

A. J. VRANA

shaky case. The second was in remission, and the third had just come out of surgery; they had a long recovery ahead before Mason would be of any use.

Raymond smiled coolly. "Why not meet with your patient, then take some time off? Consider it a paid side job while you take a vacation from these beige walls. I will double your hourly and cover all expenses."

"Most people make less than that in a year," Mason protested. "Where are you even finding that kind of money?"

Andrea laid a hand over her husband's. "Our money is worthless without Emiliya. What else are we to do with it? Money is a means to get what you want, and what we want is our daughter back."

Mason picked up his pen and twirled it around his fingers. He didn't know what else to do. Raymond had cornered him, left him with no excuse but a resounding, *I don't want to*. Of course, that would've been a lie, and standing on crooked principle, Mason felt compelled to speak the truth. The mark on his arm tingled then, and he wondered if his swift turn to honesty was because of the entity accompanying him.

He didn't want to say yes, but he found that he *couldn't* say no.

"Fine," he relented, though not without some edge. "But only for two weeks. I still have plenty of paperwork to do, and there will be new referrals coming in."

Mason hadn't taken time off since getting hired two years ago, after he returned from leave and finished his residency. The dean would approve a two-week vacation request, especially since he had few active files.

Raymond Delathorne seemed pleased with himself, his lips quirking. "Very good." He turned to his wife, and they traded triumphant smiles.

"And please," Mason interjected, "don't double my hourly." His voice dipped lower. "My conscience couldn't take it."

Raymond regarded him silently before responding, "Just your hourly, then."

Mason dropped the pen and nodded. He felt sick. And excited. His desire for the answers coalesced with the pulsing terror of where they might lead him.

What if they took him straight off a cliff?

Truth in chaos, doctor. Peace in surrender. Wisdom and prophecy have never lent themselves to control. That is for small men, petty men, fearful men.

Mason's eyes trailed up to meet Raymond Delathorne's.

Are you a fearful man, doctor? Or are you a prophet on the cusp of revelation?

No, Mason thought. He wasn't Raymond Delathorne—a man whose bone-hard façade barely concealed the maelstrom swirling beneath the surface. He was the last man on earth Mason wanted to be.

"I'm writing you a cheque for half the money now. You'll get the rest when you've made contact with our daughter." Raymond pulled a chequebook from his blazer and plucked the pen from Mason's desk.

Mason waited, at a loss for how to proceed. By the time he gathered his bearings, the cheque was torn and placed in front of him. Ten thousand dollars, just like that. How could the Delathornes be so confident Mason would follow through with their request? What was stopping him from going on vacation and *pretending* to search for Miya? After all, he couldn't promise them anything. If he failed, he simply wouldn't receive the other ten grand.

The Delathornes didn't strike Mason as trusting people. Where did their faith in his integrity come from? Beneath Raymond's collected exterior, Mason detected a man on the verge. His recklessness betrayed the hairline fractures around the edges of his icy mask.

"Thank you," Mason mumbled. "As soon as I finish my next appointment, I'll purchase the airfare and send you the details."

"Excellent," said Raymond as he stood, and Andrea quickly followed suit. "I expect to hear from you soon."

Mason nodded, his eyes scanning Andrea's face for any sign of resistance, hesitation even. Was she comfortable wrangling a doctor into this misguided wild-goose chase?

Then again, *was* he being wrangled? Raymond had manipulated him, but there was more at play. Mason didn't refuse the offer because he didn't want to. For three years, he'd tried to snuff out the burning curiosity about what had happened to Miya and Kai. He'd thrown himself into his work, sublimating that destructive impulse to pursue truth at any cost. He'd saved lives in the process, and for the most part, it worked. But now, something had changed. Now, he had the servant.

Miya's parents saw themselves out. Their certainty was unnerving. It reminded Mason of the man he used to be— the one whose ego had no room for the dregs of doubt.

Those days were over, and with good reason. His quest for certainty had nearly destroyed him. Mason Evans would never go back to scoffing at the unknown out of sheer arrogance. He no longer considered himself that kind of authority.

Yet he wanted *more* than humility. He was willing to accept outlandish explanations and supernatural intrigue so long as it gave him...something.

Mason pushed his chair back and walked over to his map. He knew Miya was no longer in West Virginia. He would always be one step behind.

"If I were a god of dreams, where would I go?" he mused.

He pressed his thumb to the map, tracing New York, Pennsylvania, and West Virginia. Miya didn't abide by the constraints of time and space. She could be anywhere. But where would she *want* to be?

Jackson.

The map reverberated against Mason's fingertips, and he jolted back. "What?"

Jackson, the voice repeated.

"Who's Jackson?" Mason called out.

...Not a person. A place.

Mason glanced at the map, eyes scanning every state on the eastern seaboard.

West, the voice instructed. *Now south.*

Mason's eyes fell on Mississippi—Jackson, Mississippi.

"Why there?" he demanded.

There was a pause. *I know not the reason. I only know it is truth.*

Mason sucked on his teeth. "That's not a good enough reason for me to buy a plane ticket. I thought you didn't know where she was?"

I do not know her exact location. I only read traces of the god. A reflection of a reflection. This is the closest I can bring you to the object in the mirror. I cannot do more until you open your mind.

Mason inhaled slowly. "You're asking me to take a pretty big leap of faith here."

What was it you thought earlier? That you would accept outlandish explanations and supernatural intrigue so long as it gave you something?

"This is absurd," Mason hissed.

You have nothing else to grab hold of, young doctor. You are grasping at the divine, and you expect to grip it with mere flesh?

Mason gnashed his teeth. "Fine. Jackson, Mississippi it is. But how do I explain it to the parents?"

The entity considered this with a low hum. *This world is overrun with those who are haunted, and that which haunts. I'm sure you will find a reason.*

Sighing, Mason sank into his chair and searched for haunted locations in Jackson. Low and behold, there was no shortage, but one particular incident caught his attention: a murder case from Cypress Swamp—a wetland that stretched along the Pearl River some fifty kilometers northwest of Jackson.

A man had killed his wife, then testified that a demon made him do it. Grief-stricken after the murder, the husband committed suicide while in custody. The coroner's office found no evidence of foul play. The defense was dismissed, and the perpetrator was diagnosed with a brief psychotic disorder.

Large wooded areas, claims of demonic possession, and women murdered by immediate family—it was more than enough for Mason to draw a parallel to Black Hollow.

A slow, unnerving chill crawled up his spine. He returned to the map and splayed his fingers over the jagged outline of Cypress Swamp. A winding ribbon of blue swirled through its center—the Pearl River. It cut south through Jackson and into Louisiana, cleaving through more sprawling swampland. *Open your mind*, the entity had said.

"It's a road," Mason realized, impressing his fingers into the glossy paper. His gaze trained on the pathway of drowned forest. He felt the tickle of Spanish moss and the smooth grooves of lotus leaves brushing against his hand. The air conditioner was on, yet a sticky, oppressive heat sopped his skin, and beads of sweat dribbled down his jaw. Mason shrugged one shoulder, wiping his face against his shirt to ease the gibing itch.

When he looked back up, foliage was sprouting from the map. The paper tore as vines sprung from the wall, and the screech of cicadas drowned the room. Yelping, Mason jumped back, but the sinewy stems shot after him, coiling around his wrists and reeling him in.

"N-no!" Mason protested, now pouring with sweat. Before he could call for help, he was yanked forward. Mason turned his face to prepare for impact, but instead of crashing with block-hard drywall, he was propelled through a barrier where his cool, dry office, sweetened by air freshener, collided with the humid stink of wildlife.

Heaving for breath, Mason's eyes shot open as he was thrust into a shallow river the colour of mud. Flailing and wild with confusion, he pushed his head out of the pungent water. He was in a literal—and metaphorical—morass.

"Not this!" He spun around. "Anything but this!"

The price, the servant's voice echoed, *of truth.*

"I don't want this!" Mason kicked through the water, stumbling as he overestimated his strength.

Are you a simpleton, or a man of truth? the voice challenged. *Are you a small man? A petty man? A fearful man?*

Mason reached for a bow-like root curving out of the river. Leaning against it for support, he closed his eyes and fought to regain his senses. He knew there were worlds he couldn't see. Surely, this was only a glimpse into one of them.

Look, the voice directed, and Mason did as he was told.

Something was caught in the umbrage between two gargantuan cypress trees—a woman, her face half-obscured in the shade. She was thin, hungry-looking. Her lips stretched over sharp, yellowing teeth, and her bulbous, reptilian eyes grew larger as her emaciated hand sought Mason. Her fingers spindled like spider legs before curling into a fist. She hooked her forefinger in a familiar gesture.

Come hither.

Trapped by her sorcery, Mason was pulled in like a fish on a lure, his body sluicing through the swamp at break-neck speed. He would have screamed if not for the insects splatting on his cheeks and the tree limbs battering his neck and forehead, leaving welts all over.

He'd lost sight of the woman, but it didn't matter now. He just wanted it to stop.

When the blustering finally ceased, he was deposited at the edge of a river, the swamp at his back. There, wedged in the grass by the riverbank, was a bloody king of spades. Mason grasped for the card, only to have the ground fall out beneath him. He tumbled past a sign by a two-lane freeway —*Orme's Rest*, it said. The green letters were faded and mottled with mud so dark, Mason wondered if it was the same dried blood staining the king of spades. He tried grabbing onto the signpost to stop his whirling descent, but his hands slipped as though covered in raw eggs. Then, he passed through the soil and crashed into the stiff, scratchy carpet of his office.

Mason jumped up like a frog that'd been dropped into a scalding pot. His clothes were soaked and browned from dirty water, algae poking out from his shoe. Everything smelled sour, and as Mason wiped his face, his hand came away coppery with blood. He'd seen the signs. They were brief, but nothing escaped his gaze.

Shaking with adrenaline, Mason collapsed onto the floor and waited for his pulse to slow. *The king of spades. Orme's Rest.*

Once Mason was sure he wouldn't vomit all over himself, he dragged his deflated body back to his desk. He kept a change of clothes at work and quickly stripped away the residue of his vision. Drying off with a towel from his gym bag, he slipped on fresh attire and searched for the location of Orme's Rest.

He shouldn't have been surprised, but his mind rebelled like the first time he'd met Gavran.

Orme's Rest was a small town in Louisiana, right on the edge of a swamp bordering the Pearl River—the one that wound north into Mississippi's Cypress Swamp.

"All right," Mason whispered to the room and the entity residing in it, "Louisiana it is."

When there was no response, he leaned back in his chair and glanced at the map on his wall. The fissure where the foliage had erupted was still there. "What should I call you?"

A breeze knocked on the windows, the shrill whistle sinking to a low groan. *As you have named me, Master.*

Mason gasped as fire shot through his left arm. He tore at his sleeve, the buttons on his cuff flying loose as he yanked it apart. To the left of the crescent moon, another branded itself into his flesh. It was reversed like a mirror image—two moons reflecting one another.

I am the Servant.

13

KAI

KAI PRESSED his hand over the king and pushed past the doors of *The Mangy Spade*. After the bloodbath, he fled *Mildred's Guesthouse*; the last thing he needed was a run-in with cops. He'd slept in an unkempt park on the edge of town, wedged between bushes where only the occasional possum roamed. As soon as the sun was high, he stalked back into Orme's Rest. His jaw clenched as he put too much weight on his useless leg and struggled to hide the limp. Getting stabbed usually didn't hurt much at first—felt more like a hefty punch than a shiv to the squishy bits, but Kai had sliced his leg open and fallen on it, and that had a way of kicking the shit out of his pain receptors. The worst of it had softened to a dull throb, but every so often, Kai would move funny, and his whole left side would go up in spitting hellfire. Now, his pants crinkled from the drying blood, his thigh sticky and irritated.

Crowbar lounged on a stool behind the bar, sipping gin and reading some romance novel with two chicks on a purple and teal cover—*Once Ghosted, Twice Shy*. Head hanging, Kai slid onto one of the stools. He ignored her stupor when she peeked over the pages and took in his dishevelled appearance.

"What the hell happened to you?" She slammed the book shut.

Kai let out a shaky breath, his voice low. "I did a bad thing."

Crowbar plucked an ice cube from a tray, then emptied the remaining contents of a whisky bottle. She pushed the glass towards him. "Yeah, well, you seem like the kind of guy who does bad things."

Kai watched the tawny elixir ripple from the crackling cube. "What if that's not the kind of guy I want to be?"

Crowbar plunked down in front of him. The room felt smaller, like the walls were closing in on him. "Your fire's going out, dude."

Kai threw back the booze, replacing one bitter taste with another. "Maybe for the best."

"Do you need some food?" she ventured. "Bastien—the chef you met—he's not in, but I can whip up some mean nachos."

"I'm good," Kai declined the offer, his gaze fixed on the counter.

There was a pause before Crowbar asked the dreaded question, "Where's your girl?"

"Safe," he answered automatically, but his mind was in tatters.

Crowbar's brow crinkled, her disbelief oozing from every pore, but her phone rang just as she opened her mouth—a merciful intervention.

"Hang on." She huffed and snatched her phone off the counter, then kicked her way into the kitchen where she took the call.

"Safe?" a voice rang sweetly. "You have a low bar for safety, little wolf."

Kai's breath halted, his stomach churning as the smell of acid and bog water washed over him. He could see her from the corner of his eye—the *thing* that'd nearly gotten the better of him. Her gibes had only been unwelcome static in his head, but now she felt *real*, indistinguishable from anyone else. In his periphery, she was a mass of grey lumps and slimy green tendrils, but he had little desire to paint a clearer picture of his tormenter.

Maybe *nearly* was too generous. She *had* gotten the better of him.

After Miya had left, he stayed crumpled on the floor, his every cell screaming. He couldn't move, couldn't speak, couldn't even feel the tears streaming down his face until he tasted the salt. Why him? Why did every fucking demon on the block want a piece of him?

"It's because you're such a sensitive pup!" She—Rusalka, he'd learned—rubbed a smarmy hand along his back.

"Don't touch me," Kai snarled under his breath. He kept one ear on Crowbar's conversation in the next room. "I got rid of that ghostly turd, and I'll get rid of you too."

Sighing, Rusalka peeled the puckered flesh from her arms. "*You* got rid of Abaddon? Oh, honey, we both know it was that witch of yours that did that." She leaned in close, her sour breath tickling his ear. "Your lamb did all the work, little wolf. You just reaped the rewards."

Kai's heart seized in his chest. "How do you know that name?"

"Spirits talk," she shrugged.

"Not inclined to believe a mouldy washcloth trying to kill my girlfriend."

"Why not?" she feigned innocence.

"Abaddon loves dramatic entrances." He glared stonily

into his glass. "There's no way he'd let his name slide by someone like you without an introduction."

She leaned her elbow onto the bar top and cupped her chin with her palm. "He sounds dreamy."

"You'd be a perfect match," said Kai. "The devil and his siren."

He'd seen it all when they'd connected; he knew she'd bewitched Sydney Baron's husband and driven him to murder. He wasn't even the first. How many had there been before him? Their faces had flooded him, each of them indistinct. Did Rusalka even keep count?

"How do you do it?" he whispered, clutching the glass to keep his hand from shaking.

Her shadow slithered closer, her voice like honey laced with arsenic. "You'll have to be more specific, pup."

His grip tightened when a small, ashen hand slipped over his calloused fingers.

"It'll break if you squeeze any tighter."

Kai bit the inside of his cheek and flinched away. "The men," he growled. "How did you make them do it?"

"It doesn't take much." She retracted her touch. "A seed of resentment needs only to be watered. I don't plant the seed, pup. I fertilize the sapling. The men decided what must be done on their own."

"Then why the grief? They didn't *want* to do it." Kai mustered the courage to look, his eyes dragging up her waifish form.

Pale blue lips curved into a cupid's bow and tresses like seaweed framed her sallow face. Her dark eyes, bisected by green irises, bulged from beneath her brows like glass spheres, and her torso shimmered with iridescent scales that caught the light like silk. When she shifted her weight and crossed her legs, Kai didn't know if he was seeing drooping skin or draped linens.

"Men are fragile creatures," she cooed. "When they can't handle the weight of their choices, they shatter. Some forget entirely. Others blame their victim. Oh, she was a madwoman! An adulterous whore!" Rusalka threw her head back and unleashed an undulating cackle. "A psychotic episode, the doctors say! Such coddling. Those men knew exactly what they were doing while they were doing it."

Kai pressed his fingers into the rim of the glass, half of him wishing it would just break already. "Bullshit. I wasn't in control."

"Ah, but you were!" Her hand snaked up his arm. "You crushed your basest instincts, your unyielding itch for freedom. You cut into your own body to protect your beloved." She leaned in close, her vinegary voice dripping with ire. "People think men don't kill women they love, but it's *always* about love. The problem is that men hardly know the difference between a woman and a toy. They kill women as children break toys that displease them." Her fingers spidered up his shoulder and splayed across his cheek. "Then they cry that the toy is broken. They beat their fists and scream that it wasn't their fault. That they didn't know. They want to take it back, but they can't, can they?" Her face was so close that a shudder ran up his spine. "No one ever taught them the difference between love and possession. And the world even pities them for it."

Kai jerked back and swatted her arm away. "You're still *making* them do it. You think I shanked my leg because it's Tuesday?"

Her mouth curled upward. "I can't give you something you don't already have."

"But you can twist it into something it's not," he observed.

The smile crumbled from her face.

Kai's lips tugged into a triumphant smirk. Abaddon was

a piece of shit, but he'd taught Kai an important lesson: even hell wasn't black and white. That dick waffle claimed the pot of crap he was stirring had long been on fire. Of course, he was right. Black Hollow had a hankering for mass murder. The people weren't blameless, but that didn't mean Abaddon was off the hook.

"You prey on assholes who can't tell their heart from their nut-sack," said Kai. "Instead of helping them, you mess them up."

Rusalka's brow arched. "I can't cure cancer, pup."

Kai gave her a withering glare. "If you know how to fuck with someone, you know them well enough to un-fuck them too."

"A fair point," she conceded, "but not what I'm here for."

Kai washed down the last drops of whisky. He smiled darkly and gestured for her to come closer. "So, who broke your little black heart?"

Rusalka glided forward until there was barely a breath between them. "What's this? Trying to get to know me?" She chuckled. "I knew you were a sensitive one."

"Careful," Kai flashed her a wolfish grin. "Something tells me you've got shitty taste in men."

"It won't work," she warned him tenderly. "You can't get rid of me with your opportunistic sympathies or your rakish charm...as much as I enjoy it."

"In that case," he narrowed his eyes, "you should have nothing to hide."

Her mouth wrinkled, then quickly ironed out. *Of course* her baggage mattered; she was still a malicious spirit. They were vengeful things that acted out their traumas, again and again, multiplying their hurt until it ate them up and there was nothing left.

The kitchen doors swung open, and the demoness'

scowl melted into a chorus of girlish giggles. Kai ignored her, his eyes following Crowbar as she clunked a brand-new bottle of *Bulleit* on the counter. She looked tired all of a sudden, shadows clinging to her face.

"So, you going to talk?" Her fist curled around the neck of the bottle with surprising force. "Or would you prefer bourbon?"

"Bourbon's *great*," Kai evaded. He wanted to tell her the truth. That he'd nearly killed his best friend. That he was sitting next to the demon who'd pushed Vincent to murder his wife. Sydney Baron's death was on Rusalka's hands, but did it really matter? Would it bring Crowbar peace to know Vincent hadn't lost his mind? Would she move on, or would it drive the knife deeper?

Crowbar pulled out the cork and poured him another shot. "So, what's up?"

Kai sighed, sloshing the booze around. He could hear Rusalka humming quietly next to him, though he resolved not to expend a single nerve on her. "It's complicated, and I'm not good at talking about my problems."

"Bitch, please," Crowbar scoffed. "People go to bars *just* to talk about their problems. All they need is some hooch to hold their hand through it." She nodded towards the drink, the gesture more of a command than a suggestion.

Kai cracked a wry smile. He raised his glass, tilted his head back, and let the bitter medicine burn down his throat. "You better not be charging me for these," he said as he slammed the tumbler down.

"You going to pay me for the therapy then?" she asked with a wide grin.

"I didn't ask for therapy," Kai pointed out. "You're prying."

"True," she sighed, "but you look pretty wrecked, man.

And who doesn't like a good story when there's blood, you know?"

"Bleeding's not as fun as you seem to think." Kai glanced down at his lap. "Besides, I'm clearly not the only one here who's got shit to unload."

When she didn't respond, Kai looked up to find her turned away.

"Give me a sec," she said, then hurried into the kitchen as Kai stared after her.

Salt and sorrow wafted through the air in her wake. Something had changed after she'd gone to retrieve the bourbon. Propping himself up on the bar, Kai held his mangled leg as he swung around to the other side and helped himself through the doors.

Amidst the old grease and fried meat, Kai could still smell the death that lingered on Crowbar's skin. He found her sitting on the floor by the sink, her knees curled into her chest and her face tucked away from sight.

Kai leaned his shoulder against the wall and crossed his arms over his chest, observing her with a tepid frown. "Crying in a dish pit is probably a health code violation."

"Shit!" Crowbar jolted, her eyes wide as her head jerked up. Her face was blemished with tears. "What the hell, dude! You're not supposed to be here!" She pressed her palms to the tiles and jumped up, then grabbed his arm to turn him around. "You're seriously sketchy, you know that?"

Kai didn't budge as she tried to usher him to the dining room. "Didn't realize floors were so comforting. I'll be sure to give them a try next time I feel like dogshit."

Crowbar's jaw clenched as her thumb dug into his bicep. "It's nothing. Just had a rough phone call. Your not-so-fun bleeding made it worse."

Kai's brow shot up. "What was the call about?"

"You know what," a syrupy voice whispered. He ignored it.

Crowbar's hand dropped to her side. "Syd's case."

Rusalka's laughter reverberated in his ears. She relished the pain she caused. "And?"

Crowbar's face paled with grief, her voice quaking. "I haven't said it out loud. If I do, it'll become real, and I don't want it to be."

"Whatever it is, drowning in a bottle of bourbon isn't going to turn your turds into farts." Kai knew the price of avoidance better than most, so he added begrudgingly, "You'll just puke like a freshman, and you'll still have shat your pants."

Silence followed; Crowbar's reckoning was palpable before she answered.

"Vince is dead."

Rusalka was ecstatic now, twirling through the kitchen and clearly pleased with her handiwork. Kai's scowl could have been mistaken for a look of surprised disgust. "You seem upset about it," he said. "I thought you hated him."

"Of course I'm upset!" Crowbar threw her arms out, the tears flowing freely now. "I wanted him to have a trial—a fair trial—and *live* with his mistakes." She spun away, swaying left and right as she ran her hands through her hair and wiped the wetness from her face. "I wanted answers!"

Kai choked on his words. His idea of retribution was so...simple. He thought the human impulse to imprison the guilty was merely sadism. Why not just put them out of their misery? End the pain for the victim and the perpetrator. It wouldn't raise the dead, but it buried them for good.

Or so Kai thought until he remembered that Alice never really died—not in his heart or his memories. He didn't even remember what his family before her looked like, but they still lingered, their absence robbing little pieces of him every day. And their killers? They'd taken something Kai could never get back.

He understood now; Crowbar needed meaning from the heartbreak. So long as Vincent lived, there was a chance he'd one day explain himself to the people he'd harmed. He'd feel the weight of what he'd done. Crowbar wanted a reason, a motive—anything to quell the horror that came with the absurdity of his crime. Now, she would never get that. Her sister's death—a senseless tragedy—could never be anything more.

At least, as long as she remained oblivious to Rusalka.

The demoness ceased her chaotic twirls and sneered. "Don't even think about it, pup. She won't believe you. Even if she does, you'll just get her killed."

"I'm sorry." Kai lowered his gaze. He'd come so dangerously close to becoming the reason for another grieving family. Despite his cool exterior, his every vein pulsed with molten fury; the source of the sickness was right in front of him, yet he was powerless. He couldn't bring Sydney Baron to justice, and he couldn't say anything that would ease Crowbar's pain. He wasn't good with words, and Rusalka had effectively castrated him, stunting his ability to do the only thing he did well: violence.

Grinding his teeth, Kai pushed past his impulse to flee. He lifted his arm and clumsily dropped it around Crowbar's shoulders, offering her a consolatory pat. "My parents were murdered," he said at last. "The people who did it...I never got to look them in the eye and ask why. Never even saw them again."

Crowbar pulled back to look at him, her face a mural of anger and grief. "They were never caught?"

Kai shook his head, holding her steady as he led her to the dining room, his arm still slung around her. As a kid, he overheard the shrink using words like *traumatized* and *socially withdrawn* while talking to Alice. Then, when he got older, it became *delinquent* and *anti-social*. Abaddon's voice was chalked up to auditory hallucinations from PTSD. He never believed it, though he'd taken his sweet timing admitting that he was, in fact, traumatized.

"Fucked me up for years because I never talked about it. That made me a pretty shitty person, too. Did a lot of bad things—still do, I guess." His arm slid away as he circled around the bar and found his stool again.

After he'd attacked the hunters who'd shot his parents, he awoke to the blare of sirens, barely conscious with blood in his mouth and a shooting pain in his jaw. The sky was there, and then it wasn't, replaced by the steel panel of the ambulance truck. In the end, Alice Donovan took him in. To everyone else, she was a crotchety, chain-smoking old woman with a bad hip and magenta lipstick, but to Kai, she was Superwoman with a walking stick—her weapon of choice.

"Damn." Crowbar sniffed and wiped her nose. "That why you're so emotionally constipated?"

Kai snorted, then broke into a grin. "If you think I'm constipated now, you'd have shoved an enema up my ass a few years ago."

Crowbar's cheeks puffed like a hamster's before she burst into laughter. "Gross, dude!"

The tension left Kai's body as he fell into the comfort of her mirth. The demoness was quiet, and Kai welcomed the momentary peace. Maybe he wasn't so bad at talking about his feelings.

The front doors of *The Spade* swung open, the hinges shrieking to announce the end of their brief respite.

The intruder yelped as he stumbled in backwards and barely managed to untangle his feet. He muttered as the doors slammed shut behind him.

"Clint!" Crowbar barked as she straightened up. "I thought I told you not to show your drooling mouth-hole until you cleaned yourself up!"

Her words had little effect as Clint tripped to the bar and caught himself on a stool. "Just—give me a drink!"

Kai wrinkled his nose and leaned away only to feel Rusalka's mouth clip his earlobe. "This one's in danger," she hissed.

Kai's elbow flung back. Glancing over his shoulder, he saw Rusalka skulking in the corner with awaiting eyes and a sly smile.

"I'm not serving you," said Crowbar, pulling Kai's attention to the drunkard cascading over the bar.

"Come on, sweetie, just one drink! I swear I'm not that soused," he whined, his bloodshot eyes trailing down her body.

Kai heard Crowbar's pulse quicken as she cheated a step back. He could tell she was sick of Clint's crap. Revulsion radiated from her as she quietly balled up a fist at her side.

"A concussed shih tzu learns faster than you," Kai cut in.

Clint's bleary gawp wandered over. He swooned to the side and squinted. "What the hell? You again!"

Kai smiled wickedly. "Did I leave an impression?"

"Hey," Crowbar touched his arm. "I got this. Let me do my job."

Clint's bloated face rouged like a squishy, bulbous tomato. The colour around his pasty neck was a spreading wine stain as he ground his jaw. "You got some balls on you, kid."

Crowbar's pacifying hand slid off Kai's arm as he stood up and cracked his neck, then levelled his stony gaze on Clint. "Eyes up here, buddy."

"You going to start shit, asshole?"

Crowbar swiped the bottles and glasses off the counter.

"Hey! No fisticuffs!" she snapped as she ducked down to hide the booze.

But neither Kai nor Clint was listening, both fixated on their stand-off.

Strike him, chimed Rusalka, her voice now ringing between his ears as though she were inside him. *You know you want to.* He could feel her bony fingers slide over his fist, squeezing it tighter, but her lips didn't move even as the words pulsated through his skull.

Fuck off, Kai growled inwardly. Clint may have been a douchebag, but Kai wouldn't attack him without provocation—even if he wanted to.

The demoness sighed against his neck, then floated over to Clint and stared at his profile. Her lips quirked as she opened her hand to reveal a black spider quivering against her palm. Rusalka leaned down and whispered something to the vermin before it scurried up Clint's face and crawled into his ear. Kai grimaced, but Clint didn't seem to feel a damn thing.

That is, until his eyes widened, he clenched his fist shut, and swung wildly at Kai. Lunging out of the way, Kai watched as the belching ragdoll lost his balance and shambled forward.

"What the hell was that?" Kai taunted, then pointed a thumb between his legs. "They're right here, shih tzu."

The bulbous tomato looked ready to explode, then roared in fury.

See! Rusalka hissed. *He's trying to hurt you!*

Kai scoffed. *Didn't* you *say he was in danger?*

Or was I referring to you? She chuckled, weaving confusion into his mind. Distracted, he hardly noticed Clint hurling himself forward. Glimpsing a fist from the corner of his eye, Kai leaned back against the bar, the breeze from the clumsy strike tickling his nose.

Rusalka's reverberating laugh shook his senses. He was lucky Clint's organs were practically fermenting; the guy was likely seeing doubles as he pushed forward a third time and hucked a fist at Kai's shoulder. This time, Kai didn't move out of the way. He blocked the attack and grabbed Clint by the collar of his shirt, spinning him around and throwing him towards the door.

"Come at me one more time, and I'll rip out your liver," Kai menaced with a feral snarl.

You want *him to get back up, don't you?* Rusalka goaded. *To give you a reason to hit him until he can't get back up at all.*

Kai's lip curled as he prepared to intercept another attack—the last one, he told himself. One more swing and he'd pummel Clint into the ground.

"Enough!" Crowbar slammed her fist down on the laminate counter, the sound jolting Kai out of focus. "If you two want to brawl, take it outside!"

Kai glanced over his shoulder and saw her glaring right at him, her eyes spilling with disappointment. *You should know better*, they said.

Her disapproval felt like barbs pressing against his chest, so he tore his eyes away. He reached down and clutched his aching thigh. What he would've given to see Miya. She'd been his equilibrium; she tempered his worst impulses, and after nearly unleashing them on her, he had no one to restrain him.

Restrain yourself, you dick. His self-chastisement did little to help. He was fighting off a mouldy washcloth as she toiled away with his mind, shaving off pieces of his sanity.

Before his emotions erupted out of control, he clamped down hard, battering the anger and helplessness away. Bundling them up, he imagined whipping them behind a reinforced steel gate. Then, he pictured the only key that could unlock that gate and threw it into the ocean. Once it sank, it was gone forever.

Exhaling slowly, Kai opened his eyes only to see the doors of *The Spade* crawl open. Clint leaned against them, his eyes glassy and his cheek raw with scrapes from face-planting the floor.

"You're a bully," he grunted, then hobbled into the alley-way, the doors clanking shut behind him.

Kai considered himself many things, but a bully wasn't one of them.

He was outmatched, and you knew it. You could've chosen not to escalate, but you did, Rusalka tutted. *You were cruel, like a child plucking the wings off a helpless butterfly.*

That's one gnarly butterfly, Kai retorted, but her words stuck like rancid sap. He'd been eager for a fight, but instead of knocking the bastard out cold, he'd toyed with him just to delight in his own power. It was no wonder why; he'd never felt more powerless. Turning towards the bar, he pulled out his wallet and placed a few bills on the counter.

"Sorry," he muttered, staring at Crowbar's silver-studded belt. He couldn't bring himself to meet her gaze—wasn't sure he wanted to know what he'd find there. Kai turned on his heels and stormed out, the dripping, spectral footsteps of Rusalka stalking close behind.

❦ 14 ❧

MASON

APPREHENSION TUMBLED through Mason's chest as he dropped into the driver's seat of his rental Chevy Impala. The backs of his eyes prickled with déjà vu. When he'd last driven from a large city to a middle-of-nowhere town, it hadn't ended well. Yet here he was at Louis Armstrong New Orleans International Airport, signing off on a two-week contract and directions to Orme's Rest charted on his GPS.

Through Bayou Sauvage and across Lake Pontchartrain, the trek northeast shook him from his ennui; he was crossing into another world. The bridge stretched for miles over the deep blue water, the summer sun glinting off every dip.

Mason pushed down the impulse to seek out the Servant for answers. Whatever *it* was, however benevolent it seemed, Mason didn't want to deepen his dependency on it for the truth.

But God, how he yearned for truth.

The mirror-image moons on his forearm ached like a

spider bite, every brush of fabric a scorching itch he had to resist scratching. The Servant wanted to be called; it wanted to be asked. Still, Mason refused.

"I'll find the answers myself," he said, and the needling finally subsided.

If Black Hollow was a village of secrets that wove through forest and fog, Orme's Rest was the silent scream of a living, breathing gravestone. The town, while picturesque, had a heaviness to it that stank of pestilent winds, like one of the four horsemen had already ravaged the riverbank.

Mason's lips twitched as a haunted laugh escaped him. He never would've entertained the possibility of a town having an aura, but he knew better now. He didn't have to ask the Servant to glean he was in the right place.

As Mason turned onto the main road, he spotted a police cruiser parked outside a three-story brick-house inn —*Mildred's Guesthouse*, according to the sign. The officer was speaking to a frumpy, greying woman holding an oversized tuxedo cat. Its bushy tail whipped back and forth as it observed passing traffic. Mason needed a place to stay, and where better than a possible crime scene?

He parked his Impala in a narrow side-lane and plucked his suitcase from the back seat. Poking his head around the corner, Mason waited for the police cruiser to drive off before he approached the inn.

"Excuse me, ma'am," he called out just as the woman headed inside with her feline companion. She stopped with her fingers around the door handle and blinked at him.

"May I help you?" Her voice was nasally, every syllable lethargic.

"I was wondering if you have any vacancies." He offered her his best smile—the one he gave to nervous patients.

Her brows knitted together like she was unsure why

THE ECHOED REALM

anyone would *want* to stay in her establishment. "Yes, we do. It's just—where are you from, son?"

"Vancouver," he answered. "Is something the matter?"

The woman sighed and gestured for him to follow her inside. "We just had an incident recently," she said as she held open the door, "so I'm surprised you aren't taking your business elsewhere."

"What kind of incident?"

The woman—Mildred, he assumed—plunked down in the armchair behind her desk, jostling her cat as she did. "Bad one. Had a couple come in the other night. The girl seemed nice, but the man," she shook her head, "the man looked like trouble. Awfully rude. Paid with cash straight from his pockets. Just hours after handing them the key, I heard a loud noise, then screaming! There was a terrible sound, and when I finally got my old knees up there, they were both gone."

Mason frowned. It wasn't quite as juicy as he was expecting. "Maybe they had a fight?"

Mildred choked back a laugh. "The hell they did! There was a giant pool of blood on my carpet!"

"Oh..." Mason trailed off. "You said the man looked like trouble?"

"Sure did." She leaned back. "Tall, dark-haired fellow. Broad shoulders, nasty eyes. Real menacing, you know? Didn't seem to give a hoot about anything."

Mason blanched. Few people in this world gave less of a rat's ass than Kai Donovan. Their time together had been short, but it was one of blood and bonds. Mason had peered into the wolf's eyes and seen what he was made of. Kai was all edges—stone-hard grit and bare-boned reckoning.

"The girl," began Mason, "was she about this tall?" He held his hand up to his nose. "Brown hair? A little tan, maybe?"

Mildred's jaw slackened. "How'd you know that?"

Mason's hand dropped to his side. "Just saw it on the news." It was a poor lie, and anyone with sense would've known it, but Mildred only nodded.

"I suppose it would've been on the local news," she said slowly. "The station sends an officer every day to check on me, just to make sure everything's been handled."

"That's very courteous of them."

"Small town police," she shrugged. "What else they got to do around here?"

"Well, seems like they've got a crime to solve now," Mason chuckled, earning him a toothy smile.

"I'll say! You seem like a nice young man." She pushed her chair back and shooed the cat from her lap. "Go on, Petunia!" Mason watched as she fiddled with the old wooden drawer and barely managed to yank it open by the blackened handle. "It's been a bit slow, so I can give you a room for cheap."

"That won't be necessary," Mason interjected. "I'm happy to pay full price, ma'am, precisely because it's slow." It was coming out of Raymond's pocket, anyway.

Mildred's knobby hand flew to her chest. "Oh, you sweet boy!" She reached into the drawer for a room key. "What brings you all the way to this little bayou town?"

Mason considered his answer. "Just some business. I'll be staying for a week, I think. Two at the most."

"Second floor, dear. First door to your right." She smiled and dangled the split ring from her forefinger. "Just let me know if you need more time with us."

Mason pulled out his wallet and handed her a card before taking the key. "Thank you." When his payment went through, he retreated up the narrow, winding steps.

Caution tape meekly blocked the staircase to the third floor. Mason elected to ignore it for now, wondering if he could charm Mildred into showing him the bloodstains she was so upset about. He unlocked the door to his room and creaked his way inside.

The accommodations were a total eyesore. The walls were covered in lilac floral patterns accented by light brown curtains framing the window. Against the cream-coloured carpet, the frilly yellow duvet draped over the bed seemed like the yolk of a giant egg. Mason winced.

After unpacking and organizing his impeccably folded clothes in the wardrobe, Mason slipped downstairs and smiled at his overeager hostess on his way out. The late afternoon light sank below the treetops, and a dark shadow crept overhead as a gargantuan cloud blanketed the sun. The town's charming façade crumbled beneath the weight of the stormy curtain. Historic buildings now seemed derelict, and the flower beds garnishing the sidewalks drooped as if overheated. Unsettled by the jarring change in atmosphere, Mason meandered down an adjacent alleyway in search of a bar or pub. His nerves felt like they'd been hooked up to a three-hundred-volt battery, and he needed to cool off.

The dream stone hummed to life against his leg. Rattled by the vibration, he reached into his pocket and grasped it, then stopped to look around. Above him, an old wooden sign hung from a brass post fastened to the rust-coloured bricks.

The Mangy Spade.

The door was speckled with playing cards, and Mason's eyes fell on the king of spades. The eidolon of the blood-speckled card by the swampy riverbank invaded him like a fever. *What were the odds?*

Mason pushed through the heavy, laminated doors to find himself in a gold-lit tavern with a long bar stretched across the back wall. A woman with short, two-toned hair was drying glasses, then looked up and nodded in greeting. "Welcome," she said gruffly. "Looking for lunch?"

"I'm just here for a drink." Mason helped himself to a stool several feet from the bartender. He smiled and shrugged mildly. "It's five o'clock somewhere, right?"

"That's what I tell myself," she laughed, setting aside her towel. "What would you like?"

Mason was a sucker for craft beer, but today he felt adventurous. "How about something local?"

"A visitor!" She leaned back. "Odd times, these are."

Mason didn't know what that meant, yet he couldn't stop the disorienting blur of tiny black spades floating before his eyes. "I'm in town on some business." It was a half-truth, at least.

"You and everyone else." A pensive smile crossed her lips as she glanced towards an empty whisky bottle sitting by the sink. "All right," her probing hazel eyes shifted back to Mason, "I recommend a Ramos gin fizz."

"Is that different from a regular gin fizz?"

"It's...got some alterations." She grinned and raised her chin proudly. "The usual stuff, plus lime juice, egg white, cream, orange flower water, and soda water."

Mason felt the curls on his head bounce as he reeled back. "I have to admit, the mad scientist in me is intrigued."

The bartender snorted, waving him off. "It's hardly mad science, hon." She turned and snatched the gin from the shelf. After what felt like ten minutes of potion-brewing, she slid over a straight collins glass frothing with whipped egg whites. Mason stared, dumbfounded, then poked the foam with his straw and took a long drag of the strange elixir.

It was delicious, he decided, and sucked up the rest in a single breath.

Just then, the pub's doors screeched open, and a woman with thick white tresses walked in. Her nails drummed against the door frame, and her eyes—golden like honey—dragged across the playing cards encased against the wood. She greeted them with a quirk of her lips, then floated into the room like an apparition, her navy slip-ons soundless against the aging boards beneath her.

Mason gawped as she slid into the stool next to him. The bartender on the other side fiddled with a pair of tapered scotch glasses, struggling to arrange them on the shelf.

"If you turn every other glass rim down, they'll fit more snuggly," the white-haired woman's velvety voice echoed through the near-empty taproom. Mason still couldn't speak. The bartender startled and hissed several choice words.

"Shit!" she exclaimed, slapping a hand to her chest. "I did *not* hear you come up to the bar, lady."

Ama's plump lips curved into a lovely pink arch as she slipped a silvery strand behind her ear. "Sorry, old habits die hard."

"Were you an assassin in your yesteryears?" the bartender asked, pressing her fingers into her cropped hair.

Ama chuckled and rested her cheek against the palm of her hand. "Well, if I was, I wouldn't tell you, would I?"

"Fair point."

"Could I have a drink, please?"

"Oh," the bartender blinked, "of course. What would you like, assassin lady?"

"A Black Russian should do." Ama's eyes trailed the conspicuous *MANEATER* tattoo on the bartender's forearm. It disappeared as she reached for a bottle on the top shelf.

A. J. VRANA

Mason watched as their mixologist swiftly measured each ounce of water-clear vodka and dark liqueur.

"Here you are, assassin lady." She set a small green napkin on the counter and placed the old-fashioned glass just over the corner.

Ama lifted the glass to her lips and tilted it just enough for a grazing sip. She clamped her teeth over the rim, then set her drink back down and smiled. "What's your name?"

"Huh?"

"Your name," Ama repeated. "Surely it isn't *Maneater*?"

The woman with short hair turned her arm over and pressed it to her side, her face scarlet. "Dahlia," she said shrilly.

The white wolf simpered. "It's a beautiful name—"

"Ama," Mason cut their flirtation short.

Her glossy, navy-blue jacket hugged her waist as she shifted on the stool and finally acknowledged his presence. She took her time peeling off the garment to reveal strong, well-muscled arms and a sleeveless, charcoal mock neck tucked into waist-high jeans. Glowing, sunlit eyes locked onto him, and rosy lips pulled apart in a knowing smile.

Air caught in Mason's throat as the stone's song rang louder, more urgent. His heart hammered behind his ribs. "What are you doing here?"

Ama picked up her drink and swirled the black liquid around. "Waiting for a friend." She paused as she took a sip. "Not you, I'm afraid."

"Does your *friend* know where to find you?" he asked, eyebrow raised.

Ama set down her Black Russian and cradled it between her hands. "She will."

A small gasp slipped from Mason's lips. "Miya?"

Ama canted her head as she glanced down at his fizz.

"Order another drink, Dr. Evans. There will be little daylight to spare by the time our Dreamwalker arrives."

"She's coming?" His words were ecstatic. "Here?"

Ama's mouth curved. "Isn't that what you wanted?"

"If there's one thing I've learned from Black Hollow, it's that what I *want* isn't always what I need."

❧ 15 ❧

MIYA

SILVER AND GOLD *speckled the cobalt river carving the land. In some places, the streams ran as blue as the ocean; in others, they were as clear as glass. The nook near the Emerald Shade saw the river shimmer like liquid pearls. Nowhere in the waking world did such a wonder exist, and Miya loved curling up by its shores to watch the water dance for hours.*

"You don't have hours," her predecessor warned. "Go back."

"I live here," Miya replied, adamant.

The Dreamwalker clicked her tongue. "Have you forgotten already? Go back, girl. You're still near the surface."

"Why should I trust you?"

"I've kept you alive, haven't I?"

Miya's eyes drifted from the sparkling brook and settled on the cloaked figure next to her. "I don't even know your name."

The Dreamwalker sank her fingers into the earth and crept forward like an animal stalking its prey. Her mask floated closer until the two women were nose-to-nose. "My name is Ekaliya..." She hesitated as though remembering something. "Kali."

"Kali," Miya echoed. "Why are you here?"

The Dreamwalker's lips pulled back into a cutting smile, the bone-beak mask hugging her chin. "You're nodding off again…"

Miya jolted with a gasp, exhaustion searing through her veins.

"Shit," she choked, then rubbed her eyes until they felt bruised.

Her butt hurt from sitting on the ground, and her cheek was imprinted with divots from the brick wall. Miya had resolved to stay away from hotels; the urge to sleep was too strong. Regardless, biological need had won. When she sat down to rest her legs, she'd wound up thumping her head against a building and dozing off.

The Dreamwalker had saved her—and Kai—again.

Miya's lack of sleep was hardly the result of insomnia. No, she *had* to stay awake; she couldn't drift off for longer than twenty minutes at once, or Kai would be finished. Deliberate dreamwalking was even worse. Travelling during sleep ended when she awoke, but she could only return from a willful descent when her spirit found its way back to her body.

Instead, she'd entrusted her odds to a wild shot in the abyss and a stolen egg timer.

Her wall-snooze may have been an accident, but she'd slipped into the dreamscape multiple times during the quiet hours before dawn in search of allies. Finally, one of those trips yielded results.

She thought back to the waspish exchange, the raven's protests still a din in her skull. Not that it mattered. To save Kai, Miya would graft her will over both realms—the toll be damned.

"You can't stay awake forever," Gavran had chivied, but Miya's limited time had worn as thin as her patience.

"That's why I need Ama," she'd insisted. "She can keep

tabs on me, so I don't get distracted by a shiny flower or a talking squirrel. Do you have any idea how many power naps it took to find you?"

She recalled Gavran's bristling, his hair rising like hackles. "He tried to kill you! Why care for him still?"

"He's possessed," she'd replied while gritting her teeth.

"He's always possessed!" Gavran had thrown his arms up, his feathered cloak sprawling like wings. "He's weak! Undeserving!"

Relentless, Miya had spurned the condemnation. "Kai isn't weak. Rusalka's corrupted countless men. Kai resisted her. He'd kill himself before letting anything happen to me."

At that point, the boy had stopped his pacing and loured.

"Why do you hate him?" Miya had asked. "Why do you want us separated?"

She remembered the horrid gurgle, the words barely passing through his snarl. "Because he brings only destruction. It's all he knows."

"Give him a chance," she'd pleaded. "He's got good in him, I swear."

Gavran had tried to mollify her. Miya could still feel his pale, icy fingers around her hand. "It's not about whether there's good in him," he'd said. "It's about whether he can fish it out from the dark sea it's buried under."

Miya's hope clashed against Gavran's pragmatism; she knew he was right, but she was too stubborn to give in.

Before departing the dreamscape, she'd squeezed the boy's hand and spoken her command.

"Just get me Ama."

GAVRAN PROMISED Ama would be there by nightfall.

The sun was sinking just below the horizon, but Miya could still see the giant orange globe burning behind her eyelids.

Just a little longer, Miya bargained with herself. *Ama will know what to do.*

Taking a laboured breath, Miya headed for *The Spade*. She faltered after only a few steps. Stars bloomed before her eyes, but she caught herself on a nearby wall and waited for the dizziness to pass. When her insides settled, she resumed her disoriented amble.

The stone nestled against her breastbone trembled in the copper raven's talons as she slammed through *The Spade's* doors shoulder first.

Crowbar looked up from behind the counter. "Hey girl! Saw your angry arm candy a little while ago. Guy looked pretty wrecked. Everything all right with you two?"

Miya's bones felt like they'd crumble. She bit back the truth. "He just had a bad accident." She held the words steady, her voice threatening to crack. Her throat worked, and she quickly sought a distraction from the storm brewing inside her. Fleeing Crowbar's scrutinizing stare, her eyes fell on two figures sitting at the bar.

Ama...

...and Mason Evans.

Something about the doctor was askew. He'd always struck her as a touch overconfident, but the air about him seemed unsettled, shaken even. His shoulders were stiff despite the company, and there was a thick film—something cold and unnatural—caked over his body. It darkened him like a fog darkened a thicket of dense trees.

Something was attached to him.

"There she is," Ama said without turning. Mason spun so furiously that Miya thought the stool's legs would snap beneath him.

Crowbar leaned over the bar between her two patrons. "You all know each other?"

"Old friends," Ama replied, and Miya could hear her smiling through the words.

Miya dragged her weary limbs towards them, but she didn't sit.

"Are you all right?" asked Mason, oozing concern.

Miya's unsteady breaths came slow and haggard. "I've seen better days." She caught Crowbar trying to mind her own business with little success. Guilt knotted into a tight ball in the pit of Miya's stomach. She knew the truth about Sydney, but her lips wouldn't form the words.

Wood screeched on wood as Mason pushed his stool back and stood. "Miya, you've been gone for three years. Your parents—"

She raised her hand to silence him. "I know, Mason. I can still count the days just fine."

He looked as though someone had twisted his arm, fiddling with the cuff of his shirt. His fingers scrabbled at the flesh under the blue cotton—the source of the dark film. "Everyone thinks you're dead! Your parents are desperate and need closure!"

Crowbar had made herself a mouse in the corner, furiously dusting off shelves, though Miya was sure she was plucking details from their conversation.

Miya didn't care. She was inundated by a skein of unwelcome emotions. Her presumed death couldn't have been more trivial. Miya wanted to banish the doctor from her sight for daring to mention it, but when she glanced at him, infected with something sinister, scraps of lingering compassion cleaved through her mounting anger. He had no way of knowing what was at stake for her—no way of knowing that Kai was *maybe* trying to kill her and that she was being hunted by Rusalka.

"It's just—" Miya tripped on her own tongue. She ground her teeth as something sticky and repugnant crawled up her throat. Shame was ready to burst from her body and devour her whole. "I didn't mean for this," she said, her voice quaking. "Please, just tell them I'm okay. That I'm happy. Tell them not to worry."

"M-Miya," Mason stammered, awkwardly scratching through his straw-coloured curls. "You don't look like you're okay."

Miya squeezed her eyes shut and cast out the haze drowning her clarity, then bore holes into Mason's arm. She could feel whatever was there, tugging at loose strands—the unresolved questions, the persistent doubts. It would tug and tug until the threads unravelled, and Mason's sanity alongside them. Although she didn't have a name for the thing he harboured, she knew it was a parasite that fed off people's uncertainties, a predator that preyed on those seeking answers. It was a truth demon, an entity that knew all and wished for only one thing: a companion whose thirst for knowledge rivaled its own.

It couldn't end well. The human mind wasn't built for boundless truths flitting across multiple realms. Miya had seen it first-hand with Black Hollow: people craved a code they could follow. The residents of her hometown had found theirs in the myth of the Dreamwalker, and this had taught Miya that knowledge wasn't so different from a fable. Both were stories that weaved fragments of truth into something useful. Without a story to create meaning, the mind would break in chaos.

People weren't made to know everything, but the truth demon had no awareness of this; it thought it was helping, giving its victim what they wanted until they couldn't tolerate any more. Miya squared her shoulders and took

Mason's hands in her own. Her tone was harsh, but her eyes welled with salty tears.

"Listen to me very carefully, you stubborn, single-minded man. I need you to know—no, to *believe*—that everything is real. Know that I'm fine, that I'm able, and that I don't need saving. Not from you," her voice wavered, "not from Raymond, and not from anyone else. All I need is for you to have faith that I'm doing everything I can to set things right. Please, be satisfied with that, and go home."

Miya dropped his hands like bricks. Her eyes tore from his face; she didn't want to see whatever was there. Grabbing Ama's elbow, she turned to Crowbar and said gravely, "I'm sorry we dragged you into this," then pulled the white wolf from the bar.

"I'll see you again." Ama winked at her new friend, then called to Mason. "There's more than one way to the truth, Dr. Evans."

"I don't under—" He was cut short as the two women disappeared into the alleyway.

MIYA LURCHED FORWARD as she let Ama go, bile rushing up her esophagus. Dropping to her knees, she wretched until the acid left her body.

"You look awful." Ama hauled her to her feet.

Miya spat out the sour taste in her mouth and wiped herself clean. "We need to talk. Then I need some damn sleep."

"Agreed." Ama wrapped an arm around Miya's waist to steady her. Although she appeared stout next to the long-limbed Dreamwalker, her hold was firm and her frame sturdy. "Where to?"

"Graveyard," Miya instructed, her hand splayed on the

grainy wall for support. "It's quiet there, not too busy. I can nap on a bench."

Ama chuckled. "Classy."

Miya scrunched her face up as the light greeted them beyond *The Spade's* dark lane. "I gave up on class years ago. At this point, I'm just trying to survive."

The smirk fell off Ama's face. "So I've heard."

"From Gavran?" They hobbled down the street, and a middle-aged woman walking her poodle slowed, slack-jawed, as she watched them pass. Miya would have welcomed a friendly interaction with the pooch had her owner not looked so offended. Then again, Miya realized she looked day-drunk after a bad break-up. Perhaps it wasn't far from the truth.

"We share knowledge," Ama replied.

"So, you know." Miya winced, inching up the hill that led to the cemetery. The sky ahead was a luminous sapphire as the sun dragged the light westward. She missed the dreamscape, the roiling waves of colour that radiated from the hanging star.

Miya's legs wobbled like caterpillars when they finally reached the top of the slope and passed the lily-paneled church with its coppery brick spire. Spotting a rickety bench, Miya collapsed onto the slats and plunked her head on the backrest.

Ama sank down next to her. "I know your life is in danger. That brute tried to hurt you." Her humour had evaporated like dry ice.

Miya's heart kicked against her ribs as the memory of Kai's face came back to her—the rage, anguish, and confusion all spiralling into a maelstrom he couldn't fight. He'd been ripped from the ground like a shrub caught in a cyclone.

Run, he'd said.

"Go back to the dreamscape," Ama broke in.

"What?" Miya peered at her.

"You're wasting away," said Ama, "Return to the dream-scape and recover."

"Kai can't go back without me." Miya sat up straight as the clamour between her ears grew louder.

"And?"

She wasn't sure if Ama was feigning innocence or being stone-cold serious. An elderly couple, bouquet in hand, passed them languidly, and Miya held her breath for several intolerable seconds until they were gone.

"He'll *die*," Miya emphasized. "Why do you think I've been awake forever without a wink of sleep?"

Ama shrugged, unconcerned. "It's his own fault he needs you to survive this plane. Whatever happened to him isn't your problem. Return to the dreamscape and put the dog out of his misery."

"What the hell!" Miya snapped, the fatigue bleeding out of her. "I didn't call you here to plot murder!"

"And what were you expecting?" Ama's lip curled, her canines shining like a threat. "That I'd care about his life? That I'd risk yours on the off chance that he can be saved? He's weak, Miya. He wouldn't be in this position other-wise, and I won't gamble your life to free him from his demons."

Miya blanched, the woman beside her suddenly a stranger. "I thought you'd care about what I want. About my happiness."

Ama stared off into the distance, her expression unchanged. "Your happiness is your responsibility. It's not carved in stone, not like these tombs." She gestured at the charcoal obelisks scattered around them. "It's childish to think Kai's the only thing that'll ever make you happy."

The world around Miya faded away. The sky could have

turned into a fiery apocalypse, and she wouldn't have noticed.

"Fuck you," she spat, her eyes like a forest ablaze. "Don't patronize me. We both know you'd give your life to save Gavran's, and it has nothing to do with how capable of happiness you'd be without him. The point is you don't *want* to be happy without him."

Ama risked a gander, clear amber clashing against dark, muddy green.

"You're wrong about Kai," Miya continued. "He fought against his demons. He hurt himself so I'd escape. And frankly, you and Gavran are worse. Kai would at least look you in the eye before cutting out your heart."

Silence hung between them like a cloud heavy with rain.

"Fine," Ama sighed. "But you know Kai is like a grenade with a loose pin." Her gaze narrowed. "What you perceive as Kai's self-sacrifice is no different than my instinct to throw him under the bus to protect you. It's not virtuous or kind; we're just trying to defend our own, and I've been watching over you far longer than that overgrown puppy."

Miya raised an eyebrow. "So, you'd murder each other for my sake?"

"Something like that."

"Well then you can both fuck off." Miya flopped back against the wooden boards. "Neither of you are in any position to tell me what to do, and I'm not letting Rusalka get her way either. If you force me back to the dreamscape, you'll be giving her what she wants."

"And what *does* she want?" scoffed Ama. "Why you?"

"I don't know, but I'm not about to kill someone I care about to outplay her. And for the record," Miya raised a warning finger, "if the tables were turned and Kai suggested killing you, I'd tell him to sod off too."

Ama blinked at the fingertip grazing her nose. Her lips

pulled back, and she swatted Miya's hand, her laughter echoing from the top of the hill. The cemetery was mercifully empty now, the last of the visitors having trickled far out of earshot. "He would offer to do it himself, I'm sure!" She winked. "Trust me, his wretched little heart is no saintlier than mine."

Miya smiled despite herself. "Then we can agree you're both rotten."

"I suppose you're right about that," said Ama. "Have it your way, Dreamwalker. Perhaps the calls for execution were premature." She tucked away a strand of Miya's dark brown hair and lightly traced the contours of her face. "But I should warn you. If I'm ever forced to choose between your life and his, I won't hesitate to rip his throat out and paint the walls red with his blood."

Miya's mouth dropped open. She reached for Ama's wrist when a small hand clasped her shoulder. *The white wolf speaks the truth*, came a boy's familiar voice, but when Miya turned, she saw a raven perched where the hand should have been.

"Gavran," she breathed out, then fixed him with a scowl. "Threats won't change my mind."

The raven cocked his head, his beak slicing open in silent protest as his feathers stood erect. She could feel his disapproval sinking into her from his talons.

"You can't coerce me with prodding and scratching," she said. "If you really want to do me a favour, find Kai and help him."

The raven thrust out his wings and chortled, then bowed his head, his blue-black feathers brushing Miya's jawline.

Smiling, Miya scratched his silky neck. "Thank you."

Ama slouched against the bench and grumbled. "I maintain my promise."

"We'll see about that." Gavran hopped along his make-shift roost. "You know what you have to do." She swept up her arm and propelled him into the air.

The raven crowed his farewell, gliding towards the trees and disappearing into the maze of earthy hues.

"Don't worry," said Ama as she caught Miya staring pensively into the distance. "Gavran will find him."

"How do you know?"

The white wolf leaned her head back and smiled towards the sky. "Ravens always hunt alongside us. They're scavengers. They feed on our kills." She took up Miya's hand and squeezed reassuringly. "Where we go, a murder is sure to follow."

✤ 16 ✤

KAI

"Do you feel that?" Rusalka hissed in his ear. "The pain, the impotence, the stubborn belief that they matter."

Kai had never much given a shit about people's feelings. Perhaps it was a nasty side effect of refusing a second glance at his own, but since Rusalka had wormed into his head like a brain-eating amoeba, she'd taken every opportunity to point them out. And God, people had a lot of fucking feelings.

Whenever someone attacked him, he never thought about why. He grinned and savoured the pleasure of defending himself—usually by putting the other guy in a coma for a week. But Rusalka showed him just how deep the roots ran.

If survival drove Kai to violence, then fear drove men to it. Kai was no stranger to fear, but what lurked below it, why it was so dangerous, never registered until now.

Fear was Rusalka's weapon of choice, and in her deft hands, she moulded it into anger like a sculptor perfecting an art form. She showed Kai a world festering beneath people's actions—a world to which he'd been blissfully unaware. People, it seemed, were terrified of each other... and themselves.

"Over there," she instructed, the shadow at the edge of his vision nodding towards a woman standing at the street corner. It was a busy day, chattering voices echoing from every direction as people peppered the main road for their weekend splurge, but this girl was alone. She smoothed out her knee-length skirt and pressed her rouged lips together. Her dark bob was perfectly styled, the straightened locks dead in the wind even as the gauzy fabric whipped around her thighs. She was waiting for someone.

A man about Kai's age approached her then, his hand brushing her elbow to grab her attention. He smiled and began speaking. Kai couldn't discern the words, but he knew exactly what was happening. The girl pulled away with a tense smile; the man was leaning in too close.

"What do you see?" Rusalka's voice chimed like a bell.

"An embarrassment," Kai replied without looking.

Rusalka laughed shrilly. "Accurate, but what else?"

Kai sighed, uninspired to analyze a stranger's cringey cock posturing. "His socks don't match, and that plaid shirt looks like vomit-themed Tetris."

"I don't care about what's on the outside," she warned, drumming her fingers on his shoulder. "I care about what's inside."

Kai's breath halted; her nails were like icicles digging into his skin. He focused on the interaction. The smiling faces and the pealing laughter fell away as he permitted himself to open the door to his senses, if only just a crack.

"He's anxious," Kai observed, noting the beads of sweat pooling around the man's collar.

Rusalka's mouth lifted, her nostrils flaring with excitement. "And the girl?"

Kai's gaze drifted past Gary—that's what Kai was calling him now; he looked like a Gary, and Gary was the perfect name for a plodding pedestrian with mismatched socks. The girl clutched her handbag, a tight-lipped smile plastered on her face as she blinked heavily and nodded. She glanced past him as though trying to flag for help, then choked back a laugh and quickly shook her head. "Looks like she'd rather walk barefoot over a sea of pinecones than bump uglies with Gary."

"Gary?" Rusalka blinked at him.

Kai shrugged. "Know any mouth-watering specimens named Gary?"

She frowned and slanted her head as though scanning her memory stores. "Can't say I do."

Kai flashed her a wolfish grin. "Exactly."

Something warbled in Rusalka's throat. "Stop diverting. Your petty resistance is meaningless."

His mouth curved into a vicious smirk. "Small victories, you dead-eyed bitch."

Grey skin swiftly found his thigh, nails like rust and cold tunnelling into his wound. Although the tendons had sewn themselves back together, his leg was in no condition for another mangling. Kai clenched his jaw and grimaced, his eyes like blood and fire. Patience whittled to a mere splinter, he grabbed Rusalka's wrist and squeezed with stone-crushing force. "Your kitty claws are tickling me," he menaced in a low growl. "Remove them."

"You're a strong pup," she snubbed, "but if you don't play by my rules, I'll do more than tickle you, little wolf. Perhaps a scuffle with Gary? Or a visit to your favourite bar? A lone woman tending to an establishment with such disreputable clientele—well, there's no saying what might happen, is there?"

Kai wanted to crush her waifish wrist, tear her hand free, and feed it to the crows, but he was powerless without Miya. A living person couldn't clobber a spirit manifesting in the physical plane, and a spirit had no way of ending another spirit in the dreamscape. No, these were two different realities. Miya knew how to find the in-between, a limbo where all things existed inseparably from one another. That was the only place he could do damage.

The infuriating catch: only Miya could navigate that liminal space, and only she could bring others into it. She found the borderlands between dreams as they rippled out from their dreamers. In rare instances, dreams touched like strangers brushing past one another on a crowded street. Miya's true power—the Dreamwalker's true power—was to inhabit that sliver where two worlds became one, and to move between them unfettered. Sure, Kai could reach a fist into the in-between and slug a bastard in the face, but they had to be brought there by the Dreamwalker first.

Kai loosened his hold. "The girl's nervous," he said, staring dully at the woman with the black bob. "She wants to get away, but she's meeting someone, so she can't."

There was a sharp sting as Rusalka retracted her nails. His wound was still closed, absent of marks where she'd sliced into him, but the ache persisted.

Just then, another man—this one with matching socks —approached the awkward couple and slinked an arm around the woman's waist. His bulging eyes glued to the peacock invading his territory. Gary immediately backpedaled, raising his hands as he addressed the man with matching socks. The woman he'd been hitting on was quickly forgotten, shrinking into the smog of escalating dickmanship. Although Kai couldn't hear Gary's words, he knew they were a rapid-fire apology.

"I'm so sorry," Rusalka dubbed the exchange. "I had no idea she was your girl!"

Kai's eyebrow arched as he watched the trio, a series of guttural barks and catty hisses sounding next to him as Rusalka enacted the scene.

"Oh! What do you think he's saying now?" she gasped into Kai's ear, clutching his arm in giddy anticipation.

"I could punch your face through the back of your skull," Kai muttered in monotone, intentionally vague about who, exactly, he was referring to.

Rusalka pouted. "No jab at his manhood?"

Kai refused to acknowledge her.

She gestured towards the two men. "This isn't even about the girl anymore, is it?"

When Gary finally retreated, tail between his legs, he didn't give the woman with the black bob so much as a second glance. She was leaning against the wall, her arms crossed as she stared at her shoes. Her human football of a boyfriend knotted his fists as his eyes darted left and right in search of the next threat. Then, his glare landed on his girlfriend, lingering on her hemline.

"Isn't it funny," began Rusalka, "how men always apologize to other men for disturbing women?"

Kai was too engrossed to reply. Body language was a dialect he spoke well, and he tensed in response to the man's barely contained aggression. Kai glanced around the square, but other passersby seemed oblivious. The girl was a hair's breadth away from being yelled at by Biceps, yet no one noticed his clenched-up asshole and the veins ready to burst under his purpling neck. How did *no one* notice?

"It's because the girl doesn't matter," he said to both

Rusalka and himself. "It's not about her. It's about their egos."

Rusalka purred in his ear, "Well done, little wolf."

"I'm not a toddler," he snarled, his scorching stare still on the football-man with misdirected anger.

"They're treating her like toilet paper," Rusalka's voice dripped with disdain.

Kai couldn't disagree with her. Both men feared they'd lost something, but while one was forced to slink away, the other had the perfect outlet for his frustrations: the possession he thought almost lost.

"They're all afraid," Rusalka whispered like it was a well-kept secret. "The man fears he is now less of a man. The woman," she added darkly, "the woman is simply afraid." She laughed like an omen before a catastrophe. "How easy it would be to turn them on her. To tear down the fragile barrier between anger and action."

"What's that got to do with me?" Kai asked, his spine tingling with the heat of kinetic fury.

"Nothing, perhaps." She smiled sweetly. "Or everything. Your fear is what brought you to me. Fear whispered, *open the door*," her lips found his ear, tongue darting out like a snake's, "and you did. You let me in."

Kai pulled away, repulsed by her rancid breath. "I'm not some jealous asshole."

She threw her head back and cackled. "*Jealousy?* Dogs get jealous." She waved her hand dismissively. "No, this runs far deeper than mere jealousy. This is entitlement. Entitlement over your women, your egos," she cast him a sideways glance, "your freedom."

Kai turned to stone beside her. *His freedom.* He'd never thought about it before Miya, but since being tethered to her in the dreamscape, he loathed his dependence on her, even if she was his best friend. The tether demanded his trust, and no matter how hard he tried to surrender it, every inch he gave left him bitter, angry, and—

"Fearful," Rusalka finished his thought. "You were afraid she'd never unshackle you. You're still afraid. Just like they are." She gestured towards the throngs of people in the square.

Kai watched the couple disappear into the crowd, his eyes lingering on the man's large hand clasped possessively around the woman's. He wondered if it hurt, if her fingers felt like they were breaking in his grip. If she was in pain— and he sensed that she was—no one would know. Her boyfriend didn't notice; he was so focused on grasping on like a child with a stolen toy. They would go home, and she would swallow whatever accusation seethed under the lid of public propriety.

Breath hitched in Kai's throat, waves of panic crashing through his chest. He'd spent the last thirteen years teetering between repression and unbridled rage. He didn't have the energy for this, but now that Rusalka had coerced his animal senses into perceiving things he'd never considered, he found himself paralyzed by the onslaught of others' emotions. They were so...leaky. Sure, most people shoved their bullshit so far down that an oil drill couldn't excavate it, but it was still there, oozing like pus, pooling around the edges of Kai's mind.

How hadn't he seen it before? Humanity was the most destructive force on the planet because they lived in constant fear.

And the irony of it all?

Those in whose likeness he was made were the most fearful and destructive of all. Men were violent because they'd been promised the world, yet no kingdom had been delivered to them. They hadn't realized there were no more kings.

"Why are you telling me this?" Kai asked, cutting the thread of his spiralling thoughts. "Your bullshit won't work on me if I know how you do it."

Rusalka blinked, her mouth a thin line before she howled with laughter. "Oh, my sweet, little wolf. Just because you know how something works doesn't mean you can stop it. Nothing is more painful, more terrifying than watching a spider spin its web around your paralyzed body." Her spindly fingers caressed his arm as her eyes trailed over him, admiring his physique.

Kai felt sick. Between her probing questions and her cloying affection, he was dizzy with doubts. He shot to his feet, shaking off her syrupy hands.

"And where do you think you're going?" Her voice was now laced with venom.

She was worse than Abaddon. At least Kai's former nemesis let him go where he pleased. Rusalka wanted him to believe that Miya had him on a short leash, yet nothing in Satan's playground could've compared to the chokehold this mouldy washcloth had on him. She was a plague. Not only did she dictate his movements, but she'd also weaseled into his mind during his weakest moments. His best defense was to keep a level head, stay calm, and dole out sarcasm like it was candy corn on Halloween.

Easier said than done. She'd unsettled him more than once in thirty minutes of idle chit-chat. How long until he cracked? Until he lost agency and did the unthinkable? No. He would rather die. He'd made that abundantly clear with his leg and a sharp blade.

But Kai was first and foremost a survivor, and he was good at getting by against the odds, no matter the cost. He doubted Rusalka would be torn up if her new doll ripped itself to pieces before she could. There were countless others she could replace him with, and that made the prospect of dying less appealing. If she was after Miya, any number of men were candidates: good old absentee Raymond, or that golden turd, Evans. What if she dug up old acquaintances—some disappointment from college who clung to an old flame that was never kindled? And what of those who straddled more than one world like Kai? Could Gavran be turned against the person he was most loyal to?

"I'm hungry," Kai grunted, though it was an excuse—an attempt to shield the panicked spate flowing through his bones. Yet in his mind's eye, he only saw one thing: a boy with waxy skin and eyes like depthless pools of black ink.

Gavran.

He needed Gavran.

KAI SURVEYED the trees peering over the gabled rooftops of Orme's Rest. He scrunched up the wrapper of his freshly devoured burger and tossed it into the trash. The raven had always been near, both in Black Hollow and in the dreamscape. Would Orme's Rest be any different?

Where are you, Shit-for-brains?

"What shall we do next?" Rusalka interrupted his surveillance as she twined her arm with his.

Kai weaved away from the bustle and meandered towards the outskirts of town. The colourful boutique shops and restaurants were gone, leaving a trail of dilapidated depots along a pockmarked road with no sidewalk. Weeds poked through the craggy pavement, and the bulbs of overarching streetlights were blown out or broken.

"Thought you'd force me to murder someone," he said dryly.

"Why, of course!" she trilled. "In due time, that is. It's no fun if you're expecting it at every turn. Maybe we should do something to relax you first."

Kai's thoughts wandered to Miya. He felt a prickle of

discomfort every so often—a sure sign she was slipping into the dreamscape—but no burning agony, no eviscerated cells marking lengthier departures. His heart twisted as a caustic lump tugged at his throat. She must have been exhausted. One bad night of insomnia typically had her glum and implacable. He couldn't imagine what several days without rest would do. Was she eating? Had she found shelter? He wanted to see her, tell her he was rebelling, and beg her not to give up on him—to take a goddamn nap for more than ten minutes. He'd last at least thirty. Maybe forty.

"Tell me," Rusalka leaned on his shoulder, "what do you enjoy?"

"Killing, fighting, fucking." It was an evasive response, but he was torn in two—one part of him aching to find the raven while the other fought to keep collected.

"Hmm, so basic. Though I suppose it explains your mulishness. You *are* irritatingly true to your instincts."

"Eating too. I like eating."

Rusalka rolled her eyes. "Now you're boring me."

Kai kicked at a pebble on the worn-down asphalt. "I also like being alone. You wouldn't mind fucking off, would you?"

A caw echoed from above. Kai glanced up to find a raven settled on a rusted lamppost, and the scavenger wasn't alone. There was an entire congress of the bastards, circling overhead as though searching for the perfect head to shit on. Kai reckoned they'd found it.

"How rude of you," Rusalka chided. Her pupils darted around the bulging twin cases of her serpent-like eyes as she caught sight of the looming threat. "Is that any way to treat your guest?"

"You're not a guest," said Kai. "You're a parasite."

"I'm a gift!" she roared, her nails slicing into his forearm.

Glowering at her hold, Kai whipped his arm free. "Sure, a gift." His mouth quirked. "Pickled meat for the crows."

The raven from the lamppost divebombed her in a blur of muddy black. All wings, feathers, and talons, his beak thrust into her hair and face. She swung her arms and spun like a pinwheel, shrieking as purulent blood oozed from her cuts.

The raven chortled, and the others descended in one fell swoop, swarming the demon in a cloud of darkness. Her cries were swallowed by the cacophony until the first raven —the largest in the group—freed himself from the frenzy and perched on Kai's shoulder.

She won't be held down for long, the boy's voice echoed in his mind.

Kai didn't need to be told. He bolted down the street and turned sharply behind a run-down garage with a junk-yard at the rear, the raven fluttering close behind. "What the hell do you mean she won't be held down for long? Pluck her to death!"

A wet hiss escaped the raven's throat. *Feathers and air, you gargantuan oaf.*

Kai peeked around the corner.

The unkindness was gone. Rusalka flailed and screeched like a banshee, but she was entirely alone. It was all a goddamn mirage.

"No shit," Kai muttered, then rolled off the wall and hurried down the lane. Hopping the chain-link fence, he slid past a wrecked car. The dumpster-lot was ass-up against the swamp, and it would buy him precious time.

"We need to talk," said Kai.

Not here. Shit-for-brains flew on ahead and disappeared into the quagmire.

Despite his aching leg, Kai was forced into a sprint. "Asshole," he grimaced.

The wet earth sloshed beneath Kai's boots as the raven glided through knitted foliage and skirted around colossal cypress trunks. He could hardly keep up, let alone heed his surroundings. All he registered was the eerie familiarity. With every step, his spine tingled in anticipation of vines coming to life and coiling around his ankles.

When the cypresses cleared away, Kai skidded to halt, his toes against the shores of the black lake. He saw the islet in the distance with its towering dead elm. Only then did he recognize where they were.

"Why the hell would you bring me here?" Kai's demand rang into empty air.

"Because," the boy said from behind, his words shadowed by a second voice, rough like sandpaper scraping against glass. "Here, we touch the dreamscape."

Kai spun, the thing before him more jarring than the scenery. Gavran was no longer a corpse-child with bloodied teeth. Now a man almost as tall as Kai, his body was woven with wiry muscles and a long, angular face. Glistening black hair peeled back against his scalp, revealing a broad forehead with harsh lines curving over thick brows. Only his eyes remained the same—dark as coal and deep as the cavern they'd been mined from.

The raven—its edges blurred like dye in water— swooped down and clasped Gavran's slim shoulder, greeting him with a gentle peck on his drooping ear.

"It's the Grey Gnarl," the two voices coalesced into one.

Questions stuck in Kai's throat like a chicken bone. When had they tumbled into the dreamscape? Usually, there was a sign—a change in the air or a sudden drop through the earth. Kai felt *nothing*.

Would Miya sense he was gone? How would he get back without her?

"I can bring you *in* but not *out*," said Gavran.

"So, I'm the only dingus who can't go in either direction?"

"So it seems." Gavran sighed, then gazed wearily into the swamp. "Ah, *her* eyes see again."

"Rusalka's free," Kai swallowed.

"Speak quickly, wolf. Though I hope you aren't here to plead for help." His lips sliced open, carving a smile into his face. "I will not give it."

"Then you're a useless pigeon," Kai scowled.

"I am kind enough to grant last requests." His grin widened, inky pools bubbling with glee.

"Damn," Kai choked on a laugh. "Sounds like you *want* me dead."

Gavran scoffed. "The Dreamwalker only suffers because of you and your fragility. Had you been stronger, surer, you never would have been infected."

"Cut the shit," Kai snapped, shame gnawing at the pit of his stomach. Rusalka was closing in, and the borders of his mind dimmed with her miasma. "I've only got one favour to ask. Consider it my last request."

Gavran pursed his lips, shoulders shuddering as though he could barely contain his contempt. "Speak."

Kai clenched his fists to stave off the juddering dread. Eyes hard like ice, he stared down the man Gavran wore as skin.

"Take me to Abaddon," he ordered. "I've got business with that whimpering bitch."

❧ 18 ❧

MASON

"I DON'T UNDERSTAND!" Mason called after Ama and Miya, but he was met only by the heavy tavern doors slamming shut.

He *never* understood. Not when it mattered.

"Want another drink?" asked the bartender as she flung the dusting cloth over her shoulder. "You look like you could use one, and frankly, I've got a pretty intense itch for some gossip."

"Can't blame you." Mason slumped his shoulders and dropped into the stool. "Give me the strongest thing you have, Dah—"

"Call me Crowbar." She nodded. "And you got it."

"Crowbar," Mason chuckled.

"That's right." She poured something dark and earthy over ice. The bottle was tall and tinted deep brown, with a wide, rotund neck and no label.

"What's this?" he asked as she pushed the drink towards

him. He picked it up and chanced a whiff, then wrinkled his nose and pulled back.

"Moonshine." She grinned proudly. "Made it myself."

Mason took a cautious sip before slamming down the glass. His eyes watered as he sucked on his teeth to pull back the burn. "Jesus Christ," he coughed. "What's in this?"

"That," she leaned over the bar, "is not to be divulged to medical personnel."

Mason groaned and plunked his head down. "Please tell me it's legal."

"Probably."

"Probably!" He sat up and squinted at her.

"What?" She shrugged innocently. "You're feeling better, aren't you?"

Begrudgingly, he took another gulp. "It's been a long week."

"Yeah?" She pulled up a stool on her side of the bar. "Well, it's my job to listen to people and give half-baked advice, so I'm all ears. What's eating you? Something to do with Miya?"

Mason considered her for a moment. The jet fuel in his tumbler was warming his stomach and melting his brain. Despite that professionalism demanded he practice discretion for his client's sake, the impulsive detective had surfaced and was fast taking over. Mason had always been a lightweight, but whatever Crowbar had given him was strong enough to put a rugby player under after an extra-large pizza and a bucket of wings.

"Ok, fine," he almost slurred, then lifted a finger. "But you can't tell *anyone* about this, all right?"

"Yeah, yeah, I got you, girlfriend. This isn't high school." She swatted his hand down. "Don't wag your sausage claw at me."

"Sorry," he mumbled. "I'm a doctor, you know? I'm used to telling people what to do."

She rolled her eyes. "You are *so* Ivy League, you know that?"

Mason's mouth dropped open, his brow creasing. "What's that supposed to mean?"

"Jesus, man, just tell me the fucking story!"

"Okay, okay, yeesh," he whined with an exaggerated huff, then stared into his glass. "Miya's parents hired me to find her."

"So, you're a doctor *and* a stalker?"

"No!" He glared. "She's been missing for three years! Legally, she'll be dead next year. I was the last person to see her alive."

"What the shit?" Crowbar snapped upright.

Mason risked another quaff of moonshine. "I *knew* she was alive. I kept it to myself, tried so damn hard not to think about it. Didn't tell anyone because I knew she probably didn't want to be found. But her father," he shook his head and chuckled quietly, "that son of a bitch. He's smart. Used my guilt against me, got me to agree to this wild sheep chase. My curiosity didn't help. Always gets the best of me, so here I am."

"If she doesn't want to see her dad, she shouldn't have to," Crowbar said sternly. "She's a grown-ass woman. She can do what she wants."

"I don't disagree." Mason drummed his fingers on the counter. "There's just...so much more to it. So much that's happened." He glanced up at her. "Have there been strange things going on here lately? Anything out of the ordinary?"

"It's backwater Louisiana," she snorted. "I bet everything that happens here is weird to outsiders."

"I'm serious," he said more urgently. "I'm not here just

to look for a missing girl. I'm investigating something bigger. Something bad."

Mason saw the colour drain from Crowbar's face as her lips ironed out. "Like a strange murder?"

"Exactly like a strange murder."

She took a deep breath. "Well, you've come to the right place then."

The mark on Mason's arm began to sizzle. "Will you tell me about it?"

Her mouth tugged downward as she scrutinized him. "Why?"

"Because I might be able to help. But I need information. I need to know what happened if I'm to put the pieces together," he insisted.

Her caution didn't crack. She studied him like a jaded stray sniffing a too-easily proffered steak.

"I'm not here to bother anyone," he reassured her. "I'm just trying to understand why women are dying. Miya might be in trouble with whatever's behind all this."

Mason glimpsed a chink in the armor as Crowbar's gaze widened with intrigue. "What do murdered women have to do with Miya?"

"They're connected, I know it. But I won't be able to understand how and why unless I have as much information as possible."

Crowbar shifted her weight, her jaw clenching and unclenching as she blinked away tears. She poured herself a shot of moonshine. "Fine," she said. "For Miya."

Mason was compelled to complete silence. He listened as Crowbar explained how her sister, Sydney Baron, was inexplicably murdered by her husband, Vince—a man who was nothing but adoring, devoted, and kind until the last few weeks of Sydney's life. A man who, upon killing the woman he loved, muttered about being coerced. As far as anyone could tell, he had no motive, but he'd claimed that *something* had convinced him his wife needed to die.

"Is he pleading guilty?" Mason wondered if Vince would use the insanity defense.

"He already did in his own way. The bastard's dead." Crowbar fiddled with a bottle opener. "Guards found him on his cell floor. Suicide, apparently, though they have no idea how he managed it."

Mason withered in his seat. He knew this pattern. "Cause of death?"

She shook her head. "The detective who called said the autopsy report's classified. No fucking clue why. Seems like an excuse to hide their incompetence."

Mason's brain was swimming in a dangerous cocktail of alcohol and awe. Crowbar's story was almost identical to the case from Cypress Swamp. Returning to Black Hollow and its troubling cycle, Mason was confronted with the same puzzle pieces: a large wooded area known as a spiritual repository, a young female victim mistaken for an imposter, and a perpetrator who kills the person he loves most without explanation.

"How are you here, working after all this tragedy?" he asked, questions tearing him apart at the seams.

"It's all I've got," Crowbar said with a shrug. "I live alone. Not many friends in a town like this. Except Bastien, the chef here. Syd was the only family I had left. Mom and Dad kind of kicked me to the curb after I wasn't down to pray the gay away. And since my only real friend is in the kitchen, I've got nowhere else to go. Besides," she smiled, "listening to other people's shit reminds me I'm not alone."

Mason had stopped processing her words. His arm was on fire, the mark blistering with newfound fervor. It spread deeper and faster as if feeding off his tryst with revelation.

Black Hollow, Cypress Swamp, and Orme's Rest were all junctions in the same web.

"I-I'm sorry," Mason stammered, pulling out his wallet as he stood abruptly. "I just remembered I forgot something really—" he could barely speak, his every nerve erupting with agony, "—important." Hands trembling, Mason fumbled for a twenty, but it slipped through his fingers, floating past the bar and onto the floor next to Crowbar.

"Hey, doc, you all right?" She rose to follow him, ignoring the bill.

Mason didn't answer. He stumbled towards the door, barely squeezing through as he pushed it ajar. The scalding pain didn't subside even as he threw himself into the light. Tearing at his arm, Mason ripped the buttons free from his cuff and yanked back the sleeve. Breaths drawing shallow, he stared down at the twin moons, the symbols etching deeper into his flesh. A burnt scarlet line cleaved slowly through one of the arcs, then halted its approach, leaving the other crescent unscathed. From somewhere deep within, the servant's voice rumbled like an impending earthquake.

Soon, my master, we will be as one.

❧ 19 ❧

KAI

"Have the magpies snatched your tail?" Gavran's mouth warped, pointed teeth clipping his bottom lip. "You've gone rabid, wolf."

"Says the useless pigeon wearing a corpse," Kai replied, unshaken. "The request stands, Shit-for-brains."

Gavran canted his head to the left, then jerked it to the right as he spat on the ground. "You think Abaddon yet lives?"

Kai betrayed a sliver of a smile. "The cycle was broken. That's all. I know he's lurking. I can feel the bastard moping, scratching at the back of my skull."

Gavran scrunched up his face like there was something tart on his tongue. "Fine, yes." He sighed. "The Dreamwalker's spirit banished him far from Black Hollow. His end was not part of their bargain, and she was not yet strong enough to make it so." His lips slithered out. "She is far more honourable than I."

Before Kai could question him, an ear-piercing shriek shattered the sky and rattled the treetops.

"You *worm*," came Rusalka's throaty growl as she shambled into the clearing, her shark-eyes ablaze with hatred. The air around her radiated with blighted heat; the grass at her feet writhed and browned, and behind her, a serrated stream of death and decay plagued the ground she'd doddered over.

Gavran's head wound a hundred-and-eighty unbearable degrees, his shoulders still squared to Kai. He leered at Rusalka, his bloodied grin impossibly wide. "I *eat* worms, little fish."

Kai detected hesitation in the demon who'd ensnared him in her schemes. She slowed to a stop, her eyes a storm as they darted between the wolf and the raven. Did their shaky alliance compromise her control? Kai looked hopefully to Gavran, who offered only a low, menacing chuckle.

"Very well," he said, twisting his head back to where it belonged. "You shall have your wish, wolf. You and the devil can devour each other for all I care." Clasping his hands behind his back, he strolled towards the Grey Gnarl—a scarecrow against the slate-coloured sky.

"Don't you dare go with him," Rusalka threatened when Kai turned to follow.

"Ignore her," Gavran drawled when Kai paused mid-stride.

"Can't you kill her *now*?" Kai fought to keep his back turned to Rusalka, his animal instincts berating him.

"I cannot!" Gavran barked, then stepped into the black lake. The water didn't hinder him as he ambled straight through, sinking inch by inch until only his head bobbed between the algae. "You know as well as I that spirits cannot be killed here or there." He nodded towards the dead elm that separated them from the physical plane.

"Only in the place between. Only by the Dreamwalker's bidding."

They were powerless without Miya. Kai glanced over his shoulder to find Rusalka trailing from a safe distance.

"I see you," she hissed, teeth bared.

Kai snarled back. "Good. Then you get to see what comes next."

Her flesh peeled from her face as her jaw unhinged, and she released a bone-shattering scream. Wincing, Kai followed Gavran into the water and waded across. The algae scrabbled at his ankles like souls trying to hew their way from the underworld. Maybe there *were* things in the abysmal lake—dead things that only surfaced when they found someone to grab onto.

"I told you to ignore her," Gavran tutted as Kai climbed up onto the island after him. Despite the humidity, the island was bone-dry. Had the elm sucked all the life from it, then withered when it had nothing left to feed on? Maybe Rusalka and the Grey Gnarl echoed one another.

Kai glimpsed the evil siren slithering through the water. "Let's go," he said, and they stepped through the gateway.

His stomach nearly flew into his mouth as beaming light seared through his vision. Mercifully, the sensory whirlwind only lasted a moment, and he was able to keep his innards where they belonged.

They landed on solid ground, and Kai was pleased to find himself still balancing on two legs. The air was tolerable now; the iron stink of sludge and quagmire dissipated into the crisp scent of pine, fresh river water, and old campfires. Up above, thin clouds weaved through the sinking orange dusk. Gavran wound sharply into the shrubs and guttered like an apparition. Swaying spurs hung all around like a thick curtain, obscuring Kai's line of sight. He knew this place.

"Where are we going?" Kai brushed aside a low-hanging branch.

Gavran didn't respond. His steps were effortless, like he was gliding rather than trudging through terrain paved by endless seasons.

"S-stop," came Rusalka's cry, quiet and far away.

They moved further into the trees until only an occasional flicker teased through the foliage. The crevice Gavran led them into smelled like fire, ash, and blood.

They were close.

The glade was so dim, Kai could barely see three feet in front of him, but he recognized it as though it were part of his own body. Up ahead, he saw the ramshackle paneling of a cabin—his cabin.

How many nights had its walls sheltered him from the elements? Last time he saw his old home, it was burning to the ground as Black Hollow's residents frothed like rabid dogs. Yet here it was. The smoke was still fresh, wafting from blackened splinters.

Every breath felt like sand caught in his throat. He reached out and placed his hand against the door. "How did we get here?"

His question was met with silence. Gavran was gone.

"Please," came Rusalka's strained voice, "don't go in. You don't know the cost of what you seek."

Kai dug his fingernails into the charred wood. "If it'll get rid of you, I don't give a shit."

The door chirred open, and the cabin extended its uncanny invitation. Home beckoned him inside. Kai only hesitated a moment before he stepped over the threshold, and the shadows swallowed him up.

The last thing he heard from the world outside was Rusalka's fading whimper—a hopeless plea lost to the wind.

❧ 20 ❧

THE CABIN WAS BARE, swimming in darkness save for a dash of silver moonlight spilling over the bathroom door. Kai's animal senses were hampered by the dreamscape's midnight haze. Seconds yawned by, yet his eyes didn't adjust. Pulled to the only thing he could see, Kai reached for the rusted knob. His fingers numbed by the time he turned his wrist. Again, Kai stepped into blackness, and the door slammed shut behind him.

Cold breath washed over Kai's ear—ragged as it fought to form a single word—an accusation.

"Monster," it said.

Kai swallowed down the bile. He knew exactly who it was. "Brother."

"What's the matter?" he sneered. "Forgotten my name?"

"It's a boring name," said Kai. "So...biblical."

Quiet chuckles chimed against the ceramics. "A fitting name. You'd know that if you could remember."

"Remember what?"

"There's no sense in telling a man who he is if he doesn't already know."

The space was claustrophobic, reminding Kai of the years he'd been trapped with Abaddon. It'd felt just like this —a barren cell with mouldy walls and a cracked, distorted mirror. *Of course* his nemesis had chosen it for their reunion.

Kai took a step forward and growled. "You know I hate riddles."

The reply droned from all around. "I am the First."

"You got a name, or you just like winning races?" Kai mocked, sickened by the smell of fumes.

Another piercing silence followed. The First's voice, suddenly crisp, rumbled directly in front of Kai. "My name," a face in the bathroom mirror cleaved through the murky shroud, "is Velizar."

Kai's hand struck the old porcelain sink as he stumbled back. The man in the mirror was Kai's own spitting image, but where Kai's gaze was scarlet fire, this man's eyes were a cold metallic gold. His face was gaunt like he'd been starved of the malice that sustained him, and his jet-black hair had grown into a wild mane that barely passed his shoulders.

"Velizar," Kai began, the name bitter on his tongue.

The man tilted his head, his gleaming eyes hollowed out, his skin waxy and pale. His mouth cracked open in a dazed smile. "Poor baby brother—I forget names mean nothing to you." He braced his arms against the walls, something oily-slick splattering around his fingertips. Pulling forward, he emerged from the mirror whole.

The shroud lifted, the sink and the mirror disappeared, and the brothers found themselves standing in the cabin's main room. The walls were spattered with human silhouettes made of ash, and Kai's furniture was ripped to pieces; his wool blanket was in tatters, and his mattress had been gutted, the inner sponge littering the floor like confetti.

"Why are you here?" asked Kai, his eyes trailing the

charred remains of all the people who'd perished that night. "You hate me. Why stay here?"

"Hate you?" Velizar wrapped an emaciated arm around his bulging ribs and laughed, the sound identical to Abaddon's maniacal cackle. The mirror image grinned and repeated Abaddon's words. "What would I do without you?"

Memories of trauma kneaded into Kai's skull. "Fucking with me was the core of your existence. That doesn't make it anything less than hate."

"Oh, little brother," Velizar sighed. "You know as well as I that the line between love and hate is paper-thin. And paper is *so* easy to tear, and even easier to burn. It's more fragile than life itself."

"Cut the shit. Say what you mean."

A chilly hand reached for Kai, clasping his shoulder. "I will always hate...and love you. That is why I need you. And I suspect," he smiled like a threat on the edge of a blade, "that you're here because you need me too."

Kai's muscles tensed, his face aching from the scowl he'd been wearing. How he loathed himself for what he was about to do; he would've rather cut out a piece of his own heart. But if Rusalka was a cancer and Velizar the nauseating cure, he'd have to endure the oncoming sickness.

"I have...a problem."

Velizar closed his eyes and inhaled deeply, swooning as he hummed. "Ah, yes. I can smell her now. But I don't see how she's a problem I'm obligated to help with."

"You're not. But I know you want back in." Kai mustered the courage to close in and grab the phantom by the back of the neck. "I also know you won't share me with her. If I invite you in, she'll fuck off."

The corners of Velizar's lips tugged up. "You want me to force her out. What's to stop you from exorcising me afterwards, little brother? As I recall, you have a fledgling Dreamwalker in your pocket."

Something sticky and sour filled Kai's mouth, but he gulped it back down. He'd always been self-reliant, even when Alice took care of him. Somehow, she never got angry about all the trouble he caused. Maybe she knew he'd already had enough anger in his life. On his sixteenth birthday, he'd come home late after a week of fistfights and his second suspension, but that didn't stop her from sticking a candle into a rack of pork ribs she'd made—and she *hated* cooking. She ignored the bruises, pretended there'd been no phone call from the principal, and then handed him the lilac birthday card.

He never asked for help, but he also never took responsibility. Finding Miya had only disguised that. He'd taken for granted the solace they found in each other; Miya tempered the worst of his impulses while he emboldened her to push through obstacles without trepidation. Yet their victories gave way to new trials, and those trials blew back the cover on Kai's shortcomings. Now, the only way out was through the very hell he'd fought to be rid of, and it disgusted him down to the marrow of his bones. He was about to uproot everything he'd built, everything he'd become.

His gaze hardened as he held fast to his resolve. "What if it's something more permanent?"

Velizar's brows shot up, and he scoffed. "Are you proposing an integration? Two become one?"

"Why not? I won't be Miya's burden anymore." His grip tightened on the back of Velizar's neck, bruising the cool, pale flesh. "You're my problem now."

Kai felt goosebumps against his fingertips. Velizar was grinning like a madman, his eyes teeming with sheer ecstasy.

"Show me this demon that haunts you," he hissed before his tone softened, "and let me protect you from the monsters outside."

Kai's hand dropped to his side. Every fibre screamed that this was wrong—that there was no returning from this Faustian bullshit. Gavran would be vindicated. Ama would sneer, reminding him that she always thought he was garbage. Miya would never forgive him. She'd leave him, and he'd be alone.

Kai started towards the door. He never imagined he'd have to betray Miya to protect her from Rusalka.

"Don't worry about your precious Miya," Velizar broke in. "I can give you everything she kept from your grasp."

"You mean eternal torture?" Kai snorted, welcoming the distraction from his suffocating shame—the menace's mind-reading be damned.

"That," Velizar chuckled, "and the tools you thought only she had." His fingers brushed the hilt of the hunting knife strapped to Kai's belt. "There will be no border you cannot cross, no enemy you cannot slay. Not when you're with me, brother."

A flutter rose in Kai's chest—the prospect of freedom—but he knew better than to believe pretty words. He would test those promises very soon.

"Poor thing," Velizar crooned. "You don't even know why the chains buckled around you."

Kai's throat worked. The dreaded question—why—burned in his mouth, begging to be spat out, but he wouldn't let it slip.

The cabin pealed with Velizar's sickening laughter. "No need to hide your curiosity. If I'd been shackled, I'd surely want to know why."

"I don't care why," Kai deflected, but it was a lie, and Velizar knew it.

"When your *precious* Dreamwalker broke the cycle, she unbound us. She is chaos, after all, and in sowing it, she became something more while unravelling us both. She reduced us to our simplest forms: the will of the First," his gaunt cheeks stretched as he smiled like a sickle, "and a wolf under a willow tree, waiting for a girl he'd become dependent on."

Fire raked up Kai's esophagus. He didn't know who he was angry at anymore. *It's not her fault*, he reasoned. *She had no way of knowing.*

"She tethered you to her," Velizar swooned close, his voice hoarse. "It *is* her fault. You were free before her; you were free with me. She *always* rips you from me and leashes you like a dog. When she awoke on that fated night, you become a casualty."

Something ancient and terrible stirred in Kai—a gutting familiarity with the emaciated creature next to him. Velizar was telling the truth.

It doesn't matter, Kai insisted, guilt corroding his anger. Velizar and Rusalka were a bane; he would rather spend an eternity with the Dreamwalker, hitched by iron links.

"She's not here," Velizar reminded him. "Now, only I can give you power...and freedom."

Kai kicked the door open, the snap of wood cathartic as he stepped into the foggy glade. Rusalka hadn't moved. She clung to a birch tree like a leech hanging from salted skin, a puddle of melted flesh and grey pus pooling around her feet as she wheezed. She was weak here. Her eyes widened as she stared past Kai, her slit-green irises dilated into perfect spheres of terror.

"What have you done!" she shrieked, trying to mask her fear with rage. But Kai knew the smell of fear better than anything; it was an elixir to the predator in him.

Roused by the intoxicating scent, he unsheathed his

hunting knife and twirled it smoothly around his fingers. Striding forward, he seized Rusalka by her slimy hair and drove the blade into her heart. "I hope you bleed," he growled through clenched teeth, twisting the hilt for good measure.

Rusalka jerked forward, retching as the steel pierced her chest. Coughing up a tarry liquid that smelled like asphalt, she grabbed Kai's wrist with a trembling hand and squeezed.

He was on the verge of breaking out into a triumphant grin when she suddenly tugged his arm and plunged the knife deeper between her ribs. With an iron hold, she pulled him close and locked her fingers in his dishevelled hair.

"Men like you are the reason I'm here. Men harbouring their fear like a fugitive until they find the right woman to blame, the right one to kill." A puppeteer pulling strings, Rusalka forced him to twist the knife a second time. She held him steady and pressed her lips to his, then cooed sweetly as inky life spilled from her wound. "Go on then. Carve up my heart, little wolf. Carve it up until yours is finally still."

As blood soaked over skin and clothing alike, Kai's teeth began to chatter. His hand trembled until he couldn't tell if he was clutching the knife or trying desperately to let go. Reeling from the loss of control, something inside him cracked. His mouth opened, and he released a grief-stricken roar. Tears that'd been waiting for decades flooded his vision as he ripped Rusalka's hand from his hair and pushed her back, his fist still closed around the haft. The once silver blade came out black as sin.

Kai dropped the weapon. He fell to his knees and gashed at the soil and stone with his bare hands. Knuckles shattered and fingernails came free, but he welcomed the pain—anything to get her off him.

For the first time in years, he wanted nothing more than the metamorphosis that came without his say-so and broke his every bone in a torrent of unyielding change. How much simpler that'd been—how much easier to endure than this wretched thing that burrowed in his mind and gnawed at his heart. Guilt. Shame. Self-loathing. This was the language of the tormented, not wolves among men.

He wanted the pain back. He wanted himself back.

"And you will have it," snarled Velizar, his icy hands closing over the sides of Kai's skull. "You will have it all and more."

Cold seeped into him. Velizar's voice—once outside of him—rang from the empty cavern behind his ribcage. Darkness tore through Kai like starving teeth tore through flesh, and the breaths he once called his own stilled as his heart now beat for two souls.

The earth shifted on its axis as something wicked rippled through the dreamscape. Kai's bloodied hand withdrew from the soil as he retrieved his knife and rose to his feet. Inhaling deeply, he lifted his gaze—hungry red eyes turning Rusalka to stone. The storm had passed, but the beast had awoken.

🐾 21 🐾

MIYA

A PUNGENT, death-like odour filled Miya's nostrils. Her stomach churned like spoiled butter, and she lurched forward off the bench.

Ama was next to her before her knees hit the grass. "What's wrong?"

"Something's off." Lightning pain shot down Miya's arms and erupted through her fingers.

She bit back a cry, but she had bigger concerns. Closing off her senses, she scanned every crevice of the dreamscape —at least those she could reach with her mind. Yet no matter how forcefully she pushed past the border between worlds, she felt only the tide of panic rising rapidly through her chest.

Miya's muddy green eyes swirled with naked dread. "Something's happened to Kai."

Ama's lips parted. Though her expression was mild, Miya could see past her calm façade. Hawk-eyed, her shoulder twitched in anticipation. "What is it?"

"I don't know," said Miya. "He's there, I can feel him. He's just...different." No matter how far apart they were, she could always feel Kai. He was an open window of clear, brash intention. Now, it felt like peeping through a hole in the wall, cold and shadow drifting in from the other side.

"I don't like it," Ama growled.

"Ow!" Miya jolted back, startling them both. Heat oscillated against her chest where the dream stone rested in the copper raven's talons.

Pulling the pendant out, Miya found the rock glowing with mordant energy. Purple, green, and gold shimmers snaked around inside their casing as though trying to burst free. She rested it on her palm and felt it pulsing faster and faster, like a heartbeat in distress.

"No, no, no. Not you too!" Miya feared for her talisman. It was her totem—her compass in the dreamscape. Without it, she was as lost as any other dreamer.

Ama's eyes were like blazing sunstones. "Get up," she ordered, pulling Miya to her feet. "We need to go."

Miya stumbled as she was yanked forward. "Go where?"

"To save an idiot," Ama barked.

"Which one?"

The white wolf turned. "The one with the other half of the dream stone."

Miya gawped, taken aback by the disclosure. "You know where it is?"

Ama sped down the cemetery hill, Miya at her heels. "He wasn't ready to part with it, so we broke it in two."

"Who's *he*?"

Ama faltered as they hit the main road. "Mason Evans."

"What?" Miya halted. "Why?"

A car whizzed by, children laughing as they stuck their hands out the back windows. Ama slowed at the mouth of *The Spade's* alleyway, her anxious retreat to the tavern foiled by Miya's heels planted firmly on the ground. Finally, she answered, "Gavran placed it in the doctor's care knowing he'd eventually find his way to you. His grief and obsession with answers made him the perfect vehicle to deliver the dream stone to its rightful owner." She arrested Miya with her gaze. "Gavran sprinkled breadcrumbs to feed Mason's fixation, to show him a path to something beyond himself. It was all good fun for a mischievous raven—tricks to stave off boredom. He hadn't anticipated the doctor would cling to you so intensely—that he wouldn't give up the stone."

Miya's throat nearly closed as the woven tapestry of Gavran's and Ama's schemes revealed itself. "You manipulated a grieving man to get to me?"

"We didn't trust Kai. He's always been volatile. There was no telling if he'd overcome his demons or succumb to them. But the stone—it would've at least opened a door for you to escape Black Hollow."

"Then why not just give it to me?" Miya strode forward and grabbed Ama's hand. "Why put Mason through hell?"

"Because he sought hell out. He asked to be called." Amber eyes glowed against the twilight. "Grief reverberates, shaking things from their slumber."

"You thought you were helping him?" Miya asked, incredulous.

"We are not benevolent gods, Miya. We answer those who seek us on our own terms. He wanted to be the hero of someone's story, so we let him try."

"He was your pawn!"

"And he is better for it."

Miya swallowed down her anger. She didn't have time for this. Whatever was happening to Mason was severe enough to give her half of the dream stone a sweltering fever. If she didn't hurry, it would implode. "We can argue later." She pushed past Ama and thundered into the alleyway where she felt the stone's thrum grow louder.

"You weren't ready," Ama called after her, her voice breaking.

Miya whirled on her. "What?"

"You asked why we didn't give you the stone." Ama sighed. "The truth is, you weren't ready. You had battles to win first. Fears to conquer."

"How would you know that?"

A thin smile tugged at Ama's lips, melancholy settling into the lines of her face. "You wouldn't have wanted the stone, Miya. All you wanted was to find your own way. If we'd given you the dream stone, you never would've known if it was your strength or ours that saved you. And that would've eaten you alive." Her expression warmed, her eyes distant and wistful. "I wanted you to know you're strong enough on your own. I wanted you to believe in yourself before you believed in magical rocks or hidden worlds."

A hush loomed over them. Tears stung Miya's eyes, threatening to overflow. All the bitter things that clung to her heart began to dislodge, falling away and striking her where it bruised deepest. How naïve she'd been to think fate was an impartial arbitrator—a random hand that determined everyone's beginning like a child grabbing a toy from a dark chest.

No, fate was a sheer will, exerted on her by forgotten gods with familiar faces. They were neither heartless nor cruel; they loved fiercely, dedicating their every moment to a singular cause—one Miya still didn't understand. But they used people as throw-away chess pieces, cogs to be manipulated towards this unspoken end.

Brimming with hurt she could no longer stifle, Miya opened her mouth to scream but was silenced by a man's sudden wail. The sound pierced the air between her and the white wolf.

Ama rushed by like a furious wind. Bled dry of all she'd clung to, Miya followed wearily. The childhood memory of the white wolf grabbed her by the throat and twisted. Nothing was ever as it seemed.

❧ 22 ❧

MASON

MASON FLATTENED his palm against the mark, wishing in vain that the pressure would somehow suppress his rising panic.

"Go away." He closed his eyes and focused his remaining willpower. "Please, just go away."

Do you not seek truth, Master?

"I don't want to be one with you!" Mason bellowed to the walls.

There is no other path, said the Servant. *Truth demands surrender.*

"I don't understand what you want!"

It is not what I want, but what you want that drives me. I am but a humble servant.

Mason detected no deception in the words. This entity meant what it said—that it only sought to give Mason what he wanted: the truth.

Yet with every passing day, the reality of their attachment grew heavier; this *thing* was consuming him.

Mason pressed his back to the grainy brick wall and wiped the sweat from his brow. "Fine. I don't want the truth. I don't care. I'll do what Miya asked. I'll be satisfied with what she told me. I don't need more. If she's happy, nothing else matters—not even her parents."

The lingering pain in Mason's arm faded to a dull ache, and the Servant's voice quieted.

But the respite was short-lived. The silence wasn't a submission, but a calm evaluation preceding judgment—a final verdict.

Every lie you speak in an attempt to fool me is a lie with which you poison yourself.

Mason felt the cold, weighty hand of shock strike him across the face. His "servant" was patronizing him.

It preached on with religious fervor, *You are not satisfied with subjective experiences and relative truths. You are a man of absolutes, an inquisitor in search of the universal. Particulars...are meaningless. If there is no objective measure, no greater law, then there is nothing but chaos.*

"The Dreamwalker transcends every law I thought was absolute," Mason countered. "Yet she's real; she's meaning-ful. She saved me from hellfire that night in the woods. Why can't that be enough?" Was he asking himself or the Servant?

She is your scourge, the voice of the Servant rumbled, *a puzzle with a missing piece. She must be put in order and made sense of. Isn't that why you are here?*

"No." Mason shook his head, ignoring the maddening itch under his palm. "I came here to find Miya. For her family—to confirm that she's alive, that she's okay."

The Servant tutted, *More poison for your soul. The family's suspicions have been confirmed, yet you still yearn for something more. Be honest, Master. The girl's happiness means nothing to you. What you really want to know is—*

"Why..." Mason whispered. He could feel the Servant probing his brain, tugging on the threads he couldn't stitch into a simple pattern. Why was she here? What'd happened to her? Why did his insides feel like withering every time he imagined himself doing the right thing—respecting Miya's wishes and returning to Raymond with the only truth that mattered: Miya's truth.

But was her truth what Mason needed?

A hand curled around Mason's throat. Nails dug into his neck, squeezing the air from his lungs. "No one gives a damn about what you need," came a woman's raspy snarl.

Mason's eyes flitted across shadow-kissed walls, then fell on the creature seizing him. She was a monstrosity. Tangled seaweed hair slithered like snakes over her near-skeletal frame. Her flesh was grey and sickly, slopping from her bones like sludge. Her eyes were craters, void save for a ravaging hunger that screamed from the abyss. He'd seen her before—from his vision in the map.

"You've caught quite the bug." A mocking smile tugged at her lips, thin and ashen with death. "No matter. I have use of your parasite, little man."

She grasped Mason's forearm and lifted the mark to her dark, tunnelling eyes.

"What are you doing?" Mason croaked, but the question was met with bony fingers bruising his neck.

Her thumb grazed over the mark. It burned as though she'd rubbed salt into a fresh wound. "Come out, you coward!"

Mason didn't know who she was referring to, but he tried to shrink back against the wall.

I do not answer to you, the Servant's voice echoed, suddenly strained.

The rotting woman's grin widened, her cheeks like caverns. "I wish to know of the girl." Sharp, crooked nails drilled into the brand on Mason's arm. "Tell me, and I'll leave you in peace to suck the sanity from this blubbering infant."

Mason's breaths came fast and shallow, his arm searing in agony like nothing he'd ever known. He would've cut the limb off just to be free of it all: the woman holding him, the Servant haunting him, and the pain jutting against his heart.

When he thought he couldn't bear it any longer, the creature's head snapped back with a sharp gasp. Her eyes widened and her mouth dropped open, her face frozen in a silent scream until finally, her grip on him eased.

Mason dove towards the pavement, scurrying into the farthest corner of the grime-covered alley.

"Of course," came the woman's ecstatic breath. "The girl *is* compassionate." Her neck bent to an impossible angle as her gaze fell on Mason. He no longer saw a corpse of moulting flesh and brittle bone, but a young woman with plump, flawless skin—still pale but glowing like pearls under crystal-clear water. Her large reptilian eyes shone like emeralds, her hair flowing like a river down her back. Her movements were spellbinding, each step graceful and measured. The very sight of her was sweeter than a siren's song.

"Thank you." She smiled graciously as she crouched in front of him, her chilly, porcelain fingertips grazing his cheek. "You've been a tremendous help."

She rose to her feet and sashayed into the gleaming light of the open street, then vanished like she'd been nothing more than an unpleasant fever dream.

The soles of Mason's shoes scraped against the stone as he tried to push himself up. "W-what the hell was that? What did she mean?'"

The Dreamwalker is compassionate, came the Servant's answer. *I showed her how to use it.*

Mason's stomach knotted like a ball of rubber bands,

each one fighting to break free from the others. "Why would you do that? That monster—it's clearly after her!"

I did it to save your life.

"How did she even find me?"

Your uncertainty is too loud. It attracts predators.

Frustrated heat rose to Mason's face. "Couldn't you fight her off? Are you really that powerless?"

Only as powerless as you, Master. My strength matches that of my host.

Mason swore under his breath and kicked a loose pebble across the way. "Host...*host*. So, I'm just food then? A sack of meat for you to leech off of?" His voice cracked, giving way to laughter that threatened to erupt into tears.

It was a fair exchange.

Mason ran his fingers through his hair, gripping and tugging at the unruly curls. "You exchanged one life for another!"

Perhaps. But that is not all that was exchanged.

"Stop with the riddles!" Mason paced the narrow corridor. "Say what you mean!"

The buzz of traffic and the chatter of pedestrians on the main road fell away. *There is not a thing in this world that can touch me without consequence. All those who seek truth seek me, and all those who accept my truth surrender some of their own.*

Mason stilled. "So, you know about her?"

Shall I show you, Master?

Mason squeezed his eyes shut and swallowed down the bile. What a fool he was; he'd been had by this parasite, and now Miya was in danger because of him. "Let me guess. You tell me everything about that woman, and I become one with you?"

Your assessment is correct.

Rolling up his sleeve, Mason closed his fingers around the back of his forearm and peered down at the mark—now nearly complete. If he agreed to the Servant's terms, would he be lucid enough to help Miya with the knowledge gained from this unholy transaction?

I will not impede your cause, Master. I am always, unequivocally, your humble servant and ally.

Did it really have no concept of the damage it was causing? Then again, could it really be blamed for acting on its nature? Mason was a human with agency. He had free will while spirits were slaves to the impulses governed by their traumas. He'd chosen wrong...again.

Still, he had to do *something*. Miya was in danger, and he couldn't ignore that; he had to rectify his mistakes. Dealing with the Servant was the only toolkit he had at his disposal.

"Fine," Mason said at last. "Show me the truth."

The moment the words departed his lips, the mark on his arm lit up like someone had taken a blade of fire to his skin. The horizontal line that'd struck through the first crescent moon resumed its crawl, inching through its twin. Mason's consciousness slipped, and a tidal wave of images battered his senses.

He saw the woman's—Rusalka's—arms slip around Kai's neck as she whispered vile temptations in his ear. He watched as she seduced Vincent, twisting him up until he did the unthinkable. Before him, a man from Cypress Swamp, and before that one, another, and another, and another. Her body was animated only by the tragedy she sowed, yet life bled out of her, oozing from her pores. It wasn't hers to begin with. She'd stolen her vitality: a chemical mix sloshing around an ill-fitting container. It was like she'd been punched full of tiny holes that wouldn't seal. No matter how often she refilled the vessel, topped it up for good measure, that strange concoction called life resolved to leak out, to drain slowly, quietly, until the final drops could only pool in the tiny crevices near the bottom of her rotten soul.

Mason's skull felt like it was cracking open, the volume of information unbearable. His heart broke as he endured every moment of Rusalka's machinations, witnessing her repeat the cursed cycle of infection, corruption, and violence. The memories dragged on in reverse until she was no longer a demon, but a corpse floating in a creek—a woman who'd suffered the ultimate betrayal. That betrayal, it seemed, was Rusalka's beginning.

Mason fell to his knees and heaved for breath, his lungs screaming like he was trapped underwater. He tried to push his head up, neck straining, but something held him down from behind, forcing him under.

Rusalka's final moments assaulted him. Mason fell to his side and began to convulse, his eyes pinned open as the memory interlaced with every neural pathway. If vicariously experiencing her death didn't kill his body, he was certain it would kill his soul.

Mason bit down to keep his teeth from slicing into his tongue, then dug into his pocket and clutched the dream stone, pleading for it all to stop. As the stone warmed against his palm, the shaking gradually subsided, leaving him with a residual tremor.

Disoriented, Mason fought to get a hold of his surroundings. "You're in Orme's Rest," he gasped. "Orme's Rest. This isn't the forest, the creek, the water. Green, not black. Elms, not willows. Swamps. Monsters," he prattled on, gravel digging into his palms as he pushed himself up only to collapse again.

He was losing grip—or had he already let go? Every word was woven with the Servant's voice. When Mason closed his mouth, the entity's whispers invaded him, imbuing every minutia with hidden meanings and unspoken histories.

The world was a conspiracy.

How did people exist in their bubbles? How did they fail to see the connections?

Mason was alighted with rapturous horror. He could feel the ripples in the very fabric of time and space, the consequences of every action, every reaction. His mind was fracturing with the sheer insurmountability of the Servant's perfect knowledge.

Mason had been right all along. Black Hollow. Cypress Swamp. Orme's Rest.

They were all connected.

Miya. The Dreamwalker. A god born of violence. A god fated to return to violence.

He needed to show her the truth.

KAI

KAI HADN'T MOVED from the muck, Rusalka's poisonous kiss still bitter on his lips. He'd watched her flee, emaciated legs buckling as they barely carried her weight. He didn't have the heart to give chase—not after what she'd said to him.

"She's long gone," Kai remarked.

She is. Velizar seemed unconcerned by the loss.

Kai felt his brother like a second heart, pulsating next to his own. His presence swirled through every cell.

Tasting iron in his mouth, Kai spat out a dollop of blood. Rusalka's tongue had been acid on his own. "You're still full of shit, *brother*." Kai nearly gagged on the word. "Guess that hasn't changed."

Something wasn't right. Driving a blade through Rusalka's heart had been as effective as misting bug-spray on a nest of homicidal wasps, yet she was tripping over sloughing globs of her own putrid meat to put distance between her and Kai.

Perhaps it wasn't Kai she was so eager to get away from.

"That mouldy washcloth was shitting her skirts the second you put your hands on me." Kai ran his tongue over the inside of his mouth, feeling out the damage. "Why?"

A trifling concern, Velizar's voice reverberated from within and without.

The bastard was being evasive. Kai recalled his conversation with Rusalka at *The Spade*, the way she too had dodged him when he'd prodded her about the name *Abaddon*.

These two knew each other. The nervous heat rising in the back of Kai's skull warned him that Rusalka and Abaddon's connection was anything but *trifling*. Now sharing a consciousness with his nemesis, Kai felt Velizar trying to suppress his knowledge of Rusalka. Memories of her, just barely within Kai's reach, were abruptly yanked away, and Velizar's sharp familiarity with her dampened in Kai's awareness. There was only one thing Velizar couldn't camouflage: the fear Kai had seen in Rusalka's eyes as she slunk into the shadows. What Velizar inspired in her was quite intimate.

Hearing a rustle from behind, Kai glanced over his shoulder to find Gavran standing slack-jawed between the trees. The voice of the boy and the old man echoed in unison.

"You...lunatic!"

Wring his neck.

Kai considered it, then breathed away the spuming rage. When the storm in him subsided, he turned to Gavran. "Fuck you. You brought me here hoping we'd tear each other to shreds."

Gavran sneered. "You wanted to eradicate the shadow. Now you are one with him! The shadow she nearly died freeing you from!"

"I needed it back...for now."

"It consumes you, mangy dog!" Gavran gestured to Kai's hand, still gripping the hunting knife and painted in Rusalka's ink-coloured blood.

Kai's hold on the hilt tightened, and his fingers twitched against his say-so. Velizar was trying to wrest control, little by little like a coaxing parent. The panic struck deep, propelling Kai into unrestrained fury. "At least this is shit I'm used to stepping in!"

"You should've stayed in the hut permanently," said Gavran.

Kai ground his teeth as he snarked back, "Tell me how you *really* feel, Shit-for-brains."

The skin-bag roosting the raven bristled. "Now, she will only grieve more."

Kai took a threatening step forward. "I'm not going anywhere. I've still got a fish to grill. I'll cut out the cancer when I'm done."

Gavran regarded him through slit-eyes. "You best hurry, then, or your cancer will metastasize. I'm sure you've noticed...how light it feels...how the weight slips away. You invited him in." His mouth twisted into a scornful rictus. "Guests are never a burden."

A wave of nausea wracked Kai as Gavran's words sunk in. It was true; Abaddon had always felt heavy, unwanted. Now, Kai felt almost nothing. Save for the disconcerting tingle running through his left hand, he felt better than he had since Rusalka had abducted him. He stared stonily at Gavran and said, "I'll figure it out."

"So you say," Gavran mocked, then turned on his heels. "Your last request has been honoured, wolf."

Kai didn't bother watching him leave. He squared himself to Rusalka's scent, the residue of rot and fear washing over him. "You said I'd be able to end the bitch."

Velizar's grainy laugh rattled around the inside of Kai's skull. **You speak as though the woman has never been stabbed through the heart before. Come now, even you must know how such a monstress is born.**

Kai arched a brow as he sheathed his knife and inspected his hand. He curled his fingers into a fist, then shook them out, wiggling each digit to ensure he had control. "Violent death or something, if you're meant to be our cautionary tale."

Rusalka was brought into the world by a man's violence and hatred. Another man's violence and hatred can only make her stronger, rooting her more firmly in her cause. It's her entire reason for being.

There it was again—that twitch. Kai's eyes darted to his hand, stiff as a board as he tried to suppress the tremor.

A man's violence.

For so long, he'd denied being a man. It felt too...human. He was a wolf. He was only trapped in a man's body, fated to be held to humanity's puritanical laws.

But would Rusalka have targeted him if he were merely a wolf? Did the malice fuelling her give a rat's ass about how he understood himself? For Rusalka, he existed as a man. He moved through the world as a man. He'd treated her with the same violence she expected from men.

He'd driven a knife through her heart, and he wasn't the first.

If Rusalka's diet was any indication, Kai was as much a man as the piece of shit that'd turned her into a trash-fire of rotting fish meat. The wolf would always be there, but he couldn't pretend it was the only part of him that mattered. Not anymore.

You always did think you could solve every problem by smashing it to pieces, Velizar's voice cut through the fog.

Kai dropped his hand to his side. He was still by his old cabin—at least, its dreamscape equivalent. "It's cute how infatuated you are with me," he smirked. "Sounds like you're jealous."

Of your smashing? Never. But I *do* know you, brother. Why do you think I've been waiting for you, here, where our story first began? I always knew you'd come back.

Kai glanced around the murky glade. "You and I go way further back than this damn shack."

Not the shack, the voice dipped lower, **but the land on which it stands.**

"Black Hollow?"

You always return to the Hollow. Life after life. Death after death. You're drawn to the tragedy of this place.

Kai took a long step into the woods, leaving his old home behind. "The only consistent tragedy in my life is *you.*"

Oh, my dear Sendoa, how little you know.

"Sen-what now?" Kai barked as he ducked under a branch.

You were not always Kai, Velizar scoffed the name. **You were Sendoa. And *we* were living gods. Creation and destruction—two sides of the same coin—brothers sharing the same bones.** Then, he murmured, **All I ever wanted was to be with my brother.**

Kai kept his gaze fixed on Rusalka's trail, her swampy odour and tarry viscera staining the foliage. "So, I was destruction?"

A *god* of destruction. And I, a god of creation.

Kai stalked past a fir tree, some of the pinecones swiped clean off. Rusalka must have groped at them as she stumbled through the woods to get away. "And the Dreamwalker?"

Chaos! Velizar snapped, his hostility vibrating deep behind Kai's ribcage. **She stole destruction, unsettled the balance we brothers created.**

Kai paused mid-step and narrowed his eyes. It sounded like horseshit—the deluded ravings of a narcissist. "What do you mean, she *stole* destruction?"

The answer came softly, an accusation coated in candy. **She stole you, baby brother. You forsook your duty, your role as the destroyer, all for your blind love of that woman.**

"Sounds about right." Kai crouched and eyed the fading footprints. They were so small and slim, like she'd wasted away and ossified in the mere seconds it took to flee. "You're a stick up the ass and a killjoy. Besides, the Dreamwalker's pretty hot. I stand by my choice."

Make jokes to your heart's content, little brother, but *you* betrayed *me*. *You* damned *me* for your selfish wants. *You*...left *me*.

Kai rose to his feet and balled up his fist. His hand was quivering again. "When are you going to get it through your thick, ghostly skull? That person you knew—Sendoa or whoever—that's not me. My name is Kai Donovan, and I'm not your goddamn brother anymore. That was lifetimes ago. I never did shit to you."

That may be so... Velizar murmured as Kai approached an aspen. The milk-coloured trunk was smeared with a bloody handprint. Kai reached out and splayed his fingers over it, mirroring the impression painted on the bark.

...But has anything really changed?

❧ 24 ❧

MIYA

MIYA ROUNDED the corner of the narrow lane and nearly slammed into Ama. The white wolf was like concrete, her arm outstretched as she held Miya at bay. Lips pulled back, her canines flashed in warning.

What could possibly frighten the snowy huntress with eyes like balefire?

"Stop." Ama swatted Miya's probing hand down and clasped it tightly. The answer to her question was lurking in front of them, at the end of a dark alley.

There, where light atrophied to a guttering flicker, the shape of a man emerged. He was slumped against the chipping brick wall, crumpled like a discarded note bearing an unpleasant message.

"Mason?" Miya stepped forward, her movements mirrored by a rigid Ama.

As pebbles cracked under Miya's rubber soles, the doctor stirred with a judder. His head hung limply to the side as he jerked liked a marionette. Blood dribbled from his nose and mouth, and the whites of his eyes were webbed with pink.

"There's something possessing him," said Ama. She clutched Miya's arm with an iron grip. "Be careful."

"I know, I feel it too." Crouching down, Miya clasped Mason's face between her palms. "Hey, Dr. Evans, can you hear me?"

A low, raspy breath seeped from Mason's chapping lips. His pupils rolled up before falling on Miya's face. "We...are not...the doctor."

Trembling fingers raked against Miya's forearms. His hands were like ice, the tip of each digit pale blue. His touch left burning streaks on her skin, and with every fiery pulse, she could glimpse swirls of madness flashing inside him.

"Mason!" She gave him a light shake, but his head only lolled. "Tell me what's hurting you!"

I warned you not to reveal yourself, Kali's—her predecessor's—voice echoed in her mind.

Miya ignored it. A life was at stake. She couldn't stay hidden. "Show me," she said to him. "Show me what's haunting you."

"Mi...ya," he wheezed and fell into her hold. His voice penetrated her skull, suddenly strong and clear: *I know the truth*.

Behind her, Ama gasped. "Miya, get away—"

The white wolf's words were swallowed up by a velvet-thick haze. It pulled Miya underground, beneath the pavement, where earth turned to charcoal smoke, and all that was solid melted away.

MIYA FOUND *herself in a foggy corner of the dreamscape, the light muted like a dim sunrise.*

"Welcome, child."

The voice was all around her, reverberating like a penny in a crystal chalice.

"Who are you?" Miya called back. "What do you want with the doctor?"

"Only to serve," the voice replied, "for I am the Servant."

"The Servant," Miya muttered to herself, measuring her next words carefully. "Why do you serve this master?"

A low hum of contemplation rumbled beneath Miya's feet. "We share a vision, a singular desire."

"A desire for what?"

"The truth."

Miya clenched her teeth and pushed down a grimace as the dream stone seethed against her skin. It was as she suspected; Mason's greatest weakness was his fear of the unknown. No wonder he'd been preyed upon by something that claimed its wish was for truth with a capital T.

She knew truth demons couldn't lie; they swore allegiance to their victims and vowed only to speak facts. They masqueraded as allies, then corrupted their host's worldview with lofty claims to knowledge. Truth demons were parasites. They fed off the insanity they induced in their victims while leaving their bodies to rot from the inside out.

"Why show yourself to me now?" Miya asked. "Haven't you already achieved your goal?"

"There is a truth my master wishes to share with you. It was the purpose of our merging."

Miya snorted. The saddest part about these demons was how they failed to see the truth about themselves; they really believed their actions were in the service of their prey. They didn't think themselves menacing, nor did they understand their intentions as self-serving. Ironically, the ghoulish authority on truth never understood the only truth that mattered: the servant was the master.

Miya's heart sank. Mason had let the monster in to help her; she was responsible for his plight. "He can't share anything with you gagging him. Let him go."

"Let him go? Or..." A pause, then a groan. "Was there no threat to follow, child?"

Heat prickled Miya's cheeks as anxiety knotted in her gut. She'd forgotten; she was the hand to Kai's blade, and right now, she had no weapon to wield.

"A weak thing like you would never pay the price for my death."

Miya frowned. "What price?"

A light wind weaved through the fog, ominous whispers riding on the breeze. They crawled into Miya's ears like ants, each one carrying a tiny mote of truth. The spirit was right yet again; the price for his death was steep—perhaps too steep.

Before Miya could weigh her options, a warm hand grasped her shoulder and tugged her back through the mist. It was Ama— reaching for her from the other side.

Come back, *she beckoned. After their time together in Black Hollow, they'd developed a symbiosis. Ama was the anchor that reined her in when she wandered too far. Miya reached for the white wolf, eager for something familiar, something safe. She closed her eyes and surrendered to Ama's voice, falling through the haze and crashing onto the cobblestones on the other side.*

Her face collided with a slab of rock. Grains of dirt and gravel scraped her cheek as the road rattled her jaw. The world spinning, she pushed herself off the ground. Guiding hands steadied her, but she swooned and nearly toppled over.

"That was reckless," Ama chided.

When the dizziness subsided, Miya opened her eyes.

"Ama," she mumbled, a lump in her throat. "I can't do it. I can't help him."

"What are you on about?"

Falling on her behind, Miya glanced at Mason. He was wasting away, and she was powerless to stop it.

"I'm useless without Kai," she whispered, the admission cutting to the bone. She curled her knees to her chest. "I have nothing to fight with. I'm just a bird lost in a storm." She'd grown arrogant next to Kai, syphoning his strength to compensate for her weakness.

"This is exactly what I was talking about!" Ama grabbed Miya's shoulders. "Has it ever occurred to you that Kai doesn't think he's strong? That maybe he also feels vulnerable and helpless? Stop measuring your worth by that buffoon's capacity for destruction!" She sought Miya's eyes. "You *are* enough. Just you. You don't need Kai! Do you hear me?" Ama gave her a gentle shake. "You are not the hand that wields the sword. You *are* the sword."

Miya wiped the streaks of salty tears from her face. "I'm not a sword, Ama. I never have been."

"I don't care what metaphor you use!" Exasperation flowed off Ama in waves. "You can be a wooden spatula or a dead end on a cliffside road for all I care! Find your own damn way!"

Miya felt like a shaking swallow, vaulting out of control as thunderous clouds knocked her around. How could she soar through the gale and make it to clearer skies?

Before Kai, Miya never fought back; whenever she felt wronged, she withdrew and wilted in her pain. Visceral peril and Kai's unyielding force of will simmering beside her gave her courage to wage a war. Now, in his absence, she felt like a sail without its wind.

It was unsustainable. Kai had given her the thrust she needed to claw her way out of a rut, but she couldn't depend on him forever. Miya was alone. Kai wasn't there to do her dirty work for her. She would have to do it herself.

In her frantic efforts to return to a normal that no longer existed, she'd rebelled against a terrifying possibility that demanded she forsake one piece of herself to discover another:

I'll find my way without him, she resolved, *because he might not ever come back.*

🕸 2 5 🕸

MIYA RAKED her nails against the cobblestones and pushed herself to her feet. Wiping her bleary eyes, she sucked in a shaky breath and turned to the doctor slumped against the wall. His eyes were blank, bloodied half-moons that shone no light. Yet amid the stillness, she felt a faint thrum.

Miya pushed aside the folds of Mason's jacket until she felt three pointed edges prodding through a mesh interior pocket. Her fingers trailed the rough line where the object had been broken.

It was the missing half of the dream stone.

Inverting the pocket, Miya retrieved the stray fragment. Her heart squeezed behind her ribs as the stone's magic saturated her fingers. The dream stone was a part of her—a splinter of the Dreamwalker that cradled her power in its iridescent glow. As Miya slanted the labradorite, black veins and a streak of shimmering gold cut through the undulating violet and emerald gleam, barely discernable in the dour alleyway. The dream stone was a totem, a tether, and so much more.

Fishing out the pendant that seethed against her breastbone, Miya pressed the two broken edges together and watched the fissure disappear. They fit like star-crossed lovers.

It was as though the two pieces had never parted.

Miya too felt more whole. A delicate seed had sprouted in her mind, and one day, it would grow into the sturdy belief that she was enough—with or without Kai. The conviction had already taken root; it simply needed to be nourished.

But Miya's newfound valour hadn't been imparted by a piece of rock. On the contrary, it never would've called to her had she not proffered some resolve. Ama's strident words had rattled the doubt from Miya's mind, forcing her to dig under the rubble of her insecurities and to find something more, something not-so-easily broken. The dream stone was just a compliment—a jewel to embellish the crown.

Mason shuddered and grasped at his left arm. Turning his wrist over, Miya traded glances with Ama, who sidled up to her and examined the markings seared into the doctor's skin: two crescents that mirrored one another, and a line that sliced straight through their centers, dividing the arcs into four perfect quarters.

"Truth demon," said Ama.

Miya peeked at the white wolf. "How'd you know?"

Ama nodded towards Mason's marred forearm. "That symbol—a cord tying two minds together. The curves represent separate consciousnesses—opposed but alike, one reflecting the other. One is for the demon, the other for the victim. The line that cuts through them is the cord, binding them together. It appears last, when the victim finally succumbs to the demon."

"I have to go back in," said Miya. "I need to untangle him from this...*thing*."

"No." Ama clutched her shoulder. "This isn't something you can just untangle like a knotted shoelace."

"Then I'll sever the damn cord!"

Ama's fingers dug in hard. "Killing a truth demon isn't easy, and there's always a price for it. It's their defense mechanism. Whatever you do to the demon, it'll come back to you."

"I know," came Miya's mousy response. "But I can't get away unscathed every time, and I can't leave Mason like this. He came here for me. Because of me."

"That was his choice."

"He doesn't deserve this," Miya protested.

"Sacrificing yourself won't fix anything." Ama kneaded the taut muscle over Miya's once-bony shoulder. She smiled. "You used to be like a gazelle. Now you're a huntress in your own right."

Miya laced her fingers with Ama's. "You and Kai are the hunters—the wolves. I'm the raven that follows."

"Ravens are scavengers," Ama scoffed.

"They're also smart. They make tools, solve problems. They observe, then bend the world to suit their needs." Miya raised her eyes to the white wolf's, drinking in the warm amber glow she'd known since childhood. "You and Kai...you *break* reality like a brittle stick. All teeth and maws. Let me do what ravens do. Let me play with the stick."

Reluctance flashed across Ama's face, but behind it, a quiet confidence burned like a spark in kindling, waiting to be stoked. "All right."

The concession was strained, but it was all Miya needed. Kneeling, she cupped her palm against the brand on Mason's forearm, closed her eyes, and let the world fall away —the bustle in the nearby street, the cars whizzing by, and the light glaring through her eyelids, painting her vision red.

She could feel Ama anchoring her, pacifying her spirit's penchant for flight. It'd become so easy for her to tumble into the dreamscape, but with Kai's life at stake, she needed someone to drag her back in time.

"If I'm still under in fifteen," she swayed forward, "pull me out."

"I understand," said Ama, her voice as firm as her grip. "Once you force the demon into the in-between, you should be safe. *Kai* should be safe."

"Good," Miya mumbled as her body surrendered to gravity, the demon's cord burning feverishly against her palm. Somewhere in the distance, the spectre snarled. She followed the sound out of her body until the garbled roars grew clearer, and she could make out the demon's threats.

You come seeking death, it hissed.

Yes, Miya replied. *Yours.*

❧ 26 ❧

MIYA GLIMPSED *the hanging star hovering above the surrounding haze.*

She tilted the dream stone towards its faint light, and the labradorite's vibrant colours painted the pallid fog in mulberry and meadow green. Where colour gathered, Miya sank to her knees and pressed her hand to the ashen soil.

Follow the roots, *Gavran had said. Her fingers seeped into the earth, and with them, violet tendrils ploughed through the darkness until they coiled around something cold and ancient: a maze of serpentine roots. She could see them mapped out underfoot, veins beneath white, sandy skin. The entire dreamscape was a living, breathing organism, and the ground she stood on was merely its flesh.*

Miya kept her eyes trained on a single road in the network: a decaying root mottled black with sickness. It wound thinly between the rest, curling around sturdier lifelines and using them to obscure its path. It didn't matter; Miya now knew her way.

The dream stone sang with power, and her fingers tingled with its vibrations. The labradorite's melody spoke to her, guiding her through the labyrinth below and the mist above. For the first time in three years, she didn't hear Kali's whispers telling her where to stop and where to go. She no longer needed her.

Miya could part the curtain on her own.

Her heart soared with wonder. Like a child at home in her favourite playground, she relished her newfound mastery over the ethereal domain. Miya waved her hand, and the pall lifted on command. Sensing her footsteps, the plump, healthy roots snaked away from the blackened veins hiding amongst them. They recoiled, unravelling from one another to reveal their diseased sibling—a path leading Miya directly to her target: the truth demon.

A shadow huddled at the end of the winding streak of decay. The impish figure was crouched, its elbows tucked into its sides as it fiddled with something in the sand. Thick, pointy ears that curved like cupped hands bowed with the weight of boundless revelations. Miya heard scraping, like teeth against hardened clay. She resisted squinching and kept her approach steady.

The creature swivelled its head and peered over its shoulder. Wide, deep-set eyes bore into Miya, plumbing the depths of her soul. Their colour morphed—at first an overcast sky, then a vibrant teal lake, and finally, a still ocean at midnight. They were like planets, dwarfing a tiny nose lying flush against the creature's bile-coloured face. Two dime-sized nostrils flared in time with Miya's every step. It had no mouth, and where she expected to see lips, dark, grainy scar tissue weaved from jawbone to jawbone like a gristly braid.

The demon reached out, and four clawed digits with a joint too many grasped at the putrid root and yanked it from beneath the sand. The cord rose like a shark breaking water, then retracted into the creature.

It was too late to hide the trail; Miya had already found the source of the pollution.

"Truth demon." Her voice sounded muffled like it'd been swallowed by the fog.

The creature canted its head. The shining globes consuming its face flashed black and blue. "You are back," he intoned, the declara-

tion one of neither surprise nor expectation. "Have you forgotten the price for my death, Dreamwalker?"

"My memory's not that bad."

"Anyone who wishes to slay truth must first destroy the truth in themselves," he cautioned.

Miya recalled the whispers—the revelation of what she'd have to sacrifice to save Mason.

"I heard you the first time." *Fear clotted in her throat as the warning came back to her. She tugged her necklace and banished the thought. Mason was here because of her—because of the questions she'd left in her wake. She wouldn't let him die for a couple of loose ends.*

As Miya advanced, strands of purple and black shadow penetrated the milky haze. They swirled around her, cloaking her body in smoke and feathers. The mercurial vapour glided up her neck and contoured over her skull, then glissaded down her face in the shape of a V. The point of the bone-beak mask curved over her chin, and inky black spiralled with violet, melding into the ivory grooves.

Your connection to the Dreamwalker will be severed, *the whispers invaded her,* as that is your greatest truth. You *are* the Dreamwalker.

The demon's curse upon death was simple. It found some essential truth about its slayer and distorted it. Now, Miya had to make a choice: her identity, or Mason's life. If she followed through, she'd be lost. Would she forget the person she was saving?

Would she at least remember Kai?

Raw dread needled her heart. Even if she never saw him again, she couldn't bear forgetting the wolf under the willow. Her heart pummelled against her ribs, begging to be released from the truth demon's portent.

Then, the recently departed call of her predecessor echoed inside her:

The witch and the wolf will always find each other.

The assertion tugged on Miya's lips, pulling them apart until she broke the silence. Her declaration rang out in unison with Kali's, their voices like thunder piercing the earth. "The witch and the wolf are bound, as the sky and sea are bound by the horizon."

Ama was right; Miya could be whatever kind of weapon she wanted. She wasn't a fragile swallow, and she wouldn't be at the mercy of the storm any longer.

She would become the storm.

Whipping her arms back, Miya catapulted through the fog like a raven slicing through the sky, her feathery cloak billowing behind her. Her hand shot out, nails elongated like talons, and she snatched the creature's throat. Now inches away, he seemed so unimposing— not unlike a grand claim to truth.

"The most painful truths are never grand," he hissed, something viscous warbling in his throat. "It's the little things that kill."

Miya sneered, defiant. He was seeing into her mind, but that no longer frightened her. Lifting him with ease, she spun him around like a ragdoll and thrust him into the silvery sand. He thrashed to break free, but the roots below eagerly ensnared him, pulling him towards the boundary between the dreamscape and the waking world—to the borderland in between.

Miya's grip never left his jugular. They plummeted into the alleyway, a thin, murky veil separating them from the physical realm. The red brick wall was muted to a dull copper, and the cracks in the cobblestone wobbled beneath the seam. Ama was statue-still, her eyes trained on Miya's body some feet away. Next to her, Mason was covered in a thick, shadowy film—the truth demon's oppression made manifest. From Miya's side, the doctor's arms looked bone-thin, his torso emaciated. A yellow, fleshy cord, blotchy with mould, wound tightly around him. She heard his ragged breaths, but he made no attempt to break free. His head hung low, chin to his chest as he struggled for air.

Driving a knee into the imp's torso, Miya pinned him to the ground. Her touch was poison; black veins spidered out from where her fingers dug into his sickly flesh.

The scar tissue on the demon's face unbraided, and he released a mind-shattering screech from his toothless, blood-tinged mouth. Wincing, Miya turned her face away as an odour like sour meat washed over her.

Then, Mason's head jittered up, and his distant eyes caught hers. His lips moved, barely forming words.

I...need to...tell you...the truth.

He tugged weakly at his bonds, then toppled over with a wet smack. The cord around him roiled with life, tightening as he tried to drag himself towards Miya.

"Mason!" She whirled from the stench and grasped the vising tendon with one hand. It squealed in protest, lashing out and striking Miya across her face. Scorching hot welts rose on her skin, but she wouldn't let go. With a vicious jerk, she ripped a piece of it away.

Mason's withering arm—tainted by the truth demon's mark— came loose from the restraints. He scrabbled for Miya's hand, his cold fingers closing around her wrist as she held fast to the vampiric tether. The unexpected contact summoned a surge of harrowing visions.

Miya found herself transported to pine-clad hills. She could smell the rain on the blustering wind and the moss dappling the trees. She'd known it all her life—the smell of Black Hollow.

A woman floated along the river face down, her body bloated and pale. When she hit the bank, her fingers tensed and dug into the leafy earth. Elbows snapped to grotesque angles, and her face rose from the brown water. Mouth agape, her pupils darted around jaundiced eyes. Her decaying flesh sloughed off, and as she inhaled to force a scream from her lungs, she choked, the cry catching and dying in her mouth.

Pressure filled Miya's lungs. She lurched forward and coughed up musty green liquid. The truth demon blurred before her eyes, and she dropped the cord.

"*I understand,*" Miya heaved, then squeezed Mason's hand. "*Thank you for showing me this.*"

Rusalka's dark history would have to wait.

Miya shook away the visions, and the truth demon came back into focus. She tore the pendant from her neck. Purple wisps percolated from her fist, then coalesced into the silhouette of a weapon. When Miya opened her hand, the fang-shaped dream stone had morphed into a dagger, the blade a wide, curved animal claw. It shimmered like volcanic glass, streaks of gold, amethyst, and emerald splashed along the iridescent edge. The haft was made of bone and carved into a raven, wings flush against its torso. With the raven's head at the butt of the blade, the beak doubled as a slim hawkbill.

"*Is this truly...what you want...?*" the imp questioned.

Miya closed her fingers around the hilt of her dagger and plunged it into the truth demon's heart. His body juddered and convulsed. Life bled out of him, leaving only a shrivelled carcass.

"*All my life, the truth's been distorted.*" She pushed the bone-beak mask up over her hair and peered into his fading planetoid eyes. "*Go on, then. Do your worst.*"

❧ 27 ❧

MASON

MASON AWOKE WITH A KEENING GASP. He shot up from the wall, and, unable to keep himself upright, careened and fell over.

He tried to fill his lungs with air and barely managed, so he pounded a fist against his chest. He retched, gagged, and when the bile came up, he rolled onto his knees and vomited. Nearby, Ama knelt beside Miya's still form, not offering so much as a peep of concern for the doctor. He wiped his mouth and spat out the remaining sick.

Ama rose to her feet, then strode over and shot Mason a strident stare. "Anything else lurking in your gut?"

Mason yelped and scrambled back, disoriented. He pulled up his sleeve and groped around his arm. Only a faint scar remained in place of the mark—a reminder of his brush with insanity. He thumped back against the wall and sighed.

A groan drew Ama back. Miya was stirring, her body quaking with feverish chills.

Ama rushed to her side and placed a hand on her cheek.

"She's burning up." She lifted Miya's arms, searching her skin. "No sign the demon's taken up residence in a new host. This sickness—whatever it is—it's infected Miya after the creature's death."

Mason stumbled over and dropped to his knees, then gently pulled Miya's eyelid open. "She's out cold." He pressed his fingers to her neck and checked his watch. "Pulse is slightly elevated, but nothing too concerning. Fever is likely the cause." He turned to Ama. "We should get her to a hosp—" He stopped, realizing the absurdity of what he was about to say.

"You can't help her, doctor." Ama slunk her arms under Miya's shoulders and knees, picking her up with ease. "I'll take her to someone who can."

"And who's that?" Mason asked, his urgency mounting.

"To Gavran." Ama peered at the dream stone resting against Miya's collarbone. Only then did Mason notice it was a lustreless grey, and no matter how the light caught the glassy surface, it remained as leaden as quarry rock. Its power was gone.

"Can I come?" he asked.

Ama frowned but didn't protest. "I'm not sure there's much you can do."

He shrugged. "Monitor her physical health? Even if your work is spiritual, I've seen how it can take a toll on the body."

"Very well." Ama turned on her heels.

"Is this my fault?" he asked meekly.

"Don't be so piddly," Ama dismissed him, yet beneath her facile response, he detected a sliver of discomfort. *Who was to blame?* Was Mason's insatiable curiosity culpable? He didn't get the impression that Ama held him accountable—at least not entirely. Did she blame herself, then?

Mason staggered after her, alarmed by how frail he felt.

The world tilted on its axis, and when he tried to correct for the sudden sloping of the walls, everything teetered the other way. He faltered and caught himself on a nearby bicycle stand. Only then did Mason realize his breathing was laboured and his pulse was erratic.

He was dehydrated and hungry, sapped of strength by the thing that'd attached itself to him. Now that it was gone, his mind no longer suppressed what his body had been trying to tell him: he'd been wasting away.

"I can't carry you too," Ama called from a few paces ahead. "Think you'll manage?"

He glanced up, amazed she could parade Miya bridal-style like the girl weighed less than a handbag. Miya had a few inches over the white-haired woman, her limbs dangling like tinsel.

You did this to her, his conscience chided.

"Would you like me to carry—" His offer was silenced by Ama's raised brow and a downward quirk of her pink lips. "Never mind," he went on. "You must be stronger than me, anyway."

"Damn right I am." She turned to leave when a nearby door swung open and almost socked Miya across the head.

"What the ever-loving fuck..." It was Crowbar. Her cigarette popped out of her mouth as she held open the back door of *The Spade*, fisting a sulking bag of garbage.

"Hello," said Ama, smiling pleasantly at a perplexed Crowbar.

The bartender arched a brow as her attention shifted to Miya. "Do you need a hospital or something?"

"No," Ama strained after a short pause.

Crowbar lobbed the garbage bag into the dumpster. Arms akimbo, she leaned back against the brown-painted doorframe. "Look, I get it, healthcare's a bitch here. I don't know how many times I skirted going to the doctor

because I couldn't afford it. But you'll never forgive yourself if something bad happens to someone else, you
know?"

Ama loosed a breathy chuckle. "I promise she doesn't
need a doc—"

"I'm a doctor," Mason volunteered, raising his hand
sheepishly.

Crowbar's face scrunched as she bent over and picked
up her stray cigarette. "Well, then what the fuck are you
doing? Shouldn't you be helping?" She bounced down the
steps and looked him up and down. "Why are you making a
girl half your size carry that Amazonian string-bean, huh?"

Mason's jaw dropped as he scrambled for a response.
How was he *always* the bad guy? "I-I offered, but—"

Crowbar waved him off like he was a nat. "Come inside,"
she instructed. "Whatever your girl's been smoking, she can
ride it out behind the bar."

"What if you have customers?" Ama hesitated, no doubt
wanting to get Miya to Gavran sooner rather than later.

"We're closed. Besides," she looked over her shoulder as
she headed back, "you weirdos have some explaining to do."

"What are we going to do?" Mason hissed when
Crowbar was out of earshot.

Ama sighed and shook her head. "It's fine. I'll have
Gavran come to us."

"With the bartender around?" he asked incredulously.

Ama cut him with a glare. "Really? That's what you're
worried about? Tell me, what did you think when you first
saw Gavran?"

"That he didn't make any damn sense?"

"Exactly." She slid past the door. "No one thinks twice
about a kooky old man muttering nonsense and lighting
sage. We'll say he's a spiritual healer. It's not even a lie,
really."

Mason mumbled and followed close behind. "Still feels dishonest."

"I know," said Ama, "but we can only afford partial truths for the time being. She's already suspicious, and if we blow her off now, she might get herself into trouble digging around the minefield we've created."

She had a point. Wasn't that what Mason had done— not just in Black Hollow, but during his search for Miya too? Wasn't that the reason he'd attracted a parasite? He was weak. Even the Servant knew this; the invader had peeled the scabs off Mason's festering traumas, then gibed him with his own failings. The Servant was only as strong as the host, and the host was quite feeble.

But what did it mean to be strong? Mason had always believed that knowledge was power, so he sought it out at any cost. It'd nearly killed him, and it'd possibly done worse to Miya, yet he couldn't force himself to deny his need for answers. He'd tried to suppress his impulse towards cold, clinical understanding, but it was a lie that only made him vulnerable. How could he teach himself to accept the unknown? If his quest to save Miya had been misguided, how was he to know the right way to help someone in need?

Perhaps Miya wasn't in need of Mason Evans at all.

The painful reversal—that she always wound up saving him—gnawed at his conscience like a rat gnawing through a cage.

Mason's gaze trained on the unconscious girl in Ama's arms. She'd taken the fall for him. After losing himself to the Servant, he'd felt her somewhere beyond the endless threads of knowledge puncturing his sanity. For those few minutes of total, mind-shattering comprehension, he was privy to everything. Miya had taken the dream stone and made it whole, only to fracture herself to slay the spectre that'd claimed Mason.

How could he have been so ignorant? Had Black Hollow taught him nothing? *Why* did he continue to tug on loose ends regardless of what they'd unravel?

"All right," he conceded. "We'll give her something, I guess. Whatever she needs to make sense of this."

Ama nodded, and they entered the dining room to find Crowbar setting up a fort of blankets on the floor behind the bar, the arrangement complete with fluffy pillows.

"Do you sleep here?" Mason asked.

"Sometimes," she answered. "When I don't want to be home alone. Grief will do weird things to your brain, even when you don't feel it sawing through your insides."

Mason and Ama traded glances. Did the white wolf know about Crowbar's sister?

"I'm sorry," he said automatically.

Ama laid Miya down and cleared her throat. "Excuse me a moment." She squeezed past Crowbar, her eyes warming as their shoulders brushed. Crowbar's gaze lingered, and Ama offered a reassuring smile. "I need to call someone. They might be able to help."

"Help?" Crowbar tossed her thumb Mason's way. "Isn't he a doctor?"

"Her problem is not of the medical variety."

"Oh?" Crowbar waited expectantly.

Ama hesitated. "Think of it as more of a spiritual crisis."

Crowbar looked like she'd bitten into a lemon. "I didn't think you were *that* sort."

"I'm not, it's just—" Ama tripped over her words. "I'm sorry."

For what, Mason wasn't sure, but she was already retreating towards the rear.

Crowbar turned to him. "Okay, what's wrong with your girl here?"

"No clue," he chuckled nervously. "She's always been a bit abrasive, I guess. Since I've known her, that is."

"Not the voluptuous goddess!" Crowbar rolled her eyes. "I'm talking about the heap of limbs lying unconscious on the floor. You know, your friend, Miya?"

Mason mouthed, *voluptuous goddess*, then stuttered, "She was like this when I woke up."

The words sounded strange coming out of his mouth. What exactly had he woken up from? One minute the universe's secrets filled him up, stretching his every mortal fibre until he burst at the seams. The next, they were gone, leaving him with a gaping void in his chest. Yet he couldn't deny that he felt better with that emptiness inside him.

Mason threw his hands up in defense when he saw Crowbar about to skewer him. "I performed a physical exam, and she's perfectly stable. Nothing's wrong with her body."

"This is all so weird." Crowbar shook her head disbelievingly. "I know you're hiding something, man. You all are. And where's Kai? The dude just *vanished*." She gestured to Miya. "He was a wreck just like this one."

Mason's face flooded with heat at the mention of Kai. The memories and insults still haunted him. He'd been permanently scarred after witnessing the carnage Kai had wrought that night in the cabin. Even with their guns, the mob was a herd of sheep, and Kai was the wolf among them, whetting his teeth on their blood and meat. Mason had underestimated the danger Kai posed; he was a magnet for destruction—volatile and without empathy for those who didn't stir his affection. After nearly losing his life, Mason had no interest in putting his throat against the blade a second time.

"What?" Crowbar goaded. "You got a crush on the guy?"

"What? No!" Mason's voice garbled in disgust. "He's an ass—"

"*Hole! Hole!*" The slur was cut short by a piercing squawk. From under the window well, a dark shadow bounced atop the backrest of a worn booth. The corner was scantly lit by waning sunlight that spilled through the steamy tavern. "*Hole! Hole!*" the intruder hooted.

Mason felt the hairs on his neck go static. His heart hammered in feverish anticipation like some primal part of him had become tethered to the creature and its master.

"Is that a crow?" the frazzled bartender asked.

"Raven," Mason corrected, clearing his throat. "It's a raven."

"Well, whatever it is, how the hell did it get in here?"

"Same way all the lost ones do," a voice rasped from behind them.

Mason whirled around in time with Crowbar's startled gasp. There, after three long years, stood the old man from the redwood. His slicked, silvery-black hair shone like an oil spill, and his cavernous eyes tugged with glee as he offered them an eerie, doll-like smile.

"What the fuck!" Crowbar jumped back.

Gavran's lips cut wider, his teeth jagged as broken glass. He pointed to the window. "They come through the door."

The raven chortled and beat its wings, then glided to Gavran's shoulder where it found its perch.

"That's not a door, Gavran," Ama's voice echoed from the rear. She looked worn, shadows like bruises clinging beneath her eyes.

"Did you find who you were looking for?" the bartender asked cautiously.

Ama didn't respond, her attention fixed on the old man.

"I am not found," Gavran tutted, then sank to the floor. "I am that which finds." His tone softened, the final syllables dragging his voice into a low, unsettling whine, like the trill of a dying animal.

His lifeless smile contorted into a pained rictus; it hurt Mason to watch. The shine in his inky irises dimmed, flickering between black and grey as the raven on his shoulders twitched and let out a heart-wrenching screech.

"She's gone," Gavran muttered, and only then did Mason realize the whirr in the old man's throat was the sound of grief, seeping out when it could no longer be contained. He peered up at Ama. "I must find her."

"Can you?" Ama asked.

Gavran's head canted and clicked, then juddered as he turned back to Miya. His knobby hands brushed her cheeks —fingers stiff and curled like claws. Despite the rough callouses marring his weathered skin, he grazed Miya's brow with the tenderness of an anguished parent. The lines in his face—long and sharp like the edge of a blade—cut deep as chasms. They betrayed his age and the bittersweet warmth of a reunion come too late.

"I may not return," he said at last.

For the first time since knowing Ama, Mason saw her falter. Her expression collapsed like the air had left her lungs. He'd seen this look on every person he'd told what they most dreaded hearing: someone they loved was going to die. Ama stifled it better than most, but if there was one thing Mason knew well, it was the pallor of raw sorrow.

"No," she revolted, meekly at first, then with defiance. "No, you can't!"

Gavran's fingers still hovered over Miya's face. He seemed content next to her. "So many memories," he sighed. "Windows and gateways to so much suffering."

"Which is why you can't—I can't," Ama's voice broke, and she pressed a palm over her mouth. Mason caught a slight tremor and a suffocated whimper as she clamped down hard on the rising flood. Ama was a proud woman; she never showed her cards. She was warring with herself, trying to keep every hair in place. Mason wanted to tell her to stop—to let herself feel before it was too late, before she'd regret losing what precious time remained for a meaningful farewell. He wanted to, but he didn't dare. Drawing a deep breath, Ama took a moment to compose herself, then tried again. "I've been with you all my life. We always find another way."

Crowbar's fingers curled around Mason's forearm, squeezing where the Servant's mark had been. From his periphery, he saw moisture prickling her eyes. Was she choking back the questions? Letting the impending sacrifice soak into her all-too-fresh wounds?

Loss hung in the air like a looming threat, potent and unyielding.

Gavran's free hand wobbled towards Ama's. He grasped her fingers, his eyes dulling like fog caked over asphalt. "Worry not. I am never far." He smiled like a ghost on a quiet battlefield, the gesture belying all the mirth and mischief Mason had come to know him by. Then, he said, "Nothing in the world ends, little wolf. It only changes, like water to mist, like bones to dust."

Ama clutched his hand and nodded. She didn't seem convinced, but the old raven had taken the fight out of her with his gentle conviction. Her arm shook as she released him, and she scooted back like the distance might quell the pain. Her shoulders caved in as she lowered her gaze, thick silvery tresses obscuring her face. Like a child abandoned to the rain, she shuddered, her silence punctuated by an occasional whimper as she succumbed to silent tears. With nothing left to say, Gavran eased himself to the floor, his movements slow and stiff.

His neck creaked like an old hinge as he turned to Miya.

"I have come to fulfill my promise, Dreamwalker. But for that, you must first be found again."

The room fell silent. Gavran's eyes—black holes to another plane—slowly drifted shut. The old man went still, his lips parting as delicate breaths came and went like the final embers of life. Yet they persisted, steady and immutable.

Gavran had descended into the dreamscape.

"This is *her* fault," Ama growled, jolting Mason and Crowbar from their stupor. Anger steeled her sadness. "None of this would've happened if not for her meddling with Kai..." she trailed off, the armor chinking as she struggled to displace the blame. "And if not for me. If not for my arrogance...my selfishness..."

Crowbar was shaking, each tremor passing into Mason's arm like a sympathetic vibration. There would be no lying to her now—no half-truths or cleverly disguised rationalizations.

"Who are you talking about?" Crowbar asked, and Ama finally looked up, her eyes ablaze like a thousand hells.

"Rusalka," Ama hissed, the name surely meaningless.

"Why don't I go make some coffee?" Crowbar released Mason's arm, then headed towards the kitchen. "Looks like we're in for a long night."

When the doors swung shut, Mason stepped over the dreamers. "Rusalka isn't what she seems, Ama."

Her expression was distant and forlorn, but she engaged him nonetheless. "What are you talking about?"

"I saw her," Mason blurted out, eager to speak his piece before Crowbar returned. "I know...*everything*."

This caught Ama's attention. A spark of sunlight returned to her eyes, her fiery stare ensnaring him.

"When she attacked me, she was trying to get to the

Servant—the truth demon. She wanted information. But the Servant gives nothing away for free."

Ama squared her shoulders to him. "So, she gave away a piece of her own truth in exchange for one she wanted."

"Yes! And because I was linked to that parasite, everything it extracted from her found its way to me." Desperation and terror caught on his tongue. "I know her whole history. I *know* what she wants."

"And what is that?"

"Retribution. She wants to hurt the man who hurt her, but she can't because he's dead. Instead, she keeps re-enacting the same scenario using other people as her puppets—people who're in love, who think they can trust each other. She worms her way into their heads, exploits their insecurities, then has them commit the same crime that was committed against her. It's the only thing she *can* do because her own revenge is impossible."

"But why Miya?" Ama demanded. "Why Kai?"

Mason's jaw clenched. The horrifying truth invaded him against his will—the labyrinth of dark forest, the shallow river gashing through its knolls.

"She wasn't always an implacable monstress. She was once someone quite different, someone far too close to home." Mason's palms were clammy with sweat as he shifted his weight. The words were stuck in his throat, fighting their way back down as he tried to force them up. "Rusalka was a girl from Black Hollow."

II

THE HOLLOW THAT BURNED BLACK

❧ 28 ❧

KAI

THE AIR where Rusalka had torn through the veil was thick with foreboding.

Transitioning from Black Hollow's dark woods to Louisiana's bayous had been seamless. In the dreamscape, distance had no meaning; how the environment morphed around Kai hardly mattered when he had a scent trail to follow. One minute, he was tracking Rusalka's blood through pines and maples, and the next, he was wading through opaque swamp water. Velizar had tried distracting him with his yammering, but Kai's sense of smell never failed him.

Rusalka's tracks ended at the Grey Gnarl, leaving Kai with one option: to return to the physical world.

Thanks to his nemesis, he could peel back the curtain and step onto the other side without Miya's help, but would she be there to anchor him, or had she returned to the dreamscape?

It didn't matter. Velizar had promised he'd be safe.

Kai had to find a way to end Rusalka before she possessed someone else. Once she was gone, he could apologize to Miya—that is, if he got the chance.

What would he tell her about Velizar? That everything she'd sacrificed to get rid of Abaddon was for nothing?

Dread pooled in his stomach like gasoline spilling over a freshly burnt match.

You're getting ahead of yourself. First, he needed to subdue the rotting mermaid, but if the blade didn't cut, what good was he?

Velizar's question pricked his conscience. *Had* anything really changed?

Was Kai still a monster—a destroyer—lifetimes after he'd destroyed his brother? Was he no different than the scum who made Rusalka?

Kai shook away the thought. He placed his hand on the slippery tree trunk, the bark soaked in Rusalka's slime. He was done with this place.

So quick to use my gifts.

"You offered them up," said Kai. "I paid a hefty price for the all-access pass."

Now, now. You didn't think I wanted inside your head just for the fun of it, did you?

"I lived with you for years. I think I know what I'm in for."

Velizar chuckled. **I am not Abaddon. My purpose isn't so...violent. I'm quite sentimental, really.**

"Save it," Kai snapped. "I'm losing time." He ground his palm against the elm and focused on what awaited beyond, yet no matter how hard he willed it, he saw nothing—no doorway, no parting mist, no tunnel through space and time.

He had no idea how to work the gates between realms. They were knots, tangled too tightly for him to understand.

Kai dropped his hand. "How does this work?"

I can show you, Velizar cooed, **if you'll do your brother a favour.**

"Haven't I done enough?" Kai kicked at the dirt around the bottom of the tree when he couldn't stamp out his frustration.

I wish only to speak, Velizar reasoned. **To tell you my story.**

His story? Kai didn't give a flying fuck. He hated this place. He hated the eerie lake swimming with algae and the fog eating its way over the water, closing in like a shroud. He hated how dead the island felt. Soil everywhere pulsed with life, and when he stopped to pay attention, he felt the vibrations between his toes. But here was different. The land around the Grey Gnarl was dry as a scorched roast, all the juice sucked away by Rusalka's vampiric tree. The silence was even worse. No matter how he strained to hear that frail heartbeat, he was met with cold stillness. It was like his feet weren't even on the ground.

"You're trying to win me over," Kai realized. "Is this your messed-up way of reconciling?"

Perhaps. Kai felt him waver. **Even gods wish to be understood.**

"What's with the sudden purge?" Kai sneered. "Spectral brain tumor got you reflecting on your sins?"

I'm not the only one who ought to reflect on his sins. But the matter is simple: a willing host is superior to a resistant one. Co-existence. Symbiosis. The better you understand me, the better we'll get along.

"How fucking quaint," Kai deadpanned, now having dug a half-foot pit in front of the elm. "Is this where you convince me the Dreamwalker is evil incarnate, and you're a saint who martyred himself?"

No, he grunted in disapproval. **I wish to apologize.**

235

"What?" Kai's voice betrayed his surprise.

The Dreamwalker came between us. Instead of cutting her out like the cancer she is, I lashed out at you.

"I thought you said *I* was the one who put the knife in your back."

You were, but only because she'd gotten to you first. You couldn't have known better.

Kai narrowed his eyes. "Sounds like you're calling me stupid."

Not stupid, Velizar hummed. **Perhaps only a bit... impressionable. Impulsive.** Kai could feel him smiling, mouth and teeth stretching across his ribs. **Am I wrong?**

Unnerved, Kai scratched under his shirt where he felt the severed grin burn against his skin, but his fingers didn't cooperate. His left hand shuddered, pulling away as though repelled by something behind the itch.

Velizar wasn't wrong. Impulsivity had gotten Kai up shit's creek more than once. He didn't put it past himself to royally screw up and leave a trail of destruction. It was the reason he was forced to flee Washington—the *how* and *why* of his entire existence in Black Hollow. Yet it was also the force that propelled him to Miya. Without his temper, they never would have found each other.

Weak logic, Velizar chided, reading his mind. **A series of events strung together is not a case for causation. You, of all people, should know that. You don't believe in fate, remember? What was it you used to say...?**

"Fate is the beginning," the words sprang from Kai's lips without his say-so.

Ah, Velizar sighed contently. **Already finishing my sentences.**

Disgust crawled up Kai's throat. Fighting to keep his

cards close, he glanced down at the hole he'd carved out. He wished he could bury all the monsters in it, but for that, the grave would have to run far deeper. "So, between me and the Dreamwalker..."

I will always hate her most. It was her fate to die, but she manipulated you into interfering. You grew soft, forgot your duties. It was your role to destroy and to reign over chaos so that I could create.

Create what? His riddles were worse than Ama's.

Nothing as superficial as life, said the spirit. Despite the humidity of the swamp, a chill seeped into Kai as Velizar's next words rattled his insides. **Fear. Obedience. Order.**

"I don't get it." Kai hated that he was interested—that he was trying to understand. *Why* was he trying to understand? "What was I supposed to be destroying?"

Those who disobeyed. Those who strengthened chaos, giving her a realm to sow her poisonous seeds.

"That makes no damn sense," said Kai. The legend—the beginning of it all—mentioned no gods of creation and destruction, of chaos and order. It was just a story about a girl who could walk through dreams and an injured wolf she met in the woods—Kai, apparently. Above all, it was a story about a pants-shitting town that turned their fear into hatred and cast out what they didn't understand.

Yes, brother. That is the tale humans remember. It is a...partial version, but it is not the one gods and spirits remember. There can be many iterations of a story, and a story is never told the same way twice.

Kai hated how Velizar heard everything, but he kissed his teeth and bowed theatrically. "Enlighten me then, god of creation."

The Hollow was not always in the New World.

"Places don't move like ethereal farts." Except for the

damn willow tree. That green bastard turned up wherever it wanted to.

But the people move. And they take their gods with them. The Hollow's cradle was an ocean away, in a craggy forest that sits on the suture between east and west. I was the ruler of those people, he claimed unironically. **And you, dear brother, were the black wolf—the monster in the woods that kept the villagers in check.** The itch returned, invisible teeth scraping against Kai's abdomen. **You were there to clamp your jaws around the necks of those who disobeyed me.**

Kai's brow arched. "We were partners in some fucked up scheme?"

The voice of Velizar bellowed with a deep, reverberating laugh. **What else is godhood if not scheming among mortals? The villagers didn't know we were divine— that their king was a god in human form. And the black wolf they dreaded? That god's brother. Creation and destruction,** he echoed, **two sides of the same coin.**

The weight of those words struck heavier than the bus had three years ago. The poetic nonsense about coins wasn't just metaphor; there was truth to it—devastating truth that Kai didn't want. Yet here he was, asking the questions himself.

His eyes were fixed on the Grey Gnarl, his jaw set as myth and history weaved into a terrifying tapestry that showcased a distant past he loathed to accept as part of himself. Yet it explained so much, gave meaning to everything he once considered the universe's arbitrary cruelty.

You were the stuff of nightmares, said Velizar when Kai didn't respond, **and I was there to harvest those nightmares, to mould the fear they inspired into law.**

It paved the way for an orderly society—one that thrived in my hands. We were born divine, and we were born to rule men.

"Foiled by the Dreamwalker?" Kai mocked.

Ah, that woman, Velizar sighed ruefully. A girl born with the power to traverse realms. She defied order. A god of chaos in her own right.

"She was like us?"

Velizar growled, sounding offended. Like us? No. But what does it matter? She always brings about the same result, whether she means to or not. She healed you when you should have died.

That's right. The girl from the village found a dying wolf. Kai had assumed he'd been shot by hunters; it seemed a common enough theme in his life. But perhaps there was more to it. "Why was I dying?"

Why don't I show you, brother? he offered sweetly. Then you can decide for yourself who the villain is.

Shaken by his bald-faced confidence, Kai faltered. "Are you serious? I've got a demon to hunt down, and you want to take a trip down memory lane?"

Cooperate, and I'll take you to the other side, Velizar twisted his earlier promise. Resist, and I'll lock you here until you submit.

"You piece of sh—"

And I wouldn't take too long deciding if I were you. It's only a matter of time before Rusalka reaches your precious Emiliya—that's her name now, isn't it?

Something struck Kai like a hammer to the knee. What was Rusalka's beef with Miya? Her MO was manipulating men into killing women they loved—a sick revenge shenanigan, no doubt. If she was going for Miya directly, there had to be more to it. Kai figured Velizar knew Rusalka somehow, though the bastard was well-practiced in guarding his secrets.

It was unfair. Kai's every racing thought was transparent to his antagonist. Their power dynamic was lopsided, just as it always had been.

"Forcing my hand isn't very endearing," said Kai.

Unlike you, Velizar rumbled, **I have always made the hard decisions. You took the easy way out. You're still trying to.**

Kai felt an uncomfortable prickle in his chest; a kernel of truth had burrowed its way in.

Through my eyes, I will show you the world you've forgotten. Soon, brother, you will understand. Violence is not strength. The power to kill is not strength. Strength is neither wild nor free, as you have always fancied yourself. Strength is found in discipline—in loyalty to a cause greater than oneself. It transcends your petty impulse towards self-preservation. It is the resolve to obey when your heart yearns to rebel. It is the persistence of faith in spite of doubt. Strength is quiet, patient...and unyielding.

Kai's vision began to blur. His feet sank into the earth and tangled into the Grey Gnarl's roots. Abaddon had been a menace, but nothing could have prepared Kai for the eloquent knife Velizar twisted into his heart. Survival at any cost. Animal rage in the face of any threat. These made Kai who he was. They made him resilient—or so he thought. He enjoyed towering over those who thought they could hurt him, and he enjoyed hurting them back.

He still tasted Rusalka's bitter lips, felt her blackened blood spilling over his hands. He'd wanted to hurt her too.

What if Velizar was right? What if Kai's brutality was

nothing more than a fragile façade to hide his weakness? What if true strength looked nothing like him?

Of course **it looks nothing like you,** Velizar replied, and Kai could hear the smile as he spoke. **How do you think I've survived this long while you have died a thousand deaths?**

Kai gasped for air, but he was already underground. Roots like snakes coiled around his limbs and embraced him in a vise-like grip. All the physical power in the world couldn't have helped him break free, so he surrendered, closing his eyes and giving in to the darkness.

He'd already invited one monster in.

Why stop now?

❦ 29 ❧

VELIZAR

FOR ENDLESS MOONS and eternal suns, Velizar had been drawn by the Hollow's impervious mists and its thick, devouring forest. The warren nestled in the heart of the viridescent sea was a prize—a wild colt to be tamed.

Velizar would be its equestrian.

He stood half-hidden amongst the woodland, paces from the tiny settlement. Milky flower buds spotted the surrounding apple trees as they stirred from their winter slumber. Basked in moonlight, dewdrops glimmered on the petals like nature's ephemeral diamonds. Wildlife beckoned, but the chaos of the animal world bored Velizar. He didn't care for nature's equilibrium or the blind instinct that drove baser creatures. He sought something greater, something higher—an order extricated from man's greatest gift: the will to power.

The Hollow's people needed a leader. They needed a king.

He called to the figure behind him, "You know what to do then, brother?"

Sendoa sidled up to Velizar, his wild black hair blowing around his neck, uneven edges just barely grazing his shoulders. His footsteps were quieter than the breeze.

A true predator, Velizar thought.

"Kill those who stray too far," Sendoa echoed his brother's earlier instruction. "Seems simple enough."

A slow, satisfied smile crept up the side of Velizar's face. His sable mane hung lower than his brother's, tied back by blue yarn. "Careful, executioner. You are only to snuff out the lives your king commands you to."

"My king?" Sendoa laughed indolently. The word should have been weightier, yet it left Sendoa's lips with the lightness of a sparrow's feather. "Go on. Claim this hole as your kingdom. It doesn't make you *my* king."

A sour taste filled Velizar's mouth. "Oh?"

"I'm not a pawn playing house with your little village," said Sendoa. "I'm the monster keeping the people docile behind its walls."

"Just do as you're told, Sen." They exchanged pointed looks—cold, gleaming gold clashing with dark, molten red. "Destroy as you were born to, so that I may create as I was destined to. We cannot thrive without each other's cooperation."

"So you've said," muttered Sendoa, breaking away from their terse battle. He skipped a pebble across the shallow stream that threaded through the trees.

"Do as I say, and all will be well. We will have balance and purpose. We will have order. I promise you that."

They needed human faith to sustain them, yet Velizar had learned that belief was fickle; when the tides changed, so too did people's loyalties. He needed to be more than ethereal; he needed to be visceral.

The whims of human imagination would not subdue him.

To be a king was far nobler than to be a god.

Sendoa rolled his eyes, then stalked into the woods. "I'll humour you...for now."

Velizar studied his brother. How alike they were in appearance, even as the younger scoffed at the pursuits of his elder. "Why?"

Sendoa flashed Velizar a wolfish grin. "Because we're gods. What more do we have than a wretched abundance of everlasting tedium?"

"For once, you speak wisely." Velizar's smile glistered against the night. "Now go, brother. Sharpen your claws and bloody your teeth. There's fear to be sown."

Sendoa's lips twisted into a sneer. "As you wish, *my king*."

VELIZAR STOOD at the precipice of the village plaza. Nestled under a crooked oak, he was caught in the sharp divide between shadow and light. The spring sun brought new life with it, yet death lingered like the final blusters of winter winds.

A thick, knotted tree trunk rose from the dirt at the center of the commons. Stripped of its branches, the totem was cloaked in furs and decorated with tokens: bones, claws, teeth, arrowheads, and the odd piece of jewelry. A bear skull hung from the top, its cavernous eyes boring directly into the settlement's new guest.

At the foot of the grotesque display knelt a woman with luscious tresses, dark as midnight and restless as the sea. Her shoulders shook, and her sobs filled the still air. She was grieving.

Velizar slithered from the shade. As his steps crunched

closer, she met him with a tear-stained gaze.

"Are you well?" he asked as he folded onto one knee.

"Where'd you come from?" she answered his question with another, then looked past him into the woods. "You are not one of us."

"I am a visitor," he said.

She wiped her eyes, her hand calloused from long days of labour. "Why are you here, stranger?"

"I followed the sound of sorrow," he answered truthfully, "and found you at this peculiar altar."

Bowing her head, the young woman clutched her cloak tighter around her shoulders. He sensed she was too timid to interrogate him. "I was imploring the Viyest to be kind to my husband in the Silent Place."

"The Viyest, you say?" Velizar looked upon the great bear skull.

The young woman nodded. "My husband, Decebal—the Viyest was his winter kill. Its flesh fed us through hungry days, and its fur kept us warm during long, frigid nights. We place the Viyest's skull here as thanks for its sacrifice, for protecting us throughout the year until the next Viyest is hunted."

"It must be difficult," said Velizar, "placing your fate in the paws of a dead animal."

She smiled, clement and reserved. "It's not for outsiders to understand, but the Viyest is sacred."

"And how do your people choose their Viyest?"

The woman averted her gaze. "The Dreamwalker chooses."

"The Dreamwalker?"

"Yes," she nodded. "She travels to the dreamscape and finds the next Viyest every autumn. But now...since Decebal went into the woods...since the black wolf took his life... we're doomed."

"I am sorry for your loss," Velizar consoled her. "Surely, your Dreamwalker will find your next Viyest?"

The woman shook her head. "The Dreamwalker was killed in the hunt with Decebal. Bartha summoned her to assist him in tracking the black monster that roams close to the village, dragging off goats and hens. We fear for our children and what little livestock we keep."

Triumph pumped through Velizar's veins like a stormy current begging for release. Sendoa must have killed them both—the Hollow's greatest huntsman and this Dreamwalker. Though primitive, the Hollow's people were hardy. There was no creature they feared, and their hubris was not unfounded. The Viyest's head, dangling from a stick, was proof of their ferocity.

But with each arrow knocked, fangs crept closer to the throat. Since the Hollow hunters were unmoved by profane beasts, Velizar had given them an infernal one to contend with.

Sendoa had made himself their harbinger of death: a stygian wolf with eyes like blood and teeth like daggers. He inspired all the dread Velizar required to subdue even the bravest—and the most foolish—of men.

Nothing tasted sweeter than courage liquefying into helpless terror.

When Velizar reined in his glee, he placed a hand on the woman's shoulder. "What is your name, girl?"

"Lana," she replied, her large russet eyes meeting his.

"Lana," he coaxed. "Thank you for your patience with me. I believe I know this creature that prowls nearby. Perhaps I may assist?"

Her suspicion melted away, and she rose to her feet. "Bartha would want to know we have a visitor." Her cheeks blossomed with colour, her smile sweet as a fresh peach. "You must have travelled from far away. There is nothing but forest between us and the horizon. I can't help but wonder where you've come from."

Velizar chuckled as he towered over the girl. "Perhaps I did come from the horizon."

She burst into a laugh—the most pleasant of songs. "If that were true, I'd think you something from another world."

Velizar only smiled.

"I will not pry," Lana assured him, then turned away from the Viyest. "Come, I'll take you to Bartha."

"You have my deepest gratitude."

Now with her back to him, she didn't see his eyes glint like gold—this mortal with the instincts of a fawn.

Lana had invited the beast's brother straight into her home and offered him the hearth.

THE FOREST HAD ALWAYS BEEN plentiful. Sustenance was easily procured from its verdant depths, so the hunters never acquiesced to an outsider. Yet with Sendoa's savage attacks, their unwieldy pride fissured. A single summer was all it took for Velizar to harness the Hollow—to break in the colt.

"You were once a stranger to us," said Bartha as he fought the tremor in his hand. The bear skull at the center of the commons had yellowed from neglect, its power lost with its magnificence. Bartha wobbled closer as others gathered around him. Autumn leaves peppered the grass, and a chill settled over the village. The elder bowed his head in humility. "Velizar—you are as a great king. You have proven yourself our savior."

"Please, Bartha, I am simply a man like any other here."

Velizar placed a firm but gentle hand on the old man's shoulder.

"Your modesty betrays your station." Bartha further lowered his head, nearly crumpling like paper. "Before you came to us, we feared for our lives—preyed upon by a demon in the woods. Now, the creature's influence has dwindled, its familiars decimated under your miraculous guidance."

Velizar had confidently led the hunters to packs of wild dogs loitering near the mouth of the woods; he'd convinced them the scavengers were thralls of the great beast. With each animal slaughtered, Velizar chipped away at Bartha's reservations until the armor flaked off and the elder was left vulnerable, and so too his people.

Now, Velizar had them eating from the palm of his hand.

"I wish only to bring prosperity to the Hollow. I am overjoyed to have staved off the darkness with good sense," said Velizar.

Rapture coursed through him, the Hollow's worship filling him with life. With neither the Dreamwalker nor the Viyest to compete with his authority, he had come to replace the old ways with his own. He'd given enlightenment to a nascent and unsightly culture.

Order and structure could only be inspired by fear—a thing like raw dough, easily moulded.

As much as it disgruntled Velizar to admit it, his success was due in large part to Sendoa's bloody efforts. His brother —a god of destruction—would always be the monster lurking in the shadows, the villain the Hollow would perpetually seek to eradicate. With the demonic black wolf sowing fear, Velizar had engineered his throne.

"The perils beyond the Hollow have not abated," Velizar called to the villagers. "Ghoulish horrors stalk the woods, lying in wait for innocents to stray. Please, remain here. Do not disobey, for disobedience leads only to tragedy."

"And what of the Viyest?" a voice shouted from the back. Pavel, an eager young hunter, stepped forward. "I have a wife and two children to feed. Between your rules and the beast haunting the woods, we'll starve by mid-winter!"

Murmurs rippled through the crowd. Velizar levelled his gaze on the teething whelp. Pavel's sharp grey eyes were in stark contrast to his muddy hair. With a well-muscled frame and an imposing presence, there was something wild and unruly about the boy that reminded Velizar of his brother.

"The Viyest is superstition from a cruder time, my child," said Velizar. "Do not place your faith in such myths. There isn't even a Dreamwalker to guide your hunt."

Pavel pressed on, "How many beasts have we slaughtered in your name? How many times has the purge of wild dogs and coyotes lulled us into complacency? Yet our best men fall to the black wolf no matter your words!"

"That is why you must keep from the woods," Velizar reasoned. "The danger is endless. I promise the creature's army has been weakened. Heed me, and all will be well."

Pavel threw his arms up. "Our people are born hunters, yet since you arrived, we run scared like barn cats. *You* keep us as such with your portents. You destroy our way of life!" He cast a finger towards the gnarled branch where the Viyest hung like a tired ornament. "We need the Viyest. It has protected us for generations. Why should this winter be any different?"

Velizar's insides bubbled like lava. Humans only prayed when they wanted something, and *that* was a precarious source of power for a god. Absolute power was in the blood and body: the authority to let some live and make others die.

Velizar's gaze drifted towards the trees where he caught a pair of candescent red eyes witnessing the strife. He inhaled deeply, then peered into the roiling darkness. The wolf melded into the shadows as though a part of them, waiting for the king's next command.

This one, Velizar instructed, his aurous stare shifting to the mouthy hunter. "I only seek the safety of our people, dear Pavel. Surely, a single night of hunger is not worth your life."

"Too many nights of hunger, *my king*," Pavel sneered the words, "and my daughter will lose hers."

A collective gasp echoed through the town commons, but Pavel was unfazed by Bartha's cautionary glare. "I will hunt!" he declared, pounding a fist to his chest. "Who will join me?"

No one dared answer the call until Velizar stepped forward and surveyed his flock. "Our brave hunter should not venture out alone. Who will aid him?"

Velizar's rally roused the villagers like fresh liver to the hunter's hounds. Whispers crescendoed until Jove and Marko, two ruffians several years Pavel's senior, stepped forward and playfully struck the boy's arm with their burly fists.

"We will go with him," Jove proclaimed, ruffling Pavel's hair in good humour.

Velizar relished the sour shame that crawled up Pavel's face. The moral high ground had always been his sharpest blade.

Good, Velizar thought. *There must be witnesses to the dissenter's demise.*

Sendoa would tear Pavel to shreds. Jove and Marko would then return to the village and decree that Velizar had been right all along: disobedience was indeed a grave crime.

❦ 30 ❦

MIYA

MIYA AWOKE BLIND. All around her was a thick, impenetrable blackness. She had no idea where she was. At first slowly, then more urgently, desperate heat ravelled up her spine. Terror shackled her in place. She couldn't see her hands or her feet in front of her.

The world was a depthless abyss, and she was lost in it.

Her bones rattled with cold beneath her veins. Rubbing her arms for warmth, Miya spun and squinted into the darkness.

"Hello?"

Her voice rang through the void, and a chilling question resounded in her mind: Who am I?

She knew the basics: She was Emiliya Delathorne, daughter of Raymond and Andrea Delathorne. She was born and raised in Black Hollow, British Columbia. Her father often travelled for work. Once, she'd wanted to be a journalist, but found university life disillusioning. Her best friend's name was Hannah. Hannah had moved to Burnaby, and Miya missed her very much.

Beyond that, it was a blur. She dug deeper, concentrated harder, but discovered only swirls of sable and violet smoke. Somewhere in their midst, she glimpsed a man. His face—a not-quite-dry painting plunged under murky water—invaded her memories. Yet when she tried to pull the painting to the surface, the colours bled from the canvas, distorting the image. All she could make out was his unruly black hair and red-tinted eyes.

Did he really matter if she couldn't remember him? From some hidden place within, a tiny voice cried, Yes! But what could she do? Some vital part of her was missing.

Then, she felt something in her hands. Her fingers grazed rough, thinly woven threads. She was holding the painting she'd tried to fish out of her subconscious. A lump of panic hatched in her throat, barricading the breath from her lungs.

Who am I? The words pummelled closer to home, but the picture remained unclear. How had she come to hold it? Had she conjured it from her mind—a thought made physically manifest?

"Man made mirrors to reflect the soul, but only memories gleam against the glass."

Miya searched for the source of the voice. A gravelly laugh sang through the endless chasm around her, and she spun to come face to face with a small figure about half her size.

The boy shed a peculiar light, his shadow flickering around his feet. He was a lantern in the midnight fog. Waxy skin and coal-coloured eyes cinched around Miya's heart. His luminous blue-black hair reminded her of plumage; it swayed like there was a breeze, yet the air was entirely still. He donned a shaggy cloak that swallowed up his limbs and coalesced with the darkness where it licked the ground. Perhaps Miya should have been alarmed, but she was unfazed by the boy's sudden appearance.

"It's a painting..." she ventured, tilting the canvas towards her visitor.

He smiled like a wide, curved blade. "Is a painting not a mirror? A doorway to the deep?"

Miya examined the barely discernable face bleeding over the

plaited threads. "This person isn't me. It's someone I know." She looked back to the boy. "Just like you."

His smile faded, and he croaked, "Yes."

"Are we friends?"

"Friends..." he repeated as though she'd spoken a foreign language. Then, he sighed, his spindly fingers poking free from his bushy robe. "We are family."

"Family." Miya's fingers grazed the streaks of colour dyeing the woven threads. "Is he family too?"

The boy didn't answer. He stepped closer and peered over her arm, his inky eyes trained on the image.

"I feel so lost. I'm scared that I'll never find my way back..." she trailed off, her breaths growing shallow. Back to...what, exactly? She didn't even know what she was meant to go back to, but there was no path forward, either.

The boy grasped Miya's wrist. Although the movement was abrupt and his skin cold to the touch, she recognized the gesture as one of commiseration.

"Gavran." The name came off her tongue like muscle memory.

"Look again," he commanded, nodding towards the painting.

Miya's eyes trailed from the bony fingers gripping her arm to the piece between her hands. The man's face was now clear.

"Kai."

She knew him; she knew his name, but beyond that, there was nothing.

"You said the painting's a mirror. Does that mean he's part of who I am?" she asked.

The boy's cheeks puffed in displeasure. "He is not needed. You are lost and found without him. You are whole without him. But," he hesitated when she bore into him, "he stood by you on all four paws."

"He supported me," she translated.

"Yes," said Gavran, though the admission struck Miya as a bitter one. "Put that down." He tugged on her wrist. "It won't help you find your way."

"Then what will?"

"It's not the first time you've been lost." He swept his cloak back as he turned and retreated into the darkness.

The asphalt-coloured mist parted around his faintly glowing form, and up ahead, Miya caught the silhouette of a towering tree. Its base was as wide as a truck and sprouted high into the would-be heavens. If there was a sun or moon in this place, Miya was sure the leaves could caress it. There was only one species she knew of that approached such a mammoth size.

"Is that a redwood?" She craned her neck.

"It's the Red Knot," he answered in confirmation. "Come," he beckoned, "sit with me. I will tell you a story to pass the time until the fog clears."

Miya stumbled forward, following the dim light curled around the boy. As worry spooled around her body, she yearned to return to a simpler time—one of bedtime stories, when fairy tales drew magic onto life's pages. She knew that magic was close. All the wonder she'd ever wanted was hovering nearby, waiting for her to snatch it back up.

Having reached Gavran, she could see the tree more clearly as it loomed overhead like an ancient guardian.

"We'll be safe here," Gavran assured her, then sat under its protective limbs and patted the spot next to him.

Silently, Miya joined him and was startled to find the earth warm and mossy against her palms. "What's this story you wanted to tell me?"

Gavran clasped his milky hands together, clapping in delight. Despite his momentary lapses into child-like jubilance, there was something deathless about him. "The story of the Hollow." He swayed closer, his breath tickling her cheek.

"The Hollow? Do you mean Black Hollow?"

"Yes, yes!" He leaned against the redwood and pressed his ear to the bark as though listening for whispers. "The Hollow...and the gods that turned it black."

Miya too rested against the tree's massive bole. "I thought Black Hollow was named after the dark green forest surrounding it."

"Names have more than one meaning," Gavran chuckled. "A hollow in a black wood, and a hollow that is itself black. A god deep in the Hollow, and a god that is deeply hollow."

"The gods of the Hollow are hollow?" Miya raised an eyebrow.

The boy's teeth glistened like broken pearls as he pulled himself free from the voices inside the tree. "Shall I tell you how they became that way?"

Miya wavered. This didn't sound like the kind of bedtime story her mother used to tell her as she hung dried lavender from the handles of her bedside drawer.

This story sounded like an omen, a doorway to a dangerous world.

Miya knew her heart was waiting there. That vital core that eluded her would not come calling. She would have to find it.

"Tell me the story." Miya pushed aside her doubt. "Show me what I've forgotten."

Gavran raised his arms in revelry, his feathery mantle erupting around him like wings. Poised as the keenest of storytellers, he began his tale:

"When a babe was born without breath, the people of the Hollow believed the child's soul was lost. Wandering too far into the dreamscape, it became unmoored from its earthly form. But all souls must find their bodies at birth, or life is little more than a dashed hope.

"A newborn's soul is curious, easily lured away by spirits' mischief. Thus, when a babe is born breathless, it often remains so. And yet, every so often, a raven will find the child's soul meandering to its plight. The raven snatches up the soul and flies it back to its rightful body. Reunited with itself, the child lives."

"This is what the Hollow's people believed?" Miya asked.

The boy nodded, his eerie grin never faltering. Crossing his legs and clutching his ankles, he rocked forward and back, then contin-

ued, "And so there was once a girl. A girl who had been born twice. A girl whose soul was returned to her by a clever raven." He drew close and cupped Miya's cheeks, his hands thin and cold as buried bones.

"A Dreamwalker."

KALI

MILENA'S HAIR was the colour of a burning sunset. Even now, when her tawny skin had turned wan, her long, wispy curls seared red with life. It was somehow dissonant, unsettling. The dead weren't meant to hold such colour.

Beside her, Lana sobbed quietly, and Kali finally allowed her gaze to drift from Milena's beautiful hair to the second figure lying in a wooden casket atop the pyre.

Decebal.

Kali drew her arm around Lana's shoulders and pulled her close. Dark strands clung to Lana's wet, ruddy cheeks, and Kali pressed her forehead against the grieving widow's. Together they'd survived famine and disease, love and loss. Lana had been there for Kali when her parents disappeared, devoured by the woods. She'd been there when the other children teased Kali and the adults shooed her away. Kali's father had been a poor hunter, and her mother frequently suffered from illness that would leave her bedridden for days. The Hollow hunters said her parents didn't contribute, though they simply hadn't been allowed to contribute in their own way.

Some said her parents' absence wasn't from a blundered hunt. Some said they'd deserted.

They'd abandoned their child to the village's paper-thin charity.

"I'm s-sorry, Ekaliya," Lana stammered, pulling back. "I don't mean to fall apart like this."

Kali managed a weak smile. "You have every reason to fall apart." She glanced at Decebal. "He was your husband."

Lana pressed a hand to her stomach, and Kali's eyebrows shot up. "Are you with child?"

Lana shook her head. "I don't know. We'd been trying, but my womb has always been disagreeable."

"Perhaps it's for the best," Kali said softly. "Some women...hate the reminder."

Lana stepped away, her expression torn between hope and dismay. "Have you seen it?"

Kali hesitated, Milena's fiery aura prickling the edge of her vision.

Milena. The Dreamwalker. She'd been with Decebal, hunting the beast that terrorized the Hollow. Her wounds were cleaned and sewn shut, but Kali glimpsed dabs of blood staining her pristine funeral garbs. Would she be allowed into the Silent Place with them?

"Now and then," Kali went on, "I walk into widows' dreams. Some mourn the loss more deeply when they see their husbands. And after they awaken, they have nowhere to put their sorrow, so they raise a hand on their child. They don't realize what they cling to."

Lana grabbed her hand. "You must tell Bartha. Milena is dead. Without a new Dreamwalker, the Hollow's doomed. We'll have no means to find the Viyest in winter. The sky already darkens quicker; the season of the dead looms only three moons away."

Kali curled her long, dainty fingers around her friend's. "Bartha already knows, and he knows I won't take up the mantle."

"But why?"

Kali's voice quivered despite her resolve. "This village drove my parents to their deaths because tradition was more important than compassion. I won't enable the beliefs that orphaned me."

Lana's shock rushed from her wounded expression and travelled down her arms until Kali felt the jolt against her fingertips. "You would doom us all because of your personal grudge?"

"It's not a grudge," said Kali as Lana dropped her hand. "It's principle. The Hollow ostracizes anyone they deem unfit for the hunt, but why must everyone be born a hunter?"

"To contribute to the community," insisted Lana. "It takes all of us to hunt the Viyest."

"Can't you see the Viyest is part of the problem? Insisting on the hunt drives the Hollow's cruelty towards its own people!"

"Not everyone in the Hollow is cruel," Lana rebuked. "What of the nights I stole cured deer and wild barley from my own family's table so you wouldn't starve in your parents' ramshackle?"

"But you would have me take part in the very thing that spurs cruelty?" asked Kali.

"For the greater good."

"We are a dozen villagers in a forest that stretches to the edge of the world! How would we know what the greater good is?" Kali challenged.

Lana was shaking as she gripped the edge of Decebal's

casket. "You're being selfish."

The words corroded what little patience Kali had left. *I'll show you selfish*, she thought, then spun on her heels and left Lana alone by the pyre.

As Kali stormed past the red maple at the mouth of the Hollow, a voice, smooth as silk, lilted from behind, "You must forgive her."

Kali turned to find a stranger standing several paces away. "I'm sorry?" An uneasy shiver spidered up her spine.

"Your friend." He offered a taut smile. "She is an ordinary woman. Such folk need something to adhere to—something to make meaning of chaos. To give life order. The Viyest fulfills that purpose."

Kali regarded the stranger—a tall man with cold yellow eyes and a dark mane. It was tied back, barely contained by a blue string. She wondered if he'd tolerate a single hair out of place. "I too am an ordinary woman, and Lana is my friend. We may disagree, but she is no simpleton."

The stranger chuckled. "It doesn't matter if the dove crawls through the mud. It'll always have wings to fly with."

Kali narrowed her eyes. "I don't quite follow your meaning," she lied.

His smile widened before he dropped his head, like his disguise had slipped. "You shouldn't go into the woods," he warned. "The beast that murdered your predecessor lurks there."

How had he known she could walk dreams?

"Maybe that beast only wished to be left in peace." Kali's words dripped with venom. She lingered just long enough to see surprise flit across the stranger's golden eyes.

Satisfied, she turned her back to him and wandered into the woods.

THE WORLD DIMMED as Kali left the village. While the sun touched the cleared earth of the Hollow, the woods were a labyrinth of shadows, fluid like water and nimble as a sprite.

Kali had never learned to hunt, but she had a way with the forest. Though she occasionally bartered for leftover rabbit or the drier cuts of cured meat, she mostly survived on edibles from the land—the best of which could be found in the untrekked parts of the forest. With a stygian wolf on the prowl, fewer people dared journey so far for a basket of berries or mushrooms.

Now, with her only friend angry and an entire village frothing to preen her as their next Dreamwalker, Kali found herself aching to meander farther, to risk getting lost. If she knew where she was, she would find her way back, and if she found her way back, she wasn't truly free of the Hollow. Her escape would remain fleeting.

No matter how much she enjoyed teetering on the verge of disappearance, Kali was spiteful by nature. She wouldn't vanish like her parents did, if only to deny the villagers the satisfaction. With nothing better to do, Kali reckoned she'd gather some willow branches to weave herself a new foraging basket.

She wound through the dense woods with ease. Looking for a challenge, she set her sights on a gulch, slung an arm around an aspen, and pulled herself up the ravine. Hiking up her raspberry skirts with one hand, Kali dug the other into the earth for balance and climbed like a child racing towards a prize. By the time she reached the summit, the village was far out of sight.

Kali descended the other side of the gully. A stream of clear water cascaded over a rock bed, and she followed its path as it gashed through the landscape, bending stone and soil alike. Through shrubbery and undergrowth, Kali caught a glimpse of a small thicket with a white oak enveloped in paper birch trees. The white oak's leaves were as red as Milena's hair and shuddered like flames in the wind. Kali wondered if her spirit rested there—if perhaps it was a doorway to her home in the Silent Place.

When she finished admiring the sunset foliage, Kali ventured farther. The woods grew heavier again, then tapered into a glade where daylight sparsely punctured the shade. Wisps with emerald petals swayed through the still air.

A willow tree unlike any she'd ever seen was nestled in the gloomy crevice. Slender branches laced together like a sprawling curtain. The willow's bole was as wide as a chariot, the world beyond it completely obscured from view. Kali's breath caught as she reached for its fluid limbs. They ran through her fingers and caressed her palms, and beneath her feet, she felt the willow's roots breathe life into the earth. They were pulsing with sentience.

She exhaled with wonder. The willow felt like her dreams—like the thrum of a hidden world teeming with fey spirits and ancient gods. They were quiet, revealing themselves only to those who listened carefully enough to hear their whispers.

Then, a crunch of leaves shattered the silence. The spell broken, Kali spun to see a dark mass moving beyond the willow's wickery branches. Sweeping them aside, she watched as the silhouette came closer; its edges sharpened into pointed ears, an open maw, raised hackles, four lithe legs, and a long, thick tail.

A black wolf was standing guard in the glade.

He circled forward as Kali backed up beneath the willow's canopy. Undeterred, the beast stalked closer until his coal-coloured nose parted the branches gilded in emerald blades. Fangs like daggers dripped with the animal's thirst as his hot breath thundered through the air. If Kali had hoped the tree would shelter her, she was mistaken. The wolf crossed the threshold, now only a modest lunge away. Two blood-red eyes pierced the darkness between them.

Swallowing down her fear, Kali focused on the willow's bark pressing into her back. This was the monster tormenting the village—the one that savaged hunters and snatched dairy goats. With dwindling milk and butter, and with the hunters yielding fewer kills, the children grew thin and hungry. And it was because of this wolf.

Decebal and Milena were dead...because of this wolf.

Yet Kali couldn't help but wonder: why was the wolf alone? Wolves lived in packs; those who broke away risked dying if they didn't find a mate.

Perhaps he's no ordinary wolf, a tiny voice chimed from within. *Perhaps he's the Viyest you're to mark for the Hollow hunters.*

Anger boiled up Kali's throat where the fear once lurked. *No.* She wouldn't be a part of that. She didn't want to end the stygian wolf's life, but she had no intention of becoming his next meal either. "I just wanted to make a basket and pick some herbs," she laughed breathily.

The wolf, suddenly appearing bored, plunked down on his haunches. Throwing his head back, he released a high-pitched squeal as he surrendered to a gaping yawn. Stunned, Kali straightened. The wolf had lost interest in her.

"It can't be," she muttered.

The wolf's ear twitched, pupils darting towards her and then back to the forest. Tail up, he lowered his head to the ground and stretched, then ambled from the glade. The border between black fur and foliage fell away as the wolf melted into the shadows like a dark mist.

The menace was gone.

❧ 32 ❧

VELIZAR

A BONE-SHATTERING scream pierced the sky. Birds fled the treetops, and the shrubbery near the mouth of the Hollow rustled as twigs snapped, branches shook, and leaves the colour of dandelions fluttered to the ground.

Out stumbled Pavel, wide-eyed and bloodied from elbows to knees, sweat and dirt painting every patch of pale, fear-stricken skin.

Bartha rushed from his workbench towards the young hunter. "Merciful gods, where have you been?" The old man caught Pavel as he collapsed like a newborn fawn, then stared into the darkness beyond the trees, waiting. "Where are Marko and Jove?"

The young man's head shook in sharp, spastic motions. Even Velizar couldn't tell if it was a willful gesture or a violent tremor.

"The wolf?" Bartha whispered, and Pavel nodded.

Heat crawled up Velizar's face. Sendoa was to leave Jove and Marko alive; they were to be witnesses to Pavel's dismemberment. Why, then, had his brother spared the dissenter?

Pavel's seething gaze found Velizar. He might've conceded that Velizar had been right; the forest was too dangerous. Yet this was no triumph. Pavel's wounded pride would be a threat to Velizar's control. What if he lashed out to restore his ego?

Moreover, the slaughter of two innocent men—men who'd volunteered to help Pavel on Velizar's behest—would only fuel the villagers' righteous anger.

"This cannot stand any longer," said Bartha. "The black wolf must be put down."

Some approached the injured Pavel, his leg mangled. Murmurs of discontent swelled. Facing the crowd, Velizar raised his hand to soothe them.

"My good people, now is not the time to act in anger—"

"Now is not the time for your sermons!" Pavel spat. "We can no longer stand idly by while this monster devours us like sheep."

"Yes, yes!" a voice cried from the growing mob.

"Who will avenge Jove and Marko? Will we leave their spirits restless and unappeased?" another challenged.

Velizar's jaw clenched. "I warned you all of the danger. Young Pavel did not heed me. Jove and Marko offered their support in goodwill, and this is the result."

"The result is always the same!" Pavel threw out his uninjured arm. "We heed your warnings, and people die. We ignore them, and people still die. All that's left is to gather our best and pierce the beast's heart with an arrow—something you've discouraged since you arrived!"

Nods of agreement. Declarations of resolve. Velizar could no longer keep track of who was defying him. He clasped his hands behind his back. "Do as you will," he said tightly, "but mark my words: more will die if you disobey."

"Is that a threat?" Pavel called. "This began with your arrival. Perhaps you're behind it."

Silence. Uncertainty.

Velizar spun on him, eyes ablaze. "A threat? Dear Pavel, if I were actually responsible for this savagery, it would be you who lies rotting in the woods, not Jove and Marko." He bore into the hunter, towering over him even from afar. "I implored you to be prudent, but you chose to ignore me, did you not? You were ill-equipped by virtue of your own ignorance, were you not? Are Jove and Marko not dead, then, because of your own boyish pride?"

The anger crumbled from Pavel's face. Nourished by the shame and guilt that replaced it, Velizar continued.

"Your choices led to this tragedy." He parted the crowd with smooth strides until he stood before the defeated hunter. "I'll not tolerate such heinous accusations from a child scrambling to shed responsibility for his actions, though I suppose it would be unreasonable to expect a boy to act with the wisdom of a man." The corner of his mouth quirked. "Worry not, Pavel. You may be too young to understand, but it is my role as your king to ensure that you learn." Velizar turned to two men. "Take him to the cellar, where he may think on his actions."

"What?" one of them balked. "He nearly died!"

"And his actions led to the death of two others!" Velizar roared. "Do we not have laws? Do we not punish those who trample on them? Or will we rely on false accusations and far-fetched conspiracies to bring peace and order?"

The two men turned to Bartha. The lines on the elder's face cut deep with worry as he glanced between Velizar and Pavel. Finally, he nodded. "Take Pavel to the cellar. His wounds will be treated, and he will be fed, but Velizar is right. Pavel was brash, and it cost us all dearly."

Pleased, Velizar smiled, but his satisfaction was short-lived.

"However," Bartha continued, "I sympathize with Pavel's frustrations. We will hunt the wolf, but we will do so out of necessity, not anger. We will ensure no more lives are lost."

Velizar stood frozen as Bartha beckoned the throng to disperse. The men led Pavel away, though not before Bartha placed a gentle hand on his shoulder.

This simply could not stand. Velizar would have absolute obedience. Even Bartha was challenging him, and it was Sendoa's fault.

He stalked toward the woods, radiating fury. Unchecked power leaked from his mortal form, and the grass withered beneath his heavy steps. Fighting to contain it, he didn't notice the figure traipsing through the trees until he crashed into her.

She cursed under her breath and reeled back from the collision. "Forgive me," she said. "The branches are so thick here."

Only when she spoke did Velizar recognize the cloaked figure of the Dreamwalker. "What were you doing in the woods?"

She raised a bundle of willow branches. "Collecting supplies."

"I see you too have chosen to defy orders."

She clutched the wicker. "Those of us not protected by the rules have no choice but to break them. The village abandoned me, so I sometimes abandon them. It's survival."

Her words struck a chord in him—one that gave rise to a peculiar medley of indignation and understanding. He loathed having anyone outside his flock, yet this one girl remained a pariah, hovering beyond his domain. Worst of all, he couldn't blame her for it.

"Take care of yourself, Dreamwalker," he said stonily, then pushed past her. He felt her probing eyes on him as he disappeared into the woods. She no doubt wondered why he was exempt from his own code. The conjecture made him smile.

He may have resented her boldness, but at least she was interesting.

VELIZAR SLOWED as he stepped into the glade. "You're ruining everything."

A growl rumbled from the shadows, followed by the grizzly crack of bones. Sendoa emerged into the clearing, dragging a dead deer behind him. "Don't be dramatic." He tossed the carcass at Velizar's feet.

"What's this?" the elder asked, his nose wrinkling in revulsion.

"A peace offering." Sendoa plopped down onto a stone. "Take it to your people."

"What?"

Sendoa leaned back and raised a brow. "You can't expect them to honour your decree if you don't feed them. They're not angry that you have laws. They're angry because your laws don't provide. No one cares about safety when they're starving, brother."

"Well, perhaps I should let *you* be their king," Velizar sneered.

A smirk crept onto Sendoa's face. Sucking deer's blood off his thumb, he ran his tongue over his teeth but said nothing more.

Velizar turned brusquely away, unable to tolerate the sight of him. Sendoa was already half-animal, unbothered by the taste of raw flesh. Velizar had hoped those unsavoury qualities would stay confined to the wolf, but he realized now how meaningless the distinction between *Sendoa the wolf* and *Sendoa the man* had become.

Ultimately, he was neither man nor wolf. He was a god, and he could take whatever form pleased him. Clearly, he preferred the beast.

Velizar raised his eyes to the colossal willow witnessing their quarrel. Its slim leaves pulsed with green life even as the surrounding foliage browned and withered. The tree's ancient roots plunged deep into the earth and through other worlds. Pieces of faraway realms flaked from it like granules of magic.

The old guardian was neither here nor there, but a doorway to everywhere.

The bundle of branches under the young woman's arm was speckled with those fey flecks; they could have only come from here. How fitting that the Dreamwalker should find the gates of the dreamscape and strip off pieces of it to weave herself a basket.

"You spared the girl," Velizar said at last.

"What girl?" the younger asked dryly.

Velizar turned to his brother. "The Dreamwalker. The one who found her way to the heart of these woods, to the sacred places no mortal should ever find."

"Does she threaten you?" Sendoa's molten gaze glinted with mockery.

"She defies me."

The beast's raffish laugh rolled through the glade like thunder. "The gravest of insults!"

"No," seethed Velizar, "but do you know what is? Having my brother spare the wretch I condemned to death while murdering those destined to behold my divine punishment."

Sendoa howled until the birds fled their roosts. "Clearly,

they weren't destined to behold your divine punishment." He grinned with menace. "I ripped their throats out."

Velizar stepped forward. "Have you any idea the trouble you've caused?"

His brother shrugged, picking dirt from under his nail. "Pavel didn't deserve to die. The other two, however—"

"I ordered him to die. Therefore, he deserved to die!"

Sendoa's good humour dissipated, his eyes gleaming red as the blood from his hands. "Your creed isn't universal, Vel. I have my own too."

"And pray, tell, what creed does a wild animal have?"

Sendoa's jaw clenched, and momentary hurt rippled across his face. "Pavel was trying to feed his family. He treaded my territory with care and respect. But those witless sons of bitches you sent with him were too stupid to live."

Velizar gnashed his teeth. "I counted on their stupidity, Sen. I needed those witless sons of bitches to cement my rule. Pavel is what threatens it."

"And the girl, apparently."

"Why didn't you kill her?" Velizar demanded, incensed by Sendoa's gibing. "You know what she's capable of."

"She's harmless," his brother scoffed. "She came looking for food and wicker. I may be a god of destruction, but ending a helpless girl's life serves no purpose. I destroy the old so that the new can flourish. And that girl is *not* old, in body or belief."

"She represents old beliefs."

"The Hollow's beliefs," Sendoa corrected, then chuckled, his gaze turning to the willow. "She looked me dead in the eye and said she just wanted to make a damn basket. How could I say no? You don't often stumble upon a woman willing to face off with a devil."

"You're too easily impressed." Velizar sighed and rubbed

the bridge of his nose. "The hunters will come for you. I cannot stop them."

"Let them," he welcomed the challenge.

"You will ruin everything I've worked to build with your flippancy!"

Sendoa strode up to Velizar and bared his teeth, his snarl low and seething. "The Hollow may be your kingdom, but the forest is mine. Here, I decide who lives and who dies. Here, my law presides. Not yours."

Immobilized by the destroyer's ferocity, Velizar took a meager step back. Although he was the conniving of the two, Sendoa was the force that snapped what couldn't be bent.

"Very well," Velizar relented. "But I warn you, brother, this cannot end well. The way of beasts is inferior to the rule created by higher minds."

"Save your warnings for fearful men," said Sendoa. "I am only a beast, after all. What do I know besides teeth and blood?"

Velizar's thoughts slowed as something dawned on him then, and he offered a careful smile. "How right you are, brother. How right you are."

"EKALIYA," Bartha implored sombrely, "We need you."

Velizar stood in the corner of the elder's longhouse, the warm glow of guttering candles leaving shadows dancing on the timber walls. Although Velizar still sulked over his loss of authority, he'd managed to maintain his calm façade. He watched quietly as Bartha and the Dreamwalker faced one another, each of them rigid as their dying beliefs.

"I don't see how I can help you." She pretended to be

oblivious, but Velizar saw through the act. She knew what she was. She'd known all her life.

Bartha sighed and leaned on his walking stick. He tossed a scrap of grouse to his mouser cat, its thick winter coat signalling the impending freeze. Outside, the clouds hung heavy with unfallen snow. Their looming presence served as an ominous reminder that the Viyest remained unhunted. "Let us dispel with the lies. You are Milena's successor; you are the Dreamwalker. Hence, you are the only one capable of finding the beast that torments the Hollow. The black wolf is...not of this world. He must be the Viyest."

"I'm not convinced," said Kali, smoothing her dark ash-brown hair over her shoulder. "In fact, I've met this wolf—the one responsible for the deaths."

Bartha straightened, his knee buckling as he clutched his staff more tightly. "You what!"

"If I'm the Dreamwalker, then you ought to listen to me. I say the Viyest only wants to live free of our bloodthirst. What if your traditions have birthed a vengeful spirit? What if it's merely striking back?"

Flames of fury licked at Velizar's ribs. *This arrogant wench. Who does she think she is?*

Just then, her murky green eyes turned on him, piercing him like a dull blade. Had she somehow read his thoughts? Just how deep did her power run?

Fear vised around his throat. How many times had she rendezvoused with Sendoa? His treacherous brother had spared his greatest enemy, and Bartha was now turning to her for aid, ignoring Velizar as though he were a broken tool that'd ceased to be useful.

The Dreamwalker was chaos incarnate. His brother was destruction made manifest. They must have been in leagues. Even if they didn't know or intend it, they were natural allies. Together, chaos and destruction would erode order—everything Velizar had sacrificed to create.

He'd never anticipated the scathing love affair that could result from destruction flirting with chaos. What did they care if they unravelled all that was good in the world?

They were drawn to each other, and their union spelled Velizar's demise.

"Bartha," Velizar cleared his throat. "What if I could lead you to the beast?"

Bartha frowned. "You know I love you as my own son, but the people have lost faith in your methods, Velizar."

"Then let me restore their faith," he beseeched. "How many have died in pursuit of the black wolf?" He pushed himself off the wall and brought a solemn fist to his chest. "I promise I've not been idle. I've taken steps to locate the wolf's den."

From the corner of his eye, Velizar saw the Dreamwalker's disdain melt into shock. He resisted the smile tickling the corners of his mouth. "I know where the wolf is," he insisted. "I can lead the hunters there and have the beast killed once and for all."

The Dreamwalker opened her mouth but was silenced by Bartha's hand on her arm. "Girl, if you will not help, then at least do not interfere."

"You're making a mistake." She tore her arm away, heading for the door. She stopped next to Velizar. "That wolf is no monster," she said loudly enough for all to hear. "We're the monsters."

Sweeping her cloak aside and throwing on the hood, she stormed out the door, no doubt heading for the forest.

"I-I apologize," Bartha stammered. "Ekaliya has always had a temper."

"Judgmental little thing," Velizar said, unfazed. "I would not place my trust in someone so erratic, Bartha."

"Yes," the elder bowed his head, "you're right."

Velizar rested his hand on Bartha's shoulder. "I promise to rid you of this beast. It won't take another life. That is my oath to you."

The Hollow elder peered up at him in awe. Velizar had been a fool to trust Sendoa, but he was sure this would win him back the Hollow, restore order, and reinstate him as the rightful king.

He was sure because he really meant what he said.

The black wolf was destined to die.

KAI

KAI SHIVERED from the biting cold, his heart sinking with burdens from lifetimes he didn't remember. As the spectres of ancient history finally faded, he resurfaced exactly where he'd gone under: on the islet in the black lake. The Grey Gnarl loomed over him, mocking him.

But the tree wasn't the only fossil lurking nearby.

"You fucking killed me," Kai wheezed. "You sicced the villagers on me."

Your time had come, Velizar responded. **To maintain order, I needed to be rid of the monster. Fear had escalated to anger.**

"So, you *killed* me."

The Hollow would never have trusted me otherwise. I did it because *you* weren't doing your job. You began protecting instead of destroying. You aligned yourself with that wench. You cornered me, left me no choice!

"You're unhinged," Kai growled. "I made a friend, and

you seriously thought it was some scheme to overthrow you, so you *killed* me."

You would have been reborn anyway, Velizar dismissed. **It was only right, given your betrayal, your sabotage.**

"Are you fucking kidding?" Kai dug his fingers into the mossy, wet earth and fought to stand, but his limbs bent like old rubber. He collapsed to his knees, his pulse racing from the strain. He considered using the elm for support but decided against it. He was sure it wanted him dead as much as Rusalka did. "Sounds like I was done playing Big Bad Wolf for you."

You scorned my creation! Velizar bellowed, rattling the inside of Kai's skull like a set of iron marbles. **I ushered in a halcyon, and you spat on it! You valued your little forest more than my world of men!**

"I believe you!" Kai shouted back. "Fuck your world of men, you elitist prick."

Velizar scoffed. **You loved the girl precisely because you knew she was an interloper in my flock. Your affection for her nearly destroyed me. *She* nearly destroyed me. You left me no choice but to let them have you.**

"Love?" Kai spat. "I met her once!"

It was enough.

"You really believe your own bullshit, huh?" Kai choked on a laugh, his breaths ragged. "I didn't want to be your lackey, and you thought it was a betrayal."

You were my partner. My brother.

"I was a tool that grew legs and fucked off!" Kai's voice cracked. His mouth was parched, his throat sore like he'd been screaming for days.

You were an unpredictable variable, Velizar said calmly. **And you needed to be eliminated.**

"I—"

I'm not yet finished, brother. Restrain yourself.

Paralyzed, Kai fought the takeover to no avail. The air fled his lungs like he'd taken a kick to the gut, and the darkness overcame him. Velizar was older, stronger. He'd waited centuries to tell his story, and no amount of protest would spare Kai from his Lifetime special.

Trapped and desolate, Kai squeezed his eyes shut and waited. His last fading thought as the blackness consumed him was that he missed Miya. God, he missed her more than anything in the world.

He just wanted her to know how sorry he was.

❧ 34 ❧

KALI

CRISP AUTUMN AIR spilled over Kali's face; winter was an icy breath away.

The village was quiet with pungent suspicion. The Hollow had decided—or rather, Velizar had decided—the black wolf would replace the Viyest. All the able-bodied men and women armed themselves for the hunt. Having refused to help locate their prey, venomous stares pierced Kali from every direction. She wrapped herself in her dark cloak and hid amidst the trees near the mouth of the Hollow, watching from the safety of the periphery.

Velizar stood at the town square, drawing the people to him with his otherworldly magnetism. Kali had known from the start that he was something from someplace else. He didn't belong. In this regard, she supposed they weren't so different, but that was where the similarities ended.

"I know I've been resistant to the Hollow's traditions," he began, waiting for more to gather. "But if there's such a thing as the Viyest, and if there is sincerely a Dreamwalker

283

among you, then is it not the Dreamwalker who has doomed you?" Eyes dancing with malice, he cast his callous gaze on Kali, somehow finding her amid the camouflage. "By refusing her duty to the Hollow, even after the elder's insistence, has she not betrayed you? Or perhaps there is no duty for her to shirk? Perhaps she is a witch crushing the Hollow under her curse."

Nods of consensus followed. Some of the hunters scanned the border as though sensing Kali nearby. She retreated further into the maze, biting down the bile as her stomach churned. Bitterness and treachery coalesced into an overpowering wave of nausea. Velizar had turned the village against her. Not that they'd ever needed much convincing. She had never been welcome; Velizar had simply given them the excuse they'd always wanted.

Spite settled in her spine as anger cauterized the hurt, sewing it shut like hot iron on wounded flesh. But beneath it all, she felt an overwhelming urge to escape— to run from those leers that cut her whenever she walked by.

Only when Velizar retreated and the hunters marched into the woods did Kali spot Lana among the scattering mob.

Things were different between them now. Kali was the Hollow's defected Dreamwalker—a choice Lana would never forgive.

The fortunes of their friendship mirrored the dwindling warmth of summer.

Pain rippled across Kali's chest as she noticed that Lana's belly had swelled; her friend was with child after all. Was she wrong to protect the wolf? Had she denied Bartha's plea out of conceit, or worse, a malevolent desire to see the Hollow consumed by what it hunted?

"Kali!" Lana called when she caught her skulking by a

barren pear tree, then sauntered over with a water pail in hand. "What are you doing here?"

"Watching, I suppose. The hunters have all gone." Kali was surprised by how solemn she sounded.

"Velizar was right to rally them," said Lana. "I don't know how he found the black wolf, but I'm glad he did."

Kali swallowed like she had nettles prickling her tongue. "He's only speaking the Hollow's language now to win favour back. He doesn't care for the Viyest."

Lana shrugged. "I'd rather have a king who adapts to his people's needs."

"He's not a king, Lana. He's a man who thinks his piss is wine."

Lana clutched the pail so hard one of her nails chipped against the craggy wood. "You mock him, Ekaliya, yet you're the reason the black wolf continues to kill. You refused to succeed Milena."

Kali raked her fingers through her hair, tugging hard enough to tear out a small tangle. "Velizar has scant faith in the Dreamwalker. He called it superstition."

"Even so," Lana's voice rose, "you were born and raised here. Velizar didn't believe because he was an outsider. But you...you should know better." Her next words came quiet but deadly. "He asked us to consider what kind of a person would refuse the duty bestowed by her people."

"You...agree with him," Kali realized aloud. "You think he's right about me."

Lana placed a hand over her growing belly, her russet eyes seething like embers. "By helping the wolf, you're only making the Hollow a more dangerous place."

Kali shook her head. "Refusing to be the Hollow's puppet doesn't make me responsible for every bad thing that happens. You're acting as if I conjured the damn beast."

A. J. VRANA

"That's certainly what Velizar thinks."

"You can't really believe that," Kali's voice broke. "How do you know it wasn't Velizar's doing? All of this started right before he arrived!"

Lana hesitated, then said, "You've always hated the Hollow. Even though you mask it with cold criticism, your contempt bleeds right through. Decebal and Milena are dead because of the wolf, and you'll be to blame for all those who'll die in this hunt."

"How can you—"

"You're the Dreamwalker," Lana hissed. Where the title was once revered, it suddenly sounded like a slur. "You're the only person who can guide the hunters to the Viyest. Those who perish will do so because you refused to lead them!"

"The black wolf is not the Viyest," Kali insisted.

"Even so! That wolf is a harbinger of death, a destroyer. And you—our conduit to the other realms—won't lift a finger to stop it! You *are* responsible!"

Kali folded her hands in front of her to keep them from trembling. Her pulse hammered in her ears and her throat worked, half-formed words stumbling from her lips. *How did it get like this?*

Lana set her jaw, her reservations gone. "You're not like us, Ekaliya. You never have been. Velizar is different too, but at least he's trying to better us. You want nothing less than our suffering—maybe even our downfall. That's why you care for this wolf. You want him to hurt us. To punish us. You have a grudge, and it's poisoned our home."

The itch to flee beat against Kali's ribs until she thought her insides might splinter. Whirling in confusion, she bolted into the woods—anything to escape the Hollow. This warren, lost in a sea of dark green, had become her prison.

With her cloak covering her from head to toe, she blended in like a shadow at dusk. Yet no matter how far she went, she couldn't outrun her fear that Lana was right: Kali favoured her grudge over her best friend. The wolf had slain Lana's husband and brought their people to the brink of famine. Why did Kali continue to defend the killer? Maybe she *did* want to punish the village for what they'd done to her family.

Kali's foot clipped a winding root that slithered above ground. The sharp pain sent her colliding into a nearby tree, branches nicking her cheek. Reaching up, she felt the thin cut well with blood.

No, a voice rebuked inside her. *The Hollow's cruelty is not a thing of the past. They marked you from birth, so you'd never be their equal. They've given you no reason to help them.*

But Lana had sacrificed for her. Why couldn't Kali sacrifice in turn?

Because, the voice replied, *Lana is wrong. You can't save the Hollow from the wolf. No one can.*

Indeed, the wolf wasn't the problem; Kali knew this in her bones. Velizar had done more to harm the Hollow than Kali ever could, yet she was being blamed.

The sound of heavy footfalls and shouting severed Kali from her turmoil. Realizing the hunters were nearby, she scrambled into the shrubs until the voices faded. Brittle autumn leaves caught on her wool cloak as she crumpled to the ground, dizzy with relief. She didn't want to be seen anywhere near the hunt.

Between tattered breaths, Kali caught the whine of an animal from somewhere nearby. She stilled, holding the air in her lungs until the cry cut through her senses a second time. Kali perused her surroundings but didn't recognize a thing, so she wandered in the direction of the plea, her limbs igniting with excitement. Trapped in a labyrinth made of twisted roots and arching spurs, she had no inkling of how to find her way back. Finally, she was lost.

Kali moseyed on into thickening underbrush and weaved through a grove of crooked oaks. As she traversed the verdant maze, the treetops blotted out the apricot sky. She ducked under a far-reaching bough and stepped into a dimly lit glade streaked with the cinders of a waning sun.

The grand willow awaited her, and beneath its emerald shade, she glimpsed a dark mass bundled against the trunk.

Kali swept aside the swaying stems and fell into the shadows.

A black wolf lay under the canopy. The earth was painted rusty red as blood pooled around him, matting his thick fur. He'd been pierced by a hunter's blade, his chest rising and falling so slowly that Kali could hear her own heart pounding between each breath.

The black wolf was dying.

As the life seeped out of him, despair poured into all the hidden places Kali had kept shielded from her hatred of the Hollow—the corners of her heart where the darkness didn't reach, where she'd hoped something good would write itself onto that blank space.

Would she allow the Hollow to steal everything from her? She was the Dreamwalker; the hunters were supposed to depend on her, not the other way around. If she was as powerful as they claimed, if she could truly conjure stygian beasts and wreak havoc with little more than the will to say *no*, what chaos could she rain with the spite to say *yes*...

...*Yes*, the black wolf was dying, but he wasn't dead yet.

35

MIYA

MIYA FELT the wolf's coarse black fur tickling her palm. It was like she was right there with him, sharing in his final moments. She remembered now—getting lost in the woods and finding the wolf. She'd dreamt it in this life and lived it in so many others.

"Gavran," she spoke the boy's name with more certainty now, then gazed up at the ancient redwood. "The Red Knot is your home. It's close to the Emerald Shade, where I found the wolf."

"Yes," he nodded, something sad and lonely colouring the grooves of his face. "You always find the black wolf."

Miya twined her fingers together. They felt cold, but more like her own. The fog had thinned, specs of rose-coloured light streaming through from the distance. "The wolf was the king's brother."

Gavran blinked. "You remember?"

"The wolf told me after I healed him," she recalled. "When he led me home."

"You were so lost," Gavran cackled. "Like a carpenter in a quarry."

Miya reached out as though tracing the wolf's invisible silhouette. "He helped me find my way back. To thank me." She frowned then, the pieces mismatched. "But he was dying. How did I heal him?"

"You're the Dreamwalker," Gavran reminded her. "All you needed was the spite to say *yes*."

Miya didn't understand, but she figured she didn't have to...not yet, anyway.

The boy grinned ear to ear. "He was so angry when he realized his brother had sent the hunters to butcher him as a prize."

"He was hurt."

"Anger is nothing more than hurt with teeth." Gavran's jaw sliced open, eyes wide like perfectly round pools of ink.

Miya settled back against the Red Knot. "I want to remember more." With each tale the boy told her, the fear that'd been wax on her skin peeled away.

"And you will." Gavran nestled into his feathery robe, his eyes suddenly distant. "You will."

✣ 36 ✣

KALI

As KALI FUMBLED towards the Hollow, the woods at her back, every inch of her screamed to stop, to return to the wolf. When she couldn't bear it any longer, she glanced over her shoulder to see him standing on the precipice of their two worlds—the peripheral row of trees a barrier between his realm and Velizar's. Ears erect and tail stiff, he watched her with uncanny attention. Was he making sure to fulfill his promise and safely deliver the Dreamwalker home? Or was he considering his next move—plotting revenge against the people who'd nearly killed him?

Kali now knew a truth she'd suspected all along: The Hollow's beliefs had the substance of mud. There was no Viyest, and Velizar was no king. The black wolf that terrorized the Hollow was a god of destruction and Velizar, his brother, a god of creation. The creator was conniving and cruel, and the destroyer capable of gratitude and compassion.

How upside-down the world was.

Kali ripped herself free from the wolf's gaze and stared at Bartha's lodge up ahead. She could hear laughter booming from inside. The villagers were no doubt celebrating, believing their tormenter to be slain.

Kali slunk into her parents' ramshackle like a wisp, the door creaking loudly as she scuttled inside. Peeping through the cracks in the shutters, she found the world outside wholly still save for the smoke rising from Bartha's chimney and the cheer roaring from inside his longhouse.

Kali retreated from the window and crawled into her hay bed. Wrapping herself in a purple blanket she'd knitted from goat's wool and dyed in blackberry mash, her eyelids drifted shut. Her feet ached, and her muscles were sore; it felt like she'd been in those woods for days. As exhaustion settled into her bones, the late autumn chill subsided, and Kali felt the pull of slumber drag her down, deep into the dream.

IN THE SLIVER between waking and sleep, Kali heard the wind sing. Or so she thought. The bellowing gale transformed into something else, something living.

A wolf howled—mournful, harrowing. At first, it was far away, beckoning from another world. Then it was closer, louder, until the cries reverberated within the walls of Kali's home.

She awoke with a gasp. Sweat slicked her skin, and damp hair clung to her neck. She expected quiet after her restless visions, but the howls suddenly resumed.

Bolting upright, Kali clambered out of bed. Through the shutters, she glimpsed firelight peppering the darkness. Several figures rushed by as shouting ensued, but the howls continued, drowning out the clamour.

Kali threw on her cloak and burst outside. Cressets flickered from the shallows of the forest, and commotion collected around Bartha's longhouse. A crowd had amassed, and as Kali approached, she saw women weeping. Their fear-stricken expressions were trained on something at their feet. Throwing on her hood and lowering her head, Kali pushed past them.

At the center of the throng lay Velizar's lifeless body. The king's head appeared disjointed from his neck; his throat was ripped open, viscera spattered around him like a bloody crown. His eyes were glassy and blank, his blue lips parted as death stole the colour from his skin.

"Gods," Kali breathed out, taken aback by the grizzly sight. Whatever had done this had intended to savage and kill, not eat. It was like the culprit wanted to crush Velizar's greatest weapon: his voice.

Kali dragged her eyes to the bone-coloured moon, the midnight sky an abyss behind its pale glow. She knew who'd done this.

"It was the black wolf!" a hunter proclaimed.

"That's not possible," Bartha wheezed from the entryway of his longhouse as icy winds whistled all around them. "The black wolf is dead. Velizar led the hunters...they killed him!"

"I saw the corpse with my own eyes!" someone shouted.

"I pierced its belly with my sword!" said another.

From the corner of her eye, Kali caught Pavel hobbling towards the ruckus. He was free of the cellar, but his broken leg was still healing. He watched from a distance, then glimpsed Kali's way. Without a word, he retreated into his home.

Then, from deep in the woods, a howl rang out like a war cry, shattering the villagers' confusion and driving them into a panic.

A. J. VRANA

"The wolf lives," Bartha realized. With a grief-stricken sob, he collapsed against his doorframe as several villagers rushed to his aid. "It's a demon...a demon from the underbelly of the Silent Place."

"It's the Dreamwalker," one of the women hissed. "She was missing from the village when the hunters went into the woods."

"She brought the beast back with her! And who knows what else!"

Fear clawed up Kali's throat as every pair of eyes in the wretched night turned on her. For once, they were right. The wolf lived because of her.

Before they could hurl another accusation, a woman shrieked from across the Hollow.

"Help! Please!"

Kali spun towards the plea, recognizing the voice. "Lana!" she called out, then rushed past Velizar.

Lana's family was already there, holding the widow's arms as she sank to her knees. Her father barred Kali's path.

"Stay back, witch!" He threw his arms out, and several other men gripped the hafts of their blades.

Kali skidded to a halt, shock coiling around her limbs. *Witch?*

"I mean no harm," she declared, but they allowed her no further.

"You've done enough." Bartha grabbed her shoulder from behind, tugging her back. "Go home, Ekaliya. You're not needed here."

Kali tried to look past the bodies blocking her view, but all she saw was the earth around Lana darkening with blood.

Surrendering to Bartha's pull, she headed back to her cabin. The howls persisted in the distance, but the hunters had given up their search.

Kali buried herself under her blanket and waited for the

294

wolf's sorrowful song to stop. It didn't. The aching call wrenched at her heart, echoing her loneliness. Was he searching for her? Did he miss her? Was he telling her where to find him?

Or perhaps it wasn't that at all. Perhaps he simply mourned the death of his brother.

***

A DARK PRESENCE clung to Kali as she descended into a nightmare. A shadow—viscous like black smoke—spooled around every home in the Hollow. The villagers breathed it in like a sweet fragrance, intoxicated by its rancor. Whenever Kali tried to banish the shadow, it retreated into the woods. As it lurked behind a tree, two gleaming aurous eyes bore into her.

It was watching her, waiting to strike.

***

KALI COULD NO LONGER SEPARATE her dreams from her waking moments. She thought the entity, like the howls that came before it, were conjured only in her sleep, yet the phantom crept from Kali's dreams and into the sunlit world. The soil had hardened with frost, mirroring the villagers' hearts. Their gazes clouded with malice, and the shadow's grip tightened. Two weeks passed, but the miasma of suspicion did not abate. The shadow grew claws that sunk deep into the hunters' minds, puppeteering them like marionettes.

Even in death, Velizar continued to reign.

Some demanded Kali's life in retribution. Bartha held them at bay, if only by a thinning thread. Another seven days passed before Kali was permitted to see Lana.

She sat up in bed and fisted the covers resting over her

belly. Her skin was lily-white, her russet eyes guarded as she watched Kali enter the room lit only with a guttering candle.

"Lana, are you well?"

"My womb is empty," her whisper lashed through the air.

Kali had suspected as much when she saw blood soaking the ground between Lana's knees.

"Well?" Lana hissed.

"Well, what?"

"Did you do it?" Lana's knuckles drained of colour as she gripped the fabrics.

Kali sighed. "You'll have to be more specific. I've been accused of quite a few crimes."

Lana whipped the blankets off her legs. She was still bleeding, crimson life pooling at the front of her muslin gown and staining the sheet beneath her. Rage seized her and she screamed, "Did you trade my child's life for the wolf's!"

Kali was calm as a lake in winter. "And what if I did? You didn't want the child to be a cruel reminder of Decebal's death, but it was, wasn't it?" She took a step forward, and Lana jolted with fear. "I've seen the truth."

Lana drew her knees to her chest, inching back. "What are you talking about?"

Something tugged at Kali's lips—a morose, bitter smile. "Your heart was left with no way to speak, so it revealed its most dreaded desire in the only place it could."

Lana shivered as the season of the dead announced its arrival with an icy gale, battering the windows like a longing ghost. "And where's that?"

Kali waited until the silence grew unbearable, until Lana finally met her stormy gaze. "In your dreams," she answered. "Or perhaps it was a nightmare."

Lana's hostility moulted like snakeskin, and raw terror glistened in its place as grief threatened to implode.

The ground beneath their friendship had finally fissured and collapsed.

Kali had nothing left to tether her to the Hollow. She was entirely bereft. Every drop of love bled out of her, and the absence left behind was more than a mere emptiness; it was a living presence, and it consumed every crevice of her heart. Without a word, Kali turned and abandoned Lana to the pieces of her broken life.

THAT NIGHT, Kali barred her door. She would have already gone if not for the bitter cold. With the forest soon to be blanketed in white, she couldn't possibly survive outside the Hollow on her own, so she stayed in her hovel, protected only by the villagers' fear of her. When they slept, she ventured outside to scavenge for sustenance and returned before dawn. As the weeks wore on and the forest slumbered under snow like ashen dust, Kali's cheeks grew sunken, her hands became frail, and her ribs stuck to her skin. Two moons passed, and the silvered earth finally browned with mud.

The Hollow knew her time had come. Kali slipped on her hooded cloak and traipsed towards the mouth of the village. A mob awaited there, holding up torches and gibbering prayers as she approached.

"Dreamwalker," they dared utter.

"Dreamwalker," they broke into cries.

"Dreamwalker," they cursed with venom.

Once they'd needed her. Now they damned her. They spat on the ground she trod upon, but none dared approach. Their courage had evaporated with the loss of their leader and their once blessed seer having turned on them.

The shadow with golden eyes was there too, gliding from one villager to the next, whispering dark temptations in their ears. Soon, they'd be frothing like wild dogs.

Kali paid them no mind. She'd made her decision. While Velizar had once sought control and order, his lurking shadow now infected the Hollow with the only thing he actually knew how to create: fear.

But she would not be afraid.

She would not be controlled.

She would not be subdued.

She was the Dreamwalker. Of all the horrors the Hollow had hunted to sate their hunger for blood, she was the only one left that had teeth. She was the only one that was real.

37

KAI

TRAPPED IN THE NIGHTMARISH FABLE, Kai locked onto his brother's face. Velizar's lips twisted into a sneer, and his eyes widened with something between hatred and dismay. Kai's teeth—sharpened to kill—rent through the king's soft flesh, and his strangled scream died in his mouth as they both bathed in scarlet.

Horror seized him the moment his brother's pulse slowed, the seconds yawning out between each waning thud. Kai fought to wrest himself from Sendoa's memories, to shake the empathy ensnaring him, but it was too late. Velizar's death was already on his hands.

This was how it felt when he cut into Rusalka's heart.

Tremors wracked Kai's body. His muscles seized as fire seared up his esophagus until he began to choke on something thick and metallic—Velizar's blood. He coughed and coughed and then laughed and laughed and laughed. His lungs burned and his shoulders shook, but he couldn't suppress the damn laughter no matter how hard he tried.

"*I got* you, fucker!" His eyes opened to the dead grey sky. "You killed me, and what'd you get for it? A mangled throat." The triumphant declaration was a tin-foil shield against the invading grief. *That's not your shit*, he told himself. *You aren't Sendoa.*

She was the reason you survived. The reason I died. I failed the Hollow, and you, dear brother, ended me for it.

"Rightly so, you sadistic fuck." Kai sat up and rubbed his face. He should've been elated by the sweet retribution, but Sendoa's regret dithered in his chest.

Yes, you killed me, but in doing so, you gave me exactly what I needed.

Kai's heart sank like a stone. *The shadow.* It'd been there three years ago when he knifed his way through swaths of rabid townsfolk. It was in the doctor's dreams; it must have been there in the beginning too.

With my mortal coils cast off, I was finally free. The phantom's voice turned syrupy sweet. **You showed me a better way, brother. You taught me that control over men means nothing when you yourself are a mere man. My final acts before my spirit succumbed to the wretched cycle of rebirth were surely my finest.**

"You turned the town against her," Kai realized.

Yes, cooed Velizar. **And the good people of the Hollow cast her out for it.**

"No," Kai shook his head, tightening his stomach to keep the knot from rising. "She chose to leave because there was nothing left for her there. She went back into the woods for me and left the Hollow behind."

Velizar rumbled low like thunder, **And *the cycle* has continued ever since.**

"Seriously?" Kai's guilt evaporated like a fart in the wind.

"It wasn't enough that you turned everyone against her, made life so unbearable that she opted to fuck off into the woods and take her chances there?"

I wanted the witch gone, Velizar spat. **I wanted them to expel her like the infection she was. And then I wanted her to disappear. I wanted her forgotten.**

A smirk crawled up the side of Kai's face. "But they didn't forget, did they?"

No, Velizar confessed. **They didn't.**

❧ 38 ❧

VELIZAR

VELIZAR never truly left the Hollow. Although his body lay buried in the ground, his essence poured from his flesh and blood, soaked into the earth, and ascended like vapour.

Gods were hardly omnipotent forces ruling the skies and seas. They were living spirits, their mortal containers the very personification of ideas, of pure want. And only the fleeting beauty of impermanence made that want worthwhile.

When Velizar rose from the tainted soil, the Hollow looked different. Where he once saw bodies made of meat and bone, he now perceived collections of colours, each hue a different desire, every shade a new dream. Some shimmered with hope while others blanched with fear.

He could tug on those dyed human threads to bring out the tones he wanted and drown out the ones he didn't. He drew them in, absorbed them until he became all colours condensed into one. He was the myriad brought to order. He was the abyss where no light could penetrate.

Then there was the Dreamwalker. Her colour was not like the others. There were no clear boundaries between her shades of fear and the tinctures of hope and want. She was iridescent, the shine of her multitudes blinding him to her threads. Or perhaps there were no threads for him to manipulate. Sometimes, he caught glimpses of violet and black swirling like oil in water, but every time he reached for her, she slipped right through his fingers. It was like grasping at smoke.

He turned his attention to the villagers instead. First, there was Lana—the sweet, heart-broken widow whose belly now ached with emptiness. She spilled slate-blue grief that blurred the contours of her longing. Her desire shuddered helplessly like burnt orange grass in an arid summer wind.

He took hold of that dust-coloured grief and pulled. It blossomed like a dark dahlia, consuming Lana until she stumbled to the edge of the Hollow and cried to the woods that'd stolen everything from her.

She stopped eating and sleeping, and then the speaking went. When family and friends tried talking sense into her, she'd lash out in waves of grey and copper that swarmed her surroundings, repelling loved ones until they stopped trying to reach her.

The villagers whispered that she'd gone mad. Save for the occasional visit from her mother, who brought fresh milk and flowers, the Hollow hunters abandoned her to her isolation.

As for those hunters...they were toys to be toiled with, their sticky yellow-green pride slopping off like sludge. Their colours were the easiest to skew—the most satisfying to paint with. Pride was so easily warped into shame, its vibrance fading to something sickly like moulding straw. One could not exist without the other.

Velizar slid his slick, shadowy hands over the hunters' bile-coloured conceit and shook it loose. **I'm still here,** he hummed. **Your king still lives.**

He wanted them to remember him; he wanted them to be ashamed for forgetting, for moving on, but in the fragile border between Velizar's world and that of the hunters, something had gotten lost. Where he declared his presence, they saw only hers—the Dreamwalker's. They grew paranoid beyond his desire, believing she lurked in the woods, waiting for the right time to strike.

I am here! Velizar bellowed, yet all they understood was that *she* was here.

The Hollow had forgotten their king, but they remembered their monster.

Velizar had expended so much energy villainizing the Dreamwalker to solidify his rule. Now, she was etched in the Hollow's memory. Trauma, it seemed, was a remarkably enduring scar.

Enraged by the Hollow's insolence, Velizar plucked at the strings of the hunters' paranoia. If they worried the Dreamwalker was watching them, he would make them sure that she was.

He had the perfect scapegoat.

Go to the woods, he whispered to Lana in her bleakest moments. **Confront the beast that robbed you of your life—your love, your child, your friend.**

And so she did. She wandered the woods for days, slashing at the trees and tripping over rocks in a half-wake frenzy.

"It's the Dreamwalker," her mother cried when she returned, clothes torn and face bruised. "She's taken hold of my girl! She's haunting us!"

The more Lana wandered the woods at Velizar's command, the more ill she became. Her father began to wonder if perhaps the husk lying in his daughter's bed wasn't his daughter at all. Perhaps she was something else.

"There's nothing left of her," Lana's father sobbed to Bartha. "She's a thrall—the Dreamwalker's thrall." He braved a glance at his emaciated daughter, who sat slumped in the corner. "Look at her! I don't even recognize her."

Yes, Velizar goaded them. **She's been consumed, her spirit corrupted. The Dreamwalker has possessed Lana and will take her cloying soul. Were they not friends? Your rebellious daughter ignored your warnings since girlhood. She took pity on that witch, and now she's been overtaken by her. Her own foolishness is to blame.**

"She never listened to me," her father spat. He slammed his fist on the table, spilling Bartha's ale. "I told her...years ago I told her...that orphaned brat was trouble. But she didn't listen. Even after she married, she didn't listen. She's always sympathized with the witch. Now the witch has her."

Bartha hesitated, but he was too old and frail to oppose the overpowering will of a bereaved father. "You're certain?"

"We must do this." Lana's father took up the old man's leathery hands, and Velizar wove their ashen fear into a knot. "We must purge the Dreamwalker, or my daughter's soul will be lost. She'll never find her way to the Silent Place."

Bartha's eyes sunk to the floor. "Your wife will not consent."

"She'll see reason," Lana's father insisted. "She must." He dropped Bartha's hands and sat back. "There's only one way. We must destroy the Dreamwalker's thrall."

If Velizar was capable of smiling, he would've grinned like a child plucking the legs off an ant. Lana had become the village's stand-in for the Dreamwalker, and once she was gone, they'd finally remember their king.

LOST TO MADNESS, Lana didn't fight them. They dragged her to the village square and tied her to the totem of the Viyest—an ironic place to die. Her mother had been barred in the house, her screams piercing the walls as she threw herself at the door. Desperation like an indigo storm cascaded from the seams. The poppy milk and valerian tea had done little to soothe her, but Velizar didn't want her to be soothed.

None of them deserved it.

Lana may have been too far gone to fight, but Velizar made sure she screamed through her death since he couldn't during his own.

When the smoke rose and the smell of broiling flesh descended upon the Hollow, Velizar felt his spirit grow calm. Lana's pleas were rose-coloured melodies, melting him into the earth. He was a part of the Hollow. This wretched place would always be his home.

Barely a moon passed before Lana's mother walked into the woods and didn't return, leaving only a fading wisteria trail behind her. Her body was never found, likely carried by the river somewhere the hunters couldn't reach. With Lana's death, Velizar had hoped the initial paranoia he'd instilled in the villagers would subside, but it only intensified following the disappearance of her mother.

How Velizar loathed the Dreamwalker. How he loathed the Hollow for immortalizing her. She left willingly, but she'd never quite gone. Now that she was lost to the woods —possibly with his brother—she was out of his control. She undermined him even in her absence. She was an affront to his order.

It was untenable.

The Dreamwalker had a legacy; Velizar had a grave. He was nothing but a forgotten leader.

He'd become a victim of the Dreamwalker's myth.

Powerless, all Velizar had left was the Hollow's fear. Although he'd been the one to spark it, it was now out of his control—a self-perpetuating monstrosity. He couldn't squash it, but what if he could channel it?

He would have the villagers hunt her.

He would have them kill her.

He would have them kill the black wolf.

Then, he would finally be free.

✿ 39 ✿

KALI

A SILHOUETTE LINGERED beneath the ancient willow's cool shade. The figure sat relaxed against the trunk, one leg drawn to his chest and the other splayed lazily against the spring earth. With his elbow slung atop his knee, he lifted his head as Kali parted the wispy branches and entered his dark abode.

"Had you taken any longer, you would've only found bones," he said dryly.

Kali's pulse hammered all the way down her throat. He was no wolf. "Winter was long. I had no choice."

"Mm." His arm slipped off his knee as he rose smoothly. "I forget how fragile your kind is."

Kali fought to stem the tremor in her voice. "My kind? Then what are you, wolf?"

Light streamed through the treetops, stippling the dusky dwelling. As he stepped towards her, the shadows lifted to reveal a rakish smile.

Kali stumbled back, preparing to run from the familiar

face. It had to be a trick. She was seeing a ghost—one that'd stolen any semblance of joy from her life.

His brow arched, then settled as understanding flashed across his red-tinged eyes. They were deep and warm like burnt clay, completely unlike the gleaming gold of Velizar's callous stare.

He threw his head back and laughed raucously. "Do I look too much like my brother?"

"Almost," Kali managed.

"My name is Sendoa," he said.

She took him in slowly, carefully.

Although the brothers were of similar height, the way each carried himself was a difference of stillness and storm. Velizar's robes had been immaculate as they flowed from neck to toes, his hair meticulously tied back, not a strand out of place. Meanwhile, his brother's unruly mane whipped freely with the wind, and he revealed every scar that Velizar would've hidden under clean linens. His warrior's frame was clad only in trousers made of animal hide and a leather harness for the blades on his back. He seemed unbothered by the elements, and even less so by his immodesty.

Though they clearly shared the same unnerving confidence, Velizar's mannerisms had always been regal: controlled, calculated, and reticent. The red-eyed brother wore his intensity like a second skin, standing tall and fearless—not like a king, but like an executioner.

Where Velizar was ice, his brother was wildfire. And he would not be tempered.

He was the wolf under the willow.

"Are you well, girl?" He pinched a leaf between his fingers and plucked it from its stem, then smirked. "You look pale."

Kali sucked in a breath. "Again, I ask, what are you?"

He chuckled, then flicked the leaf away and watched it float to the ground. "I'm a wolf."

Kali's sigh filled the emerald shade. "But what are you really?"

He shrugged. "A god. A spirit. A destroyer. It doesn't matter."

"Of course it matters!"

"Then let me ask you," he closed the distance in a single stride and circled her, his breath warm on her skin, "what are you?"

"I'm a girl from the village," Kali replied.

His lips quirked. "A girl? Is that what the village says?"

Spite simmered up her spine. "What they say about me is a lie."

He grinned like a dark portent. "Not if everyone believes the same lie. Then it's just the truth."

Kali bowed her head, but she could feel his eyes probing her, testing her.

"Again, I ask, what are you?"

Deep beneath the uncertainty, the loss, and the pain, she knew the answer. She'd always known. Meeting his gaze, she said, "A witch. A Dreamwalker. A little piece of chaos." Her heart lightened, and she smiled. "It doesn't matter."

"No," he smiled back, "it doesn't."

❧ 40 ❧

W<small>HEN</small> K<small>ALI</small> <small>OPENED HER EYES,</small> *she was standing beneath the willow tree, and Sendoa was nowhere to be found. The leaves were blood red, and the branches' sway stilted like time had slowed to a crawl.*

The air was a thick, humid fog against her palm, and smoke rose above the treetops from the ravine where the Hollow lay. She could smell the cinders, the fire faraway yet somehow close.

The village was burning.

Kali bolted from the glade and down the hill, but no matter how far she ran, she couldn't seem to reach the Hollow. On and on it went, an endless blur of brown and green, until her lungs burned, and her legs could barely hold her upright. Collapsing to her knees, she gasped for breath, limbs tingling.

She couldn't find her way.

Kali dug her fingers into the moist earth. The beating drum inside her chest grew louder, rushing through her veins, seeping from her fingertips and into the earth.

She breathed in, and the soil rose to meet her touch. The roots curled towards her grasp as if beckoned. They were listening, and they were ready to speak.

"Show me the way," she begged, and they glimmered to life.

She could see them far beneath the forest's skin like veins delivering life where it was needed most. Each vessel was a different shade, matching the heart from which it came. She clawed through the aspens, maples, oaks, and firs until she found the winding roots of the willow.

Kali knew what she had to do.

The willow's roots burrowed far below the others, unmovable and resolute. Where some were threadbare, the willow's were thick and unyielding. They led Kali through the labyrinth until the smoke grew dense, and the smell left her stomach in knots. Finally, she descended the slope and stood at the edge of the woods where the ground lay level, and the thickets turned to meadow.

She was at the foot of the Hollow, and all the devils from every hell had made it their new inferno.

The village was in flames. Bartha's longhouse had been reduced to char. Fire ravaged every inch of the clearing, leaving Kali's childhood home in unrecognizable tatters. The sky roiled in crimson and copper waves, and the moon took on the pockmarked, sickly pallor of rotting flesh. But the screams—those horrible, spine-cutting screams—were worse than the scattered remains of her life. All around her, people clambered on mangled hands and knees, faces black and blue, eyes snaked with pink.

From the shadow and smoulder, a massive black wolf lunged atop a scrambling villager. With eyes like blood, muzzle rippling with rage, he sunk his dagger-like fangs into the man's neck and tossed him aside, limbs flailing. The wolf glanced at Kali, ensnaring her for the briefest moment before his yawning maw closed around the man's throat and tore out his voice.

A chilling cry raised the hairs on Kali's neck, and she whirled around to find the dreamer—the one responsible for pulling her into this nightmare. It was Lana's sister, Darya, her face tear-streaked and her umber eyes aglow as she raked her fingernails across her cheeks, leaving swollen, bleeding welts.

She stared at Kali.

"Dreamwalker! Dreamwalker!" Her voice rived with every syllable, and she yanked at her long, matted hair. "Dreamwalker! Dreamwalker!"

"Darya, wake up!" Kali approached the girl, who lurched in terror. Seeing it was useless, Kali squeezed her eyes shut and willed it all away—willed herself to awaken—but all she heard was Darya's strangled accusation.

"Dreamwalker! Dreamwalker!"

Kali couldn't escape the nightmare until Darya awoke.

"The Dreamwalker is here!"

The villagers were closing in. Even with their bones broken and their flesh shredded, they corralled her like a pack of rabid dogs. As she spun in search of an opening—a chance to flee—a ghastly sight from what used to be the town square seized her.

There, tied to the altar of the Viyest, was Lana's burnt corpse— her mouth agape, her eyes turned skyward. What remained of her bones twisted like blackened vines around the totem she'd once worshipped as a god.

She was unrecognizable, but Kali shared every scrap of unsettling knowledge with the dreamer: Darya.

"No, no, no..." Kali staggered back, stopping when she heard ragged footsteps approach. She was surrounded, and Lana was dead.

Someone leapt at her—hatchet raised. Before they could swing, a blear of black feathers dove at them. Talons latched onto the attacker's arm as a sharp, curved beak descended, pecking ruthlessly until flesh parted from bone and bone broke from knuckle.

A large raven unlike any Kali had seen thrust out his head, departed finger in tow, and chortled with glee. His midnight wings glistened like obsidian and sapphire as he launched from the villager's arm and circled overhead, then dropped the waxy digit at Kali's feet.

He swooped down, feathers fluttering as he perched roughly on her shoulder. She winced, feeling the talons cut into her skin, but the display only sent the Hollow into a frenzy. Darya screamed, and when Kali turned to face her, she was on the ground, limbs thrashing and body igniting in flames.

"Kill the Dreamwalker!"

"Kill the Dreamwalker!"

The villagers were chanting, the sound discordant in Kali's ears. She looked to the raven and reached a quivering hand to his silky, iridescent plumage. "Thank you, friend."

The raven cocked his head and considered her, drinking up her fear. Eyes shining like fresh ink, his dark bill parted as he croaked a single phrase:

"Wake...up..."

"I can't," she pleaded, the mob still advancing.

"Wake...up..."

"I don't know how!"

"Wake...up..."

The command rang in Kali's ears. The earth shook under her feet, and the flames eagerly licked her face.

"I'm trapped," she muttered, enclosed in a tightening halo of dread.

"Wake...up...!" the raven cried louder.

"Get away," Kali whimpered. "Get away, get away!" She swung her arm as someone got too close, striking them over and over until the shouting stopped and the horrors faded into the faint crackle of the campfire.

"Wake up!" Sendoa shook her, his face sketched with concern. As the world came into focus, she saw her fists pressed against his chest; she'd been pummelling him in her sleep. Behind him, the willow's silhouetted branches swayed against the bone-white moon—the sky pitch black and starless.

Tears welled up, threatening to spill. "I was so lost...I didn't know which way to go."

Sendoa's shoulders dropped, and he sighed in relief. She'd never seen him worried like this. How bad had it gotten that she'd rattled the god of destruction with her nightmares?

"Come on." He scooped an arm under her back and helped her up.

Kali could barely move, her body feeling brittle as shale. Grabbing his arm, she yanked herself up with all her might, nearly toppling him in the process. Her skin crawled like thousands of spiders had burrowed into her veins. She tried scratching them out until her fingernails wetted with blood.

Sendoa grabbed her hand to stop her. "What happened?"

"Lana..." Kali swallowed the sick. "She's dead. She's dead because of me." The dam broke. Kali pressed her palms to her face, but she couldn't stem the tide of salty tears.

She felt warm fingers pull her hands away and met Sendoa's stony gaze. "None of this is because of you."

"They killed her!" she roared as rage quickly swept away the guilt. "They thought *I* had taken her, but I deliberately left her behind! We fought before I renounced the Hollow!" Realization ripped through Kali's chest. "We fought...the last thing we did was fight...and I didn't wish her well."

She clamped her teeth, fighting down the sob that pushed up her throat.

"And I tore my own brother to pieces," Sendoa reminded her.

Kali's breath hitched with sorrow. "But what if I could have stopped it?"

His hands slipped free from hers as he circled an arm around her back. "Your friend made choices too. Why give your decisions more weight than hers?"

"Because I had more power!" she swatted at the ground

and scraped her knuckles raw. "If I'd used it the way Bartha had wanted, none of this would've happened!"

Sendoa squeezed her arms and glared. "Yes, it would have. Velizar never intended for your people to return to their fairy tales about the Viyest and the Dreamwalker. He spewed whatever lies suited his goal, and his *only* goal was to be king. But to be king, he had to be rid of you. Your friend was a casualty of his war. Her blood is on his hands, not yours."

She wanted to fight him—to deflect his reason and return to her shame. If it was her fault, she could fix it. If she was to blame, she had control.

"Maybe you're right, but I'd be a fool not to harness this..." she trailed off, searching for the right word, "this curse of mine. I don't want to be a victim of it any longer. I don't want to be helpless." She peered up at the willow, remembering the way its petals bore blood. "This nightmare...it won't be the last. The Hollow is scared. Terror finds them in their dreams, and they pull me into them." Her eyes drifted to Sendoa's face. "I can't get out until they wake. I have to make it stop. I need control."

"Perhaps to control your chaos, you need to lose yourself in it first."

Kali's mouth dropped open. "Aren't I lost enough?"

His lips tugged into a faint but haunted smile. "You're lost in what you fight to keep away. But when you walk dreams, you tether yourself to the Hollow's most fragile truths. The unseemly things they won't show anyone. You have those too, wild lamb."

She scrunched up her face. "I don't understand your god-speak."

"All your life you've been afraid of the Hollow's judgment," he said. "You knew they were watching you, so you locked yourself up in a stone shell. And when your body and mind grew weary of that shell, your spirit broke free while you slept."

Kali felt her heart crumble like the charred wood of Bartha's longhouse. "Lana—I told her the same thing," she recalled. "When you don't let yourself feel the truth, it speaks through your dreams."

Sendoa sighed. "And you're doing the same. The more you shut it away, the more power you bestow it. Welcome it, and you'll find yourself more at ease in the dreamscape. You may even find your way."

"I don't know where to start," said Kali. "There's so much wrong with me. Pride and spite smeared over my every intention. I came to you because I didn't trust anyone in the Hollow, but I don't trust you, either. How can I? You're the brother of the devil who stole my life. You savaged your own kin for a moment of retribution." She laughed bitterly. "I don't blame you for it; I understand it perfectly, and that frightens me because I know I'm the same."

Tears streamed down her face, years of unspoken truths cascading out alongside them. "I'm not noble, compassionate, or forgiving. I've spent my life sneering at the Hollow, holding them in contempt." She balled her hands into fists. Rage emanated from her skin, beckoning the wind to howl. "I *hate* them," she seethed, and the veil between worlds began to tremble. "I hate them with my every forsaken breath."

Phantoms slipped from the shadows beneath the trees, and spirits slithered from the depthless void beneath the earth, their yellowed fingernails poking through the soil as the edges of reality fractured. "They've caused me nothing but pain."

Sendoa snatched her hand, breaking the spell. "You've got enough hate to fuel ten lifetimes worth of grudges." He smiled wryly. "That's spite rivaled only by Velizar, Dreamwalker."

Kali breathed heavily, unable to contain her wrath. "*Fuck* Velizar."

"Rein it in." He scooted closer. "You're shredding the boundary between realms."

"I don't care," she spat. "Let it all come crashing down. Let the Hollow live their own nightmares as I've had to."

His arm snaked around her waist as he pulled her against his side. "Is that your most fragile truth?" he asked, pressing his forehead to hers. "Salt the earth?"

She hesitated, the words stuck in her throat. If she said *yes*, it would've been a lie. "I-I don't know," she stammered, then flattened her palms against his chest. "I don't know what you're asking of me."

"Vulnerability."

"I'm being vulnerable!" She pulled back when she couldn't push him away. "I'm telling you how much I loathe the Hollow! How much anger and hatred I harbour!"

Sendoa's fingers closed around her wrist as she tried to flee. "No," he said sternly. "Your anger is the stone shell. It protects what's underneath it."

"How would you even know? You killed your own brother!"

"And do you know what I did after I killed my brother?" He reeled her in and ran his fingers through her hair, soothing her fury, then brought his words a breath away from her lips. "I grieved."

Silent, Kali stared past the harsh lines of his face. He suddenly appeared worn and broken. She swallowed, then asked quietly, "What's under the shell?"

He eased himself against the willow and wrapped both arms around her. Gently lulling her against his chest, he sighed and stared up at the cerulean dawn. "Hurt."

❧ 41 ❦

Lying on the forest floor, Kali stared up at the ancient willow's soothing canopy. She breathed in, leaves crunching under her weight as she shifted against the ground.

This time, she would sink into the dreamscape of her own volition.

She closed her eyes and tuned out the song of birds, the scuttle of squirrels, and the curious rustle of foxes.

I will descend.

The words echoed in her mind, and sound fell away.

I will descend, as only I can.

Slowly, almost imperceptibly, Kali felt herself dipping into the earth. The crisp breeze grew muffled in her ears as the waking world faded. Only the whisper of the willow's meadow-green blades *and the hypnotic melody of its swaying stems remained.*

The earth tilted on its axis, and Kali found herself standing where she'd been lying moments earlier. Emerald leaves now shimmered like rubies as a viscous, pink nectar dripped from their tips.

She had stumbled into another nightmare.

Kali groaned in frustration. She'd wanted to go to the dream-

scape, yes, but on her own terms. She'd failed again. It was difficult carving her own path when her spirit was drawn to the minds consumed by her absence.

"There's no need for you to stay," a throaty voice croaked at her.

Kali glanced up to find a raven—the raven—perched on the crooked arm of a dead oak. "I wouldn't if I could figure out how to leave. The dreamers keep me trapped here."

The bird chortled, laughing at her. "Petty mortals needn't dictate your path. Go where you please. Be whomever you please."

"How?"

"Focus," he said, then spread his wings and dove for her shoulder. Kali straightened her arm, offering him a roost. "I help."

"What am I to focus on?"

The bird thrust his beak towards the red-tinged willow. "Bend the world," he cackled. "Make it your own."

Kali remained unconvinced, but she reckoned it was worth a try. She reached out and touched the sanguine leaves.

"This is the Emerald Shade," she said. "I want it restored." Her heart squeezed, grief rising to her lips. "I want to be restored."

The wind howled, and the coppery pall that covered the sky peeled away to reveal a sprawling sunset of azalea, lavender, and marigold radiating from a great white star. As the blood drained from the expanse above, the willow's ruby petals dazzled with green life. It was as Kali remembered it. She was no longer in the nightmare but stood in the unfettered dreamscape.

She had only one thing left to remake: herself.

"What do you want to be?" asked the raven.

Kali thought for a moment, then replied, "I don't know."

"Close your eyes," the raven instructed, and she did. "Imagine the Hollow's fear. What do you see?"

"A shadow," she said. "Black as death, formless as vapour."

"Do you know who the shadow is?"

"Yes," she nodded, "it's Velizar."

"Now imagine the thing the shadow fears." He waited a moment, then asked excitedly, "Do you see it?"

"Yes," said Kali, her voice soft.

"What is it?" asked the raven.

"It's me."

The raven's crow rattled low. "And how do you appear to the great king who fears you?"

Kali's eyes snapped open, revelation coursing through her veins and sparking a fire in her soul. The word left her as a wondrous breath.

"Magnificent."

Velizar's vision of the Dreamwalker erupted from Kali's fingertips. Violet and black spiralled up her arms, devouring her with ravenous fervour. Shadow and light danced around her shoulders in an impossible union as feathery tendrils cascaded down her back, forming an iridescent shroud that resembled her companion's plumage. It enveloped her like a protective skin, slithering up her neck and over her scalp. As the magic passed over her face, it hardened into bone, tapering to a sharp point that curled over her chin. Although she couldn't see it, she knew the mask shimmered with lustrous swirls of amethyst and midnight skies. They coalesced like oil and water, separate yet never apart. She knew because she'd seen it in Velizar's terror.

"Now," said the raven, "you are true chaos."

He lifted a talon from her shoulder and curled it against his belly. When he eased it back down, he was clasping a fang-shaped stone. It glinted with colours that melded into one another like shifting puzzle pieces—meadow greens, sunset golds, and vibrant purples pierced by black veins that snaked throughout the rock.

Kali held out her hand, and the raven dropped the stone. "With this, you will never lose your way again."

It hummed against her palm, steady and powerful. "What is it?"

"A piece of the dreamscape," he said. "And now, a piece of you."

Kali closed her fingers over the dream stone. She was ready to return.

"What's your name, raven?"

The bird canted his head, his beady eyes dulling as he replied, "I have no name."

"Everyone has a name."

The bird tutted, "Good names are given. Those frivolously taken are flatulent. Meaningless."

"All right," Kali smiled. "Why don't I give you a name?"

The inky shine returned to the raven's eye, and he waited.

"Gavran." Kali worked her fingers through his soft, silky feathers, and he purred contently in response. "Your name is Gavran."

❧ 42 ❧

IT STARTED with the snap of twigs and the stomping of
leather boots. By the time Kali realized what was to befall
her, it was too late to run.

They'd found her. In a miracle of the most vicious sort,
the men raided the copse, hewing through the foliage. And
they weren't alone. The shadow was there—a death-like
miasma swirling in their midst, guiding them with a sinister
tongue.

Cold yellow eyes pierced Kali with a malicious stare. She
had nowhere to flee, no way to fight back.

Sendoa was off hunting, leaving her with her newfound
friend, Gavran. After she'd pulled him from the dreamscape
in a stubborn test of power, the two had become insepara-
ble, much to Sendoa's displeasure. He'd told her the raven
had no business passing between realms, but she insisted it
was a feat—a testament to her mastery. Besides, he could
only pass into the physical plane by her will. She was his
anchor, and with her permission alone was he able to stay.

She was glad she had him. As the Hollow hunters

snatched her up, it took but a glance to send Gavran to find the wolf.

They dragged Kali back towards the Hollow, their blades striking the trees as though the boles would morph into ghouls, and their eyes glistened with fright whenever a coyote skittered by.

The men wasted no time when they returned. With wide, blood-shot eyes and shaking hands, they hauled Kali to the Viyest, still charred from Lana's execution. Yet before they could tie her to the gnarled trunk, a scream rattled the clearing.

The villagers spun towards the forest.

A black wolf with eyes made of blood and rage bounded from the green sea, his teeth dripping red with the watchman's life. Halting at the foot of the warren, he stalked the perimeter and snarled like an impending storm.

Sendoa had come for her, and he wasn't alone.

From behind him, howls ruptured the evening sky as dozens of smaller wolves descended upon the Hollow. They were led by a raven, his body a blur as he glided from the canopy and landed on the black wolf's hackles, raised like blades. Throwing his head back, Gavran spread his midnight wings and released a resounding death rattle, his beak unhinging as though trying to swallow the moon.

It was a war cry, and every man, beast, and god understood it.

Kali saw Velizar's shadow quaver with delight as it blanketed the clearing. It weaved among the villagers, invading them, controlling them. Their eyes glazed over, and their jaws hung slack. Thick obsidian smoke rushed out in time with guttural screams—a response to the raven.

Sendoa huffed, his coal-coloured lips pulled back. He sneered, daring the hunters to come for him.

And they did.

Crazed under Velizar's influence, they tripped over themselves to reach their prey. But Sendoa was ready. As Gavran took off, the black wolf lunged, pinning a man's shoulders to the ground. He tore out his throat, savaging him with a ferocious roar. When the swords swung at him, he leapt gracefully from their arcs, then smothered his next target—an insect waiting to be squashed.

The other wolves followed suit. Gavran dove for the hunters' faces, latched his talons into their lips, and plunged his beak into their eyes. Their shrieks filled the night, and Gavran gurgled with glee, pink yolk oozing from his bill while he feasted. As his victim fought to dislodge him, two of the smaller wolves gored the man's sides, sawing their way through his midsection.

Yet their brutal onslaught was short-lived. Wisps of smoke guided axes and spears; as the wolves dodged one blade, Velizar's poisonous brume guided another to their bellies. The hunters fought long after they should have died —some flailing even as the wolves wrenched out their innards. The felled villagers rose again and again. The more frenzied they became, the more inhuman their strength. Single swipes removed entire limbs and heads—and not just those of wolves. Women and children running for safety were caught in the mayhem, murdered by their own. Some took up torches, setting fire to homes and trees indiscriminately.

Then, from somewhere within the maelstrom, Kali glimpsed a glint of silver burrow into Sendoa's side. A dark mist in the shape of a hand rested on the sabre's hilt. She heard the whimper—the heartrending squeal—as the black wolf collapsed, blood pouring from his wound.

Kali begged for it all to stop.

Gavran swooped down and clawed at the hand, only to

be whipped away like a pebble. He crashed to the ground with a stuttering cry, his wing bent and his leg curled in.

Smouldering heat crawled up Kali's spine as rage prickled her skin. Breaths ragged, eyes ablaze, she pulled her bruised and beaten body from the ground and grasped the Viyest's dappled skull. She remembered Sendoa's words:

You're shredding the boundary between realms.

Every creature that'd been hunted to hallow this ground was chosen by the Dreamwalker. Kali was the last of them —the only one to refuse the rite.

Mooring herself to the Viyest, she pulled on the thread of its spirit. The force of her will seeped into the soil, stirring ancient roots that pierced the waking world and penetrated the dreamscape.

If this was a battle between gods, she was yet to make her entrance.

The Hollow would live its own nightmare. Not in dreams, but on the blood-soaked earth upon which it stood.

She would cut the seams of reality and let chaos spill out.

Roars echoed from the crumbling border between worlds as Kali drew from the Viyest's anguish. Every creature killed to slake the Hollow's bloodlust was now hers as she harnessed what her predecessors had wrought.

A scorching scream ripped from Kali's chest as a cloak of violet and black feathers erupted down her back. The bone-beak mask swallowed her face, and her muddy green eyes found the shadow's. For a brief moment, she saw Velizar's fear behind the fumes.

The spirits of the fallen wolves burst from their mangled corpses. At Kali's command, they resumed their assault, and this time, they couldn't be cut down. The hunters' blades whirled through thin air in retaliation, but the dreamscape had come to the Hollow, and no mortal weapon bore strength in the realm of spirits. Some gathered around the wounded Sendoa, protecting him from further harm.

Velizar's shadow darted towards the black wolf, but Kali was faster. Thrusting her arms back, she propelled forward, her shroud billowing at her heels. Her iridescent touch infected the phantom, dispersing it into a cloud of shimmering dust.

She was chaos, and she was here to erode Velizar's order.

The miasma unleashed a cacophonous shriek as it reeled back, undulating in a disordered attempt to flee. Howls echoed through the clearing as the wolves sang, each of them clamouring for the honour to be called *Viyest* by their Dreamwalker.

Suddenly, pain shot through Kali's chest. Her breath hitched, and the hand she'd parted the darkness with flew to her heart. She felt wetness against her fingers and something sharp between her ribs.

A sword.

The blade disappeared as it was pulled back. Crumpling next to the wolf, Kali scrabbled at her robes. She turned to find Darya—face tear-streaked and cheeks rouged—as she held Decebal's blade with tremoring hands.

"For Lana!" she cried, her voice breaking with grief.

Kali opened her mouth to speak, but the words knotted in her throat.

Did you really think you could best me, witch? Velizar's laughter rumbled in her ear—layered and discordant.

"I already...have..." she managed. Her feathery cloak had vanished along with the dreamscape. The wolves' spirits had disappeared, and Sendoa lay motionless on the tainted ground.

Obstinate little bitch. Look at yourself. You are but a girl in rags, and you are dying.

Kali ignored him, her fingers closing over the three pointed edges of her favourite stone. "Not quite," she wheezed.

Gavran had told her the stone was a piece of the dream-scape. A piece of her. With her last breath and the power of the luminous fang humming against her palm, she willed the Dreamwalker's spirit from her body, then looked upon the black wolf. She wouldn't let him go so easily.

Kali faced Velizar's shadow. "The wolf and I, *the witch*," she spat the word, "will always find each other. We are bound, as the sky and sea are bound by the horizon."

Her declaration was a spell—or perhaps a hex. Bolstered by the stone's power, Kali reached into the dreamscape and tethered Sendoa's spirit to her own. The black wolf was her familiar, her love; this would be their promise and their curse.

With her last ounce of strength, she broke past Velizar's umbral shield and grabbed his spirit by the throat. Through the haze, she saw him—cold aurous eyes, wild sable hair, and a face just like his brother's. Before he could spew venom at her, she tightened her grip, snuffing the words from the tip of his tongue.

"You will never be rid of me," she seethed. "Your control...is meaningless." Dragging herself up in a final act of defiance, she loomed close enough to feel his sour, rotting breath. "And I *will* return."

Releasing him, she whipped the stone the other way. "Gavran!" she called before her knees buckled, and she fell to the ground. The last thing Kali saw as her vision faded was the raven scrambling to fetch the dream stone.

Then, the world went black.

43

GAVRAN

WING...BROKEN. Leg...crushed.

Gavran struggled through the pain. He was a young spirit—a child, really—but what did that matter when his mother lay dead?

Take the stone, her spirit whispered. *Keep it safe until the time is right.*

And so he would. None of them had much of that vile thing called time—not him, and certainly not Velizar. The menacing spectre had roamed long enough, resisting the pull of rebirth. The god of creation was strong, but the raven was clever.

Gavran hobbled to the stone before Velizar could reach it. Taking the fang in his beak, he tilted his head back and gobbled it down. He twisted his head towards Velizar, squawked one final time, then hopped towards the prettiest corpse littering the land.

He'd been eyeing it for some time now.

It was a boy with pristine, doll-like skin and hair like a

starless night. Crawling onto the child's torso, Gavran wasted no time pecking through the boy's stomach. He tunnelled his way inside, melding with the cadaver until the strings tugged and the boy's fingers twitched. Flesh rippled and ribs bulged as the raven wrested control. With a jerk and a kick, the body sat up. The neck twisted too far, so Gavran clasped the chin and click...click...clicked it into place. This shell was stiff and bereft of wings, but it would do.

The mouth twitched, then slithered open, revealing jagged, bloodied teeth. They'd been broken in the frenzy. The tongue ran over each pointed end—too sharp for the meat. The flesh sliced open, but the body obeyed.

The boy named Gavran opened his depthless eyes, shining like wet ink.

❧ 44 ❧

VELIZAR

THE WITCH WAS DEAD, but she wasn't gone. Though Velizar detected no trace of her spirit, her memory hung in the air like a threat.

After the dust settled, the Hollow wasn't the same. All that remained were cinders and ash. Dark smoke pooled in the crevice where the village once stood. The earth was charred, reminding the survivors of the stygian wolf that'd laid siege to their home. They no longer called it the Hollow; it was now *Black* Hollow.

The name immortalized Sendoa, and the villagers' fear etched the Dreamwalker into the very stone of the land. Neither would be forgotten.

Despite having ended them both, Velizar had lost control. He was fading, pulled to his next life, but he resisted. His revenge was incomplete.

He'd spent his kingship villainizing the young woman who would become a god, but instead of fading into obscurity, her legend outgrew his designs. He'd even lost his brother. His pathetic little brother had chosen chaos over him.

With the last of his waning strength, Velizar took up the paranoia that had poisoned the Hollow and carved out his vengeance. He would cling to the fable he hated and take it with him to his next life. Although his new incarnation wouldn't remember, his soul would.

The survivors left the land soaked in their families' blood, but wherever they went, they took their stories with them, and their king followed like a shadow. The place was transported with the people, and their gods were re-homed. The hunters tried building a new Hollow an ocean away, but it too became black. Every time the village came to believe they had rid themselves of the Dreamwalker's curse, the seeds of doubt would sprout a bloodthirsty weed.

But for that, Velizar's machinations weren't necessary. The human mind was powerful enough. He'd watch as the villagers' doubt gave way to guilt, and guilt crumbled to expose shame. People would do anything to rid themselves of it. The simplest way, of course, was to ensure the monster was real, the execution justified.

Exorcise the demon, exorcise the guilt.

He knew it would all start anew...a new woman, a new Dreamwalker, and an endless supply of wolves for the Hollow to choose from. They were ravenous for death, and Velizar had full faith there'd be no shortage of portents for them to fabricate.

His incarnations would live through every new iteration of the Dreamwalker's persecution, ensuring he'd be there to see her fall. With every lifetime that joined them, he would look her in the eyes and watch her burn with a smile.

If Velizar couldn't control her, then he would control her myth. He'd destroy anyone who smelled of her. Yes, she would return, but she would return to his order. And she would die in it. Again, and again, and again, until time itself broke.

Velizar would have his legacy. Even if the Hollow forgot his name, they would never be free of the cycle he'd created. It was an order unto itself, and in the hands of history, it was as eternal as his godhood.

III

HELL HATH NO FURY

✵ 45 ✵

MIYA

As the first slivers of her memory returned, Miya sighed with relief. The sensation of not knowing oneself was akin to floating in the ocean, with a depthless abyss below and an endless expanse above. But when the full force of the past hit her, it was like someone had ripped a hole in the universe, and there was now something bigger lurking behind it.

Miya felt like she'd taken her first breath—a staggering, painful gasp that burned like thousands of glass grains scraping along her lungs.

"Now you know," came the boy's low whisper.

Miya's fingers kneaded at her ribs and chest, trying to work out the sting. She remembered everything. Velizar was the First, but he wasn't the only one. Kali was Miya's first, and Sendoa was Kai's. The three of them were entangled in ways that made death and time irrelevant. And Gavran...

"Why did you help me?" she asked. "You were only there towards the end."

His eyes twinkled with knowing. "I've always been there."

"I don't understand." Miya wracked her brain for a memory that came before the red-tinged willow.

"You were lost before you'd taken your first breath," said Gavran. "I found you, tucked you in, and flew you back to your waking home. Then I watched. I waited. Every time you dreamt, I was there. You simply hadn't learned to look up, and I wasn't ready to leave the trees."

Miya recalled the beginning of his story, and her mouth dropped open. "You were the raven that brought Kali's soul back to her body when she was a baby."

He nodded, his fingers splaying over the ground. He scratched at the dirt, thick, sallow fingernails accenting his porcelain skin. He was a spirit wearing the corpse of a child from the Hollow—a corpse that never changed. But that wasn't how Ama had described her caretaker.

"I've heard you're an old man in the physical world. Why the discrepancy?"

He cackled, throwing out his arms. "Here, I am whatever I want," he said. "But your rebirth would be out there, so I needed to stay out there as well. With you gone, I had no anchor." His crooked teeth ate up his whole face. "That's why I put on the boy's corpse. But," he raised a spindly finger, "dead things rot, so I gave his bones life. The bones grew brittle, but slowly...so slowly. My life gives more than decades. Yet bodies can only be in one place at a time." He scoffed like it was the most frustrating trifle in the universe. He leaned in close to Miya. "I needed eyes everywhere," he whispered. "Inside, outside. Everywhere and in all things. For that, I made the sentry you call Kafka and gave it my eyes."

"Your...literal eyes?" asked Miya, leaning back as the boy dove in.

"A piece of me," he said. "*Kafka* can traverse realms. The old man cannot."

"But you're here," she pointed out. "Aren't you the old man?"

The boy settled back against the tree, his expression deadening. "Yes."

"So, you *can* traverse realms?"

The boy shook his head. "Only the Dreamwalker can do that without consequence."

Miya felt her heart still, then plummet into her gut. "But you're just dreamwalking, aren't you? Shouldn't that be okay?"

"Too many worlds crossed. Too many dreams walked with old bones. And some things require more than eyes—welcoming you to the dreamscape, leading you to the Grey Gnarl, helping the wolf at your behest. And now," his eyes met hers, "fulfilling my promise to you."

Miya let out a shaky breath. "To keep the stone until the time is right..."

Gavran nodded. "You have the stone back. And now, you have your memories back." He smiled warmly. "You have yourself back. My purpose has ended."

"But we've only just been reunited!" Miya pleaded. "You still have a place in my life."

Gavran chuckled, lowering his gaze. "I always wanted to be the apple of your eye. But I knew then, just as I know now: the wolf always feasts before the raven."

"No!" Miya protested. "That doesn't mean you get to starve yourself out of our lives. What about Ama? She still needs you! She loves you!"

Gavran threw his head back and laughed until his voice broke. "The white wolf has never needed anyone." He reached out and stroked Miya's cheek, his hand cold as death. "Love is not a thing of need, Dreamwalker. It's a thing of choice. You knew this day would come eventually."

"But—"

He silenced her with a light pinch on the cheek. "Nothing in this world ever ends. It only changes...like water to mist, like bones to dust."

The fog that once barred their path swam towards the Red Knot. It gathered around the boy, swallowing him up in a sea of darkness. The last thing Miya saw was Gavran's eerie smile and glistening black eyes as the haze devoured him.

Never fear, she heard his voice echo.

Old embers ignite new flames.

❦ 46 ❧

KAI

KAI WAS WRENCHED awake by a searing pain in his side. Curling into it, he rolled over and bit down a scream. This was worse than being stabbed. His gut lurched, but nothing came up. How could it? He wasn't even in the physical world. There was nothing in his godforsaken spirit stomach, and yet he still felt nausea clawing its way up, taunting him with useless heaving. Like a cat with a hairball.

Dark clouds mounded up overhead, threatening to spill with rain. He was still in the swamp, still stranded with the Grey Gnarl in the middle of that stupid lake. Thunder rolled over the livid sky, matching the sentiment in Kai's heart.

He already knew Velizar had started the cycle, but he didn't *know* it like he did now. Velizar had forced him to live it all—to feel their relationship crumble as egos erupted and civility imploded. Not that Kai ever cared much about being civil.

He wobbled to his feet. "You sad sack. You'd think a god would know better."

Velizar had wanted to watch the Dreamwalker die not once, but every time. He didn't care if the accused girls were the *actual* Dreamwalker. He just wanted her to be the bane of Black Hollow, no matter the cost. He wanted her— the very idea of her—to submit to his diabolical designs.

Well, Velizar had gotten his wish, and he was miserable for it.

Misery was a price worth paying, Velizar replied. **Every lifetime I spent in agony because of the Dreamwalker brought me closer to my truest form.**

Kai's head pounded with every word. "You mean Abaddon."

I was perfect, he reminisced. **I was finally able to rip myself free of my horrid rebirth. Being alive is a travesty. My mortal mind forced me to bury my memories and my will into my subconscious. As Abaddon, I reclaimed my autonomy and became a true god.**

Kai felt sick, the throbs deepening until they pulsed through his skull. How was he even related to this asshole? "Hold up—you tortured yourself, repeatedly, then wiped yourself off the census for your prehistoric scheme?"

Of course, Velizar purred. **All great revolutions require sacrifices—most of all, from their leaders. I was happy to condemn my future selves to lifetimes of misery if only to prove that life *is* wretched. How cruel it is...to relive a pattern over and over and to never remember why you are the fool who cannot cease falling into the same pit.**

"Pompous prick." Kai pinched the bridge of his nose and grumbled. "You know, when you dragged me into this fever dream, I worried you'd show me something that'd make you seem like less of a dick." He threw his arms up. "Not a fucking chance! You're still the same self-absorbed piece of shit!"

But surely even you see that we were doomed to dance this dance forever. It didn't matter that we were without our memories. Life after life, we continued butchering each other, and it was all because of *her*—the Dreamwalker.

"Who cares!" Kai's voice rung in the open air. "How does being stuck together make a difference?"

Because it's the only way to end this eternal spat, brother. By uniting as one, we can finally be free of each other. We can make peace. If we aren't separate, if we are a whole, then we cannot be at war.

"You mean *you* get to force me to be your little bitch," said Kai.

You're weak, Velizar hissed. **Without me, you stood no chance against Rusalka. You were nothing but a worm for her to pull apart. With me, you are strong —no, unstoppable. *I* make you great. And only in greatness do you have what's necessary to actualize her demise. Only *I* can free you from her.**

"Then what are you waiting for?" Kai growled. "I was tracking her when you knocked me down memory lane."

Velizar's chuckle reverberated against Kai's ribs. **You did well, brother. But the trail ends here.**

Kai turned to the Grey Gnarl. "Yeah, because this dried-up stick is a gateway to Orme's Rest, and *you* wouldn't let me through it."

He hated how easy it was for the dead to move between worlds. Vengeful spirits like Rusalka and Velizar latched onto their victims from the dreamscape and leeched their strength to ferry themselves back and forth. But Kai wasn't dead. Although he no longer belonged to the physical plane, he'd never *died*. For him, it wasn't so simple. Nothing living was meant to cross realities. Nothing but the Dreamwalker, that is.

Go, Velizar commanded. **She is back in the waking world.**

Kai swallowed, fear threading through his muscles. He hadn't forgotten what happened the last time he was alone without Miya there to anchor him. What if she'd moved on?

You don't need her! Or have you already forgotten that I've promised you *everything*?

"As if I'd trust you," Kai said, but he still took a step towards the tree.

Don't be foolish. Disintegrating between realms would hardly be a fitting end for you, dear brother.

Kai knew he was telling the truth. After all, if Velizar wanted him dead, he'd make sure it was slow, painful, and orchestrated like a Shakespearean tragedy. With a harsh breath, Kai placed his hand on the Grey Gnarl's slimy bark. It was like clammy, dead skin. Under his touch, the husk began to pull apart, giving way to a dark void. This time, it'd listened.

The tree sucked him in, sluggish like a sleepy mouth clamping over a thumb. It took every ounce of Kai's willpower not to plant his foot on the trunk and kick himself back into the swamp.

Something in him relented. Miya would be there, and even if she wasn't, he still had an expiring fish to fry.

Kai squeezed his eyes shut. Sound slipped into a vacuum as he tipped onto the other side and fell, weightless, then landed like a stone hitting water.

He gasped as his body crashed against the steel-hard ground. Gravel bit into his skin and he groaned, cradling his neck with his palm. "Fuck."

The sky above was dark and starless, the cover of clouds so thick the moon couldn't be found. Fighting to sit up, Kai found himself alone in the cemetery, staring at Sydney Baron's grave.

You see? You don't need the Dreamwalker's permission. You do as you please, as any king should.

Kai nearly choked on the lump that unexpectedly formed in his throat. He was back where he started—a solitary punk with a voice in his head. Sure, he knew what it was now, but he wasn't any better off for it. Velizar's shtick was making Kai feel small and powerless, even as he called him *king*.

"I'm not a king," Kai said. "I'm just a piece of trash. A beef jerky enthusiast with a hard-on for chaos."

Rusalka's swampy stench hung faintly in the air. Although she'd gotten a decent head start, Kai had a hunch where she was headed. He stared at the epitaph on Sydney's tombstone, remembering the way Rusalka's sickness wafted off Crowbar's skin.

If she wanted to hurt him, she knew exactly where to strike.

He needed to get to *The Mangy Spade*.

No, Velizar growled. **It's too soon to charge into battle.**

"Fuck you," Kai muttered as he stood. Rusalka had already threatened Crowbar. What if Miya was with her?

She might've already skipped town, but he knew better than to gamble on that hope. If he was in Rusalka's shoes, he'd want leverage. What better way to snatch it back than to threaten the person he cared for most?

No!

Kai's legs locked like rusty joints. Tripping on weeds, he strained to regain his balance. "What the hell is wrong with you? Didn't you *want* Rusalka gone?"

A. J. VRANA

Not quite yet, Velizar cooed.

"Why not!"

The voice clucked. **Because imagine how much sweeter the kill will be once she's taken everything from you. The catharsis, the release—the euphoria! It would be wasted on a wretch who hasn't fully sinned against you. And what greater sin is there than the slaughter of your beloved?**

Panic vised around Kai's throat as he realized Velizar's game. The bastard had been trying to stall him the entire time. The history lesson, the pleas for unity—they were all a ploy to ensure that Kai wouldn't make it in time to stop Rusalka. It was the same nightmare that'd plagued him in Black Hollow—all the missing girls he'd barely missed saving because of Abaddon. Miya marked the first time he'd conquered his curse, and now, Velizar wanted to rectify that.

Oh tsk, Velizar fussed. **I just want my brother back.**

Kai knew intimately what would come next. Once he was drowning in guilt over Miya's death, Velizar would swoop in to play wingman to Rusalka's demise, leaving Kai with nothing—and no one—but his nemesis: his lonely, controlling brother who also had nothing and no one but Kai.

"You twisted fuck!" Kai roared as he fought against the paralysis. He stumbled down the hill only to be struck in the back by a crushing weight.

Stop struggling.

"I'd rather drag my balls over broken glass!" Kai grunted through clenched teeth. His shoulders sank like he was carrying a building.

The voice sighed in disappointment. **Very well.**

Kai's knee jerked to the side, his tibia nearly snapping out of place as ligaments stretched and tore. Ill-prepared for the attack, Kai crumpled and cried out in agony.

If you insist on crawling back to that wench, then you'll do so on all fours like the pitiful cur you are.

Kai dug his fingers into the dirt and wrestled to stand on his good leg, but his other knee bent back, sending him face-first into the pebbles. He didn't care. Now more than ever, Kai wouldn't be dissuaded. He dragged himself by his elbows, inch by inch, breath by breath.

The pain gradually faded, replaced by a creeping horror that Velizar was healing him faster than Abaddon ever could. The moment Kai pushed himself out of the mud, he was maimed by what felt like a sledgehammer to the spine.

Not that it would be enough. Nothing his damn brother did would ever be enough.

Kai would reach *The Mangy Spade*, even if Velizar broke all his bones, tore his innards from his stomach, and bled him dry trying to stop him.

He was one tenacious son of a bitch, and by morning, he would have a sun to fuck out of Velizar's miserable sky.

47

MIYA

MIYA SHOT up from the hard, splintering floor. Blood rushed to her head and black dots stippled her vision. Her cheeks flushed and her stomach clenched with something between nausea and hunger. How long had she been out?

She registered warm, wrinkled skin against her palm and flexed her fingers, closed around an old man's hand. He lay next to her, unmoving, his long face marked by a sharp nose, deep-set eyes, and a stark frown. His thin silvery-black hair was pulled back against his scalp with only a few loose strands framing his ears.

She immediately recognized Gavran despite his age.

They were behind the bar of *The Mangy Spade*. A blanket was draped over Miya's legs, and a pillow, impressed with her head, lay on the floor. The kitchen doors burst open then, and Ama charged in, Crowbar and Mason in tow.

"You're back!" Ama's arms encircled her, dampness smearing across Miya's cheeks.

"I'm back," she exhaled, her insides squeezing with

dread. She'd returned with more than she'd left with, but in exchange, she'd lost something precious.

Miya's eyes drifted to the old man as Ama shuffled over to him on her knees. The white wolf had always been like a thunderstorm—loud, unyielding, unapologetic. Now, she shrank like a wilting flower.

"He's gone," Miya answered her silent question. "I'm sorry." The truth burned in her throat. "It's my fault. He did it to save me."

Ama bit her lower lip. Her eyes—usually warm like sunlight—now glistened with untold heartache. Despite her best efforts to keep it all in, a single lonely sob slipped out. It was all the permission the dam needed to break. She covered her face and folded with grief. Muffled cries seeped through her fingers, dying in the space between her and Gavran.

Miya was paralyzed, unsure of how to support the woman who'd always propped her up. "I-I'm sorry," she stammered, and Ama shook her head.

"It's not your fault," she said, then groped for Gavran's hand. "He made his own choices."

Miya still felt far from blameless. "I brought Rusalka into our lives. I messed up with the truth demon. All of this is because of me."

Ama sighed, then smiled shakily. "If it wasn't Rusalka and the truth demon, it would've been something else. It's my fault as much as anyone's."

"Miya," Mason interrupted softly, his voice tepid. "I'm sorry too...for whatever role I played in this. I shouldn't have gone after you." He ran a hand through his curls. "I should have just let you be."

Ama's face darkened with shame, but she said nothing.

Crowbar hovered behind Mason as he blocked the door.

She peered over his shoulder, her face sheet-white. "Is he... really dead?"

No one answered her. The ruse was up, and none of them had the energy to conjure excuses—not with their friend splayed behind the bar like a ritual sacrifice.

Suddenly, Gavran's body lurched up, then collapsed with a dull thud. Mason and Crowbar yelped, grabbing hold of each other in their fright. Jumping to her feet, Miya swooned as a wave of dizziness overcame her, and she toppled a vodka bottle while fumbling to grab the countertop for support.

"He just moved! He fucking moved!" Crowbar pointed while gripping Mason's arm.

Ama remained frozen on the floor, unblinking as she studied the body. For a long, tense moment, no one stirred, and then it happened again. It started as a ripple beneath his tattered robes—once, then twice. The bulge began to undulate. His ribs swelled, then cracked like his heart was trying to break free. Something was inside him, fighting to get out.

Crowbar slapped a hand over her mouth. "Jesus Christ. I'm going to be sick."

Mason spun and grabbed her shoulders. "It'll be okay," his voice cracked. "It'll be okay."

Something sharp like a knife tip ruptured Gavran's midsection, his corpse convulsing from the gouging force. Everyone but Ama shrieked in response, and as if encouraged by their terror, the curved point pushed further out, then split open to release a gargling croak.

"You've got to be joking," Miya hacked on her own saliva, sliding across the bar to get a better angle.

Then came the caw, echoing in the hollow cave. Dark feathers, slick with viscera, wrung from Gavran's carcass. First the head, then a wing.

It was a goddamn raven.

He appeared caught on something, thrusting out his neck as he wrenched himself free. His other wing dislodged a rib as it tore through flesh like it was a paper bag.

Perhaps that's all the body had ever been—a sack intended to hold something far weightier.

With both wings out, the raven flapped furiously, kicked his talons loose, and hopped onto the floor. Canting his head, he looked up at Ama and crowed.

She reached out with trembling hands and cupped the bird as though he were a nesting hen. "Is that really you?"

The raven purred and ruffled his feathers in response, and Ama broke out into a smile like the sunrise. She laughed and cried, lifting the bird overhead. His wings fluttered as he was raised like a beloved infant, his beady black eyes shining even in the dimness of *The Spade*.

Old embers ignite new flames.

Miya's heart soared with relief. She let go of the bar and staggered towards her friends. Gavran—the real Gavran—pounced onto Miya's arm, his wings beating in unfettered mirth as Ama wrapped both arms around Miya's shoulders and kissed her hair. The raven's joyous dance left them spattered in blood, droplets of red splashing the walls and shelves that housed the tavern's bottles.

Their celebration was interrupted by the sound of retching. Crowbar bent over, arms around her stomach, and vomited up her dinner—the smell of bile, scotch, and gumbo wafting past Miya.

"Oh, God," Mason cursed in a nasally voice as he scrunched up his nose and pulled her away from the sick.

In their jubilance, they'd forgotten they weren't alone. Crowbar had just witnessed a bird burst from a dead man's chest, then watched as two women danced beneath the rain of viscera like a pair of devil-worshipping hags.

Ama rushed to Crowbar's side after another round of purging. "Forgive me," she said, her face painted with concern. She shot Mason a pointed look, and he slowly backed away, arms up in mock defense. "Let's clean you up," she offered, then led Crowbar to the back.

"You've got some...explaining to do..." Miya heard the bartender cough between ragged breaths as they retreated towards the employees' bathroom.

"She'll be okay," Mason said as he grabbed a drying towel from the bar and wiped his hands. "If I could come out on the other end, Crowbar will be fine."

Miya rolled out her ankles and tested her balance. "Did you, though?"

"Maybe not completely," he admitted. "Not sure it's possible."

"I don't think anyone gets out of that world once they've gone in," said Miya. "And Crowbar—she's already got one foot in, thanks to Rusalka."

Mason's eyes widened, and he threw the towel into the sink. "My message. You got it, didn't you? Rusalka—"

"I know," Miya sighed. "I saw when you touched me in the in-between. She's from Black Hollow. Abaddon's victim."

"Miya, I'm so sorry—"

"Don't," she stopped him. "There've been enough apologies for today. Besides, you fought hard to get me that information."

Mason squirmed under the weight of unspoken words. "Can I at least thank you?"

"For what?" she frowned.

"For saving my life."

Miya blinked, the gratitude somehow jarring. She smiled and patted him on the arm. "Seems like you're the damsel in distress more than I am."

"Don't remind me," he grumbled.

Miya went quiet, her mind churning. Mason was hardly the first to be swept up in the Dreamwalker's chaotic path. Rusalka, Elle, Cassia—they were three of countless women who'd perished because of Kali's battle with Velizar. She had to do right by them, but first...

"I need a favour," she said.

"You do?"

"Yes." She placed a hand on his shoulder. "And it's something only you can do."

The colour drained from Mason's face. "Okay. What is it?"

"You came here to find me, yeah? Go back to my parents. Tell them the truth."

Mason's mouth popped open. "Miya—they'll never believe the truth!"

"No," she shook her head, "I don't mean the literal *hey-your-daughter-is-the-modern-incarnation-of-an-ancient-god-spirit-thing* truth. I mean *a* truth. Something that's true for me but feels honest for you too. Something that'll end their search once and for all."

"Don't you want to see them? Don't you want them to know the real you?"

"Of course I do," said Miya. "I want it more than anything. But that's just the little kid in me, yearning for her parents' approval. I'm not a kid anymore. If they didn't get my struggles as a depressed student, they're not going to accept *this*. They never met me where I was, only where they thought I should be. I need to let them go as much as they need to let me go. And I need you to be the one to help me with that."

"But why me?" Turmoil weltered all over his face.

"Call it my way of establishing boundaries," she replied.

"I don't have the tools to speak to them the way I need to. Not yet. But you...you're good at this stuff."

"No, I'm not," his voice wobbled.

"You are," she insisted. "Besides, you've got something to gain from this too."

He sighed, sounding exasperated. "And what's that?"

"A backbone."

The shock in Mason's expression blanketed any offense he might have felt.

"Your drive for the truth has caused both of us nothing but pain," Miya went on. "You endanger the people you try to help because you want to be the hero, and I know you feel guilty for that. Isn't that why you came looking for me? To make up for what happened three years ago?"

His gaze sank to the floor. "I thought I'd conquered that impulse after Amanda. I guess old habits die hard."

"Don't beat yourself up," Miya snorted. "Just look at Abaddon, or Kai, or me. We've been repeating our patterns way longer than you."

He smiled at that, and Miya couldn't help but return the gesture.

"Listen," she began. "The point is, you need to stop feeling guilty for your mistakes. Guilt's only led you to do more of the exact same thing. If the truth demon should have taught you anything, it's that you don't need all the answers. But what you *do* need is to confront your shit for real. Why are you so afraid of telling my parents the truth?"

"Because I don't want to be seen as a failure." Mason swallowed. "I don't want to feel ashamed for failing them too."

"Which is why you're the perfect person to confront them when I can't." She stepped up to him, searching his face. "Stand your ground. Conquer your guilt and tell them they need to let me go until I'm ready to face them on *my* terms."

"But aren't you just avoiding them like I am?" he challenged.

"Yeah," Miya nodded, "I am. Only I'm making that decision with my eyes wide open. I'm doing it because I'm too tired and heartbroken to watch them lose me a second time —because I don't want to endure losing them a second time. What's your excuse?"

His shoulders slumped in defeat. "Pride."

Miya gave him a light shake. "Do the right thing, Mason. Not for your ego or for praise, but just because it's the right thing to do."

He ground his teeth, mulling over her words until finally, he conceded. "All right, I'll do this for you. Besides," he smiled weakly, "I don't want to be anywhere near this place when impossible things start getting too real."

"Wise man," she joked, then caught his sleeve as he pushed past her. "And hey—thank you. Really. I owe you one, friend."

She saw the elation in his eyes when she called him *friend.* "You got it—" he hesitated, then let out the breath he'd been holding. "Dreamwalker."

❧ 48 ❧

AFTER MASON LEFT, Miya retreated to the back of *The Spade*. She heard the faucet in the employee bathroom squeak on and halted at the door, kept ajar by a stopper. Ama was steadying Crowbar, then ducked out to let the bartender brace herself against the sink. Crowbar splashed water on her face and scrubbed the blood splotching her arm tattoos. Scouring the vanity, she located a half-empty bottle of mouthwash and rinsed out whatever sour taste remained.

"What the hell was that?" Crowbar asked when the water shut off. She clutched either side of the porcelain bowl, staring at Ama's reflection in the mirror.

"I'm not sure," said Ama, and Miya knew it wasn't a lie.

The bartender whirled on her. "Then what is *he?*"

"A living spirit," said Miya, inching a little closer.

"What does that mean?" Crowbar pressed, looking between the two women.

Ama took a deep breath. "It means you shouldn't worry about it. It's not something you want to be wrapped up in."

Crowbar balked at her. "When you brought that kid

into my bar, I thought she was on drugs!" She pointed at Miya. "Drugs don't explain a bird exploding from a dead guy like a freakin' chestburster! And I repeat—in *my* bar!" She closed in on Ama, their noses nearly brushing. "You don't want me wrapped up in this, but you brought it to my door!"

Miya felt the strength sap from her bones. They did bring this to her door; they owed her more than vague warnings. She could tell Ama felt the same way, the white wolf's expression pained as she was confronted with another person's distress and confusion. Perhaps she was finally beginning to understand what she and Gavran had put Mason through, and Miya too felt herself question if her own omissions about Crowbar's sister had done more harm than good.

"It's complicated," Ama whispered, running her hands up Crowbar's arms before giving her shoulders a comforting squeeze. "And frankly, I don't have the energy or the words to explain it all, but I'll tell you this: The stories about the things that go bump in the night—they're all true. And *we* are one of them."

Crowbar swallowed and took a step back, her forehead knotting with unease as her eyes darted between Ama and Miya. "*We?*"

As though tethered to her by an invisible cord, Ama glided forward. "The raven you saw, Miya, Kai, and me." Crowbar gasped as her backside hit the sink. Ama closed in, amber eyes glowing in the mirror behind her. "We're the monsters from your darkest fables."

"Why are you here?" Crowbar asked.

"Hunting," Miya answered when Ama averted her gaze.

Crowbar squeezed past to the doorway. "Hunting what?"

Ama snatched her hand and pulled her back. "It's about your sister."

Crowbar froze. Miya knew she'd been suspicious of the police's lazy insistence that Vincent had suffered a psychotic break. Mental illness was rarely behind domestic violence; something had been missing. Now, that twisted puzzle finally had a jagged little piece that fit.

"Oh my God," Crowbar choked on a sob and pulled her hand back, then turned the corner towards the kitchen.

Miya caught the look of devastation on Ama's face. "Go after her," she encouraged, and Ama followed, catching the door as Crowbar slammed through.

"It was something supernatural, wasn't it?" Miya heard Crowbar ask.

She padded up to the kitchen doors and opened them a crack. Crowbar didn't need both of them, and the last thing Miya wanted was for the bartender to feel ganged up on. Besides, Miya had never seen Ama so vulnerable with another person before; she deserved the chance to work this out on her own.

Miya saw Ama nod in response like she was unable to speak the dreaded word: *yes.*

Crowbar stormed up to her. "Do you know what it was? How it...m-made Vincent..."

"A malicious spirit," Ama said quietly.

"Like, a vengeful ghost?" Her head was shaking as though her mind rejected the possibility without her say-so.

"Yes. In life, she was the victim of a tragedy. One Miya found herself a part of three years ago."

Miya's heart squeezed. This was all because of her— because of her legacy.

"And now she's just...hurting random people?" Crowbar sounded incredulous, her grief blurring into rage.

The white wolf sighed. "Yes. She's gone after Kai now, which is why you haven't seen him with Miya lately."

"He's staying away from her." Crowbar drew a ragged

breath. "Vince did the same thing. Just started disappearing. Everyone thought he was cheating, but he was spending his nights away from home because he didn't want to hurt Syd."

"Dahlia—I'm so sorry." Ama finally unglued her feet from the floor. Her arms snaked around the bartender and pulled her into a tight embrace. Miya knew she should've walked away then, but the tender scene held her in place. It inspired hope that maybe there would be something redeemable on the other side of this damn crucible. Crowbar had lost so much, and what Ama had gone through earlier that day was unimaginable. First, Miya had descended into a black hole, her memories and identity obliterated. Then, Gavran went after her with no promise of returning and no guarantee of success. Just as Ama had crumbled from the loss, so too did Crowbar upon realizing that her sister's death had resulted from machinations far outside her understanding. The floodgates collapsed as she wept into Ama's shoulder, her body shaking with anguish.

"H-how do you all know this?"

"It was a team effort," Ama mumbled into her rose-coloured hair. "Miya and Kai get most of the credit, I'm afraid. I'm sure you can understand why they struggled to tell you."

"I'll forgive them...eventually," she whimpered.

Miya swallowed the lump in her throat, a jumbled assortment of elation and embarrassment flooding her cheeks in a heated wave.

"I think they'd appreciate that. You seem to have developed a bond, albeit a young one." Ama smiled as Crowbar untangled herself. "You didn't tell me your preferred name was Crowbar."

She shrugged. "For friends, yeah. But I like to give pretty ladies my real name."

"Oh?" Ama's brow arched as her lips curled into something sly.

"Come on," Crowbar chuckled. "You know you're hot."

"Beauty is in the eye of the beholder and all that," Ama joked. "I prefer not to make assumptions that might come back to bite me later."

Crowbar laughed, the sound strained before it lightened to an easy chime. "Well," she slid her arms around Ama's neck and swayed forward, "the beholder is impressed." Her rueful smile crumbled then, and her fingers curled into the fabric of Ama's shirt, ensnaring her. "It feels wrong to laugh, but I'm tired of feeling like shit all the time. I'm *sick* of losing people."

"I know," Ama murmured. "Me too."

Beneath the shallow veil of human costuming, the potent scent of bitter loneliness lingered, yearning to be tended to. Miya turned away and let the kitchen doors stall shut behind her. She'd overstayed her welcome, but she'd seen enough to know that Crowbar and Ama would be all right. They'd found each other, and they were perfect.

❦ 49 ❦

M IYA RETURNED TO THE BAR, picked up the stray blanket, and spread it over the old man's body. As the fabric contoured to his form, he melted away, leaving the quilt flat against the floorboards.

Gavran-the-raven perched on a beer tap and squawked.

Miya glanced at him and frowned. "Magic trick?" she asked, then drew back the cover to reveal a pile of dust. The body had disintegrated. Without Gavran feeding it his life-force, it'd decayed at an exponential rate—as if making up for lost time.

"Saves me the cleanup." She shook out the blanket and reached for a broom and dustpan nestled in the corner.

Now alone with her thoughts, Miya's mind spiralled like a cyclone, her newfound memories battering away at her clarity. How was she supposed to feel? Nothing about her had really changed; she was still the same person. Her name was Emiliya Delathorne, daughter of Raymond and Andrea Delathorne. A once aspiring journalist and depressed university student turned Dreamwalker. The last three years were still at the forefront despite what Gavran had shown her.

Although she'd acquired all of Kali's memories, they felt distant and murky, like a penny at the bottom of a dirty pond. They gave her information and understanding, but they didn't change how she *felt*. The remnants of those experiences— even before she'd recollected them—had made their mark long ago. The only difference now was that she knew *why*.

Kali's impact had always been there; it'd only been silent until Miya pulled back the layers of time and space, and she finally heard the screams.

Gathering up the remains of Gavran's shell, Miya carefully poured them into an empty jar she'd found under the counter. She didn't know who this body had once belonged to, but she knew it was a child of the Hollow—someone her former self had likely known. Even if Kali would've wanted the ashes of every last villager scattered to the wind and whisked from memory, Miya couldn't bring herself to want the same. The bone-dust in her hands may have no longer belonged to Gavran, but they were a tangible piece of her past—her history. They deserved some care.

"How kind you are, honouring your hated dead," a voice sneered from behind.

Miya jolted around to find Rusalka standing at the end of the bar. She looked...different. Her sultry, shark-eyed stare now dithered with a strange mix of ire and uncertainty. Her confident posture faltered, her shoulders drooped, and her chest heaved with laboured breaths. Pieces of her were sloughing off as beads of slimy swamp water speckled her sagging grey skin.

Miya set the jar aside. "I was just thinking about you. Thought I'd have to find you myself."

"I felt you calling with that cloying heart of yours," said the demoness. "But I was on my way, regardless."

"You must be strong, manifesting like this," Miya

observed. "Most malicious spirits can't stray too far from their victims when they cross over to this plane."

Rusalka's pale blue lip wrinkled into a grimace. "I'm not *most* malicious spirits. I'm Rusalka."

The dream stone tickled Miya's collarbone as she shifted her weight. It was warm again, its lustre having returned with the Dreamwalker. "That's not your real name, is it? Rusalkas are folklore."

"So are you."

"Is that why you took the name?" Miya asked. "You didn't want to be bested by the fable that killed you, so you became one?"

The melting woman smiled. "Rusalkas are terrifying creatures. There are different versions, of course, but my favourite is the woman who's drowned by her lover, then returns to lure men to their watery demise when they wander too close to her resting place."

"Makes sense," said Miya. "It's what happened to you. You're from Black Hollow. I'm sorry I wasn't there to stop it."

She bared her teeth—each one pointed. "Your apologies do me no good, Dreamwalker. You lived, weaving your way through the ages until you could safely return while others died. Others like me."

Miya lowered her gaze. She knew it wasn't her fault, yet the gnawing in her gut wouldn't stop. She took a deep breath and faced the shadow of her legacy. "When?"

"October 1948." Her lip quivered, and she gasped, milky vapour fogging the air in front of her. "The water was so cold."

"What was your name?"

"Yvette." She scoffed. "They made sure to skew the record. My *dear* husband was a decorated military man.

A. J. VRANA

They couldn't have *that* stain disrupt public perception of our brave war heroes!"

"I don't understand—what exactly did they report?"

"A *tragic* accident," she spat. "Poor, foolish woman wandered too far into the woods and slipped on a rock. Cracked her head open and drowned in the river."

"Shit," Miya whispered.

"Of course, they couldn't resist insinuating that I'd been spirited away by you. That story became especially popular when my murderer took his life," she sighed, "apparently from the grief!"

"You killed him."

"What?" She seemed aghast. "No! If I'd killed him, I wouldn't be here!" Her anger shook the chandelier. "He killed himself! Out of *genuine* grief!" She began to tremble, her seaweed hair writhing like snakes. "He didn't deserve to grieve...he had no right!"

Miya's eyes widened with realization. "This isn't just a vendetta, is it? You wanted justice...an arrest, public outrage, a corner of a newspaper page—anything."

"Instead, he died a hero. A tragic victim of his wife's selfish meandering."

"I'm so sorry," said Miya, her throat tight. "I know that doesn't mean anything to you, but you're not alone."

"Is that supposed to make it better?" Rusalka mocked. "The pain of other innocents doesn't ease mine!"

"Then why do you do it?" Miya took a step forward. "You drive people to kill other innocent women!"

"Because the pain is all I have now! It's all that keeps me here, and I will not lie down and succumb. I will not be remembered as a hapless girl or a victim, even if I am not a survivor. Revenge is the only liberation from victimhood, the only reparation for *not* surviving." She smiled grimly.

"Don't you know how to stop a rusalka? You must kill the one who made her."

Miya shook her head. "I can't do that. Your husband's been dead for decades."

"This is true," she feigned consideration, tapping a finger against her chin. "But there is another who shares responsibility. The one who pulled my husband's fragile strings."

"Abaddon." His name still tasted sour.

"That monstrosity," Rusalka hissed. "How many women have died because of him? How many had no relation to the Dreamwalker but lost their lives being mistaken for her—a mistake that wouldn't have mattered if not for Abaddon's cruelty and malice!"

Miya curled her hands into fists, clenching and releasing as she mulled this over. "What if I take revenge for you?"

"How?" Rusalka huffed, sounding bored. "Abaddon is gone...again, because of you."

"But the First isn't," Miya countered. "I saw him with my own eyes. I bargained with him. I won."

This seemed to pique Rusalka's interest. "Go on."

"You're right. This is all because of me, and I should be the one to end it. So, I'll make you a deal. I'll go back to finish what I started." Miya lifted the dream stone from her shirt and dangled it for Rusalka to see. "I can drag spirits to the in-between. I can kill them. And I'll do this for you under one condition: You leave Kai alone. You leave me alone. You disappear from our lives, and you never hurt anyone again."

Rusalka bore holes into her, digging for a trap. "And why not simply take me to the in-between and be rid of me?"

"Because Velizar is still the root of the problem." Miya dropped the pendant. "Besides, you're a vengeful spirit. Something born from violence can't be put down by it." She locked eyes with her enemy. "I'll do as the folklore says. I'll avenge you."

A slow, sensual smile spread across Rusalka's face. Her pallid tongue darted out, and she licked her lips. "You have a deal, Dreamwalker."

KAI

KAI WAS DONE WITH PROPRIETY. Done with what little concessions he'd made for humanity's delicate sensibilities. As he stumbled towards the underbelly of Orme's Rest, a passerby gawped at him like he needed an exorcism. Maybe he did.

"Fuck off!" Kai roared, his voice layered with Velizar's. Grabbing either side of his head, he tugged his hair and keeled over as the throbbing returned. This was nothing like Abaddon. Kai thought he would've been able to handle it. He'd handled it for years.

You were wrong. I am not Abaddon. I am pure.

Kai drove his fist through the downpipe of a nearby building, breaking the bottom clean off. It clanged into the gutter, the racket splitting his skull. He was so close. He could smell her—that rotting *bitch*.

Forcing himself upright, Kai wiped the sweat beading across his brow. The air was sticky, sweltering—like breathing in fumes. His vision was bleary, shapes melding into one another. Colours bled out of objects like ghostly auras. Squeezing his eyes shut, he followed the smell of death, decay, sick, and swamp all the way to *The Mangy Spade*.

The walls closed in; he was in the alley. When his hand brushed over the laminate glaze on the tavern doors, he knew he'd made it.

Kai opened his eyes to the king of spades welcoming him home. Pushing through the entryway, he stepped inside.

Still dimly lit, the orange glow of the chandelier faltered as he approached. There, sitting atop the bar, was Ama, her silvery-white mane cascading over her shoulders as she leaned back on her palms. Her legs were crossed, foot twitching as she narrowed her gaze on him.

"Where's Miya?" The words came out like gravel, scraping his throat on their way out.

"That's none of your concern," said Ama.

Kai scanned the empty establishment. Rusalka's stench was strong, but she was nowhere in sight. "Is she with Crowbar?"

The bridge of Ama's nose rippled as a fearsome snarl erupted from her lips. "You will keep away from them. *Both* of them."

"I don't have time for your shit!" Kai flung a nearby chair. It skipped across the dining room before crashing into a corner booth. "Can't you smell her? She's been here!"

"Yes," said Ama, sliding off the counter. "She has. I figured you wouldn't be far behind."

She was poised for a fight. Kai knew she didn't trust him —not after all his fuck ups. He couldn't blame her, but his singular focus was finding Miya. He didn't give a damn if the white wolf was here to protect her. He'd tear right through her if he had to.

The pain was suddenly gone. His legs felt strong, and the gutting migraine had faded to a trilling calm. Velizar had loosened his hold.

Kai made his way to the bar, eyes trained on the kitchen doors. He could smell Miya on the other side—faint but familiar.

Ama glided in front of him, barricading his path.

"You're in my way." He placed a hand on her shoulder to move her aside.

She grabbed his arm with viper-like speed. Yanking him towards her, she swung her elbow and struck him across the jaw.

Stumbling back from the surprising force, Kai braced against the bar top. She was stronger than she looked.

Spitting out a glob of blood, he straightened and wiped his mouth. "Fine," he growled, then flashed her a shit-eating grin. "I've always wondered how this would go down."

Ama snorted, shaking out her hand. "Disappointingly."

Kai didn't wait for another quip. He lunged forward, forearm to her neck. Shelves collapsed and bottles tumbled as he pinned Ama to the wall and drove a fist into her side. He felt her muscles tense against his knuckles, the blow landing softer than he would've liked.

Offering little more than a grunt of displeasure, she reached up and grabbed a bottle of Jack, then smashed it over his head. Pelted by shattered glass, Kai turned away only to feel her previously dangling feet dig into his chest. With one kick, she launched him into the counter, and he swore he felt his ribs crack. Breath hitching, he shambled back, but he barely had a moment to regain his senses when two small hands found his shoulders, and Ama's knee hammered into his groin.

Kai doubled over. Before he could gasp a lungful, she

clasped his chin between her thumb and forefinger and forced his eyes to hers, their amber glow mocking him.

"Did you think this was going to be a fair fight?" she seethed.

Impotent rage coiled around Kai's throat as he choked back a strangled cry. He heard Velizar's laughter—that cold, blood-curdling sound that rattled his core. It wound up every bone and coursed through every vein. His body felt like living fire, and his arm—that godforsaken left arm—began to move on its own. It snatched Ama's wrist like a bear trap.

Kai opened his mouth, and the voice of Velizar spiralled out with his own. "No."

Otherworldly power surged through him. Twisting Ama's arm like it was a twig, he wrenched out of her hold and dragged her to the floor. Rolling over, he nailed her down with a knee to the gut. He saw the alarm on her face as realization soaked in: she no longer had the advantage, and with Velizar's strength compounding his own, the ferocious white wolf was reduced to a whining pup.

It felt good, and Kai hated that it did. His fingers curled around her neck without his say-so. He could feel her pulse fluttering against his palm, driving him into a frenzy. Every predatory nerve twitched with an overwhelming urge to kill. Yet something inside him screamed, *No, no, no. There'll be no coming back from this.*

It'll be a new era.

"Kai." It was Ama, her voice strained as she fought against his hold, nails clawing at his hand. "Fight...it."

"Why should I?" Kai snarled. "What's the point? I'll never be free of this!"

"Coward!" she choked, but his grip only tightened.

He didn't want it to end like this. Ama may not have

been his friend, but she was a comrade. Even now, the two of them shared the same goal: to keep Miya safe.

End her.

I can't.

You can. And you will.

No, Kai rebelled, but his fingers only sank deeper, until he could feel the curve of her jugular and see the bruises colouring her flesh.

Kai looked into Ama's eyes—always warm and full of life, like sunlight breaking through storm clouds. Even now, she was fearless, confident that she'd get her way.

For the first time since knowing her, he hoped she was right.

❦ 51 ❦

MIYA

A LOUD CRASH echoed from the dining room, followed by Gavran's ear-piercing screech. Jarred, Miya dropped her glass on the kitchen floor, water pooling around her feet. Crowbar had gone to buy cigarettes after refusing to return home at Ama's behest. The white wolf had tried bribing the bartender with promises of Sunday brunch and pricey mimosas, but it was no use.

That left only one person in *The Mangy Spade.*

Squeaking the tap off, Miya blasted towards the front of the tavern. She could see the black blur of wings from the corner of her eye as Gavran followed suit, just as he had lifetimes ago.

He caught her shoulder and tugged her back as she was about to reach the doors.

Rush into danger...stupid. Sneak! Sneak! he squawked in her mind.

Miya slid to the wall and peeked through the round, greasy window just inches from her face. She couldn't see

377

much, but there were bottles strewn across the bar top—some broken, others whole. Then, she heard his voice.

"Why should I? What's the point? I'll never be free of this!"

Kai.

Desperation and despair laced his angry roar. Miya's heart twisted, but before the anguish could tear it from her chest, she threw herself through the doors.

The dining room was a mess of shattered liquor bottles, far worse than what she'd spied through her peephole. The brass chandelier swung like a squeaking metronome, threatening to unlatch at any moment. Blood smeared the floor, the crimson streaks guiding Miya through the bedlam until her eyes fell on Kai and Ama.

They were locked in a death match, their focus broken by the interruption. Kai tore his gaze from Ama, his shock palpable. It was the first time he'd seen Miya since their parting in the hotel room.

His face was cut open with glass embedded in the gashes. Blood trickled over his lips and speckled Ama's cheek. The lines on his forehead smoothed as he drank Miya in, but his eyes were as red as his wounds—a shining mural of unspoken emotions, ugly ones that didn't have words to describe them.

"Miya."

Her name sounded like fire in his throat, burning him raw.

"Get off her!" Miya commanded, taking a threatening step towards him. Gavran beat his wings as he hovered in the background, crowing at Kai.

Kai's face rippled into a snarl, his words spoken through clenched teeth, "I...can't..."

Miya saw it then—the hand around Ama's throat. It was shaking, fingers twitching like he was losing control.

Wisps of charcoal smoke wafted around each digit, painting his skin a necrotic black. Kai was struggling to keep his hand open while something tried to force it closed.

"He's fighting it," Ama said between gasps. "But it's too strong for him."

Kai whirled his molten glare on her. "I'm the only thing keeping you alive!"

"Well, excuse me...if I'm not...grateful!" She writhed under him, trying to lift her hips and dislodge him.

Before Miya could react, Gavran dove towards them, talons scraping Kai's face. Miya could feel his intentions as though they were her own—*distract, bad arm swipe up, free Ama.*

It worked. The hand around Ama's throat shot up and struck the raven so hard he flew across the room, crashing into the remaining shelves before he was able to slow himself. It was a split second, but it was all they needed.

"No!" Miya shouted as Gavran slumped to the floor and struggled to right himself. As she spun towards Kai, Ama launched up and head-butted him in the nose. He pulled back, blood gushing. Ethereal feathers of midnight and violet engulfed Miya like armor as the dream stone flashed. Taken by fury, Miya released a war-like scream that momentarily felled the border between worlds. The sound distorted as it pierced through the physical plane and the dreamscape alike, sending Kai crumpling to the floor as he clamped his hands over his ears.

Dark mist shuddered against his skin, battling to stay inside.

The anger drained out of Miya faster than it'd filled her up, her otherworldly shroud vanishing alongside it. "What did you do?" she whimpered as she realized that Kai wasn't alone.

"Yes..." came a gleeful hiss as putrid breath washed over her.

It was Rusalka, now clinging to Miya's back.

Staggering to his feet, Kai grabbed the wall for support, then curled in on himself.

"What did you do?" Miya asked again, her voice quaking with fear.

"I had to get rid of her," said Kai. "This was the only damn way."

The miasma slithered over him, coalescing in his left arm. He tried to make a fist, to contain the spasms, but the entity subdued him, bending his fingers to grotesque angles.

Kai grimaced as his joints were folded beyond their limit, but he didn't dare make a sound—a stubborn refusal to give his nemesis even an inch.

Something about him was different. Even while Abaddon haunted him, he retained his autonomy. Sure, the phantom terrorized him, made him live in constant trepidation, but Abaddon never *controlled* Kai.

And Miya had never feared him; she knew that no matter what Abaddon threw their way, Kai wasn't dangerous. The brothers were forces that clashed, but neither had the strength to overtake the other.

This was different.

They were joined—not just by an enduring grudge, but by the very fabric of their souls. It was like they'd been stitched together, the suture too deep and painful to rip apart.

"You're integrated with him," said Miya. "With Velizar."

He finally looked up, his face hidden under shadow save for the stream of red emanating from his eyes. "Yes."

A weak croak drew Miya's attention, and she glimpsed Gavran hopping forward as he shook out his injured wing. She sighed with relief, but the reprieve was fleeting.

"You knew this would happen." The words were directed to the demon at Miya's back.

"Of course I did. Why do you think I came to you?" Rusalka tittered. "Have you forgotten what Abaddon did to me? I wasn't supposed to die, but I was murdered in your place, Dreamwalker. When I said there was another responsible, I didn't just mean your enemy. I meant you as well."

She circled around like a shark, greeting Miya with her vacuous smile. "I will have revenge on all three spirits: First, Velizar, who set the cycle in motion, then his brother, who enabled him for far too long. And finally, you, who lives while I and so many other innocents died. You will lose the one you love most by your own hand. *That* is your punishment."

"No," Miya shook her head, her voice breaking. "I won't do it."

How could she? There was no promise that could bind her to murder. Even if Velizar had taken possession of someone else—Mason, or a random stranger—she would *not* take anyone's life to appease Rusalka's vindictiveness.

"But you must," cooed the demoness. "The only way to kill Velizar now is to kill the one he is a part of."

I don't care, Miya wanted to scream. Sickness swam in her stomach as memories pummelled her like stones—her first meeting with Kai, reiterated throughout the aeons. An injured wolf and a lonely girl who always found one another beneath the willow. They fit together like the two pieces of her broken dream stone.

Even if Miya could spend the rest of her life without him, he was still a part of her story—a god from her fable—and she'd be a fool to allow a promise made in deceit hold her hostage.

"I won't do it," she said, her gaze fixed on Kai. The tremors grew stronger until she knotted her hands into fists to keep from shaking. Turmoil swirled between the witch and the wolf. Despite everything he'd done, she knew he was fighting back with the only tools he knew how to use. He didn't deserve to die. Besides...

"I still love him."

Rusalka's face contorted. "This was *your* deal, Dreamwalker. It's on you to fulfill it. Or I'll simply have to find a new target—your father, perhaps? He came so close last time. You were lucky he never found you in those wretched woods."

Miya spun towards the monstress when the panic threatened to swallow her whole. "You're just like Abaddon!"

"I was his victim!" Rusalka howled back, sickly slime spewing from her mouth.

"You're a victim who's become like her abuser! You're stuck in his cycle!" Miya's muddy green eyes ignited. She refused to budge, even as Rusalka's venom spattered across her skin and burned her like acid. "You've taken his place. You're enacting his will even in his absence. You proud of that?"

Rusalka's eyes swelled with tarry rage. Her mouth drew impossibly wide, her saw-toothed maw unhinging as her nostrils flared. Grabbing Miya by the hair, she yanked her back and exposed her throat. Her nails plucked at the soft skin beneath Miya's jaw. "I will kill everyone you love. It's your choice. Lose one or lose them all.

From the corner of her eye, Miya saw Kai blunder closer. He was grasping his left arm, fingers twitching erratically as if out of his control. His breath drew in with a ragged wheeze, his skin caked in sweat as he struggled against the entity scraping away his volition. Miya stretched back and searched for Kai—the real Kai hidden beneath the heap of torment Velizar had all but crushed him with. As if feeling her call, he looked up and found her.

His eyes no longer bled fire. They'd returned to their warm mahogany brown, his pupils ringed with their usual red tinge.

With malice slicing into her jugular, Miya did the only thing she could think of. She smiled at Kai, then whispered the words she wished she'd told him aeons ago, before Velizar drove a blade through their hearts.

"I love you."

52

KAI

THE FLOOR WOULDN'T STOP TILTING. Miya's words had barely formed on her lips, but he'd heard them loud and clear, echoing in the hollow chamber behind his ribs.

But the fucking floor wouldn't stop tilting.

Kai felt like he was in a snow globe being shaken by a toddler. Every time he tried to step in the right direction, the annoying brat governing his universe shook the glass ball and left him tripping over his own feet, lost in a blizzard of helplessness.

That rotting mermaid had his girl.

Ama flung herself at Rusalka, but it was no use. She was a vengeful creature that couldn't be killed by ordinary means. Only the Dreamwalker could slay a spirit, and this one played by its own complicated rules. The white wolf plunged right through her, tumbling into a chair before jumping back up and glowering. She was joined by Gavran, who dive-bombed the monster several times before she cut a thin line across Miya's throat. It welled with blood, painting Rusalka's nails red. Her grudge was strong enough to harm the people she was attached to. For the Dreamwalker, her claws were as real as any blade.

Just then, the kitchen doors flew open, crashing into the adjacent wall.

"What the hell is going on here?" Crowbar stood in the entryway, a still-lit cigarette between her lips. She scanned the room, eyes lingering on Miya's bent form before she spotted Kai. The anger bled from her face alongside the colour. She was now sheet-white, ghostly shock invading the space left behind by the outrage. The plastic bag dangling from her wrist slid off her hand and plopped to the floor as she went slack-jawed.

Ama pivoted towards her, voice fear-stricken. "Dahlia—"

Before she could finish, Crowbar jumped onto the back counter and retrieved her namesake. Clapping the steel into her palm, she hopped down and scanned the room. "It's here, isn't it?" She was hoarse and breathless, her cheeks moist. "The thing that killed my sister!"

Rusalka threw her head back and unleashed a discordant laugh. "What's this? You actually told this poor girl the truth?"

Kai hadn't, but he saw from Miya and Ama's heart-broken expressions that they'd been left with no other choice. They'd given Crowbar new wounds to heal.

The bartender homed in on Miya, whose contortions only confirmed that something had a hold of her. Miya flinched, attempting to jerk free, and Crowbar saw her opening.

"Don't!" Kai's protest was a pathetic croak as he was lambasted by Velizar's infection.

Gavran bolted for Crowbar's weapon. His talons clinched the curve of the rod as he flapped furiously, trying to guide the bartender away from danger. Ama grabbed her from behind and pulled her farther from the demoness at the center of the room.

"What are you doing!" Crowbar fought back, now sobbing uncontrollably.

Ama tightened her grip, the human girl no match for her strength. "Stop! You can't clobber your sister's killer with a stick!"

"I don't care!" Crowbar shrieked, now kicking and throwing herself back at the white wolf.

Kai couldn't breathe. He didn't know if it was because of Velizar, or because something inside him had finally broken for good. None of this should've been happening, but it was...and it was all because he was *weak*.

You don't have to be weak.

"Shut up," Kai rasped.

The only way to stop her is to get to her first. He felt Velizar's teeth grating against his spine—like there was a second body sprouting from the dark ooze flooding his insides. **Slice up her heart, Destroyer.**

"You said that wouldn't work."

It won't work for long, but then we'll have the pleasure of cutting her down again. We can hold her down together.

Kai's left arm began to spasm, jerking towards his hunting knife. No matter how hard he tried to wrangle it back, his traitorous hand wouldn't obey, so he snatched the weapon with his good one.

His left arm was dying. Bruises settled into his finger-tips, and black veins erupted from the taint, spidering up his wrist.

Velizar was a poison—a caustic fume withering Kai from the inside. All throughout time, they'd wrestled for control, until competition devolved into brutality. Their cycle of

A. J. VRANA

killing one another had never actually ended. How many times had Kai butchered his brother? How many lifetimes had been wrecked by their contest of egos, by their stubborn refusal to do the most obvious thing in the world and simply walk away?

Kai stared at the knife, recalling how he'd driven it into Rusalka's heart, how he believed so brazenly that it would eliminate her the same way it'd eliminated his other problems—including his brother.

But it didn't work. It never worked. Violence and destruction defined him, just as Velizar wanted. His brother had once called himself the king of spades, though Kai wasn't sure which of them that applied to.

Was Velizar really the king of spades, or was he merely the king's hand?

Kai understood now why his nemesis had chosen to fester there. Hands enacted wills. They were a testament to the mind's control over the body. What better way to rob Kai of his autonomy than to take the hand that wielded his own blade?

Kai gripped the haft tighter. "She can't help you," he called to Rusalka. "But I can."

The demoness sneered at him. "What are you on about, wolf?"

"I know what you want, and I can give it to you." He turned the tip of the knife to the floor. "Let her go, and I promise I'll end this." He glanced at Miya. "I'll do what she can't."

Rusalka's grip on Miya's hair loosened, and a cruel smile spread across her face. "Oh? Will you slit that pretty throat for me, precious thing?"

Miya darted back, her wide eyes grabbing hold of him. "Don't—"

"It's all right," Kai said softly and offered her a faint

smile. He looked past her, locked eyes with the raven guarding Crowbar, and nodded in gratitude.

Gavran tilted his head to a near-right angle, and the boy's voice echoed in Kai's mind. *You are a god of the Hollow and the realm that echoes within. Reality is your playground. Shape it as you see fit.*

Kai knew what he had to do.

Velizar had tried to convince him to take the blame for what'd become of them. He wanted Kai to accept that they'd be better off as a single being so they couldn't keep repeating the same mistakes. Most of all, he wanted Kai to believe that the Dreamwalker was their enemy.

But it was all a ruse; the question of whose fault the past was didn't matter. Velizar's goal wasn't reconciliation; it was control. To destroy Kai's sense of self, to strip him of agency. They couldn't keep fighting if one of them was a slave to the other.

Kai raised the knife.

I don't know what you're planning, his brother's frantic voice interjected, **but you can never be rid of me!**

Kai's arm throbbed with the force of Velizar's compulsion, but he was a stubborn son of a bitch, and he wouldn't be bested by a clingy zealot.

You are *nothing* without me!

With his last ounce of willpower, Kai balled up his betrayer-fist and pressed the cursed thing flush against his side. Spinning the hunting knife in his right hand, he aimed the point downward. "I'll be a better nothing without you."

Then, he brought down the glinting steel.

Kai bit back a scream as the blade pierced his gut. Blood blossomed over his shirt, the dark fabric failing to disguise the wet stain as life spilled from his wound. Every cell screamed in rebellion as blistering fire erupted over his skin, but he refused to let go. Defying his impulses, Kai sawed through tendon, muscle, and bone, cleaving through ribs and moving towards his heart.

"Get out," he growled through clenched teeth, the knife juddering in his white-knuckled grip. "Or die with your precious baby brother."

You're bluffing!

Kai's lips pulled back into baleful grin. "Think I won't die for her?" He tugged the blade closer to the beating mass in his chest. "You've got a short memory, *brother*."

No!
No!
No!

Velizar's fury gored Kai's senses as he repeated the word like a futile mantra.

You dare!
You dare!
You dare!

His protests grew louder, the groans rising to a skull-piercing shriek.

The air fled Kai's lungs, and he wheezed desperately. Stars bloomed before his eyes, chairs and tables blurring into wobbly doubles as his legs shook from the strain. But Kai endured. Lifetimes of deadly conflict with Velizar curdled into an ultimatum.

He'd carved up Rusalka's heart. Now he would carve out his own.

A roiling pressure pushed on the blade from inside him. It squirmed between his broken ribs, writhing to escape. Unable to fight the thrust any longer, the knife came free. Kai reeled back and dropped it, the pain overtaking him. He crashed into the wall and fell to his knees, gripping his abdomen as it spewed red and black. A tarry, foul-smelling liquid poured out of him, and as it did, the veins that pulsed with darkness along his left hand faded to a light blue.

The thick, mercurial substance that left his body bubbled like hot oil. It undulated against the floorboards, losing itself in the cracks as though trying to disperse.

"He's escaping!" Rusalka shrieked, her voice laced with panic.

But no one was listening.

Kai detected every pair of eyes in the room on him. He curled into a ball, sight bleary and teeth chattering. He rolled onto his back and whimpered, the skin around the wound searing as though branded.

Then, he felt Miya drop next to him.

"Lambchop..." he murmured deliriously.

"Shut up, you're bleeding to death!" He couldn't bring himself to look at her—not yet.

"I'm fine."

"You just stabbed yourself!" She tried to staunch the flow with a towel, but it was like putting a Band-Aid over a gunshot wound.

He finally found the courage to open his eyes, and the worry on her face ate him alive. "Rotting Mermaid...is right."

Miya glanced at the floor, but the black ooze was gone.

"You have to go...fuck him up."

"I don't care about that right now!" Her hands shook against him.

He could hear Rusalka crying, her monstrosity giving way to something fragile now that her rage was faltering.

"Oh, get a hold of yourself!" Ama snapped at her, then released Crowbar and rushed towards Miya. "Kai's right. You should follow that...*thing*. It could be your only chance to finish him."

Miya didn't move. "But—"

"I'll take care of Kai!" the white wolf silenced her.

Miya swallowed and nodded slowly. "Just give me a minute."

Ama sighed but conceded. She retreated to the corner of the room with Crowbar and Gavran, watching Rusalka's every move. The mouldy washcloth seemed wrung out, albeit begrudgingly. Her only shot at revenge was to let the Dreamwalker do what she did best.

Crowbar had long stopped fighting to swing at a murderer she couldn't see. Her hands were pressed over her mouth, her eyes bloodshot as tears rolled over her fingers. Ama wrapped both arms around her, and she collapsed against the white wolf's shoulder, overcome with grief. Crowbar had witnessed one of the many twisted endings that might've awaited her sister and brother-in-law had things played out differently. Kai and Miya could've been Vincent and Sydney, only Vincent had no way of surviving what Kai had just done to himself.

Miya reached for Kai's hand. Twining their fingers, he squeezed to let her know he was still breathing.

"What if I don't make it back in time?" she questioned.

"Go," he groaned. "You'll make it."

"How can you be so sure after everything that's happened? How will you know it's me and not death beside you?"

Kai's mouth quirked, and he couldn't stop the laugh that rumbled from his chest. It hurt like all hell, like his ribs were about to shatter, but having Miya nearby left him with few shits to give about the sorry state of his body. Tugging her hand to his lips, he marked her palm with a bloody kiss and said, "That fucking raven could claw my eyes out, and I'd still know it's you next to me." Her murky green eyes found his, and the fear melted from his bones. "Besides, I'm pretty sure death smells nothing like you."

Miya leaned over and pressed her mouth to his. "You're right," she whispered. "Death smells far sweeter."

Silently, she lay down next to him and extended her arm, the gesture a command. Gavran swooped down, perched on her shoulder, and chortled victoriously.

"We've got prey to hunt," she said, then lifted the dream stone.

Kai's vision was fading, exhaustion and blood loss pulling him to darkness, but he resisted. He lolled his head to the side and stared at Miya's face. She looked serene as she readied herself for the greatest test of her life.

From across the room, Kai saw Ama smile.

53

MIYA

When Miya opened her eyes, she was staring at The Mangy Spade's *ornate brass chandelier. In place of the cobwebbed ceiling were thatched branches, swaying smoothly overhead. She sat up and surveyed her environment. The air was thick with otherworldly smoke, the usually warm-brown furniture now washed out like an old photograph.*

She heard weeping, a distant knelling like the voice of a solemn bell. The wolves were still and pale like marble, but Gavran's spectral body remained perched on her arm, his blue-black feathers shimmering as the bounds of his form shuddered in the haze.

Rusalka—the source of the wails—stood several paces away. Her sobs crescendoed as her head twisted towards Miya, then halted. All emotion fell from her face, her expression blank save for the tears marring her cheeks. She looked different—not like the decaying monster Miya had come to know, but like a young woman whose heart had been broken. Her once Medusan hair flowed down her back like waves of clear water, her skin shining like pearls where it had once been sickly and dull. And her eyes—previously like wide tunnels—held in them a glint of emerald.

Miya rose to her feet, her attention never leaving the demoness. "You're here."

Her mouth opened, but she struggled to speak. "Only...a little."

"Keeping one foot in each world is hard." Miya shifted her weight. "You making sure I live up to my word?"

A stilted nod, like a puppet made of wood.

"I hope this brings you peace, Yvette," Miya said softly, then turned to leave.

"I'm jealous..."

She peeked over her shoulder. "Sorry?"

Rusalka's head ground to the side like her spine was made of rusty gears. "Of all those I've compelled..." her voice reverberated against the walls, "none have resisted me...like the black wolf..."

Miya frowned, but she was willing to hear her out. "What are you trying to say?"

"Love is so rare," Rusalka wheezed. "Everyone thinks they know it because they feel it. But emotions are fleeting as dandelions in spring." She dragged in another painful breath. "Emotions...are not love. Burnished words...are not love." Slowly, agonizingly, her body rotated to face Miya, her shoulders slumping and her skin sagging as it lost its lustre. "Love is ugly, jagged, and sharp. It cuts. It bleeds. It's teeth and claws and depthless terror, and anyone who can embrace that is blessed." Her thin, cracked lips stretched over saw-like teeth, her ghoulish eyes gleaming as the emeralds corroded with re-surfacing malice. "I know this because I fed on those who thought they knew love. I devoured their pretty, gilded promises—their childish, beating hearts. Oh, how they made me beautiful. How their naïvety nourished me." She gasped, her hand curling into a skeletal fist. "But real love is like a broken wishbone in my throat. It offers me nothing but pain."

Miya averted her gaze as the grim words washed over her. Rusalka was being genuine, and what she said held true. Kai had survived her curse because he had no delusions about what it would take to be rid of her, and he was willing to bring back the foulest parts of his life to accomplish that.

"His only weakness," Rusalka grinned, her gums white as ash, "is that he is a man...and men are liars to themselves most of all."

"We're all liars," replied Miya. "I guess we only pay attention to the lies that hurt us most." Gavran croaked by her ear, and she reached up to scratch his feathery breast. "But believe me when I say I'll end this. Not for you, but for Kai. For me, too."

A low chuckle vibrated from Rusalka's chest. "Your love...will kill me..."

Something clawed at Miya's heart then—pity, anger, sadness— she wasn't sure. "Are you leaving?"

"I know you'll fulfil your promise." The smile slipped from her face, and her eyes locked onto Miya's. "Make him bleed, Dreamwalker."

Before the scraping in her chest left any more welts, Miya spun and deserted The Spade, *leaving Rusalka—no, Yvette—behind her. She would be gone soon, laid to rest by her faith in a single promise: that Miya would end Velizar once and for all.*

Miya threw open the doors and found herself staring into the dark, hilly forest of Black Hollow. Although she had no way of verifying her location, she felt it in the bottom of her soul. The roots below came to life, greeting her with their sleepy moans as she traipsed over the leafy ground.

Gavran fluttered next to her, then shot up to the sky and surveyed the land. He swooped and sliced through the wooded maze, leading the way. Even though he'd flown far out of sight, Miya could feel him in her pendant. Power thrummed through the dream stone, whispering to her in tongues only she understood.

This way, *it said, and she followed without hesitation.*

As Miya stepped deeper into the woods, the foliage around her changed; the leaves curled at the edges and shrivelled to a lifeless sable. Velizar was sucking strength from his surroundings, desperate to regain some semblance of power.

The failed creator had devolved into a wanton destroyer, and it made him so very easy to track.

The birches were charred, their milky skin like tarmac and their wispy branches dry and bent. The soil—a mosaic of earthy browns, rusted reds, and sage specs—bled into scorched black sand. As colour fled and the light vanished, an overpowering stench like burnt rubber washed over Miya. A chill coiled around her exposed neck, and as she approached, a deep, haggard breath thundered all around her.

"You've lost another wager," she called into the gloom. "Only this time with yourself."

A raspy, feral growl shredded the stillness, and before Miya could get any closer, a cacophony of gravelly voices invaded her. "Another step...Dreamwalker...and you'll be eaten whole."

She ignored the threat, and as she strode forward, a shadow rose before her, its edges quivering. Two golden eyes beamed from the abysmal form. Its face was indiscernible until something resembling a mouth—a hole where there should have been lips—yawned open and released a blood-curdling screech. The forest shook and the decay spread, wilting all in its path.

Miya raised an arm as dirt whipped past her, but she remained undeterred.

"You can't scare me," she said. "There's nothing I haven't already seen from you."

The gaping cavity widened, stretching like dough until it crawled up the side of the shadow's would-be face. "You will fear me, Dreamwalker, especially when I am gone."

"I welcome the day you're gone." She tried moving forward, but a cutting gale pushed her back.

"I have felled you countless times!" Velizar protested, pieces of his spectral shield moulting away. "Do you remember them, Dreamwalker? The faceless girls on the hill?"

Icy air slit Miya's skin like a thousand needles. The world around her vanished, and she saw the women, absent of any features, lined up in perfect rows on the sprawling knolls.

"You fear me," he reiterated from atop the mound, "because you are defined by me. And you are nothing without your enemy." The king of corpses spread his arms wide, beholding his domain with pride.

As if commanded by his gesture, the women's heads jittered like marionettes, shaking off the dregs of death. They wrenched left and right; flesh rived and bones splintered as they came free from their necks and levitated. Miya kept her gaze trained on Velizar, fighting the churning in her gut. Then, the floating heads swarmed her, skulls bumping and tongues lashing as they nipped and shrieked. Miya swung her arms to fend them off, but her fingers only grazed flesh like bruised fruit.

"You put the noose around our necks," one of them hissed.

"You tied us to the pyre," said another.

"You lit us ablaze," they chanted in unison.

Miya stumbled back and tried banishing the vision. "It's not real," she whispered, focusing on the forest floor, searching for the familiar crunch of dried leaves.

"It is real," came a girl's familiar voice. "You just never liked reality."

Miya looked up and came face to face with Elle. Her jaw was crooked, her left cheek drooping, and her jugular bruised with a thin line where her necklace had drawn taught, choking the air from her lungs. Her eyes were blotched with red, her pupils pale and blank.

"I'm dead because of you." She struggled to form the words, her lips roiling.

"No," Miya whimpered, shaking her head. "I found you, Elle. We were in the playground by the woods. Don't you remember? Your father killed you."

"Because he thought I was you!" Elle roared, slimy blood

spewing from her mouth as she hovered closer. The others crowded around, each of them muttering their own tale of how the Dreamwalker had damned them.

Miya wiped the viscera from her face. Hands shaking, she tried peering over the heads in search of Velizar but found only more victims of his cursed cycle. They were endless—a sea of women who'd lost their lives to his menace.

"We are your victims too!" Jaws unhinged, faces warped, and flesh peeled back as they keened. Their cries were followed by an eruption of flames that consumed each woman's head. Now alight, they flung themselves at Miya and battered her with sweltering screams.

Terror ravelled up Miya's limbs, binding her in place. With nowhere to escape, she clapped her hands over her ears, but her eyes were pinned open as tears streamed down her face. Somewhere behind the fear, she felt a gnawing guilt that'd followed her through lifetimes.

These women were dead because of her too. After all, she was the one who bound the wolf. She'd enslaved one god to punish another, and she'd condemned countless women in the process.

Was it true? Was the Dreamwalker just as sinister as her mortal enemy?

"The world would be better off without you," he crooned. "Without your chaos."

"No," Miya choked, heat licking her face.

"The flames are hungry, sweet girl. They yearn for your soul. But first, they'll have to eat through your body."

"No," she insisted, but something inside her wavered. She had no way out. She was trapped—doomed to be killed by the man who'd killed her a thousand times before.

"Why not sate the fire? Put an end to your pain, to this wretched existence in which you've trapped yourself."

Maybe she deserved it just as much as he did.

Velizar's shadow stretched, consuming the ground like slow-moving lava. It pooled around her feet, threatening to overtake her. "Shall I tell you one final secret before your end, Dreamwalker? Something that took me an eternity suspended in umbrage to understand?"

She was met with rotting teeth and a sickle-like grin cutting across his cavernous face. His jaundiced eyes bulged like swollen yolks as his voice warbled closer, and his sour breath washed over her. "There is no good and evil. There is only power."

If that were true, then she'd never been good, and Velizar had never been evil. They were an unstoppable force and an immovable object, bound to collide forever. Maybe the morality of it all didn't matter. Kali believed herself to be just, but Miya wasn't Kali.

Miya was the Dreamwalker now, and she would forge her own path.

Velizar's hand came over her face, and her vision blotted with darkness. Skeletal fingers bit into her cheeks and temples as his palm clamped over her mouth. He exhaled with delight, the stench worse than a corpse left out in the summer sun.

Miya snatched his wrist and dug her nails into his grey, pliant skin. With all the force she could muster, she anchored her feet and pried his crab-like hands away just enough to speak. "Is that the best you can do? Insult my moral compass?"

Velizar howled with laughter, and between his spindly fingers, she saw his mercurial shield devour the adjacent trees. "What moral compass? You are chaos; you have no compass. You are the maelstrom that spins the needle. As long as you reign, there will be no path through the storm. And yet you feel righteous, coming here to snuff out the final embers of my life?"

"I'm not here to arbitrate right and wrong." Miya unlatched his claws one by one. "I'm here to put you out of your misery."

His face twisted and he staggered back, the burning heads following suit. "My misery?" He choked on the word like it was an affront. Outstretching his arms, the shade that had spread *throughout the woodland retreated, coagulating around Velizar's emaciated figure.*

"God of chaos," he rumbled. "Remember that a storm is nothing without a ship to wreck, without survivors to tell the tale. You are nothing *without me! I am creation! I am order! Without me, there is no ship!"*

A rueful smile crossed Miya's face. She really did pity him. "This isn't about me. It never was." She inched closer, the blaze dwindling as Velizar's victims retreated. "It's always been about your brother. You grieve him, your loss of control over him." The obsidian mass guttered like a candle, then shrunk away as Miya closed in. "You once told me that creation and destruction are like brothers, two sides of the same coin. It's you, god of creation, who is nothing without your brother. And I'm here to tell you that you're never getting him back." The dream stone rose up, luminous and alive. Miya locked eyes with the phantom and said, "Your little brother's long outgrown you. He understood from the beginning that what you call chaos is only change."

Gnashing teeth and throaty snarls yipped from the vacuum in front of her, yet the foliage blighted by Velizar's taint unfolded with newfound life. As Miya breathed in, lightning flashed from above. Rain descended at the Dreamwalker's bidding and extinguished the flames enveloping the women's slaloming heads. One by one, they turned to ash and scattered to the winds. With his creation usurped, the phantom fled, and the miasma thinned.

"Change is a storm," Miya called after him. "And I am that storm."

She pursued him into the midnight mist. A dim lavender glow enveloped her as she went, permitting her just enough sight to watch her step. In the apparition's stead, she found a glistening mass huddled against the concave groove of a dead oak. It rippled and swelled, fighting to take form.

"Stop," Miya commanded. "Stop trying to be something you're not. Show me your real face."

The fiendish ooze bowed, its lumps morphing into discernable shapes—shoulders, knees, the arch of a back, and finally, a head. Miya waited patiently as the oily liquid raked into unkempt sable hair and revealed skin blemished by gashes. Finally, the head rose, and two aurous eyes found Miya's.

"You won't have me," Velizar spat.

"Yes," said Miya, "I will."

From the sky above, a raven cawed, then dove beak first towards them. The god of creation threw up his arms and ducked as Gavran beat his wings and roosted on Miya's outstretched arm. A cloak of violet and black feathers blossomed over her, and when Velizar lowered his hands, Miya was studying him through her iridescent bone-beak mask.

"I thought of having him peck your eyes out." She stroked Gavran's bill with a slender finger. "But those ugly yellow balls in your skull are the only thing setting you apart from your brother." Crouching down, she clasped him by the chin, then whispered, "And I don't ever want to forget them."

He opened his mouth to bellow something back, but Miya didn't wait. Grabbing a fistful of his hair, she slammed his head into the ground. The black sand crumbled beneath them, the ground breaking away until they both plummeted into a low, dense fog. Miya let go of her prey, allowing him to shamble about as he gathered his bearings.

She wanted him to see. She wanted him to understand. Trapped in his cell, he had nowhere left to run.

The Emerald Shade rose as he staggered. It towered over him, its mammoth bole a barricade blocking his escape.

Miya glided forward, pushing Velizar towards the willow. "I warned you," she began, repeating the words she'd said to him upon her first death. "Your control is meaningless."

The god of creation teetered back as the earth quaked with chaos' every step.

Her voice echoed in the hollow chasm of the in-between. "I promised you'd never be rid of me."

She stopped in front of Velizar, the tendrils of plumage from her robe caressing his knees. Winding her copper chain around one finger, her pendant floated up in front of her. As she tore it from her neck, sparks lit across the stone, morphing into shadows that coalesced into a wide, curved blade. The dagger flashed to life, shimmering with gold, purple, and viridian.

Clutching the ivory handle, Miya tilted Velizar's face up with the tip of her ethereal weapon, their eyes meeting for the last time. "And so I have returned, just as they always feared. And just as they foretold," she smiled wickedly, "the Dreamwalker has come."

Miya slashed the sharpened edge across Velizar's throat. His lips parted in a silent scream, and blood like wet asphalt trickled down his neck. He tried to fight it, clawing at the wound, but it was no use. His body began to convulse as his skin cracked like baked earth. His veins pulsed under thinning flesh, joints seizing and snapping as he withered. Miya watched as he succumbed to the inevitable, and those gleaming golden eyes paled like winter straw.

Finally, he went still.

54

KAI

MIYA HAD BEEN under for barely a minute, but time worked differently in the dreamscape. A fleeting moment to the living could've been an eternity to a spirit. Kai wasn't sure he'd hold out long enough to see Miya wake up. His body was leaking like a soggy basement ceiling about to cave in, rattling his confidence that he'd be able to heal. His nemesis had made him cocky.

Rusalka hovered nearby. Through bleary eyes, he saw her vibrate and shimmer like pearlescent fish scales. Her scent wafted in and out of his awareness, and he figured she was trying to keep tabs on Miya, weaving her essence through both worlds.

Somewhere in the back of his mind, Kai sensed Velizar's distress, his fear flickering on the edge of his waning life force. Velizar had hunted them for centuries, and now he was the prey. Kai had full faith Miya would curb-stomp him into a fat tree root, but he wished he could be with her. He hated just *lying* there, immobile and helpless as he watched over her comatose body.

Just stay alive, he bargained with himself. He never imagined it would be so difficult.

Ama and Crowbar had scrambled to tend to his wounds, tearing a tablecloth and wrapping it tightly around his midsection. He was so tired he couldn't even react to the pain, wondering vaguely if this was what death felt like—not a desperate grab for a scrap of existence, but a gentle lull into nothingness.

He heard Rusalka approach as fatigue weighed on his vision.

"Stay the fuck away from me," he growled when she was within reach.

"I won't harm you," she told him meekly.

He forced his eyes open and squinted at her. "Don't tell me you've fallen for me," he cracked, his lip curling into a sneer.

"Perhaps in another life." She glanced at the girl by his side. "I don't have much time left."

"Good."

"You may be right," she mused. "Now that I'm at the cusp of my revenge, I feel so...empty. I do not hate. I do not fear. I just..." She paused, considering her next words. "I'm relieved."

Kai snorted as he stared at the ceiling. "I'd be relieved too if I looked like a corpse, and someone finally put my decaying ass in the ground."

She chuckled, the sound a light chime, and it disarmed him to see her so earnest.

"You're funny," she whispered. "I never appreciated that about you."

"You didn't seem to appreciate anything, if we're being honest..."

"I'm relieved," she went on, "because I get to pass on knowing I was wrong."

Kai's eyebrows drew together, and his mouth tugged into a frown. "You want to be wrong?"

"Yes," she breathed, a smile breaking onto her face. "You proved me wrong, and now, I get to die for love. Not some facile nonsense or the violent jealousy of a fragile man. *Real* love. It'll finally end me, and it'll be my salvation." She crouched down, her hand lightly grazing Miya's cheek. "Being wrong allowed me something I never thought possible."

Kai strained to lift his head as he glared protectively. "What?"

"Forgiveness," said Rusalka. "I wanted all three of you to suffer." Her hand drifted to his face, tracing the bruises along his jawline. "But you cut into your own heart to put *us* first."

"Us?"

"Me," she beamed, then turned to Miya. "And her. You finally saw the answer someone else needed. Not the one you wanted, but the one that was necessary."

He sighed, craning his neck to evade her touch. "Don't expect me to gush for you." He faltered, then said carefully, "Velizar was a dick to me too. He also killed me. More than once."

"You weren't alone like I was," she said. "You had the Dreamwalker."

"I thought I was alone."

Rusalka didn't reply; her voice had depleted to a silent hiss. Kai glanced over to see her fading. The bony hand grazing his face wasted into nothing, and she looked up at him with fearful, searching eyes, like she was distraught that he might be looking right through her.

"I see you," he said gently, and he felt her dread quiet as the final pieces of her disappeared.

She'd only ever wanted to be seen.

"Rest well, you bad bitch."

55

MASON

THE LAST TIME Mason saw his office felt like an eternity ago. Only twelve hours earlier, he'd booked a flight out of New Orleans, and after arriving in Vancouver, he didn't even stop by his apartment before driving straight to the hospital. His immediate presence had been demanded.

The blinds were nearly shut, narrow streams of morning sunlight illuminating the floating motes of dust. The room smelled faintly of old air freshener—something that claimed to be like an ocean breeze. With a hefty sigh, Mason threw himself into his leather chair. It'd always contoured to his spine, but it no longer fit the same. Nothing ever did.

His appointment would be arriving soon, and he wasn't remotely prepared. His mind was elsewhere, replaying the events at *The Mangy Spade*.

Tell them the truth, Miya had said.

He wondered if his truth would do her justice.

A knock sounded on the door, and Mason jolted in his seat.

"Come in," he called, his voice cracking.

The Delathornes thundered into his office like a pair of storm clouds. Raymond was dressed in a stylish navy suit, a silver tie cinched impeccably beneath his collar. His salt and pepper hair was combed back, kept neatly in place by a modest helping of gel. Yet despite his coiffed appearance, dark circles rimmed his discerning green eyes. Andrea, too, looked worn, but this seemed less out of the ordinary. Her wild tresses were tied back, the grey roots peeking out just above her forehead. She clutched the hem of her jacket, her lips pursed as she and her husband silently took their seats across from Mason.

For a long, excruciating moment, no one spoke.

"Well?" Raymond finally broke the silence. "You said you had news regarding Emiliya's whereabouts."

"You found her." Andrea wrung her hands in her lap. "But you said we needed to discuss it in person. Why?"

Mason took a deep breath. This was it.

"I can confirm that your daughter's alive and well," he said slowly.

"Where is she then? Why was your location not available on the call?" Raymond interrogated.

"So that you couldn't trace my steps," Mason replied, fighting a scowl that threatened to creep onto his face. "Yes, I found your daughter, and she wants you to know that she's found something she loves. She's happy and safe, and she'll likely come back to you at some point, but until then, you need to let her go. Let her be her own person."

"But—but why—" Andrea stuttered, her head shaking with each failed syllable. "I don't understand. Why won't you tell us where she is?"

"Because she doesn't want to be found," said Mason.

Raymond's jaw clenched. He crossed his legs and gripped the chair's armrest. "Last I checked, I was the one who hired you. Not my daughter."

Mason had always been a patient man. Rarely roused to anger, he now found himself resisting the urge to pull a page from Kai's playbook. He bit his tongue. "I have my reasons."

"But why won't she speak with us? She could at least let us know she's well!" Andrea pleaded.

"She is speaking with you, ma'am. Through me. She requested that I act as the intermediary until she's ready."

"That's absurd," Raymond countered. "Do you have any proof? Even a shred of evidence that Emiliya's really alive?"

Mason was aghast. Miya's unyielding parents burdened her with needless guilt in their foolhardy attempts to locate a daughter they wouldn't even recognize. Now they wanted proof that the ghost was real?

"I have no reason to lie," Mason shot back. "I wanted the truth just as much as you, and there's nothing I can show you that'll convince you she's fine. Even if I did have something, how do you know I didn't get it from her old landlady? Or from Hannah? You don't want proof that she's well; you just want her back."

"I won't pay you for your speculation!" Raymond shouted.

"And I don't care!"

Mason could see the anger writhing on Raymond's face, but for once, he had no retort. Andrea, however, was unrelenting.

"I still don't understand why she won't speak with us. Just a phone call!"

Mason sighed, pinching the bridge of his nose. "Do you

remember the last thing she would've heard about you?" When neither responded, he looked at them and said, "You were riling up the town to hunt her down."

Raymond threw his arms up. "We weren't hunting our daughter!"

"The town was," Mason rebuked. "And you *let* it happen. You went along with it."

"She was missing. It was a strategic decision," Raymond grumbled, self-reproach flashing across his face.

Mason never imagined he'd miss Kai Donovan. If he could've, he would've teleported the brute into his office and unleashed him on Raymond Delathorne. *Meet your son-in-law*, he wanted to jeer.

"Say you found her." Mason tapped his finger pointedly on his desk. "Say you rescued your daughter from the woods, but when you looked at her, all you saw was the Dreamwalker. What would you have done then?"

Raymond sputtered, "That's a ridiculous question!"

"Is it?" Mason pressed. "Because it's what everyone was thinking at that meeting. You heard the accusations. You were there. The fact that you can't accept this is part of the problem, and it's part of the reason she won't see you."

"My God," Andrea gasped. "Of course, we wouldn't have seen the Dreamwalker."

Mason choked back the scornful laugh spuming in his mouth. If they only knew. "But if you did?"

Another protracted silence thickened the air.

Mason pushed back his chair and stood. "I can see this has been very hard on you, and I do apologize for not delivering the results you expected." His gaze washed over them both, and he exhaled. "I'll give you some time alone to process. If you'll excuse me, I have to make a phone call."

He strode over to the door, stopping as he was halfway through. "There's just one thing..." he trailed off. "Everyone in Black Hollow was so convinced your daughter was lured away and possessed. No one ever thought to consider the obvious."

Blinking away her stupor, Andrea looked over her shoulder and asked, "What?"

Mason smiled and shrugged. "That she chose to leave."

The door clicked shut behind him. Mason rounded the corner and sped from his office before Raymond could come after him. His pulse thudded in his ears. He'd finally done it. Three years ago, he'd set out into the woods to save Emiliya Delathorne. He wanted to be a hero. He'd failed then, but not this time. He'd done the right thing and helped Miya on her terms; he gave her what she needed. All it took was a little blow to the ego.

Locking himself in a custodial room, Mason pulled out his phone and dialled Hannah Cleary.

"Dr. Evans?" she answered after several rings.

"Hannah—yes, it's Mason." He peered through the small rectangular window on the door. "Listen, there's something I need to tell you, but I need your word that you won't share it with Miya's family."

"Oh my God!" Her giddiness was audible. "You found her, didn't you?"

"Yes, but—"

"She wants nothing to do with her parents. Not a shocker, honestly."

"You understand then?"

"I do." Hannah paused. "Where is she?"

"She didn't ask me to share this with you, but honestly, I'm going out on a limb here." He paced the crawlspace, then stopped. "I think she'd love to see her friend again. She's in Louisiana. At least she *was* there. No idea where she'll be going next, though."

"How do I reach her?" Hannah asked.

That's right, thought Mason. Miya was practically untraceable. Unable to help himself, he began to laugh, a great, hulking weight sliding off his shoulders.

"Call out to her in your dreams," he said. "If you're lucky, you may just get spirited away."

❧ 56 ❧

MIYA

MIYA RUBBED the back of her neck and winced. Everything hurt, but it was finally over. The entire night had passed as they waged war with spirits and ghouls, and now dawn was breaking on the heels of a bittersweet victory.

With Ama's help and Kai's remaining sliver of consciousness, they'd stumbled through the back alleys towards Crowbar's apartment. The bartender gawked at Ama as she hoisted Kai up with the strength of an Olympic weightlifter. She clearly didn't care to keep up the charade that she was a five-foot-six human in reasonably good shape. No, she was a beast, and she would let it be known. Crowbar offered directions, but Ama kept cutting behind buildings to stay out of sight, much to the bartender's chagrin.

It *should* have been a five-minute walk, but it took them four times that with Ama bearing the brunt of Kai's weight. The white wolf was quiet throughout their ordeal, mumbling that she'd left the dining room spotless and ordered replacements for the smashed liquor bottles. She only realized how many were broken when she'd restored the shelves behind the bar and saw they were half empty.

"You owe me *so* many mimosas," Crowbar had barked. "If Bastien comes back to a wrecked bar, I'm in shit."

Now sitting cross-legged on the floor of Crowbar's cramped bedroom, all seemed strangely quiet. Kai was resting on a mattress with no frame, his skin beaded with moisture as he slipped in and out of feverish dreams. Miya could hear pieces of Ama and Crowbar's hushed conversation in the kitchen, though most of it was drowned out by the portal fan blasting away the sticky summer heat. She glanced up at Gavran, perched on the bedroom's windowsill.

"What do you think they're talking about?" she asked, and he canted his head, offering a low croak in response.

Footsteps sounded, and as the door opened behind her, Gavran dove off and flew away.

"Dahlia says we can stay as long as we need." It was Ama, her tone sullen.

"Is she upset with us?" Miya asked.

Ama shook her head. "No. She's just in shock. Worried she'll be abandoned. Nervous that Kai's not in the hospital."

Miya had been more than just nervous; she'd feared for Kai's life. Abaddon and Velizar had glibly taken credit for Kai's supernatural healing, and the need for it had only ever arisen because of them. With the menace gone, she didn't know if Kai's body would work just like a regular person's. Miya's every cell had clotted with alarm when she returned from the dreamscape. Kai's blood had gathered around her fingertips, alerting her to just how injured he was. He could've been dead on the floor next to her, his final moments passing in her absence. She never would've forgiven herself.

Luckily, the god of creation had always been a liar.

Miya pulled back the surgical gauze they'd used to dress Kai's wound. By the time they'd cleaned him up, most of the profuse bleeding had stopped. He still healed quickly, though not *as* quickly. Mercifully, Crowbar kept a healthy stash of rolls in her bathroom for drunken accidents and bad fights that broke out near *The Spade*.

"He's already much better. His temperature's a bit high, but he'll be okay. Besides, he hates hospitals." Miya settled against the wall. "What's this about being abandoned?"

Ama padded over and sat next to her. "Dahlia doesn't want us to disappear from her life."

"Us?" Miya questioned. "Or you?"

Ama frowned. "Maybe more the latter than the former."

"And you shouldn't disappear. She's lost too many people already."

"Do you really believe that?" Ama probed her.

"Yes," Miya nodded. "Imagine being at your worst. Imagine meeting someone who finally makes you feel something good while you're at your worst. Then imagine having them disappear because the reason they came into your life had nothing to do with you." She met Ama's gaze. "How would that make you feel?"

"Point taken," Ama sighed. "I suppose I just don't want to screw it up."

"You won't," Miya reassured her. "You're a force of nature."

They fell into a comfortable silence until Ama spoke up again.

"Maybe I was too harsh."

"Huh?"

"Kai," said Ama, "I don't think I gave him enough credit."

Miya wrapped an arm around the white wolf and gave her a gentle squeeze. "You and Gavran both."

Ama patted her knee, then stood up. "I'll leave you alone with him. I'm sure he's cowering in some unconscious corner because he can smell me in the room."

Miya couldn't help but snicker. "I'll be sure to tell him you're cool when he wakes up. Either way, you've got more important things to do." She inclined her head towards the door. "Take your girl out for that brunch you promised her. Buy her *all* the fancy mimosas."

Ama smiled, a new light shining in her sunlit eyes. It wasn't the coy mischief Miya was used to, but something brighter, more open. It looked a little bit like hope.

After she left, Miya heard chatter in the other room, followed by the clank of keys and the rustle of shoes. When the front door shut, Miya huffed with relief.

She was finally alone.

Crowbar's tiny room was reminiscent of Miya's old basement apartment in Black Hollow, but only in size. The sage-green walls and earthy brown décor matched well, and the natural light spilling through the window made the place feel more like a home and less like a cave. Crumpling next to Kai, Miya curled into a ball and stared at the side of his face. His brows were knitted, his mouth downturned in a scowl.

As she reached out to stroke his cheek, he stirred with a deep breath. His eyes opened, fixed on the ceiling, then lowered to her face.

"Miya..." He sounded parched, straining to speak.

She rolled over and wrestled a water bottle from the twelve-pack Crowbar had left them. Kai greedily accepted it, hoisting himself up and crushing the plastic as he sucked out every last drop.

Miya grabbed another, and another, handing them to him like an assembly line until he'd emptied, crunched, and tossed aside four bottles.

He slid down with a groan, kicked off the covers, and splayed himself over the mattress. Realizing he was barely clothed, he took stock of his sweaty torso and arched an eyebrow at the yellow smiley-face boxers shielding his nether regions.

"Sorry," Miya grinned sheepishly. "It was the only thing that fit."

He clunked his head against the wall and chuckled. "Yellow's really not my colour."

Miya eased herself down next to him. His ribs were bruised but mostly fused together, and although the blood loss had left him close to death, he'd somehow managed to slug the grim reaper back across the river Styx. Now, his condition seemed no worse than a bad hangover.

Her eyes wandered down his side, stopping at his bandaged abdomen.

"I don't regret it," he said. "It was the right choice."

"How do you know?" she asked quietly.

His eyes drifted shut. "When Rusalka first got me, I blamed her for the hurt. I just wanted to make it stop." He paused, running his tongue over his mangled bottom lip. "That didn't go so well."

"Did you try to stab her?" Miya asked dryly.

"I did," he confessed. "But then I realized how much she was hurting too. I understood why. After that, the answer just...made sense."

"Velizar never counted on you hurting yourself."

"He figured I'd put my survival first," said Kai. "That's how I've always operated."

"You proved him wrong." Miya shuffled closer and rested her head on his shoulder, then pressed a hand to his forehead. "Your fever's broken."

"Thank fuck," he grumbled, scratching through his dark, dishevelled hair. "My brain felt like an egg on a skillet. I dreamt I was being chased by a bus driven by a hamster."

Miya laughed and wiped the remaining sweat from his brow. "Sounds like your personal hell."

He lolled his head to the side and squinted at her. "Enjoy my pain while you can, Lambchop."

"And why would I do that?"

"Because I don't have a good enough apology," he uttered. "Not sure I ever will."

A moment of tense silence passed between them.

"I don't think you have to say anything," Miya said at last. "What you did was enough."

He frowned. "And just like that, I'm forgiven?"

"I was never upset with you," she said. "Not once did I think this was your fault, or that you owed me anything but your efforts to break free. And you did break free."

He ground his jaw, struggling to accept the clemency.

"How many lifetimes has it been, Kai?"

"I don't know," he murmured.

"Exactly. At this point, it's all a blur. And this?" She gestured around them. "This is nothing more than a hiccup. Maybe if I hadn't remembered everything, I'd be pissed. But knowing what I know—what we know—how can I?" She smiled, elated as she caught his gaze. "We're finally free."

Kai turned to his side and studied her. "Are we really, though? We've got a lot to unlearn."

He'd changed. The intensity in his eyes was still there, but it no longer raged with the reckless abandon of youth.

It simmered steadily, as though the aeons had finally caught up to him.

"You're right," she admitted with a sinking feeling. "I'm the Dreamwalker. My story isn't done with me."

Yes, they'd shattered one chain, but other shackles remained. The past was hardly forgotten. Miya felt its bonds like a thorny rope around her limbs, and it wasn't letting go.

When they left Black Hollow, they were so triumphant that Miya had broken the cycle. How naïve they'd been. The fable permeating their community hadn't stayed quietly in its birthplace. Trauma didn't heed the borders between peoples or the partition between worlds. It clung to all those it touched, and it transformed the communal into something personal. It loathed being left behind.

Now, Black Hollow's traumas were their responsibility—the Dreamwalker's and the black wolf's. They were wounded people as much as they were spiteful gods.

"You've got it backwards," Kai's gruff voice snapped Miya out of her thoughts. "Your story doesn't own you. Write the damn thing yourself. Preferably in blood."

She squirmed under his stare, drumming against his collarbone with a nervous touch. What would their lives look like from now on? Their promise had been fulfilled, and they were no longer tethered; she could sense it when she touched him. The suture that once bound them had torn. What if he wanted to go his own way? To explore the world on his own terms? It was the first time in lifetimes they didn't *need* to find one another. The realization drowned her in a tidal wave of dread.

"Kai, I'm not sure I'm ready to start inking stories in anyone's blood." Her voice quaked, and she swallowed the lump scraping against her throat. "At least, I don't want to do it alone. I want—"

"Lambchop." He clasped the back of her neck. His molten eyes drank up her fear, absolving every lingering doubt. "Shut up and take off your wool."

Fingers tangling in her hair, he pulled her into a hungry kiss. As his bruised mouth found hers, she remembered Gavran's words.

Love is not a thing of need, Dreamwalker. It's a thing of choice.

Miya melted into him, her hands seeking his body as she surrendered to the bone-deep pull. Desire pooled in the pit of her stomach as he pressed against her, teeth snagging lips, gasps leaving shudders in their wake. Hooking a thumb over the band bordering his hips, she tugged down, and the ensuing tussle to remove their clothes culminated in Kai's frustrated growl reverberating in her ear. When flesh finally met flesh, their fervour only mounted. Their long-awaited reunion harboured not only the loss of recent days, but that of lifetimes spent apart.

She missed the tickle of his rough black hair against her breasts, yearned for the fleeting glances—red like fire—as his breath raised her skin.

Miya's legs coiled around Kai's waist as he dragged her under him. If he was still in pain, he hid it well. Breaking free of her hold, his lips trailed down her abdomen and grazed the inside of her thigh. Her body blossomed with heat as he found her center. The room tilted when her back arched, and she raked her nails through his unruly mane. Her heart hammered against her ribs, each pulse a rising overture until she finally let go, ecstasy rolling over her in waves.

Trembling from the blaze, Miya pushed Kai onto his back as he tried to get up. She straddled him and entwined her fingers with his. Their eyes locked in a brief, smouldering exchange before she descended on him, every groove and contour finding its place as sparks rippled between them and the world fell away.

The Dreamwalker and her black wolf may have spent nearly an eternity apart, but they would wrangle the very fabric of time and space to make an eternity of this moment.

They were bound, after all, as the sky and sea are bound by the horizon.

ACKNOWLEDGMENTS

There are so many people who helped make this book happen—friends, colleagues, and family to whom I am tremendously grateful.

First, I am so indebted to my parents, who have supported my creative endeavours with unshakeable faith in my capabilities and have privileged me with the freedom to pursue what makes me happy.

Thank you to my beta readers, who braved through this manuscript in its early stages and helped me fill in the gaps. Thank you, Laura, for the video-calls about the logistics of dimensional travel, the proper etiquette for breaking reality, and for helping me devise new and creative ways to make Miya suffer.

A huge thank you to Brenton, who knows it is his sworn duty to drop everything when I am in need of a sounding board. Without you, I wouldn't have a resolution to this story, and Kai would have far fewer cuts and bruises, which simply wouldn't do.

I must also thank my rescue cats, Moonstone and Peanut Butter, who reminded me when it was break time by ensuring that typing was more difficult than it had to be. Whether by loafing between my elbows on the desk or yowling for snacks an hour ahead of schedule, my feline companions never failed to provide a suitable distraction when I was in need of respite. They are also excellent muses.

I am also deeply grateful to my agent, Emmy Higdon, who saw the potential in my work, suffered through all my **very visceral** metaphors, and helped me slash the extra POVs I was initially reluctant to let go of. I swear the next book will be less complicated! Maybe...

To my editor, Malorie: I cannot thank you enough for slogging through this manuscript multiple times, helping me with continuity issues, tweaking language, and tolerating my incessant questions about the placement of every comma. This entire duology owes you so much.

Moreover, the success of these books would not have been possible without the reviewers and readers who took a chance on my debut, *The Hollow Gods*. Thank you for supporting me, my work, and for being open to my stories. That my writing means something to you is the greatest joy any writer can ask for.

Finally, thank you to the entire Parliament House team for bringing this book to life. I especially want to thank Shayne, whose tireless effort, passion, and dedication to book publishing is unlike anything I have ever seen. I truly appreciate all of the invisible work you do, and I am privileged to have started my publishing journey with The Parliament House Press.

MIYA STILL NEEDS YOU

Did you enjoy The Echoed Realm*? Reviews keep books alive . . .
Miya needs your help!*

*Help her by leaving your review on either
GoodReads or the digital storefront of your choosing. She
thanks you!*

ABOUT THE AUTHOR

A. J. Vrana is a Serbian-Canadian academic and writer from Toronto, Canada. She lives with her two rescue cats, Moonstone and Peanut Butter, who nest in her window-side bookshelf and cast judgmental stares at nearby pigeons. Her doctoral research examines the supernatural in modern Japanese and former-Yugoslavian literature and its relationship to violence. When not toiling away at caffeine-fueled, scholarly pursuits, she enjoys jewelry-making, cupcakes, and concocting dark tales to unleash upon the world.

www.thechaoscycle.com

facebook.com/AJVranaAuthor
twitter.com/AJVrana
instagram.com/a.j.vrana

THE PARLIAMENT HOUSE

CPSIA information can be obtained
at www.ICGtesting.com
Printed in the USA
LVHW022309300921
699149LV00002B/116